Priest

Ratcatchers, Book 1

by

Matthew Colville

This is a work of fiction. Any relation to actual living persons, alive or dead, is entirely coincidental.

Revised edition edited by Joshua Yearsley
Cover design copyright 2011 by Tim Denee
First edition self-published by Matthew Colville in 2010
Revised edition self-published by Matthew Colville in 2017

Follow the author, @mattcolville on Twitter!

Special Thanks

The inestimable Tim Denee for the brilliant cover.
Natalie, for everything.

Priest

Chapter One

Heden stared at the door to the jail. His heart hammered in his chest and he considered turning around and going back to the inn.

He could do it. He could turn around now while it was still early morning, no one on the street, and come back later. He wanted to do it. He told himself there was no reason not to do it.

The whole point of coming here early was to avoid this. Instead of a mostly empty jail and a few guards he knew, it was full inside. He could hear it. Full of prisoners, and as soon as he put his foot on the stone step and heard them through the door his heart started to race.

The desire to turn around, avoid the issue, avoid the unknown and the conflict was almost overwhelming. He felt ashamed that something so simple, so stupid, could unman him. That helped. The shame gave him perspective. And part of him knew he wouldn't come back later. Not once the streets filled up. It was now or tomorrow morning and tomorrow morning meant lying to Gwiddon later today. That pushed Heden over the edge.

Once his heart stopped threatening to burst out of his chest, once the tingling in his fingertips went away, he felt better. All he had to do was wait. Endure it. He was not going to die from a burst heart, the abbot had assured him. Easy to say after the fact.

He took a long breath and grabbed the thick ring on the door, pulling it open.

A riot of noise and heat and the smells of sweat and blood and oil spilled out. There were maybe twenty or thirty men policed by a small handful of guards inside the jail. It was dark and the ceiling low; the prisoners' bodies blocked the candlelight inside. The nearest cultists stopped their protest and turned to look at him and the open door.

They were men of different ages and sizes, all wore dirty black robes, and each had an eye patch over his left eye.

Heden stared at them for a moment as he realized he knew what cult these men belonged to. A thin, pale young man, his hands tied in front of him, saw Heden pause in thought and tried to make a break for it. Tried to run through the open doorway and past Heden.

Instinct took over. The door was heavy and Heden was not a big man, but his compact body was almost all muscle and so he was able, without thinking about it, to yank the door closed again, slamming it into the young cultist.

The boy made a sound like a shout and a grunt, and Heden heard a body hit the floor of the jail.

He opened the door again. The boy writhed on the wooden floor. Heden stepped into the jail and bent down, helping the young cultist struggle to his feet. The boy was helpless, his face smashed, his hands bound, his vision blocked by blood and tears. Heden did most of the work getting him up.

"It's alright," Heden said. "I don't blame you." The boy pushed himself away from Heden, turned to go back into the crowd of cultists before anyone else could punish him for trying to escape. Heden watched the young acolyte try to wipe off his face with his bound hands as he wandered away. "It was worth a try," Heden said, mostly to himself.

"Hey!" a voice called out. Heden looked across the jail and saw a guard point to the boy. "What the fuck do you think you're doing?" He pressed his way through the prisoners, grabbing the young cultist by the collar of his dirty robe.

The big guard hauled back to punch the acolyte. Heden grabbed the guard's arm from behind him.

"You get your hands off me, you slimy piece of piss!" The guard jerked his arm away and turned to attack his new foe.

Heden backed away, smiling. "I'm not your enemy," he said.

Realization dawned. "Heden!" the guard boomed.

"Hey Mathe." Heden nodded, looked around the jail. "Busy night."

"Black gods, I almost didn't recognize you!" Mathe said, clapping his hands on Heden's shoulders. "What the fuck are you doing here? Did you let this one get out?" he said, and the young acolyte disappeared into the crowd of cultists.

Heden shrugged. "I opened the door. He saw it and went for it," he said. "I don't blame him."

Mathe peered at Heden. "Yeah but it was you that stopped him, though, weren't it? Saw someone smash that door right in his face." Mathe smiled. "Shoulda known it was you. Fast," he said.

Heden shrugged again. It was a bad habit he'd picked up somewhere. "Instinct, I guess. I'm here for your boss." He looked around the room. He didn't see Domnal, but he noticed most of the cultists hands were tied with rope. Some were in manacles. None were gagged. "I thought the place would be empty."

"Heh, yeah," Mathe said. "A bunch of ratcatchers brought this lot in about a turn ago."

"For a bounty," Heden said.

"Yeah. Castellan put a price on their heads back in Bleaker. We forgot all about it."

"They dropped off thirty cultists, went off to the castellan to collect the bounty, and left you to clean it up?" Heden asked. To his eye, the prisoners arrayed before him were thin, pale shadows of the kinds of zealots he used to deal with. He wanted to believe things were easier for the younger generation, but suspected he was just getting old.

"Yeah. It's shit, but it was a slow morning anyway." Mathe smiled as he grabbed a cultist by the neck.

"It *is* shit," Heden said. "Those ratcatchers are shit, and you should get half that bounty."

"That's funny coming from you," Mathe said with a wide grin as he kicked the legs out from under the fanatic, who looked to be Heden's age, forcing the man onto a bench. "Sit down, you streak of shit!" Mathe hollered, and more than one cultist involuntarily sat on whatever was nearby.

"Yeah," Heden said. "Where's Domnal?"

"Downstairs getting all the manacles he can find. Said we couldn't leave this lot tied up with rope." Heden raised his eyebrows, impressed. *Good man Domnal,* he thought.

He noticed one guard on the other side of the room. He was tall and lean and seemed uninterested in everything happening around him. He leaned against one of the big wooden pillars holding up the stone ceiling. To Heden's practiced eye, this guard seemed to take everything in, missing nothing. He wasn't shouting at the cultists like the other guards. None of the prisoners around him seemed to be putting up any fight. He had a handsome face and brown hair with a natural wave in it. He wore a slight smile, like he was observing a secret joke. There was an attitude Heden recognized.

"Who's the new guy?" Heden asked.

Mathe looked around and realized who Heden meant. "Teagan!" Mathe shouted the name over the chanting and raving. The man heard his name and looked over. Mathe pointed to Heden and gave the thumbs-up gesture. *He's one of us,* Mathe was saying. Teagan looked at Heden and nodded once, the slight smile not leaving his face. Heden nodded back.

"He ain't new; been here a year," Mathe said. As far as Heden was concerned, that was new. "He's good. Keeps to himself. Seems happy to have a job. Good man in a fight," Mathe said with obvious respect. "You'd know him if you ever came out of that hole you got yourself locked up in all year 'round."

"Yeah," Heden said without inflection, "Listen, Mathe," he said, "you need to gag these people."

"We what?" Mathe turned his big round face to look down at Heden. "Gag them?"

"These men are Eseldics," Heden said. "They serve Saint Eseld of the Eye." Heden reached out to the unshaven, undernourished cultist Mathe had just pushed down and deftly tore his eye patch off.

The man's good right eye began to search around wildly, not seeing. He was in an apoplectic ecstasy and no danger to anyone. His left eye, the one the eye patch covered, was missing its upper and lower eyelids. They'd been carved off, and the eye underneath had grown putrid and decayed. There was a smell. It was terrible to look at, the flesh around it wincing and writhing with no lid to blink. This is what those who worshiped She of the Maddening Eye, the Eye of Hate, did to themselves. They thought it gave them power. They were right.

Mathe gasped St. Llewellyn's name and warded himself by making his right hand into a fist and then covering it, grasping it with his left hand.

"These men are dangerous," Heden said. He looked down at the acolyte. "Well, not this one. He's an idiot. But the ones who haven't lost their minds will know some potent…"

One of the Eseldics, and Heden now knew this man was no acolyte, brought his hands around from behind his back where they'd been tied. Somehow he'd untied them, or cut the ropes, or someone else had cut them for him.

Heden wasn't ready. He realized that it was his arrival, Mathe being distracted and talking to him, that gave the enemy priest the opportunity. Mathe had no idea what an Eseldic was, or that some of them could be truly dangerous. Heden should have seen that. Should have seen that since Domnal was elsewhere, he had to take responsibility. He'd regret not doing so for a week afterwards.

Before Heden could blind him or suck the air from his lungs so that he could not speak, the priest of St. Eseld chanted a quick but potent prayer to his witch-saint, pointing at the source of all his pain and trouble.

Mathe.

Heden watched the scene play out in slow motion. The fanatic priest—his single eye wide with zeal, head thrown back in a twisted form of ecstasy, mouth chanting words no one but Heden could understand—stabbed a finger at Mathe, and Heden watched the watchman's head explode in a burst of pink. Bone, hair and brain showered in every direction as a headless body slumped lifeless to the ground. All of the guards froze in shock, looking down at the blood and human remains covering their clothes and faces. All but one.

Teagan stepped smartly into view, grabbed the cross guard of his sword with his left hand and his scabbard with his right. Heden recognized the nonstandard draw and knew his instincts were right. He was in the presence of a professional.

As the priest turned to Heden to attempt his lethal prayer again, Teagan yanked the sword halfway from its scabbard, turning the pommel into a projectile, driving it up into the priest's chin. There was a loud crack. The priest was unconscious, possibly dead, and Teagan hadn't even drawn his sword yet.

The priest's body slumped to the ground while the other acolytes began fighting the guards, some of them chanting minor prayers. Heden grabbed the amulet of St. Lynwen under his shirt and began a prayer of his own. He knew the battle would be over in a moment—was already over from his point of view—and he thought it best if everyone just calmed down.

Teagan yanked his sword out of his scabbard with enough force to almost make it fly out. He gripped the blade like a mace with both of his leather-gloved hands and bashed the nearest acolyte over the head with the cross guard, knocking the acolyte out. This was a man used to fighting with metal gauntlets. Another acolyte hit the ground.

He flipped the sword over, caught the pommel and leveled the tip of the blade at the neck of the nearest acolyte.

"Halt," he announced. The acolyte stopped chanting and stared down in terror at the blade at his throat. Teagan had taken two men down and had another held at sword-point in the time it would have taken even an experienced guard or soldier to draw his blade and swing once.

The acolyte fainted. Teagan sheathed his sword, guiding its point into the scabbard without looking. *I could never manage that,* Heden thought. *I always had to look down and watch what I was doing when I sheathed a sword.*

Heden finished his prayer, and everyone in the jail, starting with those closest to Heden and moving outward like a wave, all calmed down. The cultists stopped chanting, stopped struggling. They weren't compelled into silence or submission; Heden had just returned them to normal. Many of them had been in a fanatical ecstasy for hours and would wonder now why they were in a jail.

They all moved as far away from the dead bodies as they could, while the other guards moved closer, trying to understand what had just happened. Heden had taken their fear away. Now there was confusion…and anger.

"You bastard," one of them said, looking down at the dead priest. "That was Mathe, you fucking bastard!" He kicked the dead priest's head, causing blood and teeth to fly out. "He was my fucking friend, you piece of shit!" He was shouting and crying and the other guards had to restrain him.

Heden looked at Teagan. He wasn't angry. He looked exactly as calm as he was when Heden walked in. He hadn't even broken a sweat or been out of breath. He was calm as a rock.

The tall, lanky watchman looked back at Heden, and Heden saw the accusation there. Tacitly agreed with it. *You're right,* he thought. *I should have seen this coming.*

"He was my friend," Heden said, by way of mourning. Mathe had been glad to see him. Now Mathe was dead and Heden didn't feel much except the dull dread he lived with all the time now, somewhat more exposed, closer to the surface than usual.

"Some friend," Teagan said. The slight smile gone.

Heden nodded and looked down at Mathe's body. "Some friend," he said.

Stomping boots echoed from behind the door to the dungeon below. The door opened and Domnal emerged, his shoulders laden with two dozen heavy manacles. Domnal was a big man, fat but strong. He stood looking at the scene before him, at the acolytes all staring silently at the floor. At the explosion of red on the wall and the headless body of Mathe on the floor, next to the beaten corpse of the priest of St. Eseld.

He let the manacles slide off his shoulders and in wide-eyed anger said,

"What the fuck happened here?!"

Chapter Two

"Alright, let's hear it." Domnal's voice echoed off the walls of his small office as he walked around and dropped into the chair behind his desk with a loud creak of objecting wood.

Heden followed him in and closed the door. The room was warm, made of hard wood and lit by four candles in sconces on the wall. The floor was covered with a layer of sawdust, put there by the guards to absorb any blood spilt during the execution of their duty. Several pieces of parchment covered Domnal's large desk. Heden knew the man could read and write, but only the typical phrases found in official documents. Put a book in front of him and he'd start to sweat.

"You heard it from Teagan." Heden sat down in the armless chair.

"I want to hear it from you." Domnal scowled.

Domnal was fat like the other older guards. His pale complexion meant his face went flush any time he was angry or ashamed or had exerted himself. It was currently beet red. His hair grew in short brown wisps. He was loud and brutish, but effective.

Heden recounted what happened.

"Ahh Mathe," Domnal said. "It's never the cutpurses and thieves we lose men to. Always the fucking things the ratcatchers drag in."

"I'm sorry," Heden said. "It's my fault."

"Black gods," Domnal said, wincing at Heden's distasteful comment. "Stop blaming yourself for every damned thing. Weren't your fault. You didn't bring that lot in."

"I should have said something."

"You *did* say something! You said the same thing I said. 'Need some manacles,' *and* you were right! That fucking priest killed Mathe, not you. It ain't complex and it ain't about you. Give it a rest," Dom said, deflating a little.

Heden didn't say anything. Dom needed to let it out. Heden knew that if he tried to defend himself, Dom would just get angrier.

"I'm going to have to go talk to his wife," Domnal said.

"Want me to do it?" Heden asked.

"You?"

"Sure," Heden said. "Done it before."

Domnal grunted a negative, adjusting his bulk. "It's got to be me. She'd think I didn't care, if I sent you."

He was probably right. Heden tried to change the subject.

"How's Megan?"

He saw Domnal's face flash blank for an instant and Heden's stomach turned. He recognized the sign that something was wrong between Domnal and his wife, and that just saying her name caused him discomfort. Domnal was about to lie to him.

"She's fine," he said. "Keeps saying we should invite you to dinner."

"You *should* invite me to dinner," Heden said.

Dom sighed at his friend. "You wouldn't come," he said with sympathy. "You'd find an excuse to stay in that fucking inn you never open."

Heden didn't say anything. He had plenty of reasons to stay in the inn and they both knew it.

"She says you just need a woman," Domnal said, gaining interest in talking about something other than the Eseldics and his dead friend.

Heden shrugged. "What did you tell her?"

"I asked her if she was volunteering," he said, flashing a quick smile. Heden smiled a little for show. For some reason he couldn't explain, he found that kind of talk distasteful.

Domnal took the question seriously and answered: "I told her it was too late for you. Tried to explain."

"What'd she say?"

"She don't believe that stuff. Not a romantic, like you." Dom drew out the word "romantic" to make fun of Heden. "She's got a niece she says would play your organ like a fife if you'd but loosen your belt."

Heden looked at the ceiling and blinked as though asking Cavall for strength.

Domnal chuckled at Heden's reaction and this made Heden happy. "She don't know you," Domnal concluded.

Heden waited a moment and changed the subject again.

"Did you know Teagan was a ratcatcher?" Heden asked, guessing at the new guard's old profession.

"What?" Domnal said. "Teagan? Course I did." He frowned. "Everyone does. You know what it's like here, no room for secrets."

Heden *did* know what it was like there and knew there were more secrets than Domnal would let on.

"He's good," Heden said. Domnal was impressed with Heden's evaluation.

"He's a mare." Domnal grinned.

"He's a what?"

Domnal sat back in his chair, his grin turning into a smile.

"Fancies men," Domnal said.

Heden's face went blank for a moment as he absorbed this. "Hm." He shrugged to himself. "Well he's that good in a fight, he can do what he wants with his prick. Who was he with?"

"The Sword of Silver," Domnal said, raising his eyebrows and pronouncing the words with exaggerated precision. Most people thought company names were absurd.

"Really?" Heden said. "They were good. They recovered the Blade of a Thousand Years. I always thought 'The Immortal Blade' would have been a better name for them after that."

"Ah it's all crap," Domnal said, the melancholy returning.

"True," Heden said.

Domnal remembered something and threw a sharp glance at Heden for a moment. Then, seeming embarrassed, cast his eyes down.

"Listen, Heden," he said, screwing his face up with reluctance. "Uh, listen," Domnal said again, lowering his voice as he asked a favor. "I was wondering if you could, you know after everything that happened this morning, if you could...say a blessing for me?"

Heden frowned and looked the watch captain up and down, suspicious of Dom's motive.

Heden shrugged. "Okay," he said. Dom was immediately relieved. The two men got up and approached each other.

Domnal straightened up, eyes closed. Heden grabbed his amulet with his left hand, held up his right, palm out, and prayed to his saint, Lynwen.

Both men stood there, eyes closed, as Heden spoke his prayer in the First Language. As he did so, Heden caught a fleeting glimpse in his mind of two eyes, a woman's, rolling with amusement. Heden felt his hands grow warm and knew Dom was feeling the same unnatural heat.

The prayer was not ceremonial—it purified. It cleansed in proportion with how just and fair the subject was, as was Cavall's will, but Heden prayed to St. Lynwen, who had her own agenda which none but Heden understood. The prayer would strengthen the body and cure small ills. And reveal any physical problems with the supplicant.

Heden's eyes flashed open, angry at the secret Lynwen had revealed to him even as she cured it. Now he knew why Dom was ashamed to ask.

"You fucker," Heden said.

"Heden!" Domnal said, flinching at his friend's judgment.

"You know I'm going to have to pray over Megan now, too."

Domnal half-turned, picked up a proclamation off his desk. "Well you can do that when you come to dinner." He avoided Heden's gaze and pretended to read the document.

"You complete shit, you know she dotes on you. Brags about you."

"Should I tell her, do you think?" Domnal asked, his face pained, his voice quiet.

"Should you…no you should not tell her, you should be faithful to her! You should go to the church and ask Cavall and Llewellyn for forgiveness!"

"Am I going to be alright?" Domnal asked, stung by his friend's anger.

"Not if you keep paying for whores!"

"Listen, Heden, did you come here for a reason?" Domnal struck back, angry because he knew Heden was right. "Everyone here does it, you know. If you gave it a go once in a while, you wouldn't be…" He stopped. Heden cocked his head and raised an eyebrow.

"You going to finish that sentence?" Heden asked mildly.

The small office was silent for a few moments. Then Domnal looked away and sniffed. "Nah," Domnal said.

"You've got someone here for me," Heden said. "A girl."

"What?" Domnal asked, forgetting his earlier question. "Oh fuck you're right," he said, glad to have something else to think about. He put the papers down. "I'd forgotten about her." He reached out and picked up his keychain, his thick fingers searching through the keys.

Heden fingered a small pouch on his belt as Domnal selected the right key and moved to the door. Heden stood behind him.

"Black gods," Domnal said, and Heden saw some weight pulled off him; his body sagged a little with relief. "She's been here for three days. The boys won't go near her. I end up having to bring her food and drink. She's in a terrible state. Not bad-looking though," he mused, then remembered who he was talking to. "I knew they'd send you." He smiled at Heden. "Knew you'd show up to take care of it."

"Yeah," Heden said. Domnal turned to leave.

The watch captain looked over his back. "Thank you for the prayer."

"Yeah," Heden said. "Tell Megan I want hogget." He pushed his friend forward. "Let's go."

Domnal opened the door and led Heden to the cell.

Chapter Three

The jail was one of several small, squat buildings scattered throughout the city. It wasn't designed for much except holding murderous, thieving bastards long enough for the king's castellan to figure out what to do with them.

Three levels extended down, most of them empty most of the time. The girl was in a cell on the second floor, the only occupied cell down there. She was there, Heden knew, so she wouldn't disturb the prisoners on the first floor with her raving.

Heden and Domnal arrived outside the small door. While Domnal unlocked the door and opened it, Heden thought he detected a little fear from the man. Domnal was normally fearless. But madness, possession, loss of identity did scare him, Heden knew.

"Come get me when you're done," Domnal said, turning to leave. "I'll send someone down to clear her out." He stopped and looked with a mixture of gratitude and pity at his friend, about to discharge a terrible duty, and held out his hand. "Thanks again," Dom said.

Heden took his hand, but couldn't look Domnal in the eye. "Won't take long," he said.

Dom nodded, turned and walked off into the darkness. Heden, torch in one hand, looked into the cell but out of the corner of his eye monitored the slow retreat of Domnal's light. The light eventually winked out and Heden was alone.

He stepped into the cell. It was ten feet deep, but only four feet wide. The roof was low but low ceilings had never been a problem for Heden. The cell walls and floor were dark, ruddy clay. There was a cot about a foot off the floor. The door behind him had a small metal plate that could be opened and closed only from the outside, allowing the guards to feed the prisoner. There was a bowl of food on the floor, tipped over, and a bowl of water still intact.

In Heden's estimation the girl was maybe fourteen. She was in the far corner of the cell, on the ground, looking as though she'd crawled there in an attempt to put as much of her body as far away from the door as possible.

She was gibbering. She'd soiled herself and her mouth was bleeding. Her eyes rolled around in her head. For a moment, Heden saw the mad eye of the Eseldic from upstairs.

Heden was relieved. She was in the middle of a fit, which meant she'd be easier to deal with than the last one.

Ensconcing his torch, he walked over, sat on the cot and unlaced the pouch tied to his belt.

He extracted from the small leather pouch what looked like a ball of green pipe tobacco. It glistened in the guttering torchlight. He pulled a small leather strap out from his waist and said a short prayer.

As he prepared, he spoke to the girl. Nothing in particular, in soothing tones. He knew she wouldn't respond, but thought maybe part of her could hear him. Bending down, feeling like a thief, he began his experiment.

The girl seized up, flailing around in spasms. Her long brown hair was matted on her face, and her thin arms and legs were bruised. She wore a short wool shift, courtesy of the jail. Her face was gaunt. Her dark eyes jerked in their sockets, looking at nothing.

Heden got up from the cot and sat on the stone floor next to the girl, grabbed her arm. She didn't resist. She didn't stop her thrashing, but she didn't fight him.

He turned her back towards him so he could put her head in his arms and feed her the herbs he'd brought.

She was slick with blood and sweat and in one great spasm she rolled away from him, hitting him in the nose with her elbow. Heden grunted and scrabbled after her.

He eventually got her head in his lap, her arms and legs not close enough to the walls to get much leverage. He brought the leather strap out, folded it once and forced it into her mouth. She tried to bite around it and seemed at one point as though she might gag on it, but Heden was careful. He wedged the leather in between her upper and lower teeth on the left side of her mouth, preventing her from closing. Her eyes still danced wildly, seeing everything and nothing. It looked like mortal terror.

He took out the ball of green herbs—moistened, preserved and held together with honey—pinched it in half and pushed half of it between her upper cheek and gum, then quickly did the same with the other half and the lower jaw.

He removed the strap. Making sure she didn't bite down on her tongue, he closed her mouth and tied the leather strap around her head, under her chin. Her nostrils flared as she sucked air in through her nose.

The medicine in the herbs would slowly dissolve in her mouth. It wouldn't work if she swallowed it, Heden had read. He wasn't entirely sure it would work at all.

Before she could choke or swallow her tongue, Heden said a quick prayer and she was asleep. Her whole body relaxed, her eyes closed, and it felt to Heden as though her weight on his legs was suddenly lighter.

Heden looked around the room, at the mess, the aftermath of struggle, and thought: *I should have said the prayer first.*

Chapter Four

"Heden, I said I'd…" Domnal stopped. All the guards in the main room stopped to look at him.

Heden carried the young girl, asleep, in his arms. She felt almost weightless to him. He'd taken the time to clean her face and comb her hair. They saw the leather strap he put around her head. They didn't know what it signified, but they knew something had not gone according to plan, and Domnal was upset.

Domnal scowled. "Is she *alive*?"

Half the Eseldics had been processed and assigned cells. The rest were still here, manacled and gagged. Someone had cleaned up the bodies. All the guards stood around tensely looking from Domnal to Heden. All except Teagan, who leaned against one wall, his long legs crossed at the ankles. Teagan didn't seem to be looking at anything.

"What in the horny hells are you doing?" Domnal said, looking at the other guards. He stepped closer to Heden. "You can't take her out of here," he hissed under his breath.

"I'm taking her out of here," Heden said.

Domnal ran his thick fingers across his jowls. He was unsure of what to do.

Heden began to walk out, which meant walking at Domnal. Heden didn't look at him.

"Enough people dead today," Heden said. "Don't you think?"

Domnal, upset but unable to bring himself to do anything about it, stepped out of the way.

Heden stopped at the door and threw a look at the guard next to it. The older man realized what he wanted and rushed to open the door for him, letting Heden out into the new day.

Domnal wiped his hand over his forehead and into his hair. "Shit," he said. The other guards watched him, uncomprehending.

Teagan just shook his head.

Chapter Five

She woke up in an expensive feather bed and for a moment thought she was back at the Rose Petal. Rubbing the sleep from her eyes, she realized this was not the case.

This appeared to be a room at an inn. It was long and narrow; there was a large chest and a bureau for clothes. An expensive full-length mirror told her much about the quality of the inn. Most had no mirrors.

She was upstairs. She could tell because the roof slanted down directly over her and there was a skylight in it. Greyish-white light filled the room. It was overcast outside. She sensed it was morning.

There was a noise and she realized there was a man in the room with her. His back was to her. He took clothes from a pile on a chair, folded them and put them in the bureau. They were not her clothes.

The man didn't seem aware she was awake. He seemed of shorter than average height, but gave the impression of being fit. Well-muscled. His skin was pale. He had short black hair and seemed to be in his forties. She couldn't see his face.

She knew what was expected, however. Though utterly exhausted, her mind wasn't tired. She sat up and adjusted her hair.

"So, do you want me to…uh…" She stopped when the man turned and looked at her.

He had a dress folded in one hand. His clothes, an unstylish but practical combination of leather and wool, ill fit him. His face was hard; it looked chiseled out of granite. There were deep lines in it. While old and weathered, there was something handsome about him.

The look he gave her was a kind of appraisal. She found herself unable to read him and this bothered her. He betrayed no purpose or intent, no desire. She could tell neither what he was thinking nor what he wanted and this made her shiver.

The feeling passed and left her vulnerable. She felt like she was nine again. She pulled the sheets up to her chin.

She startled when, without warning, a large and very heavy black cat appeared on the bed. It had jumped up from the floor without a sound.

The cat walked right up to her without making eye contact, stood on her stomach, and when she reached out, it pushed its head into her hand as though it had known her all its life. It had bright yellow eyes and seemed made of muscle.

She liked cats. Most inns had them to keep the mice and rats down. Some used small dogs. But she was surprised this man kept a cat for any reason.

The man opened the door and, without saying anything, walked out, leaving the way open to the hall beyond.

Petting the cat, she looked around the room, wondering where she was and what, if anything, she should do. Run for it? Her instincts told her this was not necessary.

She was in a nightshift but it was not her own. She pulled back the covers and looked at the garment. It was expensive. But it meant…

The man came back in carrying a tray with hot food on it. She was starving, she realized. But she was more angry than hungry.

"Where are my clothes?" She tried being demanding.

Heden looked around.

"I…don't know," he said. His voice sounded dark and rough. Hearing him speak, she felt awkward. She was alone in a strange man's room and he was not a potential customer. He reminded her of something, but she didn't know what. She felt very small.

"I threw out the shift the guards put you in. I didn't think to ask what they'd done with your clothes."

"The guards?" she asked, frowning.

Heden put the food down on a table. "This is for you," he said. "You're going to be hungry. Eat as much as you want."

"Did you dress me in this?" she asked, indicating her nightshift. The cat purred and tried to position itself to get petted again. She pushed the cat off the bed but it jumped back on making a little trill, walked to the end of the bed and curled up.

Heden looked at her and then at the food then back at her. He sighed, picked up the clothes he'd placed on the chair and sat down. "I gave you a bath, cleaned you and dressed you."

None of this made sense to her. She was confused and getting scared and this made her angry. She wanted to get back to the Rose Petal, back to the safety of an existence she knew.

"Who are you?"

"My name's Heden. When I found you, you'd been put in the jail. You were having a fit."

She stared at him, mouth slack. Her skin began to crawl and she understood what he meant. She realized she couldn't remember the past few days. Her chest tightened up. Her eyes started to turn red and her cheeks flushed.

"What's your name?" he asked.

"What?"

Heden got up, picked up a bowl of soup and a spoon, and approached her. She flinched away but he just stood there, proffering the soup.

There was a smell about him. He didn't wear perfume as many men she knew did, but he smelled…good. Smelled like leather and wool, metal and oil. It was an earthy smell, and though it was not familiar to her, it gave her comfort.

She took the bowl of soup and the spoon and began to eat. This seemed to satisfy the man, and he went back and sat down.

"I'm going to tell you something," he began, but she wasn't really listening. She was thinking about what he just said. She'd been having a fit. The last one she remembered lasted almost a whole day. She had wondered what Miss Elowen would do, knew she'd have to do something eventually. Cold realization struck. *She put me in jail is what she did.*

"I gave you some medicine," the stranger said. It was a term she'd heard but was unfamiliar with. "I gave you something to eat. And you slept for a long time. All through yesterday. But now, I think, you're better."

She continued to work on the soup. It was good, and she felt life and normality returning.

"I don't think you'll have any more fits," he said.

Light dawned.

"You're a priest," she said. She didn't know exactly what he was talking about, or what had happened while she was having her fit, but she got the gist of it and now all his behavior made sense.

Heden pulled a silver medallion out from under his shirt. She couldn't see the sigil on it, but recognized it as a saint's talisman. She narrowed her eyes. He didn't look like any priest she'd ever seen. Nor act like one.

"What's your name?" he asked again.

She looked at him with big, dark eyes. "Violet," she said.

Heden nodded. "What's your real name?"

She just stared at him, the near-empty bowl of soup cooling in her hands, and heard herself say "Vanora." There were not many people left who knew her real name.

He smiled. "That's a pretty name. But I can call you Violet if it helps."

"What..." she said, and to her ears she sounded small and girlish. She cleared her throat. "What do I owe for the room?"

"Nothing," Heden said. "This is my inn."

"This is your inn?"

Heden nodded.

"You own a whole inn?"

Heden shrugged.

She nodded, eyes wide, and looked around again. She looked at the cat curled up at the foot of the bed.

"That's your cat?" she asked.

"Her name's Ballisantirax."

"What kind of name is that?"

"It's a long story," he said.

She lowered her head and gave him a look from under her eyebrows. "You don't seem like someone who'd like cats," she said.

Heden shrugged. "I like this cat."

She nodded again. She'd known this person less than a turn, but his response seemed entirely typical.

He stood up.

"If you're hungry, eat. If you feel sleepy, go back to sleep. Balli will watch you. There's a chamber pot under your bed, and a bath down the hall. I'll be back up here in an hour to clear everything away."

She looked up at him with something like a sense of wonder. He looked back at her, and she realized he had blue eyes. He seemed to make some sort of judgment about her, took a quick inventory of the room, pursed his lips and nodded to himself, turned and walked out of the room, closing the door. She did not hear him lock it.

Chapter Six

Heden knew as soon as he closed the door to Vanora's room that someone was downstairs. The air changed. Something was downstairs absorbing small sounds that were usually present and making small sounds that were usually absent.

Pausing only for the moment it took to take stock of the situation, he proceeded downstairs. He made no attempt at stealth; he was terrible at it anyway.

As he descended he first caught sight of his guest's shoes. The expensive red-dyed suede-and-silk hose told him who his guest was before he ever saw his face. Gwiddon. The bishop's attaché. The man responsible for spying on the heads of the city for the bishop.

He sat, striking a pose, in a chair at a table near a window. The wan grey light from outside spilled into the room, doing little to chase the shadows away. Gwiddon rested his prominent cheekbone on a thin finger and smiled through the window at the people walking by outside. Occasionally someone would see him inside and press their faces, hands cupped near their eyes to block out the light, and look in. *There's a person in there! Is the place open? No. No I guess not. Just one man inside, nothing else.*

Gwiddon didn't look at Heden—he just kept smiling with little humor and looking out the window.

"Let me get you a drink," Heden said.

Gwiddon gave no introduction and seemed to expect none. If Heden was being rude by not saying "good day to you," Gwiddon didn't appear to notice.

"I try to tell them," Gwiddon said, waggling his fingers at the people walking by. "Roughly once a month someone mentions you and this place and they always ask the same thing."

"I have some wine, imported from Rône," Heden said as he rummaged around behind the bar. "Not even noon yet. Brandy…port…. Ale will have to do." Heden dusted off two thick glasses.

"'Why doesn't he open that place?'" Gwiddon quoted. "'Why did he waste his money?'"

Heden came over with the ale and sat down. He took a long drink from his. It was only a few hours after dawn, but it had already been a long day.

Gwiddon picked up his glass without looking at it and toasted the passersby. He spoke in a slow, measured cadence, each phrase following the next like a steady machine.

"I love the look in their eyes so I make a point to ask them to guess how much you paid for this place. They never guess high enough—they've never been inside of course—and when I tell them…well, the look alone is worth it. Then I smile and explain that the reason you don't try to recoup your investment is that for you, it was such an insultingly small amount of money," he said, with a chuckle.

"You tell them that?" Heden asked.

"Yes," Gwiddon said, absently, still looking outside. "We had the castellan over to dinner once; he choked when I said it. Poor man."

Gwiddon took a drink from his glass and frowned at it. Turning to face Heden across the oak table, he said, "This is terrible."

Heden shrugged and had some more. "It was fine when I bought it."

Gwiddon's face was thin and fine-boned, his straw hair curled naturally. His lips were thin and bright red against a complexion that matched his hair, light without seeming unhealthy. His pale blue eyes transmitted intelligence to anyone who might receive.

Gwiddon tried more ale. It wasn't to his liking, but he was getting used to it. His lips turned down in a small frown. "What do you do, buy new stock every six weeks?"

"Yep," Heden said.

Gwiddon coughed into his drink. "Honestly?"

"Honestly," Heden said, leaning back in his chair. "I have deals with the Fool and the Vine. I sell them my unused stuff. Stupid to let it go to waste."

Gwiddon looked into his ale as though expecting to make some discovery about its contents. "Now I know why I keep away from the Vine, the place serves the stuff you've had sitting here rotting." He placed special emphasis on "rotting," letting the word roll off his tongue. His sentences always came out like a performance. He was a natural. Heden always felt like a thug next to him.

"Another story for you to tell at dinner," Heden said with a sigh, feeling tired.

"You jest," Gwiddon said, flashing a wide smile, "but I *will* tell it. If they had any idea how much you came back with, they'd not turn their nose up at what you did."

"Yes they would," Heden said.

Gwiddon was among the most cultured, well-educated, well-read, well-written and expensively outfitted men in the city, and he knew it. He made sure other people knew it. He was taller and slimmer than Heden. Heden envied him for having the kind of build tailors made all their clothes for. The two of them could not have been more different. But they shared one thing in common.

"What does the bishop want?" Heden asked.

"Really, Heden, why don't you hire someone to run this place?"

Heden took a deep breath. "You offering?"

Gwiddon chuckled. "In two days I could find you a man you could trust, who knew bartending and innkeeping, and this place would produce a hundred crowns a month in profit."

Heden shrugged. "I don't need the money."

Gwiddon's loud smile was somewhat muted by this. "No, I suppose you don't. You're the only person I know who had nostalgia for a future instead of a past. And when you built it, you found you didn't want it. Now you think: better not to have built it, eh? At least then you'd still have the nostalgia, which you loved, as opposed to this, which you don't."

"You've been talking to the abbot," Heden said.

"Please." Gwiddon seemed affronted. "It is possible for mere mortals to possess insight into the human condition. Especially concerning someone I've known for—" He waved his hand. "—however many years."

Heden didn't say anything. What was there to say?

"How was your visit to the jail?"

Heden took a deep breath. "Well I was there for a quarter-turn and a guard died."

Gwiddon read his face in an instant. "Don't tell me," he said. "You had nothing to do with it but you blame yourself."

Heden shrugged. "Ok, I won't tell you."

Gwiddon smiled. "At least some things in the world are constant. How did things go with the girl?" Gwiddon looked away, gave Heden some privacy to react without being scrutinized.

"Fine," Heden lied.

"The bishop didn't think you would, ah..."

"Is that why he sent you?"

"I volunteered. First I volunteered *you*, then I volunteered to tell you."

Heden didn't say anything.

"He was surprised," Gwiddon said, meaning the bishop. "I think he'd written you off."

"Understandable."

"So now, of course, he thinks you're ready for something else."

Heden shook his head. It wasn't clear what he was rejecting.

"I told him the girl was a special case. I don't think he remembered the boy last year."

"No reason for him to," Heden said, drinking. Only someone who'd known Heden for a long time would hear the implied criticism.

"I didn't think the girl meant anything had changed."

"But you didn't tell the bishop that."

"I couldn't think of how to explain it to him. Besides, I don't mind coming here. I'm used to rejection." Gwiddon flashed a smile. When it was gone, he said, Speaking of which..." He placed both his hands flat on the table and sat up straight.

"We need someone to go into the wode," he said. As with "the church," everyone knew which of the elf-haunted forests people meant when they referred to "the wode."

Heden stared across the table, and waited until he recovered a little from Gwiddon's statement.

> "And you have some reason to think I might say yes." The sentence came out slow and ragged, like Heden was emerging from a deep sleep.

Now it was Gwiddon's turn to shrug.

"You went in with your team eight years ago. You came out unscathed."

"That's debatable," Heden said. "And there were six of us. I'm alone now." Heden restrained himself and didn't spit out the word "alone." "And we went in a year before that and lost half our company, so you coming in here—" Heden gestured to the door. "—sitting down and saying 'wode' like it's just a fucking word people say, like that thing doesn't grow old on the bones of people like me, you need to have a good reason."

Gwiddon's face pinched a little in response to Heden's minor onslaught.

Heden shook his head, didn't give Gwiddon a chance to respond. "That's not it. You didn't come here because I've been up there before. You're just trying to flatter me. Which is…I don't even know why you bother. Give me the real reason."

Gwiddon sighed. "Fair enough," he said, extracting what looked like a small sprig of holly from his vest. It had nine berries on it. Eight a pale green, one a milky white.

"You know the procession hall?"

Heden nodded.

"This is one of the knightly crests that hang on the walls."

Heden frowned and reached out for the holly. It wasn't any kind of crest.

"I don't understand, how can this be a device?"

"Good question. We think it's what you got before all the heraldry was formalized."

"'Before…?' How old is this?

"Old," Gwiddon said. "It's mentioned in records going back as long as we've looked. We all thought it was a decoration. An acolyte brought it to us when he noticed that one of the berries had turned white. That's when we started looking into it. It's magic, obviously."

"What else?" Heden asked, thinking.

"Each berry represents a knight. A member of the Green Order."

Heden nodded. "Nice name," he said, looking at the holly. He twirled it with his fingers. "Simple. Must be old."

"You've never heard of them?"

Heden looked at Gwiddon. "No."

"I was afraid you'd say that. We hoped that you, having been in the Iron Forest..."

"What's that got to do with it?"

"That's where the knights are. Their order lives in the forest, all along the border with Corwell, and protects...well, we don't know what they protect. Something important."

"They live in the wode?" Heden said, half to himself. He had a hard time imagining how any man could do that.

He prodded the sprig of holly.

"Why is this one white?" he asked, talking about the discolored berry.

"It's dead," Gwiddon said.

"Meaning one of the knights is dead?"

"Something like that."

"How did he die?" Heden asked.

Gwiddon sat up. "We don't know," he said with some import.

"Are they some kind of..." Heden thought. "Are they immortal? So what if a knight dies?"

"They're not immortal," Gwiddon said. "We think the white berry symbolizes not the death of a knight, which must be a common occurrence up there, but the..." he searched for words. "The permanent reduction of the order. Nine knights to eight. Eight forever more."

Heden nodded. "So something bad happened up there."

Gwiddon didn't say anything. He knew his friend.

"Who's their patron?"

"I, ah..." Gwiddon thought for a moment. "I forget. You'd recognize the name if I told you. I'm not good with saints."

"You picked a good job," Heden said.

"We need someone to go up there and find out what happened. We found an old ritual, very old. Maybe a thousand years. Meant to absolve the Green Order of an unrighteous death."

"The Green Order specifically?" Heden doubted that.

"This is more than just a dead knight, Heden."

"But a thousand years? How can there be an order of knights older than the Council of Aberdanon?"

"I don't understand it all. The bishop has an idea, he'll tell you about it."

"Not if I tell you to go fuck a pig, he won't."

"There is that," Gwiddon conceded.

Thinking of the wode, Heden found his heart was racing. He was having trouble breathing. Finally he spoke.

"No."

Gwiddon looked at his friend, sensing the turmoil Heden was holding back. He stayed silent for a moment, said "Okay," and leaned back in his chair.

"I'm not going back into that meat grinder."

Gwiddon nodded and fingered his drink. "I understand," he said.

"Find someone else," Heden said.

"Who would you recommend?" Gwiddon made a show of looking around the empty tavern.

Heden seemed to shrink over the course of the conversation. He was hunched over now and looking down at the table. He wouldn't make eye contact with his friend. He shook his head almost imperceptibly. Gwiddon turned away.

They both sat there: Heden looking down at nothing. Gwiddon, relaxed, looking out the window. Neither of them said anything.

"Why did you think I might say yes?" Heden finally asked, risking a glance at his friend.

Gwiddon leaned back. "I'll tell you. The bishop, ah, and I—although in this case what I think is inconsequential—are afraid this order is important. Out there in the forest handing down a tradition for thirty generations. Not much of that kind of discipline left in the world."

Heden nodded.

"We need someone who can manage a delicate situation. Someone we can trust to do the right thing, even if that means doing something awful." Gwiddon chose his words carefully. He knew his audience. "You were the natural solution."

"The only solution," Heden said, with a touch of bitterness.

Gwiddon smiled and spread his hands. "As you say."

Heden sat there looking at the holly.

"I don't like knights," Heden said to himself.

"I know," Gwiddon said, pursing his lips in a thin, affectionate smile. "But you don't like them for all the right reasons."

Heden grunted and twirled the holly around. After a moment's silence, Gwiddon prodded.

"Where's the girl now?" he asked quietly.

"What?" Heden was sharp in response.

"The girl from the jail," Gwiddon asked. "I heard from the captain."

Heden was impressed that Domnal had told anyone. But Gwiddon was discreet.

Heden didn't answer. Gwiddon wasn't really looking for an answer, he knew. He was just making a point.

"What if we gave you help?" he asked, with sympathy.

"Help?" Heden asked, unsure how Gwiddon could help.

"With the forest," his friend said.

"I don't need any help, dammit," Heden said, tossing the holly on the table and looking out the window. Gwiddon didn't understand and Heden didn't feel obligated to explain. It wasn't the forest, terrible as it was, that presented the problem; it was Heden.

"We could give you a coach. Make the journey easier for you."

"Nothing would make the journey easy for me. Where's the order now?"

"They've decamped at a priory in the forest. Near a place called Ollghum Keep."

"Never heard of it."

"It's at the edge of the forest," Gwiddon said.

Heden absorbed this. For reasons he didn't understand and didn't want to think about, the idea of facing Vanora again with having turned down Gwiddon upset him. Maybe because Gwiddon's request brought him to Vanora in the first place. Maybe because he didn't want to seem a coward in front of her. Even if she never knew he'd turned the bishop down.

"What are you working on?" Heden tried some small talk to distract himself.

"What am *I* working on?" Gwiddon asked, surprised.

"Coming here and telling me about a bunch of knights who live in the forest is a diversion for you."

Gwiddon smiled and shook his head. "Spying on the king is the easiest job in the church," he said. "Just get invited to the right parties, ply the right people with drink. Occasionally seduce a young courtesan who might know something."

"Or might not."

Gwiddon shrugged. "It helps to keep in practice," he said.

A door closed at the top of the stairs behind him, and Vanora walked delicately downstairs clad in a simple blue dress he'd left for her.

"Heden?" she asked.

Gwiddon looked at the teenage girl, then turned his head slowly to Heden, a huge, wide grin on his face. "Speaking of which!"

Heden looked at his friend and frowned.

"It's time for you to leave," Heden said, getting up.

"I imagine it is!" Gwiddon said, smiling riotously. He stood.

As Heden escorted him the short distance to the door, Gwiddon turned back to the girl again, looking over Heden's shoulder. Realization dawned.

"Wait a moment. Heden…"

Heden opened the door. "Out," he said. Gwiddon now turned a serious face to his friend bordering on a scowl.

"Oh Heden, please tell me you…"

"I'm not telling you anything, you're leaving."

"Okay," Gwiddon said, and he stepped out onto the porch. "I hope you know what you're doing." He looked at his friend for a moment.

"You're going to accept the assignment," Gwiddon said. A prediction.

Heden shrugged.

"I'll talk to the bishop," he said.

"You should see the abbot before you leave," Gwiddon offered, extending his hand.

Heden shook his friend's hand. "I'll see the abbot when I get back. I'll see the dwarf before I leave."

Chapter Seven

Vanora wandered around the ground floor of the Hammer & Tongs. The wood had been varnished several times in the last three years and never walked on, so her feet stuck to the floor a little when she walked, making little sucking noises when she lifted them.

Heden didn't make eye contact with her. He closed the door, went back to the table, picked up the glasses from Gwiddon's visit and walked behind the bar. The heavy sound of his boots seemed very loud to him.

One wall of the T-shaped common room was covered by bookshelves Heden had installed himself. Several hundred books collected dust. Vanora stared, sometimes reaching out to touch one.

Heden went into the kitchen and a few moments later emerged with a large plate, a hunk of mutton, some vegetables and some fruit. He put the plate on the bar and began slicing the mutton.

"You read all these books?" Vanora asked.

Heden did not reply. He continued preparing his lunch. Vanora gave no indication that she expected a reply.

"Where'd you learn to read?" Vanora asked, her voice light, curious.

Heden took a deep breath. "My father was friends with the prior the next town over. When I was thirteen, the prior sent me to a rectory as my apprenticeship."

Heden threw some of the fruit and vegetables on a plate with the mutton, poured himself a beer, and carried the whole thing to a table and sat down. "First person in my family to read and write."

Vanora gave no indication she heard him. With some effort, she pulled one of the larger books out and opened it. She had to cradle it in both of her arms. She frowned at the text.

"That's a good book," Heden said while Vanora looked at the pages. "It's about a girl who finds out she's the daughter of a god. It's got a lot of pictures. Inlaid with real gold." Vanora raised her eyebrows and tried to hold the book and leaf through the pages at the same time. Her brown hair fell over her face. She seemed thin to Heden and he got the impression as he often did with women from the Rose that she needed to eat more.

"I'll teach you to read it," Heden said. Not an offer, a decision.

Vanora stopped struggling with the book and just stared at the letters, absorbing what Heden had said. She shrugged and put the book back on the shelf.

Seeming very much at home in this strange inn, she crossed the floor, pulled a chair out and sat across from Heden. She watched him eat. She raised an eyebrow at what he was eating and the way he ate, but he didn't seem to notice.

He seemed entirely unselfconscious. As if having a barefoot teenage whore walking around his inn was normal for him. Something about that bothered her.

"We get priests at the Rose," she said, crossing her arms. It was cold in the large common room. "They're just like everyone else. Good priests, bad priests. They can be a lot of fun. Some of them act bothered…" She stopped. She wouldn't look at Heden. She wasn't sure what was going on, but she didn't want to talk about the jail.

"So what do you want with me?"

Heden shrugged while he ate. He hadn't thought that far ahead. "Up to you," he said. "I helped you back at the jail; maybe I'm just trying to see it through. Make sure you end up where you want to be."

She grunted, skeptical.

"You're not bothered by what I do?" she asked, studying him for any reaction or belief or attitude. "You didn't come to the jail because…" She left the question hanging.

Heden sighed and stabbed a slice of mutton with his fork. He didn't like talking and he was about to do a lot of it.

"A year ago," he said, not looking at her, "the bishop asked me to go to the jail because there was a boy there who'd been sentenced to be drowned. The church said the boy was possessed by a demon too powerful to cast out. No one there could cure him. No prayer worked. Drowning is the traditional fate for the possessed."

Heden ate some mutton and talked while he ate, his voice casual like he was describing the weather.

"He was like you," he said, giving her the merest glance. The high-backed chair dwarfed her, making her look even smaller. "He had fits and couldn't control his body. He'd spit and soil himself and his whole mouth would be torn up, bloody. He'd bitten half his tongue off when he was younger. He'd be fine for days and then have a fit that lasted hours."

Without looking at Vanora, Heden was aware he had her full attention.

"Everyone around him—" He took another bite and chewed. "—thought he was possessed and so when the church agreed and sentenced him to death, everyone was…relieved. Even his parents, you understand." He chewed and swallowed and looked at her to gauge her reaction.

Vanora was wide-eyed, fixated on Heden. She was holding her breath. She was mesmerized.

"They sent me there…" Heden paused, remembering the meeting with the bishop. "They sent me there because the church, having declared him possessed, was obligated to make sure the boy was killed. But drowning is a terrible way to die." Heden paused. "There are good ways to die, believe me. Drowning isn't one of them."

Heden stopped eating, drank some beer, and then sat back and looked behind Vanora at the books in his library.

"The bishop called for me and explained the situation. He didn't ask me to do anything, he just…explained the situation. He'd seen men drowned before, for this same reason, and he talked about how awful it was. He didn't need to tell me.

"So that's how it works. I don't think I said anything. I knew what the bishop wanted. From the church's point of view the boy had to die, but the bishop didn't want him to suffer."

"Where's the boy now?" Vanora asked, her voice quiet, timid.

Heden looked at her, hard, unflinching, with no expression, and said, "Vanora, he's dead. I killed him."

The breath exploded out of her and she put her hands to her mouth. She could not bring herself to look away from Heden's impassive face. Heden looked away for her sake and continued. He looked out the window, mimicking Gwiddon.

"He was terrified when I got there. Babbling. He wasn't having a fit, he was just…pissing himself out of desperate fear that he was about to die and there wasn't anything he could do about it and no one would listen to him and everyone and everything he knew, his parents and the church, all approved. It was a kind of waking nightmare for him." The words tumbled out. Heden had never told this story to anyone.

"I was with him for an hour. I talked to him, I calmed him down. I told him everything was going to be okay. I told him that his parents loved him, that they wouldn't let anything bad happen to him. He sobbed, relieved. That was all he wanted to hear, I think.

"I let him think everything was going to be fine and he collapsed, asleep, exhausted. Then I said a certain prayer and that was it. He was gone. Even if…I told myself that even if the church hadn't been…" He waved a hand vaguely. "The church, even if they'd let him live, his life would have been short and full of pain and I was doing him a mercy. Maybe the bishop thought the same thing."

Neither of them said anything. Vanora's face was a conflict of fear of Heden and compassion for him. After a few moments passed, Heden took a deep breath and continued.

"I thought about that every night for months," Heden said, rubbing his hand over the stubble of beard on his face. "I fall asleep thinking about what happened, thinking about the boy, about his fits. I knew he wasn't possessed. I think the bishop did too. That's not how possession works." He looked at Vanora and said, without expression, "That's not how demons work. I relived the whole thing in my mind, over and over. What the bishop had said, what I had done. I felt very sad for the boy, but…what was there to do?

"Then I remembered something a friend of mine said. He was smart, smarter than me. He and I and some others were looking over the body of a friend of ours who'd killed himself. He said something then that I didn't understand. But I never forgot it. He said, 'I wonder what kind of catastrophic failure the mind is experiencing, to view self-destruction as the only solution?'

"I didn't understand him. I thought it was in poor taste, but that moment came to me as I was falling asleep. His point of view. Which I thought I'd never understand. I got up and came down here and went to the bookcase," he said, nodding at the books Vanora had been examining earlier, "and I pulled out a book he gave me."

"He was a physician. A kind of godless priest." Heden smiled at this phrase, and the memory of his friend. "His people are the best physicians in the world. I read through the book, took me weeks. But I found a description of what was happening to the boy. All the same things. Like they'd been there when that boy had a fit and just wrote down everything he did." For a moment Heden was lost again, remembering his own wonder at how the words from a people fifteen hundred miles away could so accurately describe a boy they'd never met. He knew the gods had guided him to that moment. "Anyway, there was a cure right there in the book. Some plants, herbs. Instructions on how to prepare them. There's a little magic involved, not much.

"The next day I started collecting the plants. I don't know why. I'd never encountered anyone like that boy before, no reason to think I would again. Some of the herbs were hard to come by. I cooked it up, followed the instructions, and then put it away. Packed it in honey to preserve it. Until…yesterday."

"Yesterday," Vanora said.

"Yesterday," Heden repeated. "When I was sent to do to you what I did to him, and for the same reason." Vanora stared at him. She'd realized what his story meant, her role in it. But him saying it so plainly made it real. Horrible, but at the same time…took some power it had over her away.

"You didn't," she said. "You didn't know what I…"

Heden picked up his drink. "I wasn't going to kill another boy. Or girl," he said. "Bishop be damned." He took a drink.

"Anyway that's it. Long story. It worked, by the way," he said, putting the drink down. He smiled at her. Vanora smiled a little for the first time. "Praise the Hazarite," he said. She smiled some more, even though she didn't know what Heden meant.

"What was your friend's name?" she asked.

"Khalil," he said. She nodded.

"I should go," Vanora said, seeming apprehensive. "Miss Elowen will be upset."

Heden shrugged.

Vanora looked at him, waiting for him to say something.

"I don't think she expected to ever see you again. I doubt she knows you're alive."

Vanora looked away, and even though Heden wasn't looking at her, he knew she was trying to avoid crying. Heden was a little proud of himself that being honest with her had worked. He made a mental note to tell the abbot about this.

"You can stay here if you want. You can go. It's up to you."

Still not facing him, she snorted once and nodded. "What would I do here?" she asked. Direct. Heden liked that.

"I don't know," Heden admitted. "I'll think about it. You'll have some say in the matter in any case and if you don't like it, there's always Miss Elowen."

She couldn't tell if he thought that was a good thing or a bad thing. Heden cleared the table off, disappeared behind a door that Vanora presumed went into the kitchen, and returned a few moments later. He didn't say goodbye; he just walked towards the door, adjusting the fit of his clothes, opened the door and then stood there and looked back.

"I have to go talk to…my boss," he said, for some reason wanting to avoid mentioning the bishop after his story. "Try to keep out of the cat's way. Balli earns her keep and at the moment you do not."

Vanora couldn't tell if he was joking. She just looked at him as he left her alone in the empty tavern.

Chapter Eight

"Knights must die all the time."

It was a small room and the bishop's writing desk took up most of it. The ornate wood paneling on the walls had at some point been covered over with expensive tapestries. They absorbed sound and Heden felt like he was packed in cotton every time he came in here. It was dark, lit with the steady golden light of four candles in sconces on the walls. Heden was dressed in his ill-fitting plain wool, but the bishop was wearing nearly his full regalia. All in blue and silver and black, the ceremonial colors of the largest church of Cavall.

"Are you sure you…" The bishop indicated an untouched tray of biscuits.

Heden raised a hand. "Please, your grace, no. I've been eating or drinking or watching people eat or drink all day."

The bishop smiled. Bishop Conmonoc was tall and gaunt with a hawkish face. His rheumy eyes betrayed his age. Conmonoc had ascended to the hierarch's position when Heden was a boy, and though he remembered his father talking about the previous bishop, and he knew there would be one after, Conmonoc would always be "the" bishop to Heden. The archetype. Heden found it difficult to judge the man as a result.

"Gwiddon didn't think you'd come," the bishop said, his lips curling at one corner.

"He's known me a long time," Heden said. Giving a nonanswer to a nonquestion.

"But you're here," the bishop said. Heden wondered if he was going to congratulate himself on being right. "I've asked Gwiddon for your service...perhaps three times in the last year and in each instance you refused."

Heden squirmed a little in his chair.

"I wouldn't say that."

The bishop made a discreet flourish with one hand, encouraging Heden to elaborate.

"I just didn't think I'd be any use to you."

"That may be," Bishop Conmonoc conceded. "But don't you think that's for me to decide?"

"If you believed that," Heden said, looking straight at him, "you wouldn't have let me say no."

The bishop seemed to find that answer amusing. "We both know that's not true. What made you change your mind?"

Heden shrugged. He hadn't thought about it. He said the first thing that came into his mind. "I didn't want to disappoint..." He wasn't sure how that sentence was going to end and for some reason didn't want to follow the thought. "Anyone," he said.

The bishop studied him for a moment. Heden was obviously not talking about disappointing the bishop or Cavall.

He lifted a biscuit from the silver tray and took a bite no larger than a bird's, careful to cup his other hand under it to catch any crumbs. After he'd eaten three tiny bites, he threw the rest away, picking a damp cloth out of a small brass bowl to clean his fingers. Heden watched this without comment.

"As you say, knights die all the time," the bishop said. He flashed a brief, humorless smile, tossing the cloth back into the bowl. "The question is *how* the knight died, you see. Normally a dead knight is replaced by a squire trained up for the purpose, but if the death is *unrighteous,* well then. The order's patron reduces the size of the order by one. It's a form of judgment. The order shrinks for every such death. Until the unrighteous death is atoned for."

"The murderer punished," Heden concluded.

The bishop raised a single finger of his right hand.

"It's unclear that there is a murder. The order is so remote, we have no real idea what goes on up there. The idea that they could operate up there for centuries without anything like this happening means this is an extraordinary circumstance. Or they are extraordinary knights."

"So murder or suicide."

"You grasp these things so well," the bishop said with a sigh. He knew Heden didn't like it when he congratulated him on his insight, but he didn't understand why.

"I figure out how he died and...do something about it."

"You understand that if the death was unrighteous, justice may be very hard to attain. The whole order may bear some burden."

"Yeah," Heden said, turning away to look at one of the tapestries. "I understand that."

"My apologies," the bishop said. "I don't mean to sound patronizing." He wanted Heden to like him, and he suspected he didn't. But like so much about this man, he didn't know why.

"I know," Heden said. "You can't help it."

The bishop flashed a smile again, vaguely aware he'd been insulted, but unsure how to respond. An awkward silence settled between them.

Heden felt bad for his jibe and filled the silence.

"Who's their patron?"

"Halcyon," the bishop said, raising an eyebrow.

Heden searched his memory and sunk back in the plush red chair. "I'm not familiar with the name, your grace."

"There's no reason you should be. She's one of a handful of saints who predate the Age of Saints. In her case, by almost five hundred years."

Heden nodded.

"That's how she has knights older than the Council."

The bishop nodded once.

"What should I expect?" Heden asked.

The bishop spread his hands. "We've done quite a lot of research, none of it very helpful. They live in the forest, they fight all manner of creature, specializing in the kind of thing you used to do when you were younger." He smiled in what he must have thought was a sign of camaraderie. "They have a reputation. It's the environment, you see. Only the strong survive up there.

"We know precious little else. We're trying to find someone who's been up there and can tell us more. They report to the local barons, they have a priory. Apart from that, whatever's happened must be…unusual. Deeply wrong, morally or perhaps spiritually. Otherwise we'd never have learned of it."

"You could send the White Hart," Heden said.

"I could," the bishop said. "Especially if I wanted the Green Order hunted down and destroyed. The Hart are not that kind of tool, as well you know."

"What are your wishes?" Heden asked.

"Only that you do what you think is right. You're going to have to, ah, make a judgment on the spot, as it were."

Heden shook his head, frustrated.

"Cavall has yet to reveal to me more than a sense that the order protects the people from the forest. From the things in the forest. And that they are critical to our safety."

"That covers a lot," Heden said.

"You seem skeptical."

Heden wouldn't look at the bishop. "The wode is…it's massive. I don't think people have any real understanding of how big it is. And the things that live there, a lot of them were made by the celestials, remember them. Carry their power. The place is a nightmare. Yeah, I'm skeptical. What could nine knights do?"

"One of the reasons Gwiddon recommended you. I don't think either of us knows anyone who's ever been inside the wode. Of course, if my instincts are correct, you would have been the only choice in any event."

"Because your instincts tell you…"

"That this is a thorny problem requiring a nicety of judgment. I believe that when this is done, you'll have had to do…things you may never be able to reveal to me.

"The order must survive, Heden. They've been guarding our people from the forest for a thousand years. But everything ends. The order must end someday. I had never heard of them before a week ago, but I don't want them to fail their mission, ah...on my watch, as the castellan would say."

Heden thought, and said nothing.

"You'll learn more when you get to Ollghum Keep. The people there, they live with the threat of the Iron Forest. They know the order. They know more about the order than they do the church or the king. You'll be able to speak on my behalf though, obviously, not on my authority."

Heden didn't seem impressed by this.

"The people up there won't want to talk to me. They're suspicious of strangers."

"The knights won't be happy to see you either. I doubt they know who I am, or that their order falls under my influence. Everything we've read describes them as zealots, devoted to the forest."

"They sound like a bunch of druids."

"I came to the same conclusion," the bishop said, smiling. "We'll give you the ritual. Once you've meted out justice to those who transgressed, the dead knight can be replaced and you can come home."

Heden looked concerned. The bishop looked at him sympathetically.

"I can't obligate you to go. Not anymore." He smiled again.

Heden took out the holly and looked at it. Eight pale green berries never ripening, and one milky white berry.

"What if the ritual can't be performed?" Heden asked, implying there might be no absolution for the unrighteous death.

The bishop tilted his head to one side. "Then the order shrinks to eight members. If that's what you decide," he said, emphasizing "you."

Heden took a deep breath and held the holly up in the candlelight of the bishop's office. He twirled the branch. He let his breath out slowly and, when he was done, put the holly back in his vest.

He got up and offered his hand to the bishop. The two men shook hands. A special ceremony only Heden could observe. Saying nothing, Heden walked towards a bookcase behind and to the left of the bishop's desk, pulled on a nondescript book, and the bookcase swung away, revealing a lit passageway beyond. The same way he'd come in.

Heden exited. As soon as the false bookcase swung closed with a click, the main door to the room opened and Gwiddon walked in. He flowed into position before the bishop, bowed, pulled his cloak into his right arm with a flourish and sat in the same chair Heden had recently occupied.

He braced his hands together and smiled widely at the bishop.

"I was right," the bishop said with some satisfaction as he wiped his hands with a damp white cloth.

Gwiddon bowed his head.

"Your instincts were correct." Gwiddon betrayed a little amusement and chose his words carefully.

The bishop threw the damp cloth at the younger man and scowled without malice. Gwiddon snatched it out of the air.

"I was lucky," the bishop said. "I see that now. Something's different. I almost didn't notice it, but our friend has changed somewhat."

"He's certainly changed," Gwiddon said, remembering the girl back at Heden's inn.

"He's so humorless and dour."

"He's got a sense of humor. At least he did."

"Ah?" the bishop prompted.

Gwiddon crossed and uncrossed his legs, delaying. He didn't want to say what he was about to say.

"I mentioned this last time. After Aendrim..." Gwiddon left it. "You know their knight killed himself? Heden at the inn, it's...it's the same thing. I don't know why he said yes, I'm not sure he knows. And then into the wode of all things. I have no idea what it will do to him. I was surprised he accepted."

"Perhaps his own way of ending it. Going into the wode to die."

"Hah," Gwiddon said. "No, your grace. Heden would never do that. He's too..." He was at a loss to explain. "He'd consider that dramatic," Gwiddon said, putting special emphasis on the last word. "Self-important. He's too stubborn for that, your grace."

The bishop nodded his understanding. Gwiddon leaned forward and took a biscuit from the bishop's silver plate. A bee had ridden in on the back of his cloak and now took the opportunity to buzz into flight and land on the colorful biscuit. He brushed it off, annoyed.

"Should I be afraid for our friend?" the bishop asked, frowning. The bee flew away.

"Afraid? For Heden?" Gwiddon shook his head. "I know of no one in Celkirk less deserving of concern. Rather, be afraid for the order."

"He'll be far from the city," the bishop said. "And he doesn't know what the Green Order can do."

"Well, as to that." Gwiddon tilted his head in deference. "None of us do. A week ago we'd never heard of them."

"Mmm," the bishop said, turning to look at the bookshelf Heden had disappeared behind.

Chapter Nine

Heden arrived at the smithy just after noon, already weary from a long day getting longer. Though it was grey and overcast, it was hot and humid and he wasn't dressed for it. He had a mail shirt on under his jerkin. When he realized it was the mail that was causing him discomfort, he was surprised to learn he'd put it on. He couldn't remember doing so. Obviously, he thought, a part of him decided it was appropriate for some reason.

The smithy was known as the Sun & Anvil because the signs over the entrances had a stylized dawning sun rising over an anvil. The name had been Dawnforge, but very few people knew that. Unlike in the vastly more advanced city of Capital, where shops and streets were named and the names printed on signs, shops in Vasloria used symbols to communicate what kinds of services you could find inside. It was only by intuition and common consensus that places acquired names. Having been to the distant city of Capital, Heden was surprised that signs without words worked so well.

The dawning sun was one of a handful of symbols—the moon and stars being other common examples—which meant magic could be found within, for a price. Heden couldn't remember when he learned this, but he was certain the majority of people who came and went didn't know it. There was no reason they should.

The Sun & Anvil was more than a blacksmith shop; it handled metalworking of all types and employed over two dozen workmen, including specialists in precious metals and jewelry.

As soon as he was standing outside the wide stone archway, he felt the powerful heat radiating from the shop. The throng of people on the street gave the place a wide berth to avoid the thick heat in the already humid day.

Heden stepped inside. It was busy. In the center of the warehouse-sized building was the main forge where metals were heated. It was built into a column of stone that went from floor to ceiling. The octagonal building's ceiling tilted upward into a central chimney, turning the whole building into a flue.

There were customers from across the strata of the city talking with workmen. Almost all men, but Heden could see a handful of polder as well, their short, diminutive frames making them look a bit like children, but the way they held themselves and moved revealed their inhuman nature.

There was nothing subtle about the two massive warbred urq who worked in the place. The wizards who created them decades ago bred no special love for craftsmanship into them, but they were strong and, cast adrift from the war they were made for, they searched for jobs that brought honor and kept them away from the public. Living among men went without saying; there was no question of them making a life among the urq.

The forge was loud, the ring of hammers was loud—everyone in the place had to shout to be heard. Heden stood just inside the doorway.

There was a knot of people standing off to his right. Heden looked at them. It looked like two patrons and three craftsmen discussing a project. They were all smiling as they talked. It was generally a good place to work and do business.

One of them caught Heden's eye and stopped smiling. The rest saw the man's reaction and turned to look at Heden. The patrons' faces were blank. The craftsmen all suddenly went grim.

The man craned his neck, looking farther into the shop at something Heden couldn't see. Something obscured by the forge. He called out to someone, and then turned to Heden and jerked his thumb over his shoulder.

Heden nodded and made his way through the shop. As he passed by the craftsmen, they said nothing, just watched him.

As he rounded the forge, he found who he was looking for.

There were anvils of all sizes and functions in the shop, but this was by far the largest. It was sunk into the ground in a neat bit of engineering that betrayed the influence of its creator, currently using the anvil to hammer on what looked to Heden like a long metal pike.

The Sun & Anvil was the dwarf's version of the Hammer & Tongs. Except the dwarf's dream of retirement was open and thriving. The shop's owner looked up from his work; the fierce orange glow from the heated metal illuminated his squat, square face. He stared at Heden. He wasn't the only one in the city, but to a small group of people of a certain generation that included Heden and Gwiddon and many of the people who now ran the city, he was The Dwarf. Just as there were many elvish wodes, but only the Iron Forest was The Wode.

He was roughly four feet tall and, though short, seemed massive. Heden knew the dwarf weighed a quarter ton, though he didn't look it. It seemed to Heden as though the world around the dwarf bent and bowed in an attempt to make itself smaller.

His dusky brown skin appeared to be flesh. Heden knew this not to be the case. He was one of the stone dwarfs, known to academics as the granite elementals. Any town that had one counted itself lucky. They were master craftsmen in every material, and stone was their preferred medium. His skin was a strange combination of flesh and rock. It was supple, it moved and flexed like skin, but a normal sword would spark off it, deflected as though bouncing off armor.

The dwarf stared at Heden for a moment, then threw his hammer to the ground in disgust. A watching assistant scurried up to the anvil, used a pair of locking tongs to grasp the heated metal pike, and took it to another, smaller anvil to be finished.

Heden stepped forward and looked down at the dwarf. Many people throughout the shop were watching. The dwarf's body was hairless. He wore a leather apron and leather pants. His broad face bore a thick scowl and his small eyes fired red. They gave a baleful look, but his eyes always did that. The dwarf radiated back the heat he'd absorbed from the forge.

"I need one of the swords," Heden said.

The dwarf just sneered at him, and waited. Heden realized why.

"It doesn't matter which one. You choose."

The dwarf spat on the ground and turned his back on Heden. He selected a long metal rod from amongst the scrap on the floor, picked it up and inserted it into a small metal collar set into the bottom of the anvil. He pushed it in, then pulled on it with one strong arm.

With a burst of steam, the anvil slowly rose out of the ground and slid aside, revealing a large hole in the dirt floor. It was well lit and walled, and there were steep stairs going down. The dwarf trudged down them soundlessly. Everyone in the building was watching. Many had their mouths open.

Heden had served the gods for as long as he could remember, and one thing he'd learned: they influenced the world in direct and indirect ways. There were several traditions in his culture that deliberately subtracted conscious will from a decision, in order to grant gods or saints the opportunity to step in and influence things. Heden had no way of knowing what the dwarf would choose. Let fate decide.

Heden had met people who laughed at such things, and for them, probably the saints had no interest in influencing their lives. Heden was not so lucky.

The dwarf emerged with a long, thin object wrapped in plain, dirty cloth. He held it out abruptly, unceremoniously. Heden took it from him carefully.

He unwrapped the handle, revealing the hilt, pommel and guard of a sword. It was beautiful but full of angles, as though it were built out of complex, geometric shapes. A contrast to the flamboyantly crafted sword guards that were the fashion, such as Gwiddon carried, that looked like flowing pen-strokes carved from gold.

There was a black gemstone in the pommel. Only a little of the blade was showing, a dull purple-grey metal. Unlike any in the city. The metal threw off a light few humans had seen. It was a kind of glowing violet and it cast Heden's features into sharp relief.

"*Starkiller,*" Heden said, regarding the weapon wryly. "Figures."

The dwarf said nothing. He turned his back to Heden and pushed up on the metal rod. He removed it and threw it aside with a loud clang as the anvil slid back into place, and an assistant brought forth another item for the master's attention.

Heden stared at the dwarf's back for a little while as the whole forge resumed work. He didn't say anything. He looked at the ground for a moment. Then he wrapped up the sword, tucked the whole package under his arm, turned, and left.

Chapter Ten

Heden came back to the Hammer & Tongs to find the heavy oak doors standing open. He'd left the doors unlocked and was happy to see that whoever'd come to confront him about whatever hadn't broken in and cost him a crown for the repair.

He didn't hesitate. He didn't bother unwrapping the sword. He stepped up onto the boards of his inn and walked through the doors.

Inside, taking a moment for his eyes to adjust, Heden saw a thick, heavily muscled man standing by the bar on his right, and the cat Ballisantirax, sitting on the bottom step of the stairs to the rooms above. Balli was licking a paw and then washing herself.

The man's face was scratched and bleeding. He was someone's muscle—Heden had an idea of whose—and he probably didn't feel much pain. It looked like his nose and cheekbones had been professionally broken a few times, so he probably couldn't feel the razor-thin cuts. Blood streamed down his cheeks and onto his neck and shirt. It looked bad but it was just a cat scratch.

Heden took note of where the cat was sitting, and felt, though he could not see, someone watching from the top of the stairs.

The man turned as soon as he heard Heden's boots, and bellowed: "Is that your fucking cat?"

Heden smiled and looked at Balli. Ballisantirax went into what Heden thought of as her "cat statue" pose, sitting on her hindquarters, paws placed together in front of her. Her eyes were squinted half-closed, prideful and happy.

"I'm gonna kill that fucking cat!"

Heden looked from the cat to the muscle and said, "No you're not."

"You get up there," the man tried ordering Heden, "and get me that fucking trull."

Balli, assured that her master had things well in hand, turned and trotted up the steps.

"What's your name?" Heden wondered, looking askance at the big man. Trying to place him.

"My name don't matter, get the girl," he said.

"You work for Miss Elowen," Heden said. He leaned the wrapped sword against a chair.

"That's right," the man said, on firmer ground, the cat apparently forgotten. "And she says 'Morten, you go find that bitch and bring her back here.' And here I am," he said proudly. "Found you myself."

"Sure you don't want to tell me your name?" Heden asked, raising an eyebrow.

"Fuck you!" Morten said. Heden was quite a bit shorter and smaller than the big man. Morten sensed something was wrong. Small men didn't usually give him any lip.

Heden shrugged. "Vanora?" he called out. "There's a man here wants you to go with him. You're free to go, if you like."

"It ain't up to her!" Morten said, angry and getting confused. This was not how things were supposed to go.

Heden stared at him and waited in the silence for a moment. When no response was forthcoming, he said, "I don't think she wants to go with you."

"She's a fucking whore," the tough said, punctuating each word. "It don't matter what she wants. She belongs to Miss Elowen."

As he spoke, he walked towards Heden until he was standing within an arm's length.

"I hate to say this, but I don't think you'll last long at the Petal," Heden said.

"What?" Morten asked, confused.

"I mean if Bann finds out you came over here and tried to act tough with me, he'll say 'I'm going to have to fire that pigfucker because he's too stupid to be muscle even at a brothel.'"

"Fuck you!" Morten said again, and swung a thick fist at Heden. A great roundhouse swing with his right.

Heden easily and efficiently ducked out of the way, put his foot out and pulled on Morten's right shoulder, half-tripping, half-throwing the heavy man into the table on which he and Gwiddon had shared drinks earlier.

There was a crash and a grunt. Morten was making a lot of noise.

"Did you come up with this idea?" Heden asked, looking at the man sprawled on his floor surrounded by the remains of the table. "Take the initiative? Or did you talk to Bann first?"

Morten turned over. He was trying to figure out what had happened. He looked up at Heden, a little stunned.

"You took the initiative, didn't you?"

Morten pulled out a dagger. Heden sighed.

"Really?" he asked.

Morten lumbered to his feet and came at Heden in a kind of crouch.

Heden lashed out, turning his whole body and driving the heel of his palm into Morten's face as the man ran at him. There was a loud crunch and Morten dropped the dagger. But Morten's body kept coming, smashing into Heden.

Heden stumbled back against the bar, but Morten had collapsed on the ground. He was on his hands and knees, blood and spit pooling on the floor. There was a *huur, huur* sound as he tried to breathe.

Heden straightened up. "Alright," he said. *Huur, huur.*

"You broke my fucking nose!" Morten yelled. *Huur.*

"It's okay," Heden reassured him. *Huur*. He waited. He went behind the bar and got a small glass and some port.

"Come on," Heden said, helping Morten to his feet. Morten shook off Heden's arm and stood, swaying a little. "Here, drink this," Heden said.

Morten took the small glass and drank the rich port. It wouldn't do much except taste good and get Morten's mind off the pain.

"Now," Heden said, slowly. "You're going to go back to Miss Elowen and tell her you couldn't get the girl. Tell her I was, ah, you know, waiting for you. Ready. Whatever. Doesn't matter. But you didn't get her—" He spoke like he was explaining something to a child. "—and I beat the shit out of you."

"She's going to fucking kill me!"

"Nooo," Heden said. "She didn't know it was me. You tell her the girl is at the Hammer & Tongs, and she'll know it's me. Probably feel bad she sent you. She won't kill you. I promise."

"What?" Morten said. It was getting hard to understand him as his face swelled up. When he talked, Heden could see his white teeth stained red.

"Tell her I promised she wouldn't kill you."

"Why am I, uhh…" Morten began, but didn't continue.

"Okay," Heden said. "Time for you to go." He took the now-empty glass from the stunned muscle and guided him to the door. He opened it, and the man stepped outside and looked around, confused.

Heden stood in the doorway. "Find someone to take care of that nose," he said, raising his voice to be heard over the crowd walking by. People were studiously avoiding looking directly at Morten, while just as studiously glancing covertly at his ruined face.

"What?" Morten said, holding his nose.

Heden closed the door.

Chapter Eleven

Heden looked at the mess, the broken table. He waited a moment.

"He's gone."

Vanora danced down the stairs, still in her blue dress, and stopped once her bare feet hit the common room floor. She stared at Heden. There was a hungry look in her eyes. She was scared, but she also needed something from Heden and was resisting whatever it was.

"He'll be back," she said, accusing Heden of something.

Heden shook his head. "No he won't," he said.

"Someone will be back!"

Heden nodded. "Yeah," he said. She was having trouble keeping her breathing from turning into sobbing.

"She won't try to take you again though," he said.

"You don't know that!" she said, almost yelling. "She won't just let me go!"

Heden sat in a chair next to the demolished table.

"The Petal is a nice place," he said. "Respectable." This was, he concluded, why Vanora still seemed like a fifteen-year-old girl. Elowen took pride in getting them young, and training them. Treated it like a real apprenticeship. Even at fifteen, Vanora may only have had a dozen clients. And they'd be rich.

It wasn't illegal, most of the churches had no stricture against it. But Heden couldn't shake the feeling that, in a better world, girls like Vanora wouldn't have to fuck strange men for money.

"Did you like it there?" Heden asked, as if this was a normal thing to say.

She looked at the table next to her and shrugged. Almost imitating Heden.

"Do you want to stay here?" he asked.

She nodded. "I want to stay," she said. She seemed desperate. She was desperate.

Heden accepted this.

"I don't want…I want to learn to read." Heden knew what she had been about to say.

"Okay," he said.

"You said you'd teach me," she complained, as though he'd already reneged on the deal. Literacy was not valued among the people Heden knew growing up, but it was valued in the city. Almost everyone in the city could read well enough to make out the common words and phrases used in legal documents, but even people with money paid others to do their reading and writing for them. The nobility, of course, considered it a necessity. For someone like Vanora, it could be a doorway to better things.

"I will," Heden said. "And if you don't want to leave, I promise you won't have to."

"It's not that simple," she said darkly.

Heden took a deep breath. "If I don't want someone to take you from here, there's maybe five people in the whole city who could do anything about it. And Miss Elowen is not one of them."

She dropped into a chair and crossed her arms, eyes downcast. "It's not that simple," she repeated, with less conviction this time. But with a level of resignation that Heden noted. They were sitting on opposite sides of the common room.

"You're probably going to, ah…" Heden said. He stood up and crossed the room. She wasn't going to like this part. She didn't look up at him. He took a deep breath. "Okay," he said, settling on directness. "I've got to leave the city."

Now she looked up. "What?!" she asked, panicking.

"You'll be okay," he said.

"What are you talking about? How can you…"

"Vanora," he said, lowering his voice. She stopped panicking and stared at him. "If I tell you you're going to be okay, you're going to be okay. Do you understand me?" His calmness seemed to stun her. She just nodded.

"When…when are you leaving?" she asked.

"Soon. Today."

"Let me go with you!" she said, jumping to her feet.

Heden just shook his head. "You don't know where I'm going."

She waited a moment and when there was nothing else, she asked what seemed the obvious question.

"Where are you going?"

"I have to go into the Iron Forest," he said, unable to keep the drama out of his voice.

It did not have the intended effect.

"Where the fairies live?!" Vanora asked, and clapped her hands together.

This girl, he reminded himself, *has slept with more people in more ways in three years than you have your entire life.* It seemed important to him to maintain some context.

"Yes," he admitted. "There are fairies in the forest."

"Why do you say it like that?" she asked, not happy with his tone of voice.

"They're not…what you imagine."

"They don't fly around on little butterfly wings?" This was obviously important to her.

"Well, okay," Heden said. "They are what you imagine. But they're dangerous. They ensorcell people."

"What does that mean?" She was deflating with every question. He answered, looking at the floor, avoiding her pleading eyes. She wanted the fantasy, but he couldn't give it to her.

"They trap people. Forever. They were made to serve the celestials and when they left, the fairies had no purpose. They went mad without their masters to tell them what to do. So any people stupid enough to go into the wode, any wode, the fae want to serve them. Forever. They'll magic your mind and you'll never want to leave, and they'll feed you rich food and sing songs in your ears and pretty soon you've been there weeks and you're starving to death because their food doesn't…it can't be digested the way ours can, and you're shitting and pissing yourself because you forget to go to the privy but you don't notice because you only see what they want you to see. Only hear what they want you to hear. And then you die, and they don't know why. It confuses them. But only for a few minutes. Then they've forgotten you ever existed."

He looked up at her. Her mouth was open.

"Yeah," he said. "It's worse when you're watching it happen to someone you know."

"I'll stay here," she said in a small voice.

Heden nodded. "Good. There's food enough in the pantry in the kitchen to last all the time I'm gone. Just don't be too picky. If the bread gets moldy, just pick the mold off." He remembered his father telling him exactly the same thing when he was a boy.

"I don't want to be alone," she said, quietly. Then appeared to have a thought. "Who was that man I saw down here before you went out?"

"His name's Gwiddon," Heden said. "He's probably my best friend."

"Maybe he could come by..." she began, and stopped when she saw Heden shake his head.

"He's complicated," Heden said. "I can't ask him to do things like that."

"You said he was your friend," Vanora said.

Heden shrugged. "I'd trust him with my life," he said. "Yours too. But he has his own things to take care of."

"How long will you be gone," she asked, looking out the window. She was thinking about something.

"I don't know. Could be a long time. Could be a month, but I really hope not."

She shrank more into herself.

"I'll talk to some friends before I leave. I'll have them come by and make sure you're okay while I'm gone. I know it's going to be tough."

"A month? What am I going to do?" she asked, mostly to herself.

Good question, Heden thought. He looked at the shelves of books.

"Hang on," he said. "I have an idea." He stood up and walked towards a door set against the stairs. She padded behind him with her bare feet. "Have to go down here anyway," he said.

"What's down there?" Vanora asked.

He swung around and looked down at her. "You have to promise me something." He pointed at her, it just having occurred to him.

She looked up at him with eyes wide and nodded.

Heden peered at her. She smiled at him.

He sighed and leaned back against the door.

"You remember when I said that no one could take you from here?"

She nodded.

"Do you believe me?"

"I..." she said and her face screwed up with doubt. Then she remembered something. Her face changed into a look of determination. "Yes."

Heden nodded. "For the same reasons I can say that, you can't go downstairs."

"What?" she asked, confused.

"It's dangerous."

"How dangerous?" she asked, trying to look behind him.

"You can stay here as long as you want," Heden said. "You're safe. I'll have someone come by and check on you. And Balli will keep you company. But if you go downstairs...you will not be safe," he said. He kept his voice neutral. Like he was describing a simple fact. He didn't want her to feel like he was threatening her.

"I get to play with the cat?" she asked.

Heden waggled his head back and forth, weighing the question. "You can try," he said, half to himself. "But if you break your promise, she won't have anything to do with you."

Vanora put her hands behind her back, stood up straight and nodded. She was so...young and shapeless and normal, Heden often forgot what she did for a living. Probably because that's what she wanted.

"You promise?" he asked.

"I promise," she said.

Heden looked at her hard for a second. She seemed to blanch.

"Okay," he said. "You're telling the truth."

She relaxed. "You can tell that?"

"Yep," Heden said. He pulled a small keyring out from a pouch on his belt and flipped through it for the key to the basement door.

"The door's locked?"

Heden nodded.

"Well, then why…"

"I'll have to leave it unlocked," he said, "when I go."

"Why?" she asked.

"It's complex," Heden said. He found the key and looked at her again. "If you see anything weird while I'm gone…don't worry."

"What's weird?"

"A lot of things. You'll know it when you see it."

She shook her head slowly and looked scared. Heden sighed. Gwiddon wanted him to open the inn and already his life was unacceptably complex with only one guest.

"Just watch Balli," he said. "If she gets angry or afraid, then there may be a problem."

At that moment, the cat came downstairs and sat on the bottom step, resumed cleaning herself. Vanora looked at her and smiled.

"Okay," she said.

Heden turned and unlocked the door.

Chapter Twelve

Once the door was closed behind him, Vanora pressed her ear to it and listened to Heden tromp downstairs.

She heard him speak. Once, a single word, low, and then after a pause a longer phrase…several sentences. She couldn't make out what he was saying, but it didn't sound like Tevas-gol.

She waited, breathless. After a few moments, she heard the sound of heavy objects being moved around. Heden was looking for something. Some things.

This went on for a while until Vanora got tired of standing up. She slid down and tucked her legs under her, resting her head on the door. She felt exhausted after everything with Heden and Morten.

She dozed off, she didn't know for how long, and was awoken by the sounds of conversation. It had been going on for some time. A conversation with someone she couldn't hear. He was a priest…maybe he was talking to his god? His saint?

She looked up at the door latch. Quietly she stood, pressed the latch down and opened the door a crack.

"Let's say a fortnight." She heard Heden's voice, echoing from down below. "Could be longer," he said. Then, with the door open, she could hear the response. The voice was…small. High-pitched. Rapid. Quieter than Heden's. She couldn't make out words, just a patter of noises. What was down there?

"Just someone to watch, and make sure no one comes in. Deal with them if they do. Have to be in shifts, something could happen day or night."

More chittering.

"You already eat whatever you want."

A squeak. Objection.

"I don't care," Heden explained. "It'd spoil anyway. But it seems like you've already taken payment in food for services not yet rendered. Now you can render them."

More chittering.

"Like what?"

There was a sound like a piece of metal rattling.

"No," Heden said. "What about this?"

Another sound, like a pile of pans and dishes moving. Then more squeaking.

"You wear it and it protects you from being poisoned."

Chitter, squeak.

"Most of them."

Chitter, chitter.

"No, sorry."

Squeak, chitter.

"Okay," Heden said. "Deal."

Squeak, squeak.

"Really?" Heden said. "Well, as long as she doesn't come down here, she hasn't broken any promises."

Vanora's eyes went wide, and she quickly, but quietly, closed the door. She was certain he couldn't have heard her. She walked to the nearby chair, sat and waited for Heden to come back up the stairs.

Chapter Thirteen

Eventually, after much heavy tromping, Heden opened the door and emerged from the blackness beyond. He was wearing a large backpack with many pockets. It appeared fully packed.

He gave Vanora a look that indicated he knew she'd been listening. She smiled weakly back at him.

Heden didn't feel like explaining what she'd heard, and she followed some instinct that overrode her curiosity, told her asking would make things more complicated.

"Okay," Heden said. He walked to one of the many tables in the common room, unslung the backpack and dropped it on the table. "You'll be safe while I'm gone."

She looked at the door, which he'd left unlocked. As he said he would.

Heden opened the backpack, reached into it and pulled out a domed glass case with a brass base. It was about six inches tall, and inside was what looked like a detailed carving of a man in some kind of dance pose.

Vanora was immediately drawn to it.

"This will help you pass the time," Heden said as he pulled the delicate glass dome off the base, careful not to damage it.

"What is it?" Vanora whispered, getting down on one knee and resting her arms and head on the table at eye level with the statue.

"It's a golem," Heden said.

She looked up at him quizzically. "I thought golems were huge stone or..."

Heden shrugged. "It means anything made to look and move like a man. Some are big stone guardians that can't speak or do much except try to kill you. Some are..." He gestured to the little man.

It was made, she saw now, of metal and ceramic. She could see hundreds of little joints and seams. Its face was a kind of ceramic mask. It was painted to look like it was wearing a skintight outfit made of diamond-shaped patches of cloth in bright colors. Red, yellow, blue and white.

"This kind is called a harlequin."

Vanora had never seen anything like it, and would not have known what a harlequin looked like. It looked, to her eyes, like some kind of alien jester.

"Does it...does it move?" she asked out of instinct.

Heden looked at her with a raised eyebrow. She got the feeling he knew some delightful secret and enjoyed her curiosity, but the raised eyebrow was its only hint. He was otherwise stoic.

He looked at the little man and spoke a few words in a language she didn't understand.

Nothing happened.

"Shit," he said, and coughed. Then he spoke again, something different.

Nothing happened.

"It's been years since I used this thing," he muttered. "Wait, I know...."

Another short spoken phrase she didn't understand, and she heard in response the sound of a chime coming from the little man. There was a ticking noise as of a clock, and the little figure slowly began to move. Like someone walking through water, their movements slow and heavy. But the little figure's motion sped up until it seemed normal speed.

It looked once at Heden and then at Vanora. Its mask was also jointed, she saw, and moved to show expression.

"Good afternoon, mistress!" the small automaton said, bowing deeply. "And master." It took off its cap to Heden. Its voice sounded tinny and bright.

"It's a teacher," Heden said. "They were created to instruct the sons and daughters of nobility in things like…I don't know, reading and writing…."

"Reading and writing and singing and dancing!" the small man said, twirling his body about while standing on one toe. It bowed again. "Plays and opera, science and mathematics. History and religion, diplomacy and war, I am well versed in all. 'I cannot ride a horse,'" it said, placing a hand over its heart, the little holes for its eyes closing as it quoted someone, "'but I craft mighty leaders from little boys.'" It opened its eyes and peered up, smiling, at Vanora. "And little girls," it added.

"You used this?" Vanora asked in wonder.

"I did for about three months. My friends and I had to sit in one place and wait for something and I used it to pass the time."

"No season was e'er better spent!" The harlequin said.

"Eventually I got bored." The harlequin looked affronted. "Actually I got bored pretty quickly, but there wasn't anything else to do."

"Where did you get it?" Vanora asked in awe as she reached out for it.

The little man danced away.

"Don't touch it," Heden said quickly. Vanora pulled her hand back.

"It's magic," Heden said. "But it's also extremely...delicate. It's got hundreds of little gears and pulleys in there, and if you touch it the oils on your skin will muck everything up." She nodded her understanding and now appeared even more fascinated.

"It'll work for a few hours a day, then it needs to go back in its case. It'll let you know when it needs to rest." The little man was moving in circles around the table, alternating between complex balletic dance moves and clownish cartwheels. Vanora giggled.

"Go ahead," Heden said. "Ask it something."

Vanora looked shyly at the little machine. "Har...harlik."

"Harlequin," Heden pronounced.

"Harlequin," she repeated. The little man did a backflip, landed and saluted. "Tell me about..." She looked sideways. "Tell me about Heden," she said, smiling slyly.

"Alas, milady, his story is written on pages I've yet to read," the little voice piped up.

Vanora harrumphed and screwed her face up.

"It doesn't know much about us," Heden said. "About Vaslorians. It doesn't know what Corwell is or where Celkirk is. It was made a long time ago by a people who live west, across the Bale Sea.

"But it can teach you to read and write and there's a lot of good plays and music in there you'll like. Probably better to let it teach you before you start asking questions. You can ask it anything, but a lot of common-sense stuff it doesn't understand. You have to imagine you're a long-ago princess from a faraway land." Vanora liked the sound of this.

"It must be worth a fortune!" she whispered.

"It's priceless," Heden said.

Vanora looked at him sharply.

"Means its value is beyond money," Heden explained. Vanora accepted this, though it seemed to challenge her.

"Harlequin, begin with reading and writing, please," Heden ordered.

"Your daughter will be the finest student I have ever taught!" the harlequin exclaimed.

Heden raised his eyebrows and went "hmmm" and noticed that Vanora had looked away to hide some expression. He thought she might be blushing.

Heden picked up the base and put it in front of the harlequin. It dutifully stepped onto it, and when Heden replaced the glass dome, it resumed its earlier pose and stopped moving.

"There. It'll automatically revive once you take the dome off. Make sure it can get to its base when it needs to, and then put the glass back when it does."

Vanora nodded. She put her hands on the glass and looked down at the frozen man. She took a deep breath and turned to look up at Heden.

"A month?" she asked, pleading for any other answer.

"Less," Heden said. He wanted to come back to her already and he hadn't even left. "Might be as little as a week." This gave her some hope.

Vanora desperately wanted to ask more, Heden could tell. But there was something that told her now was not the time to burden him with questions. Heden found he liked Vanora a great deal. She had an instinct for people and how to deal with them that he found very neat. Precise. The product of her experience at the Rose.

"How are you going to get there? Do you have a horse?" Vanora asked.

"I did," Heden said. "But I sold him."

"Oh," Vanora said, disappointed.

"Besides, it would take me three weeks to get there by horse."

"Then how are you…going to…" Vanora didn't want to finish the question. She felt like maybe it wasn't okay to ask.

"I have a tapestry that flies through the air," Heden said.

Vanora's eyes went wide and her mouth dropped open.

"You have a…are you *serious*?"

Heden smiled in spite of himself, and Vanora smiled back. He slung the backpack over his shoulder, walked to the front door and opened it.

"I never lie," Heden said, standing in the doorway. Light and the noise of a crowd of people passing by spilled in. He pointed at Vanora suddenly. "Tell me you're going to be alright." Heden wasn't sure why he said this.

Vanora looked at him and smiled. "I'll be alright," she said. It sounded like a promise. Like she was reassuring him.

Heden nodded. He looked around his inn. "See you soon."

He left and Vanora laughed gaily to herself. She ran to the window to look out, but pulled back.

Heden strode back in, snatched up the sword he'd left bundled up and leaning against a chair, and turned to leave again.

"For real this time," he said, winking, making Vanora smile more widely.

And he was gone.

Vanora watched him leave, but he was quickly swallowed by the crowd. She was disappointed, hoping to catch a glimpse of his mode of travel. Probably, she thought, he leaves the city before he uses it. She imagined him standing nobly on a rich, tasseled tapestry as it sped through the air and something about it thrilled her.

She turned and looked at the large common room of the Hammer & Tongs, which she already thought of as "home," and walked up to the table with the harlequin. She removed the glass dome.

The little man came to life more quickly this time. He leapt off the brass base onto the table. He bowed deeply and flourished his conical cap.

"We shall erect a mighty city of the intellect here, milady. Let us place the first brick."

Vanora dropped herself into a chair, and regarded the figure with a mixture of curiosity and skepticism.

"Okay," she said. "I'm game."

Chapter Fourteen

The door to the small inn burst open, wind and rain howling in from the night outside. The candles guttered. The fire roared.

A cluster of figures, all cloaked, dragged a man's body through the door. They were drenched. The figure they carried was unnaturally pale.

The dozen townspeople in the inn moved as one to the group and lifted the unconscious body from their hands. Two people, a man and a woman at separate tables, did not join the others. The innkeeper watched intently from behind the bar, mouth open, eyes wide.

They carried the body to a nearby table. They placed him on it like the table was an altar and he was a sacrifice, and starting pulling strips of clothing off him. His pale skin was rent in several places exposing red flesh and white bone. There was almost no blood.

"We found the carter," Dade, one of the rescuers, said. They all took off their sodden cloaks, mist boiling off them in the warm room. They were all young. The oldest only seventeen. The youngest barely thirteen.

Those who had been waiting or resting in the inn were all adults.

The young rescuers had swords, bows, maces. Backpacks. They had left ready to fight something, but returned unscathed.

"We found him with his cart," Dade's brother Jeremy said.

"It was on fire!" Wenna, one of the two girls, the youngest, said.

"On fire?" one of the townspeople said. "In this rain?"

"Lamp oil," Meliora, the older girl, said. Wenna was wide-eyed and shaking. Meliora was quiet and grim.

A middle-age woman in a plain brown dress put her ear to the carter's chest, cheek touching one of the wounds and after a moment of silence, looked up and said, "He's alive."

All the townspeople in the inn breathed a sigh of relief and started talking amongst themselves as the priestess began to pray over the carter.

The rescuers all looked at Credan, their round friend. "I didn't," he said, lost for words. "I didn't know what to..."

"It's okay," Dade, the eldest of them, said. He put his hand on Credan's shoulder. "You did fine."

"Will he be alright?" Jeremy asked.

The priestess nodded. She moved her hands over the carter as she spoke softly in words none of them could understand and the wounds began to close.

One of the guests, clad all in black, appeared to notice none of this. Kept to herself. The other warmed his hands by the fire, back to the townsfolk. A small patch of what looked like frost on his cloak melted away in the heat. It could not be frost, however, being it was the first month of spring.

After a few more moments, they could all see the carter begin to breathe normally. Though his eyes remained closed, he ceased to look like a lifeless body.

Dade and Jeremy looked at each other. Jeremy nodded.

"We're going back out," Dade announced.

"What?!" a woman cried. "You can't! Why?"

Her husband, the boys' father, put his hands on her shoulders. She instinctively grasped them.

"Boys," the father said. "Don't upset your mother. You done fine, you found carter and he'll live. Everyone's proud of you. Leave this be 'til morning. We'll get the Lord of…"

"Can't leave it 'til morning, da," Jeremy explained, picking up his cloak and making a futile attempt to wring it out.

Credan and Wenna looked back and forth from their parents to Dade and Jeremy. They were afraid to go, but more afraid to stay. Meliora just looked out the door into the darkness.

"Carter's wife and son were dragged off, Jeremy reckons," Dade said. "Might still be alive."

"Trail big enough for a blind man to follow," Jeremy said. Of the two boys, Dade was slightly taller, but much broader. Jeremy was lean and moved like a cat.

"Lord Mayne would just send to Ollghum Keep anyway," Meliora observed. "Two days. Might be alive now—" She turned back to the group and pulled her cloak on and over her head, obscuring her features. "—but they'll be dead by then."

One man, Meliora's father, stared at his daughter and said nothing. His eyes welled with tears. He realized now he no longer knew his daughter, and blamed himself for her mother's death.

"Credan," a large woman announced. "Stop this foolishness and *come here.*" Credan's whole body tightened at this sound. At those words in that tone of voice. He hated it, and the hatred shocked him rigid. He looked with fear at his mother.

Dade and Jeremy looked at him. Dade's confident gaze calmed him down. Nothing was said.

"This is madness," the brothers' father said, stepping forward. "That woman and her boy, there's nothing you can do for them."

Dade looked at his father. Both seemed calm. "You don't know that," Dade said.

His father knew the boy was right. "There could be anything out there. It's dangerous at night. Remember Beal."

"Jeremy thinks its kethat," Dade said. Jeremy nodded. "I think we can handle kethat."

The word caused a susurration. The kethat were known scavengers, but rarely attacked the town. Nothing was stopping the five children from leaving. They seemed to be waiting for some approval from the adults. The adults were wondering how far they should go to protect their families.

A barrier had arisen between them without anyone saying anything, had already opened as soon as they burst in with the carter. At no point had either side made any attempt to cross the room and make contact with the others.

Father stared at son. No one spoke.

The man at the fire stood up, appearing old and bent with age. He laboriously stretched his joints out and turned to face the gathered townspeople.

Though only in his early forties, he was older than most of the parents. He wore a plate chestpiece over leather armor. He had a plain sword at his side, and stood beside a heavy pack with many pockets. His face was grey and gaunt, his hair short, black. His eyes blue and wide. The only part of him that seemed open and expressive.

He looked at the young rescuers.

"You're going to stay here," he said, his voice rough.

They looked back and forth at each other, some looked to their parents. The parents looked confused as well.

"Listen," one of them said, stepping forward. "We don't..."

"You're going to stay here, with your parents," the man said. "With your families. And you don't leave the inn until morning."

"This is our problem. We can take care of this," Dade said, Jeremy standing so close behind him he was pressing his shoulder into his brother's back, something he subconsciously did to support his older brother.

Heden looked at the five boys and girls. "I know," he said darkly. "I know you can do it. You can find them, rescue the wife and son. Kill a lot of keth. Kill and keep killing.

"I know you can do it," he reiterated. "It's easy, and you're ready. That's why I'm going to do it. So you don't have to."

None of the rescuers understood, but each felt the palpable sensation that they stood at the edge of a gaping chasm, prepared to leap off into a darkness that would change them forever. Some were eager for it, some afraid. And this man was trying to stop them.

"It could be a whole tribe," one of the men said. "There could be a hundred of them."

Heden looked at the man, expressionless. "Not when I'm done."

"You don't know where the carter's..."

"I know where it is," he said. "I saw it coming in." This made no sense to them, but they couldn't know he saw it from a thousand feet high, had hated himself for not stopping and investigating the blazing fire in the rain, freezing at that high altitude.

"I'll be back a little after dawn," he said to the room in general, shifting the pack onto his back.

The room had changed. Heden had placed everyone in the room against him, reuniting them in a way. None of them seemed equipped to muster any opposition. Their experiences in life had not prepared them for someone like Heden coming in and doing something terrible so they didn't have to.

"You need a tracker," the woman in black said casually. The way she said it, it wasn't clear if it was a question or a statement.

Heden looked at her. "You know how to use that thing?" he asked, nodding at the woodsman's sword. That she could use the unstrung bow leaning against the back of her chair went without saying.

"Served with Duke Baed in the Fifth Irregulars," she said, matching Heden's reserve.

The name shocked Heden for a moment and his eyes unfocused as he remembered something. He took a deep breath and brought himself back to the present.

"Good enough for me," he said. "Come on."

The woodsman stood and gathered her gear. She followed Heden to the door. Everyone in the inn watched silently.

Reaching the door, he stopped and turned to face the men and women, sons and daughters.

"Any of you follow me, get any ideas, I will personally thrash the skin off you." He made a point to look each of them in the eye. "Try me if you don't believe me."

He opened the door into the black spitting rain, and left. The woodsman closed the door behind her.

Wenna's mother and father rushed forth and wrapped themselves gratefully around their daughter. The spell was broken, and Wenna grabbed them back and began to cry with relief.

Chapter Fifteen

Heden was wrong. They got back to the inn half an hour before dawn.

When the door opened, everyone in the inn stood. Fathers and mothers had, with one exception, reunited with daughters and sons. No one had left.

Heden walked in unceremoniously with the body of the carter's wife slung over his shoulder and went straight to the closest table in the inn. He carefully laid her on it. The woodsman came in behind carrying the son in her arms and stood in the doorway, not sure what to do.

Heden stood next to the table, looking down. No one moved. Heden was covered in blood, and black ichorous stains soaked his armor and covered his face.

"They're alive," Heden said.

At this pronouncement, the townspeople came and relieved the woodsman of her burden and surrounded the table with the carter's wife on it. They all began talking to each other at once.

As the folk came and gently took the unconscious boy from the woodsman, she looked at them, people she didn't know. She looked dazed. She was breathing in fits, hair matted with rain and blood. Her black leather armor was wet and slick, but it was impossible to tell whether with water or blood or both. But she smelled like an abattoir.

"He's got a..." the woodsman gasped as they took the boy from her, sweating in spite of the cold. "He's got a flying carpet," she said.

The townspeople appeared not to be listening. Relieved of her burden, she collapsed into a chair.

Heden found the innkeeper and gently pulled him away from the concerned crowd. He pointed silently to the bar. The innkeep looked in Heden's eyes, and nodded.

As he scurried behind the bar, Heden said, "And meat. And bread. And cheese."

The innkeep went through a door that led down into the cellar.

Heden leaned on the bar. Dade and Jeremy, their father behind them, stood and looked at Heden's back.

"We could've done it," Dade said. His father frowned and tried to silence him, but his heart wasn't in it.

Heden gave no response, no indication he heard anything.

"This wasn't your problem," Dade continued. "Why did you do it?" The young man was demanding now.

The innkeep came up with a large platter covered in unprepared food. He began cutting and slicing. No one had eaten while Heden and the woodsman were gone.

"Does it..." Jeremy said. "It is because of the kethat? Do you hate them?"

Heden realized that while they'd been gone, the townsfolk had been guessing at why a man would assume this burden, this risk, to rescue people he didn't know so that other people he didn't know wouldn't have to. Maybe he really hates the keth, they reasoned.

In Heden's experience, people didn't understand him even when he explained himself. And he'd already explained himself once.

He grabbed a large chunk of duck from the innkeep's plate, some cheese too, and turned to face the three men.

He took a bite of the duck and talked while he chewed.

"Doesn't matter why," he said. "They're alive, you're alive. Everyone's here, safe. And none of you had to kill anyone. You want to go out tomorrow with your friends," he said, indicating young Wenna who was trying to listen without being noticed, "go out and have an adventure. Up to you. I won't be here.

"Besides," he said before swallowing and taking a bite of the cheese. "It wasn't just kethat."

"Trolls," the woman in black, the woodsman, said. She opened her mouth and tasted the air in the inn; she breathed heavily, eyes raised to the ceiling.

"Trolls?" the boys' father said. "Trolls at the mine? That's only..."

"It doesn't matter," Heden said, finishing the small amount of food he'd taken and pushing himself away from the bar.

"Who are you to say?!" the father said, his voice bouncing off the walls of the inn. "This is our town, our farms. It's all we've got. And what happens when they come looking to avenge their dead? What happens to us, ratcatcher?!"

The confrontation, the attitude, didn't bother Heden. People acted in all manners when confused and ignorant. It was natural.

"It doesn't matter," Heden said. "Because they're all dead."

Heden's words hit the floor with the weight of finality, shocking the townsfolk.

"You killed them all?" the father whispered, looking Heden up and down, and then looking at the woodsman.

"Unless someone starts working the mine, more kethat will come. They like mines. Caves. It's natural for them. The trolls I can't explain."

"Will there be…" another man in the inn began. "What happens if there are more trolls?"

Heden didn't smile, but nodded at Dade and Jeremy. "You've got a whole passel of heroes here, champing at the bit." Perhaps a little bitterness crept into his voice at the end.

The townsfolk argued amongst themselves. One man slowly extricated himself from the knot of bickering farmers, carpenters and tanners, and approached. He was shivering and thin and wan and covered in a thick, heavy blanket. Heden knew who it was.

He came forward and extended his hand.

"That's my wife and son you rescued," the carter said.

Heden nodded and took the man's hand.

"I don't know why you did what you did, but we owe you our lives."

Heden released his grip and shook his head. "I just got your family back," he said. "The boys and their friends there rescued you. Didn't need my help."

The carter looked at him, gratitude and compassion and confusion working their way around his face.

"I'm looking for a place called Ollghum Keep," Heden said.

"Everyone here knows it," the carter said. "It's the seat of the barony. Just take the road north," he said.

"Heden," the woodsman said.

Heden turned to see her looking only barely recovered from their ordeal.

"I'm going past the keep," she said, pushing her hair out of her face. "I'll take you. But not on that thing."

Heden might have smiled a little. "Okay," he said. "But we leave now, no rest."

She nodded, looking at the floor.

"Your name's Heden?" the innkeep asked.

Heden suddenly went numb. The innkeep had stopped moving, like the harlequin after its magic had run out. He was just staring ahead at nothing.

Heden nodded once.

"You were with the Sunbringers?"

Heden didn't say anything. He didn't look at the innkeep. Everyone in the inn was staring at him. The rain outside had slowed to a trickle; grey light was starting to come through the window.

"My sister lived in Aendrim," the innkeep said lifelessly.

Heden snatched up his backpack. The woodsman stood and looked between Heden and the innkeep, confused.

The innkeep looked from Heden to the woman and boy who were clinging to the carter.

"Get out," the innkeep said to no one in particular, his voice choked.

Heden was already leaving.

Chapter Sixteen

Ollghum Keep stood on a hill like a lighthouse, warning travelers of the maelstrom that was the Iron Forest beyond to the north. Small copses of trees dotted the rolling hills, the normal everyday trees Heden had grown up with. Forests that weren't alive and thinking and malevolent. The kinds of forests a man could walk through without fear of being killed in an instant by something that considered you an enemy combatant in an endless war you'd never heard of.

Even though the wode started a mile beyond the keep, the trees dominated the small walled city. Each rose three hundred feet or more, the stark line of them looking more like a cliff or a giant wall of water about to wash the keep and its people into the green sea that was the smooth hills.

The keep was a motte and bailey built on a large hill. A stone wall in the old Golish style with no mortar surrounded the keep and a few dozen wooden buildings. Together, the keep, the buildings, the wall made a town. A small one. But the keep was, to Heden's practiced eye, easily defensible. The Gol built small fortresses with massive underground warrens that could hold thousands of people and were incredibly difficult to siege. Though it was three thousand years old and looked like it could fall apart at any minute it would probably stand another thousand years and outlast this Age of Men.

There was a crowd of people waiting to get into the keep. Farmers whose houses and fields dotted the landscape for miles around. They formed a rough and winding line, their livestock milling around them. Packing them all into the town would make life there uncomfortable. They were anxious but controlled No one was shouting. A squad of guards posted at the gate kept people from flooding in, but they didn't appear to be turning anyone away. Just noting everyone who passed through. Probably checking to make sure they knew them.

"They normally work during the day," the woman in black next to him said. "Then gather their families and spend the night in the keep. Some come early. They're expecting a siege."

"Yeah," Heden said, looking into the forest. "We had to do the same thing when I was a boy." He studied the land around the keep. The two of them stood at the edge of a copse of trees, Heden surveying the keep and its surroundings. His companion was dressed all in loose black leather, leaning on her bow.

"Sieged by who?"

The woodsman shifted her weight. "Don't know," she said. "Heard tell of urmen. Could be. Could be thyrs. Probably urmen."

"What would urmen want with the place?"

She didn't answer. It was a rhetorical question.

They were silent for many moments. A hawk cried in the clear air.

"I've got to go in there," Heden said. The woman nodded. He looked at her and did not look away.

"Are you joking?" she asked, slinging her bow over her back.

"No. Those people are all going to die and you know it."

Heden shrugged. "That hill the keep's on?" he asked.

She grunted assent.

"It's a mound. Man-made. Probably warrens under the town and stretching out under the forest. Maybe even under us, here. If they've stored food and have a couple of wells…" He left the statement hanging.

She frowned and looked at the keep.

"If it's a siege, they could use someone like you," he said.

She crossed her arms and thought, not taking her eyes off the keep. Then shook her head. "No," she said. "Stupid. Stop being so sentimental. I can be more help out here anyway. Pick off the urq commanders. Slip away whenever I want. If they had good scouts, they'd be doing the same," she said, nodding to the keep.

Heden agreed. She could make a difference out here and leverage her greatest strength: her mobility.

"Urmen, you said. Have you gone into the forest?" he asked.

"That meat grinder?" she said. "I liked you better when you weren't asking stupid questions."

Heden was silent. Then he picked up his pack, turned and extended his hand to her. She took it. They looked at each other.

"I don't know your name," Heden said.

Her pale cheeks turned pink slowly while Heden held her hand, but she didn't look away.

"Probably for the best," she said, her voice rough. She didn't let go of his hand. "I'd like to forget the last sixteen hours, if you don't mind."

Heden pulled his hand away and nodded. He turned and headed towards the keep.

"I know what you mean," he said, without turning around.

Chapter Seventeen

"Who's this then?" A large woman with a body like a walnut shell sized Heden up.

Heden looked around, as though he didn't know who she was talking about.

"Hush, Gwennog, don't be rude to the man." The man standing next to Gwennog looked too much like her to be her husband. Probably her brother. A big man with long brown hair. Heden realized this is what his father must have looked like before Heden was born. When his da was still young and vital. Each of these folk reminded Heden of someone he knew as a boy.

"Don't you hush me! And it's not being rude to ask a stranger who he is."

It was odd for Heden to feel both at home here and like a complete stranger. Aware of the way his career had changed him. Made him an outsider to these people.

The sun was low in the sky, the day was late and Heden was surrounded by townsfolk, pigs and chickens. All waiting to enter Ollghum Keep. No one seemed agitated or worried. They seemed bored, as they waited for the guards to vaguely terrorize each person entering.

"My name's…" he began, but these folk weren't interested in what he had to say.

"He's a ratcatcher, look at him," the man behind him said. Heden didn't turn in reaction; he'd heard the wiry goatherd talking before and remembered his face. Heden presumed he was a goatherd. The goats seemed to like him.

"Figures," Gwennog said, crossing her arms and looking Heden up and down. "Thieving little rats. What're you doing here, rat? Come to see what coin you can make off our misery?"

Wonderful, Heden thought. Making a great impression right off.

"What makes you say he's a ratcatcher?" a woman to his right asked, her voice high. Long, thin hair. "He's nice-looking."

"And what would you know of nice-looking, young Sirona? And you married to that pot roast Edric!"

The people laughed, but Sirona was not going to be cowed by the matronly Gwennog.

"I got eyes, haven't I? He's nice-looking, look at him. Seems honest." She touched Heden on the shoulder. He turned and tried to smile at her in what he hoped was a natural way. *What would Gwiddon do?* he wondered. Probably pay them all to go away.

"What's your name, dear-heart?" Sirona asked.

"My name's Heden," he said, and felt self-conscious. Two days ago he'd almost told the bishop to go stick his head up a cow's ass. Now he felt defenseless surrounded by a bunch of dirt farmers. "I'm not a ratcatcher," he said. *Not anymore,* he thought.

"His name is Heden and he's a liar, more like," Gwennog said with a sniff, looking out over the crowd at nothing in particular.

"Dyfan, will you tell your wife there to mind?" the goatherd behind Heden said.

"I'll tell her no such thing, she can speak as she finds." A tree-stump man standing behind Gwennog poked his head around the large woman to chime in. "And should too, I don't see how we need any more strangers here. Got enough as it is."

"Got that little birdie at the turnip," another man agreed.

There was a kind of collective sigh from the young girls and a speculative silence from the older women. Another stranger in town though.

"Who's this minstrel then?" Heden asked.

"Never you mind!" Gwennog said. "And who was it said he was a minstrel?"

"I know what a little birdy is," and Heden found his accent coming back. His voice was a traitor. He didn't want these people to think he was mocking them and wasn't enthusiastic about reverting to his family's mode of speech. The more he thought about not talking like his brothers, the more he talked like them. "Goes tweet-tweet-tweet all the day long."

Someone, probably the goatherd, pushed Heden's shoulder from behind.

"And what would you be wanting with our minstrel?" he said.

Heden turned to find several more men behind him, backing up the goatherd. None of them so far smitten by Heden's charm.

"He doesn't want nothing!" Sirona objected.

"You never said what you was here for," Gwennog said, stirring the pot.

The people felt not the least bit threatened by Heden. It was a common attitude outside the big cities. Campaigners brought trouble and even though they were skilled with sword and spell, the local farmers and carters, wheelwrights and tanners had no truck with them. Would drive them out of town fearlessly, armed with spades and rocks. And the campaigners would go. What point staying in a town where everyone hated you? The stars made a decent blanket and there were ways to stay warm and dry, even in the rain.

"What of the urmen?" Heden asked.

"There's a thousand of them, I heard tell," Sirona said, eyes wide. She was, it seemed to Heden, trying to change the subject on his behalf.

"The baron's called the order," a man next to her said. *The order*, Heden noticed. "We don't need no ratcatchers coming up here to make the forest spit out all manner of beastie at us."

"I'm not a ratcatcher," Heden said.

"Oh he's not then, with that pack and that plate and that broadsword," Gwennog said. It looked bad, Heden knew. If there was a uniform of the itinerant campaigner, Heden was wearing it.

"I've heard about the order," Heden said. "The Green Order."

"You better hope they haven't heard of you," the goatherd said.

"See through his lies right off," Gwennog said.

"I'm not a liar," Heden said, letting a little defensiveness show through.

"Let him talk!" Sirona said.

"What is he then," said the man with Sirona, presumably her husband Edric who looked, in truth, a little like a pot roast.

"I was sent by the hierarch." Heden used the old word for "bishop."

"What a terrible big lie you just told!" Gwennog said, and this seemed to be the consensus of the people.

"Come on, godbotherer," Edric said, smiling with newfound joy in menace. "Give us a prayer, then."

"I don't blame you," Heden said, "I'd be scared too if there were a thousand urmen bearing down on me, and no one to defend me and nowhere to run." He was provoking them, he knew, but he suspected that if he watched them defend themselves and their lord, he'd learn more about what was going on.

"We ain't scared of them," a new man said, stepping forward. This one was a brawler, Heden could tell, and some women were peering over the shoulders of the men to see what he'd do. "And we ain't scared of you."

"Why don't you go home, ratcatcher," the goatherd growled at him, "before you get hurt."

Heden accepted this, as though the man had given him a proper response in a formal exchange. He took a breath and the folk leaned in a little, sensing they were about to get a show.

He spoke a prayer in the First Language, just two sentences, but the act of speaking the words impressed these folk. A man babbling in a language none of them knew? That was real godbothering. They were going to get a show, alright.

A shadow covered Heden's face, his eyes burning out of it, and the folk gasped and recoiled.

"Gowan!" Heden said, his finger stabbing out like a crossbow bolt towards a man. A little man who'd been watching his friend bait Heden shrank back as though struck. He was frozen in place by Heden's prayer.

The folk looked at the man like he had the plague, pulling away from him.

Heden advanced in two quick, long strides. He grabbed Gowan by his thick woolen jerkin.

"You stole it," Heden pronounced, pulling the man up and off his feet. Everyone was silent but the pigs and chickens. The man's eyes went wider still and he looked around furtively. Heden could smell the thick odor of sweat and pig. "You stole Maelon's silver," he said.

"What?!" a man behind them cried out.

"The blacksmith wouldn't take credit or trade, so you took it." Heden's voice came fast. "You crept into his house and took it. And the dog." He shook the man, holding him up with one hand. "It knows you, it knows you don't belong in that house so it barks and you don't know what to do, they'll find you. They'll find out what a filthy little thief you are. So you killed it. You stole their silver and killed their dog to stop it barking and hid the corpse."

"Please!" Gowan cried.

"Black gods!" someone said.

"But you couldn't spend it, could you?" Heden's voice went low, but no matter how low it went the folk around him could hear every word. "Everyone would know, and where did you get that kind of cash? You who never had a streak of luck in your life. So it's to the tavern then, and women. Twenty-two silver on women, what did it get you? Three hours? Five? Did you spread it out? An hour a day for a week?"

"Gowan!" a young woman now standing behind the man cried for him. She was only five feet away but she didn't dare reach out to help.

"Gods, please. Please don't!" Gowan cried.

"Cavall sees you, Gowan," Heden said, his eyes now fire burning into the man.

"Ahh, gods!" the man cried. Heden's words, a brand searing his skin.

"I am his eyes!" Heden's voice was a trumpet.

"I did it!" Gowan confessed. As the words left his mouth, Heden dropped him. He fell to his knees, sobbing. But Heden wasn't done.

He drew his sword, the old, notched blade of his father's father and swung it back, holding it up and behind his head. His face was a thundercloud.

"Know then that I am an agent of Cavall, come to do judgment upon you!" His pronouncement was a lightning strike, and with it a score of townspeople surged forward, their hands grabbing Heden's arm, his sword, his shoulders, pulling on his pack. They shouted, they pleaded.

Heden relented. He relaxed, and the fugue was gone, that raindrop of Cavall's power, granted to him to do justice in his god's name, drained away, leaving him a normal man, with normal sight. He no longer saw the truth, the awful fetid truth of every man around him. He no longer heard a dozen voices wondering and fearing.

With care, as though tending a sick man instead of a confessed criminal, the folk picked Gowan up by the arms and carried him away. His thin wisp of a wife followed, crying and reaching out to him. All the women, Sirona, Gwennog and many others, followed. The men stayed behind and stared at Heden in awe and wonder and fear.

"By the bald pate of Nikros, man," one of them said, and the spell was broken. They all looked away. The one with the rough voice, Dyfan, Gwennog's husband, was accusing Heden of doing something indecent.

"Sirona said a thousand urq," Heden said, looking into the far distance.

No one contradicted him.

Heden sheathed his sword, turned and looked at these farmers. Men with skin wrinkled by the sun, days' worth of dirt caked casually on them.

"You're going to need all the help you can get," Heden said.

"Aye," Dyfan said, looking at the ground. The men nodded. Few would look at Heden and none for more than a moment.

"Gowan ain't a bad man," one of them said.

"I know it," Heden said, and when he said it many of the men looked at him like he was a normal person.

"You folk came to his defense," Heden said. "You forgave him in an instant. That's why Cavall is your god."

It was a compliment. A way of saying, "Cavall is proud to be your god."

"The guards at the gate," Dyfan said. "They'll let you in with us," he said. "They'll just ask your name is all."

"And I will give it to them," Heden said, "as I gave it to you." This was a mild reproach and it worked. The men showed a little shame in having been so distrustful. Heden took it easy on them.

"So," he asked, his lip curling into a smile, "where's this little birdie makes the young girls sigh?"

Dyfan's lips slowly spread into a grin, matching Heden's.

Chapter Eighteen

Renaldo stopped playing and looked down into the large cooking pot the innkeep let him use to collect payment. Gold crowns made a distinct sound when dropped amongst the copper and silver. He looked at the man standing at the edge of the small stage. Wide, honest eyes set in a chiseled, age-weathered face and a compact body.

"Please," Renaldo said, his accent heavy, no attempt made to hide his disgust. "Remove your coin and then that shipwreck of a face before you scare my customers away."

Heden looked down into the pot and then back at the bard. "I just put a gold crown in there."

"I will lose two just by talking to you and my stomach just by looking at you. Now be a good little priest and find someone more in need of prayer."

"I…" Heden stopped and looked around. The tavern was packed with people, none of which seemed to pay either him or the minstrel any mind. Occasionally someone jostled him.

"Hang on," Heden said. "Let's, ah, let's try this again." He started to speak but then Renaldo began to play again, nodding at the pot.

Heden took a deep breath, bent down and fished his coin out. He stared at it in his hand, and then looked back up at Renaldo.

"I was just hoping to…"

Renaldo played louder.

Heden clenched his fist around the gold crown and surveyed the inn. It was smaller than his. There were maybe sixty people packed in the common room, which could not comfortably seat more than thirty. None of these folk cared. Most of them weren't paying Heden any mind, but some were. Heden thought he recognized some of the men from the gate. They were spreading the word and in a small town such as this, the word didn't have far to go.

The minstrel probably worked hard to get these people to trust him. Being seen with Heden, another stranger, would alienate some of his paying audience, and so he wanted to avoid it. Another time and Heden would have respected this. But he'd come a long way, and done at least one awful thing to get here, and now he needed information.

Heden turned back to the minstrel, stepped up on the tiny stage, picking up the pot as he did so. He spun around and in one smooth motion pulled his arm back, preparing to fling the cooking pot, heavy with coin, out the window.

He felt the cold bite of steel at this throat and tensed in a blink. Motionless otherwise, his arm still flung backward. He heard the sound of the chair tipping over and hitting the stage, along with the clash of strings from the lute hitting the floor. *Black gods he's fast.* Heden was in real danger and there was a certain thrill to it. He wanted to test the minstrel, but dared not. Men in the inn would die in the battle. There was a time when he'd not have given these people a second thought.

"Now I must ask you," Renaldo said, and everyone in the inn was watching, "to trust me." His voice was casual, light. Uncaring. At the word "trust" he pressed the blade and it bit into Heden's neck. "For you feel the blade is thin and you think, ''Tis but a trifle.' Think you can make some move, push the blade away. Please believe me when I say: you would be on the ground bleeding your life out before you moved an inch. This is no broadsword like you have there, not one of those great two-handers I could dance along the blade of before a man swung it once around. Far deadlier in fact. So please do not make the mistake so many of your countrymen have made. You will naturally want to fight back…"

"Not against Jacanda steel, I won't," Heden interrupted, not moving a muscle, trying to ignore the audience watching.

"You…ah. What?" Renaldo stammered, backing out of the dancing pose he held. He pulled the blade away and looked at Heden anew. Heden moved only his eyes and raised one eyebrow.

"Not against a Riojan troubadour, I wouldn't."

Renaldo assumed a dueling pose, his rapier pointing straight down, tip touching the stage. One hand on his hip. His mouth was open.

Heden saw the man had assumed a deferent position, and he allowed himself to move.

"And not against a playwright of Capital," he said, smiling.

Renaldo clasped his free hand to the top of his head, a reflex from one used to wearing a hat.

"I..." he said, and frowned, looking around the stage as though he'd misplaced his own name.

He noticed the folk staring. He took a deep, resigned breath, and let it out slowly.

The Riojan waved a hand while he sheathed his rapier with a flourish and whistled a sharp three-tone scale, a perfect imitation of the call any of these farmers might have used to disperse their pigs.

The inn went back to its collective business, the show was over.

"Dangerous way to start a friendship," Renaldo murmured without looking at Heden. "Give me the money," he said, holding out his hand.

Heden gave him the gold.

Renaldo waggled his fingers.

Heden fished out another gold crown and handed it over.

"I will make no more coin this afternoon," Renaldo said, and pocketed the money. "These people do not like being reminded I am a 'ratman,' as they put it. Two of us talking to each other, and now I am a stranger again."

Renaldo put on his hat, picked up his flask of wine and his lute, and walked past Heden. He stepped lightly off the small stage, and a table cleared for him before he reached it. These people held him in high regard.

"A ratcatcher," Heden said, turning to follow.

"Eh?" Renaldo said. He sat down and a maid pushed through the crowd to bring him a glass for his wine, but he shooed her away and plunked the wine flask in the middle of the table, cradled his lute in his lap.

"They call campaigners 'ratcatchers.'" Heden took the chair opposite.

"Ah, yes. That makes some sense to me. I see the similarity. Filthy jobs, sometimes necessary."

"And best forgotten," Heden said.

"Well it is a dangerous business," Renaldo said, picking up a fluted bottle of wine and drinking directly from it. He wiped his mouth on his sleeve, peering at Heden. "Though you seem well suited to it."

"I was," Heden said, looking Renaldo up and down. "Once." The troubadour dressed in what Heden knew a Riojan would consider a discreet outfit. The wide-brimmed green hat on the floor held only one brightly colored peacock feather. Around his neck, a single blue scarf, no pattern. The collar of his doublet open only a few inches, revealing a tan chest and some wisps of curly black hair. The gold sewn into the doublet glittered, but there were no jewels and his red hose ran with tasteful pinstripes rather than the brightly colored checkers favored in Capital when Heden left. Understated, for Capital.

The people here would think he was a jester.

"I work for the church now," Heden said.

"The church. So you are not from the Jack?" His black eyes flashed, his eyebrows long, thin and flourished like the stroke of a pen.

"I don't know what that is," Heden said.

"It is a who."

"Oh," Heden said. "Well, ah…no."

"You have not come to extract some kind of vengeance then?"

"Nope," Heden said.

This seemed to deflate the man even more. "Ah well," he said.

"That disappoints you?"

"Many things disappoint me," Renaldo said, taking a weary breath. "The world seldom lives up to its reputation." He shrugged. "You are here for some mundane reason then and I will have forgotten you in the time it takes to drag a nail."

"You'd prefer it if I wanted to kill you?"

"Well." Renaldo gestured with a hand as though making an obvious point. "Yes."

"Give me a little while," Heden said, "I'm warming up to the idea."

Renaldo smiled a very little at this and raised his eyebrows. "Bravely said."

"So who's the Jack?"

Renaldo shrugged. Heden liked him.

"You know Capital, you know my steel. I thought perhaps you knew my work, were sent by a man I recently maligned in a popular production."

"Recently?" This was not in accord with Heden's knowledge of geography.

"Oh, a year," Renaldo admitted. "I confess I rather appreciate the idea of a man pursuing me for a year. No epic tragedy ever featured a man who was pursued for a day, or, thirty-two weeks," he said, picking a random number. "It must be a year, you understand."

"I understand," Heden said.

"The Jack is a very powerful master assassin," Renaldo said, submitting this fact for Heden's approval, obviously hoping it would earn himself some esteem.

Heden nodded. "I was friends with the Wire."

Renaldo scoffed. "The Wire has no friends."

"I was," Heden rephrased, "someone it amused him not to kill."

"Yes, he has many amusements. I, for one, remain content to bore him. So you have been to Rioja."

"I lived in Capital for six years."

"Pagh!" Renaldo said, and mimed spitting on the ground. "Built by your ancestors to rule my ancestors. All true Riojans despise that city."

"Sure," Heden said. "What are you doing here, Renaldo?"

"Ah no," the troubadour said, taking another pull from his wine. "You have me at a disadvantage. We are not wizards you and I, but names first, nonetheless. It is polite."

Heden nodded and told Renaldo his name. Renaldo doffed his hat.

"I am Renaldo de Merisi, a temporary exile, Brother Heden. The master of the Leaf thought it best if I spend some time abroad after *Catch as Catch Can* opened."

"Your play," Heden said.

"A play? No I do not write plays. I wrote plays when I was a lad, now I craft carefully aimed and highly entertaining attacks on the enemies of the Leaf. In this case, the master of the Fulcrum."

"Not wise to upset the men who hold the money."

"I reasoned they were a small guild, only newly come to power. They would retaliate certainly, but how bad could it be?"

"They could try to have you killed."

Renaldo deflated at that. "Ah yes, this is true. When they assassinated my leading man, I knew it was time to take a trip. And so here I am!" He gestured to take in the entire inn. "The Steaming Turnip. Which I, not properly decoding the sign out front, took to mean the Steaming Turd."

Heden snorted at this. The carved wood sign outside did, indeed, look like a steaming turd. "How did you know I was a priest?" he asked.

Renaldo deflated a little and gestured to the room.

"They told you?"

"I am a troubadour," Renaldo reminded him.

"Just seems fast is all," Heden said, turning and looking at the townspeople. "I came straight here."

"A mile for a man is a yard for a tale," the minstrel said.

"That's good," Heden said, appreciating the quote.

"That's mine," Renaldo said.

"You're good," Heden said.

"Occasional flashes of legend amidst a tempest of brilliance."

"Okay," Heden said. No point in getting carried away. "How much does the two gold get me?"

"How much do you need?"

"I just got here," Heden said. "You tell me."

"Fair," Renaldo said. "Less than two gold's worth, certainly."

"Everyone said there's an army of urmen marching."

"That is what everyone says," Renaldo said. No way for the minstrel to tell if it was true, they both knew. "I think it likely. These people have experienced this phenomenon before, they know the signs."

"They don't seem worried," Heden said. The townsfolk were smiling and laughing and eating. Enjoying the circumstances that had them all pressed together in the town. "Why is that?"

"They await the arrival of an order of knights, the Green, who defend these lands from all manner of incursion. They believe the order will save them."

"Oh." Heden deflated a little.

"Ah-hah," Renaldo said. "You know something of their conspicuous absence."

"Not yet," Heden said. "But I think I will soon. It's why I'm here."

"I think I understand. Well good luck finding them, my friend." Renaldo played a little tune.

"Why?" Heden asked, frowning.

"Because the forest will not permit it."

Heden blinked. "What do you mean?" he asked. Knowing the wode, he anticipated a gruesome answer.

"The baron sends men into the forest to find the order's priory. They return unscathed but unfulfilled."

"Well," Heden said and reached out to take a swallow from Renaldo's wine, "could be worse." The wine was fantastic, better than anything he had at the Hammer. He looked at the bottle and noted it bore a faded Riojan label. He decided not to ask how this man traveled thousands of miles with his own bottle of wine.

"How long until the urmen?"

Renaldo shrugged. "How to tell? Days it seems."

"Days," Heden said.

"A few days."

"You're not worried about a thousand urq days away from crushing this place?"

Renaldo's head lifted from concentrating on the strings of his lute, and he looked off into the distance as he considered Heden's question. He pursed his lips.

"No," he said.

"Why not?"

"Oh," Renaldo said, "because I will run away."

Heden nodded as if confirming a suspicion. "Smart," he said, looking at the townsfolk.

Then he looked out the corner of his eye, suspicious of the minstrel's motivations.

"So why not run now?" Heden asked, and turned back to confront the minstrel.

Renaldo appeared to be ignoring him.

"How much money are you going to make in the next few days?" Heden asked. "And do you need it? Why are you still here, Renaldo de Merisi?"

Renaldo sighed and laid his lute in his lap, cocking his head as he looked back at Heden.

"Very well, you have me. I do not trust this order of knights to arrive in a properly dramatic fashion. And so I hope to convince these people to flee."

Heden sat back, smiling smugly.

"Seems somewhat out of character, don't you think?"

Renaldo frowned. "I enjoy casting against type," he said. "I sing songs to highlight the wisdom of saving one's own skin. These simple people, of course, do not realize my intent, or my meaning. I find being direct so artless." He smiled widely, bearing perfect white teeth. "They know only that the songs are brilliant."

Heden nodded, humoring him. "Brilliant," he said.

Renaldo looked at him, studied his face.

"You will head into the forest looking for this Order Green," Renaldo predicted, his brow furrowed as he played out the events of the next few days. "Tell me, my friend. Do you think it likely your immediate future holds tales of adventure, heroism and miraculous deeds?"

Heden stared at the Riojan.

"I don't know," he said, looking at the bar. He turned back to Renaldo and looked at him with misery. "Probably."

Renaldo smiled slowly until his grin turned into a hungry, feral thing.

"Then I *must* attend you. Your death will, I surmise, fuel an excellent tale."

"My death," Heden said.

"I am an optimist," Renaldo said, shrugging. "Heroic tragedies are very popular in my homeland right now."

He adjusted his instrument and began to play. "Please come find me once the baron is done with you!"

"What?" Heden asked. Renaldo looked meaningfully behind Heden.

There were two guards behind him, one at each elbow.

"Hallo sunshine," one of the guards said with a mean smile. "Now why don't you stop bothering our little sparrow here and come with us?"

Heden turned slowly and looked at the two men, each taller than Heden. One round and old, the other whip-thin and young. He pointed at the fat one.

"I know you," Heden said. "You were at the town gate."

"That's right. And I don't know you. The baron likes to meet new people," the thick man said, smiling.

"Oh. Good."

Chapter Nineteen

The baron was a baroness. Most people in the north didn't bother with gendered terms.

She and two advisors stood behind a large oak desk at which sat a bald, elderly monk scratching ink onto vellum. It was likely, Heden thought, that the baron could not read. Literacy had never caught on here at the fringes of civilization. The writings would be posted, but first a crier would read them to a gathered throng. There was a time when this would have seemed hopelessly backward to Heden. Now he experienced a mixture of nostalgia and respect. Things here hadn't changed in a long time, because they didn't need to.

He waited, eyes cast down, listening to the baron's voice as she took advice from her privy council. One old man with white hair and a long robe, and a man Heden's age who wore a breastplate and a mace at his side. A talisman around his neck. A wizard and a priest. Heden frowned, wondering what Renaldo would think of the stereotypes presented.

The baron looked ten years older than Heden and, while all the noblemen he'd ever met wore plated armor over chain and leather, she was sporting scale armor, which Heden had only seen in paintings and tapestries. The scales were white and Heden wondered what they were made of. She seemed fit and capable. Her straight hair was cut just below her ears in the classical Golish style. She had that bronze-skinned, black-haired look of the ancient Gol that bred true every few generations. Heden guessed she was proud of her heritage.

She talked about drunkenness and curfew during the siege. There was a stack of already finished proclamations and Heden recognized she was anticipating the next week or two's events and preparing documents now while she could.

The two guards stood behind Heden in the large stone room, the ceiling an impressive thirty feet high. Shafts of pale light stabbed through tall, narrow windows onto a once ornate faded rug.

He listened to several proclamations, all very pragmatic, and then she finished. She looked at the guards. They shoved Heden forward.

Heden remembered his etiquette, bowed and said, "Thank you for receiving me, milady."

The baron tilted her head to one side and examined Heden for a few moments. "Are you a friend of the minstrel?" she asked.

"No, milady," Heden responded.

"Just plying him for information?"

Heden shrugged.

The baron shot a look at the head guard, who lunged forward and bashed the back of Heden's neck with his mailed elbow, causing Heden to stumble forward.

"When the baron asks you a question, you better come up with a fucking answer," the guard said, his voice thick and meaty.

Heden, his hand to his neck, straightened up and turned to stare at the guard. The guard tried to stare back, but after a moment seemed to doubt himself and looked at the baron for help. Heden turned back to her.

"Your people are under a lot of stress," he said. "There's a siege coming, everyone's talking about it. People may die. But you tell your warthog there that if he touches me again he won't have to worry about the siege because I will put him on his ass and he will not get up."

The guard stepped forward, ready for violence, but the baron made a gesture and cut him off.

The almost-certainly priest walked to the side of the table and looked at Heden with scorn.

"Someone called you a priest," the man said with disdain in what seemed to Heden an affected noble accent.

"I was made a prelate five years ago," Heden said. True.

The baron looked at him with something approaching hunger. The man with the mace took a step backward in a kind of shock.

"My advisor," the baron said, appearing to take a little pleasure from the confrontation. "Deacon Owlsley." With her northern accent, it sounded to Heden like "woolsley." "A prelate five years ago," she repeated. "And now?"

"I'm seconded to Bishop Conmonoc, Hierarch of the Church of Cavall the Righteous." Also true.

The baron was impressed and looked at Heden as though he were a statue made of gold and she planned on melting him down and spending him.

"What saint do you follow?" she asked.

Heden took a weary breath. "Saint Lynwen."

The baron and her priest looked at each other, neither having heard of Lynwen.

"She's obscure," Heden said. True.

"What is your name?"

He told her.

"Heden, you come to us in a time of dire need."

I bet, Heden thought.

"Everyone says there's an army of urmen on their way here," Heden said.

The baron nodded.

"Have you seen them?"

"My scouts have. My wizard scryed them," she said, indicating the older man behind her.

"How many do you estimate?" Heden asked, expecting the answer to be in the hundreds. The number he heard outside the gate, a thousand, was an exaggeration.

"Five thousand."

Heden didn't say anything. His expression didn't change. But his sense of ease and his relaxed attitude faded. Only someone who knew him would notice it.

"Five thousand urq and you're sitting here writing proclamations?"

The baroness sighed, turned to the scrolls she'd been dictating and, almost absently, asked, "How much do you know about urmen?"

"I know they were created by the dragons in mockery of men," he said. Everyone in the room looked at him, surprised.

"Is that true?" the baron asked her advisors.

"Possibly an ancient legend, milady," the wizard said.

"They live short lives," Heden continued, ignoring the wizard who, at least, was not affecting an accent above his station. "Forty years. And they war constantly. Your son or daughter might take a year to learn to walk. An urq can walk and talk a week after they're born. The only thing they understand is strength. The strong lead, the weak are killed. They're smart. You can treat with them but it's rare. They hate humans and don't really…they've never understood what makes us strong, or believe we can be strong. And they don't live long enough to learn. They take what they want, or die trying."

The baron was obviously impressed. She looked at her wizard disparagingly.

"You speak of negotiation," the wizard intoned, trying to control the conversation and make up what he had lost in his master's eye. "What, in your expert opinion, would they want in return for sparing us?"

The baron turned back to Heden hoping for an answer. A solution.

Heden shrugged. "The dragons created them to hate humans. It's in their blood. An individual might decide different, but as a race?" Heden pursed his lips and shook his head dismissively. "They're driven to attack whatever humans hold. And," he added casually, "it gives them something to do."

"Like building castles," the baron said, wryly.

"Better to be fighting you than each other. Every few years a strong leader comes around, unites the tribes." Heden stopped, the conclusion was obvious. "I'm surprised it doesn't happen more often up here."

"The order," the baron said. Heden was still skeptical. Something was missing from the equation. Nine men and women holding back everything that called the forest home?

"Could you stop them?" she asked.

Heden stared at her.

"Could I stop five thousand urmen?"

"Yes."

Heden's eyes darted around the room, looking for any sign of sanity. Everyone was looking at him expectantly. "No."

"He could do it," the deacon snapped. He seemed afraid.

"You're mad," Heden said, as though identifying the man's country of origin.

"A prelate of Cavall could summon a dominion. A whole army of dominions. He could..." The deacon stopped talking to the room and spoke directly to Heden. Any fear of Heden, any embarrassment at being made to look the fool was gone. This was a man begging for his life. "Listen, man, you could take our men and pray and bless them until each was worth ten urmen."

Heden stared at him as though he'd gone insane.

"It doesn't work that way," Heden said. "You should..." He looked at the baron. "He should know better. Is this what you've got?"

She ignored him.

"You would have the use of my men," she said.

"Your men?" Heden asked, skeptical.

"Yes."

"How many men do you have?" Heden asked, keen to hear the answer, showing a little anger at the irresponsibility in evidence.

"Two hundred regulars and maybe four hundred peasant levies."

"You'd need at least a thousand," Heden said. "Ten units of trained and experienced solders, forget farmers with pitchforks. Inside a Gol keep, with foreknowledge of the army, a thousand soldiers could defend against five thousand urmen. Until you ran out of food, but the urq don't like long sieges."

"I have six hundred."

"Then you need to get your people out of here."

"That's been suggested."

"Good."

"It's too late," the baron concluded. "We couldn't move fast enough."

"Why did you wait?" Heden demanded. "You've sentenced these people to death, what did you think was going to happen?!"

"One does not address the baron in that manner!" the wizard said. Heden ignored him and locked eyes with the baron.

She just looked at him, her jaw set, her mouth a thin pursed line, but her eyes pleading.

"The Green Order," Heden said for her. She didn't object. She at least had the decency to appear regretful. Shamed. Heden thought for a moment.

"Alright, here's what you do. You tell your people to scatter. Run like mad for any town in any direction. Don't let them group up. Send your men in squads with them, give them orders so they make sure the people don't end up running to the same place. Confuse the enemy. Make them split their forces. The urmen won't know what to do when they leave the forest, they don't like plains. They'll probably still take the keep even if it's empty. They're stupid that way."

The wizard and the deacon both looked expectantly at the baron. They were hoping she'd take the advice.

The baron ignored them and held Heden's gaze. "We're going to wait here."

"What?"

"The Green is out there, they have to come. It's their oath."

"Their *oath*?" Heden repeated.

She nodded.

"And you're willing to bet the lives of all your subjects on that?"

She said, quietly: "We always have before." She blinked as she said it, as though she didn't dare take the time to evaluate that decision

"This is madness," Heden said. "You're all mad, you know that right? You deserve to get roasted alive by an army of urq, but those people out there," Heden said, shouting, stabbing his finger at the window, "haven't done anything wrong except depend on *you*!"

"Listen, you piece of shit!"

Heden had forgotten about the guards behind him. The bigger guard clamped his mailed hand on Heden's shoulder.

It sounded to everyone in the room like Heden swore under his breath in an inhuman tongue, several words as he spun and hit the guard square in the chest with the flat of his hand.

The guard, tall, big, stupid, had the wind driven out of him and his eyes went wide with surprise as the blow lifted him impossibly off his feet and sent him sailing. As he flew backward, his skin, his clothes, his whole body flashed to stone, and what hit the ground was a kind of rough-hewn statue that shrieked when the rump of the former guard skidded against the flagstones.

The younger guard swore and fell down, scrabbling to get away from Heden. The priest and the wizard raced to put up wards while the baron looked at the statue that used to be her guard captain.

"By Cyrvis' thorny prick!" the wizard hissed. "What have you done, man?"

"I told him," Heden said, upset at himself for losing his temper. "I told him."

"Arrest him!" the deacon said and, realizing that the only man who could arrest Heden was now a large piece of art, he looked wildly around the room at no one. "Someone arrest..." He trailed off.

"I needed him," the baron said, more to herself than anyone. It seemed like Heden's action had collapsed whatever support she'd been using to hold back despair; she now seemed like someone who'd given up. "His family had been in service to mine for five generations. I was at his wedding."

"It'll wear off," Heden said, looking at the floor. "I lost my temper, there was no excuse for that, milady." He was angry at himself for getting involved in this in the first place.

"How long will he be like that?" the baron asked, her voice flat.

"Three days," Heden said.

The baron looked at Heden. "I don't have enough guards left."

Heden was upset at himself, but refused to show it. He went on the attack. "You didn't have enough guards to begin with," he said, looking her in the eyes. He stabbed a finger at her. "You never had enough. Against five thousand urmen? You never had enough."

"The Green will come."

Heden remembered his instructions. The ritual that would cleanse the order was in his pack.

"Pray they do," Heden said, and meant it.

The baron appeared to reach a conclusion. She composed herself and rebuilt whatever defenses against despair Heden had momentarily destroyed. "You are a prelate of Cavall. Even were you to simply heal the wounded, your services would be invaluable. And you just cost me my guard captain. I'm pressing you into service. You are a serf on my land, and under the contract between your lord and master you owe service, prelate or no. Consider this payment on all such debts."

"I'm sorry," Heden said, shaking his head. "We both know that won't work. Anyway, I'm already a freeman. I'm going to do everything I can to help you, but not here."

The baron looked confused. "How then?"

"I'm going to find the Green Order." Somewhere in the previous conversation, Heden discovered that he was this town's only hope. These poor idiots, just like the poor idiots he grew up with, the poor idiots his parents were. The poor idiot he was. Whatever he thought before now, he was committed.

"Is that why you're here?" she asked.

"Yeah," Heden said without conviction.

"The bishop sent you here to liberate the order from whatever prevents it from reaching us?" The baron was skeptical. She obviously didn't believe Heden.

"Something like that," Heden replied. He didn't know what he believed anymore.

He looked at the baron and they shared a moment. He didn't know why he was doing what he was doing. She no longer knew why she was doing what she was doing. Both of them were going through the motions, hoping some greater meaning would present itself. All either of them knew was they didn't want these people to die.

"Praise Cavall," the deacon said, putting his fist into his hand and pulling both up to his mouth. He missed whatever was passing between Heden and the baron.

The baron shook her head. "It won't work."

Heden picked up his pack. "It'll work," he said.

"The forest won't let anyone through. They go in, follow the trail and come out again without any memory of turning around."

Heden nodded. "I need a horse."

"A horse?"

"Just a regular horse. I'm sorry about the guard," Heden said, not changing tone.

The baron looked at him. "Me too," she said. "I'll have a horse saddled for you."

"Station people in the warrens," Heden said. "The urmen sometimes use kethat sappers. The warrens'll confuse them. They won't expect to find tunnels or people in them."

The baron nodded.

"The knight who was killed," she said. "It was the knight-commander. Sir Kavalen. He was the…" She faltered. "The head of the order."

Heden nodded. "Thanks," he said. It was useful information.

The baron walked around to the other side of the desk and from a drawer pulled a small vellum scroll tied with ribbon and affixed with a wax imprint of her seal.

She walked around the desk again and presented it to Heden. He thought she was trying to knight him or something.

"If you find them, give this to the lady Isobel."

"Isobel."

"She's the eldest of the order."

Heden took the scroll. "I will. If she's still alive."

"She's alive," the baron said.

"You can't know that," Heden said. Over the course of the conversation, he'd come to the conclusion that the order had been wiped out. If they had a pact with the forest, that would explain the mazement preventing anyone from entering and looking for them. The forest was saying "There is no order."

"I would know if she were dead." Before she continued, Heden sensed what she was going to say next. It explained her blind faith in the order.

"Lady Isobel is my sister."

Chapter Twenty

At first the horse was confused. Heden rode it through the gate and when the horse tried to turn right, where the road led south to civilization, Heden pulled the reins to the left. To the forest. Where there was no road, no path.

The horse didn't know what to make of this. Heden dismounted, fed it an apple he'd brought for just this purpose, and rubbed the horse's neck absently while it chewed.

Mounting up again, the horse was more willing to accept Heden's guidance. The two of them struck out north, across the rolling green fields, to the massive trees of the Iron Forest. Even at a mile distant, the trees loomed so high they tricked the mind. They looked like they were toppling over.

The tree line was distinct, sharp. Once they reached it, the horse became a little jittery. Remembering the stories his father told him about Sir Ollwen and his knights, Heden turned the horse so it faced due east. The forest on his left, the keep down on his right. The horse should, if it were sensible, turn right and head back home to Ollghum Keep. Probably after standing still for a quarter hour, too stupid to realize anything was amiss.

Saying something less a prayer and more a wish, Heden patted the horse's neck, rubbed its thick, short hairs, took a deep breath and let the reins go slack on the horse's neck.

The horse sniffed the air and champed its teeth, pulling the bit forward. It shook its head back and forth once, testing to see that Heden wasn't holding the reins. It murmured a horsey whinny and stamped the ground once. Heden relaxed, didn't move. Tried to think of nothing. After a few moments, maybe half a turn, the horse gently turned left and began to head into the forest.

Heden's trick was working. He trusted to fate, let the horse pick its own way. Into the forest, and towards whatever destiny awaited him there.

The wode closed in on all sides, completely denying any opportunity to get one's bearings. The sun was difficult to find in the sky, there was no sense of distance. And whatever natural connection man had to the cycles of day and night became disjointed.

The trees were taller than any human structure he'd ever seen, wider around than a house. Adding to his disorientation was the fact that the huge trees of the Iron Forest were not packed close together. Only the tips of their leaves touched. The distance between the trees, and their sheer size, created a sense of space that overwhelmed him. Each tree was like a massive pillar, holding up a green sky made of leaves above. He felt like an ant crawling across the floor of a cathedral.

The horse found a trail. Heden didn't notice when they started on it. He was daydreaming and then he looked down and they were on a thin trail, probably a foot trail. The underbrush around them, the bracken and ferns and vines, was thick, but the trail was clear. He twisted around, looked behind for the spot the trail started, but couldn't see anything. The horse obviously knew something he didn't. Probably knew a lot of things Heden didn't. Probably figured being sat on all day entitled it to an opinion.

He used the meditative time to think, go over events in his mind: Gwiddon, the carter, Vanora. The baron. He replayed the scenes over and over again. Not for any reason, just out of habit. It was something he couldn't turn off. Occasionally he would think of something he should have said, or upon remembering something someone else said, gain some insight into their motivation. Their real meaning. Also, sometimes, his own.

After a turn in the forest, the horse plodding along at a steady rate, he was startled by something out of the corner of his eye. Motion as though something had run off behind a nearby tree. And then the bottom began to fall out from his world.

It was possible, he reminded himself, even likely, that a rabbit or some other small game was startled by his passing and took flight. But as soon as the sensation passed, it was replaced by a growing suspicion. As he rode, every tree became a place behind which some enemy could be hiding. The woods were silent—were they unnaturally silent? Were they silent because of hostile humanoids lying in wait? There were birds, small noises…were they normal? Heden found he couldn't remember. He could imagine anything.

It was madness, he tried to tell himself. It didn't work. His nightmare scenarios seemed all too plausible. He'd been in a dozen situations, exactly like this, where the trees *had* concealed urmen or worse. No one knew he was here. There was no way, no reason, for ambush. But that didn't mean it couldn't happen. He could be trespassing on some inhuman creature's territory. That tree there was big enough to hide a thyrs. He stared for what might have been a full minute thinking he was seeing the hilt of a spear sticking out from behind a distant tree. Then the horse moved and he saw it was only a branch from another tree, farther in the distance.

He wished he could blame the tightening, the senseless fear, on the forest and its power to confuse, but Heden knew this was going to happen. Happened every time he left the city.

His heart was hammering in his chest and for the thousandth time he feared it would burst. He realized he was completely, utterly alone. There was no one to help him if something happened to him. If his heart burst in his chest, there was no priest to aid him, no one to go and get a priest. The fact that he lived alone and had done so for years didn't mean anything. In Celkirk, he felt safe, and so didn't think about such things.

He was suddenly gripped with fear that he had turned around, was heading back to Ollghum Keep. He twisted in the saddle, staring back the way he'd come, wondering if it was the way he should be going.

He remembered Gwiddon offering to give him help and, for a little while, seriously entertained the notion of going back to Celkirk, going south almost a hundred miles, a whole day's travel, and asking for help in getting the last few miles. The temptation to return to the known, to get away from this place of danger, was almost overwhelming.

He found the saddle constraining. As much as he had to get out of the forest, back to the inn, he had to get out of the saddle.

He swung his leg over and dropped clumsily to the forest floor. He staggered, then grabbed the leather of the saddle with one hand and steadied himself on the flank of the horse with the other. He felt normal again. Felt the madness, the fear, evaporate.

He sniffed once. Breathed heavily. Straightened up and looked around, wiping sweat from his brow.

The horse seemed to have taken no notice of the episode. Heden remembered being a young man, with no sense of fear or mortality, and a wave of sadness passed over him, not for the first time, at what he'd been reduced to. What campaigning for twelve years had done to him. It was this that Gwiddon knew made this assignment so difficult. Eventually the episodes would get longer and more frequent.

He didn't want to get back on the horse, and didn't want to think about why. He hit the horse with the flat of his hand, signaling the beast to lead the way again.

The horse neighed and wouldn't budge.

Heden grunted a question and walked up to look the horse in the eye.

The horse shook its head. No.

Heden grabbed the reins and tugged, but the horse had the bit between the teeth and was having none of it.

"What?" Heden asked.

The horse waggled its lips at Heden, showing its big horse teeth.

Heden felt incredibly tired. He was too far from home and too much at odds with himself and his mission to fight with the horse.

"Fine," Heden said. He dropped the reins. "You stay here and let the brocc find you. They love horse."

Heden turned to show the horse he was leaving, and noticed what the horse had seen.

He turned back around and looked behind the horse. Walked around the horse and looked back the way they'd came. Then he strode back around the horse and checked in every direction.

The trail was gone. The trail they were following had disappeared. It had been here when he'd stopped, and he hadn't moved, but it was gone.

"Shit," Heden said to no one and everyone.

The horse neighed.

Chapter Twenty-one

It took a long time to clear even a small path, and he despaired as sweat fell from his face. His muscles, not used to such work, ached. He paused for a moment and tried to find the sun again. Wondered at what his father would think of him getting tired after only a few hours' hard work. He enjoyed tasks like this. For which the only solution was hard work. He was his father's son.

The horse didn't appear to mind the passage of time with little progress. It seemed perfectly happy to stand there, no one on its back, nibbling at the leaves on the vines and ferns. Sometimes it would take a turn and prune an entire bush. Sometimes it would gently mouth a leaf from a bush and leave it. Probably poisonous. *How does it know?* Heden wondered. Mysterious horsey senses men did not wot of, probably.

He set back to work. He exposed a large root, curling above and below the ground, on which had been anchored a great deal of vegetation. Unable to get a good angle of attack via any other method, he climbed atop the twisting root and stood there looking down. As he prepared to hack at it, it snapped under his weight and though he tried to catch himself, all he managed to do was flip head over heels and land on his back, his cloak over his head.

He heard the horse whinny in amusement. *Stupid horse,* he thought.

He yanked his cloak off his face and froze. There was a man standing at his feet, pointing a longsword at his throat, its blade catching the sunlight streaming through the leaves hundreds of feet above. The horse wasn't commenting on Heden's athleticism, it was trying to alert Heden to the presence of the stranger.

He was a knight without a helm. He wore plate, but it was plate for the working day. None of the frippery Heden saw the White Hart sport back in Celkirk, all ornament for show. This was smooth. Worn smooth by many blows and repairs. Not gleaming silver, but dull grey. There seemed to be a pattern etched into it but it was spotty and Heden couldn't make it out. The man's sword looked just as well-used. Heden thought he sensed some sorcery on the blade, but didn't think it mattered. He guessed that any knight alone in the wode who could get the drop on him wouldn't need a sorcerous blade to be a threat to him. Not at this distance. Not with Heden on his ass.

Without moving the sword at Heden's throat, and without making a noise, the knight looked around. Checking to see if there was anyone else around.

"I'm alone," Heden volunteered.

The knight took one more survey of the area, and then a step back. But did not lower the sword or in any other way change his posture. Heden sat up a little, but made no other attempt to rise.

"Yeah," the knight said. "I can see that." He turned full around, checking for something, then turned back to Heden.

"I have a horse," Heden said in his own defense.

The knight looked at the horse deforesting the wode. It was happily ignoring both of them, thinking horsey thoughts.

"That's debatable," the knight said. He hadn't put the sword down.

A moment passed. Neither man spoke.

"We just going to sit here like this?" Heden asked.

"*You're* going to sit there like that," the knight said.

"Okay," Heden said, giving up.

The knight made his way to the horse. He moved like a wolf. When he reached the horse, he rifled through Heden's gear. Threw open the flap of Heden's pack and pushed his arm in. Heden watched the knight's eyes go wide; he pulled back and looked at the pack, and then thrust his arm in up to the shoulder. The small pack swallowed his arm.

He pulled his arm out and closed the flap. He rounded the horse, continuing his inspection. Then he made his way back to Heden.

Heden relaxed and laid his head against the root, looked up at the canopy of leaves and ignored the knight.

The knight stood over Heden for a few moments more, and sheathed his sword. He leaned down, extended his hand. "Come on," he said. Heden took his hand and pulled himself up, grateful for the help.

"What are you doing here?" the knight asked.

"I think I'm looking for you," Heden said, brushing the dirt and dead leaves off his ass.

"Me?" The knight took a step back and gave him a doubting appraisal. He had a round head, his copper hair cut so short Heden wondered what the point was. He was a little bigger than Heden, but seemed thinner. Heden considered his own judgment of men to be keen. He saw in this knight a kindred spirit.

"I'm looking for the Green Order," Heden said.

The stranger shook his head. "Not me," he said. "I can take you to them, though." He jerked his thumb to his left. "They're in the wode."

"In the wode?" Heden asked. "This isn't the wode?"

"Well, I suppose to some," the knight said. "Not by my reckoning, though. Far as I see it, the wode proper don't start until you reach the brocc."

Heden nodded, he understood. The closer, the more intimate your relationship with the forest, the nicer your idea of where the wode starts and stops.

"Who are you?" Heden asked. "What do you do up here?"

The knight shrugged and extended his hand a little bit behind him. Responding to no obvious command, Heden's horse wandered over until the knight was able to grab the horse's reins. "There's a living to be made here, like any other," he said. "Come on."

He started off, leading Heden's horse, and Heden noticed the footpath had come back.

"Where'd this come from?" he asked.

"Eh?"

"This path. We followed it in," he said, promoting his horse to a companion, "but it disappeared."

The knight smiled. "It happens," he said. "Path this small, you wander off for only a moment, suddenly you can't see it for all the brush. You spend enough time in here," he said, "you learn where they are."

Maybe this wasn't a knight, Heden thought. He seemed more like a woodsman. Spoke like any man from Ollghum Keep.

"You know Ollghum Keep?" Heden asked.

The man scowled like Heden had insulted him. "Course I do," he said. "What kind of question is that? Where are you from?"

"South," Heden said. "I've come a long way to talk to these knights."

"Well," the knight said, "they're not going to want to talk to you."

Heden sighed as the two men and the horse walked at a leisurely pace through the woods. With company the place seemed far less threatening. Mundane. Even beautiful.

"How come?" he asked, and realized he'd slipped back into the northern dialect. "How come?" instead of "Why?"

"They don't like people," the man said.

"That's a..." Heden cleared his throat and tried to master his own manner of speech. "That covers a lot."

The knight shrugged. "It's how they are."

Heden let a moment pass in silence.

"How are they?"

"Pretty high-handed," the knight said wearily. Heden concluded that this man had dealt with the Green often, and they did not come off favorably in his estimation. "Rarely leave the forest, so they don't spend much time around men. They're rude. Full of themselves. Don't seem to get along much with each other, neither. Each one," he said, and stretched his arm across half the forest around them, "covers leagues on their own. Alone for months. I think maybe they're a little mad."

"Covers the forest doing what?" Heden asked.

The knight shrugged. "Keep the beasties in line. The urq, the thyrs mostly. The elgenwights. Stop them from raiding the towns."

"You get elgenwights this far south?" Heden asked.

"Oh sure," the knight said, throwing a glance at Heden. "Them and the brocc, always at it. The brocc are mostly on our side," he said. Heden nodded, he knew that.

"The fae, too," the knight said. "Kids from the towns come into the forest on a dare, and the fae snatch them up. Don't mean nothing by it, they don't know any better. But still," the knight said.

"But still," Heden echoed, knowing the fae as he did. "How far are they?" he asked.

"Few miles," the knight said. "They have a chapel they all gather at." Heden presumed he meant the priory the bishop spoke of. "But it'll take the better part of a day. We'll skirt the brocc territory. They're devils when they're riled up. I have a hard enough time dealing with them alone. I try to bring a stranger through, there'll be trouble no matter what."

Heden realized why he found the knight so easy to talk to. *He's a campaigner,* Heden thought.

"Where's your company?" Heden took a chance.

"My company?" the knight said, his lip curling at the strangeness of the question.

"Man like you," Heden said, looking down at his feet eating up the distance. Passing the time. "All alone up here. You know the order, you know the brocc. Doesn't figure. I'm guessing you're a campaigner." *Like I was.*

"Not me," he said. "Not a ratcatcher. I was a squire," the knight said with some wistful bitterness. "Prenticed to a knight. But he...he's dead. Just me now."

Heden didn't respond. He and the knight and the horse walked through the forest awhile.

"Well, these knights sound like complete shits," he said, changing the subject.

The knight with him smiled. "Aye," he said. "So what brings you to meet them?"

Heden sighed. "I don't know," he said.

"You've come a long way for 'I don't know.'"

"Yeah," Heden said. "There's some kind of crisis in this order and someone at the high city," he said, not mentioning the bishop, "decided I should come up here and look into it."

"Why you?" the knight asked.

"I have no idea."

"Seems strange," the knight said.

"What?"

"Just seems strange to send a man all the way up here without telling him much of why. You some kind of expert on knights?"

Heden barked a laugh. "I hate knights."

"Really?"

"They're insufferable pricks. Present company excluded."

The knight hung his head. "I never earned my spurs," he said. "My master died before the ceremony." That left the squire in a perpetual loophole, but usually another knight in the order would finish his training. Probably the other knights all had squires.

"You up here all alone, dealing with the elgenwights, the thyrs. Any man would say you were a knight," Heden said. Aware that for most squires, the opinions of those outside the order were meaningless.

The knight looked at him and smiled. "Thanks," he said.

"What order are you with?" Heden asked.

"It don't seem strange to you," the knight asked, ignoring Heden, "they send someone up here who hates knights? They don't tell him anything about what's going on?"

"I hadn't really thought about it."

"You come all the way up from the high city and you didn't think about it?"

"I…" Heden started. He shook his head. "They wanted someone who could deal with the knights on special terms." He didn't tell the knight his real station. His relationship with the bishop. "Probably they thought sending their own knights up might get people in trouble. They wanted someone to solve the problem, not make it worse."

"How you going to solve the problem?" the eternal squire asked.

"I don't know," Heden admitted. "I'm not sure I care anymore." He remembered the inn. His heart clenched at the idea that he might suffer another attack here in the wode, and he wanted to go home. "I just want to do my job and go home."

The knight stopped, the horse stopped. Heden took another few steps and then realized the knight was no longer leading them, and he turned around.

"Your job?" the knight asked, tilting his head a little to one side, weighing Heden's statement.

Heden was confused. "Yeah," he said. "Deal with their crisis and get out of here. That's my job."

"How workmanlike you make it sound." The knight's voice had changed a little. His accent was different. "Like a carpenter hired to set a beam."

Heden shrugged, no defense. "Sorry," he said. He realized he sounded like a mercenary. He wondered what the knight's interest in all of this was.

Then he noticed the path had disappeared again.

"We're off the path," he said.

"You will not find the order," the knight said.

"What?"

"It was a mistake for them to send you." The knight seemed bitter, almost angry.

Heden looked around. Was this the exact same spot they'd started off in, after walking for a full turn?

He looked at the knight anew. Pointed at him rudely.

"You never told me your name."

"Dolt," the knight shot back. "Everything that's happened and of course they send you. A hundred children in a dozen towns could tell you who I am."

Heden got goosebumps. "What order are you with?" he asked again, remembering now that the knight had not answered again.

"It matters not," the knight said. "You will not gain the green chapel."

"I will not…" Heden repeated. "Who are you to say? What business is it of yours?"

The knight grew visibly wroth and drew his sword. "What business of mine?! No *business*, clod. Thou dunce. Thou oafish ass. What business of *yours*?"

Heden stepped back at the drawn sword. Was this a knight of the Green Order? Was he being tested?

He held his hands up, showing he meant no harm. "I'm just here to…" The knight stepped forward, closing the gap, interrupting him.

"'Just?'" he threw back. "Just indeed. Just and merely. Merely and barely. Barely here, barely a man. Thou shalt not gain the green chapel, dolt."

"Well," Heden said, trying not to let things get away from him. "Then we're at an impasse, because it's the only reason I'm here. You said you'd lead me there. Will you?"

"You are here," the knight sneered, "for no reason of your own."

Heden took this as a no. "Okay," he said, and turned to continue in the direction he remembered the knight indicated.

The knight leapt forward effortlessly, until he was blocking Heden's way again.

"Turn around," the knight said, and pointed his sword at Heden.

"I won't," Heden said. "You're going to have to deal with me here, or let me pass, one or the other." He took another step forward.

The knight took a step forward as well, until the two men were only two paces apart. He pointed his sword at Heden.

"Quit the field," the knight pronounced, and in Heden's eyes he'd changed physically since they'd met. He seemed larger, his armor brighter. The fine detail in it now recognizable as a vine with blooming flowers. "Or I will strike thee down."

"What are you doing, man?"

"I say thee," the knight spoke slowly, pressed the tip of his sword into Heden's breastplate. "Turn around and get thee hence from this place or I shall run ye through and no mistake."

Heden locked eyes with the knight and covertly dug one booted foot into the dead leaves and dirt. "You think I'm going to turn around now? Because of you?" He leaned a little into the sword point, his breastplate and leather underneath more than enough to prevent harm. This forced the knight to press back to hold his ground. "You can go stick your prick in a pig's ass."

The knight bared his teeth. "Then it be battle between us," he said.

But at the word "battle" Heden was already in action. He kicked the dirt and leaves into the face of the knight as he twisted away from the sword, causing the knight to stumble forward, losing his balance. The knight shouted, disoriented, as he tried to clear his eyes.

In the time it took the knight to recover, Heden drew his own sword, a little clumsily as he wasn't used to sword fighting now, but in enough time to clear the scabbard and then hammer the knight in the back of the neck with the pommel as he stumbled past. He could have struck with the edge of the blade, but didn't know how far the knight would take this.

"Knave!" the knight shouted and wheeled, swinging his sword around. He was an expert. Better than Heden, even in Heden's youth, and soon the two men were dancing and scrabbling through the fallen leaves and branches on the floor of the forest—Heden retreating all the while.

Heden spoke a prayer and warded himself. The knight's eyes went wide with surprise, but he smiled as well, relishing the power of his foe, and pressed the attack. As though Heden's prayers had given him permission to let loose.

It was difficult, maybe impossible, for Heden to fight back while losing ground and think of another prayer at the same time. Too many options. Too many prayers learned and forgotten, and three years in the inn, shut in, alone.

The knight got through his guard, slashed him once across his right arm, and when Heden winced, he struck again, stabbing into Heden's left shoulder.

The pain brought clarity. Prayer wasn't necessary. Anger would suffice. And Heden was very angry.

He fought back with new ferocity, and now was pushing the knight back. The more Heden fought, the more ground he gained, the more the knight seemed to enjoy it. The more he smiled. This only angered Heden more.

Sloppy, fighting more with fury than any skill, Heden left many wide openings and though the knight was forced back by Heden's wild attacks, he countered once, and then struck through Heden's flailing, thuggish offense. The tip of the knight's sword sliced at Heden's neck, cutting a thin line that quickly oozed red.

The knight seemed pleased with himself and dropped his guard, smiling, as though offering Heden a chance to yield.

But Heden couldn't see the knight's attitude, his eyes saw only red, and he did not consider yielding.

Heden slashed out. The blade of his father's father, not magical, merely very sharp, swung around and sliced through the knight's neck.

He intended to trade sharp cut for sharp cut, and was therefore amazed when his blade cut clean through the knight's neck, through bone and muscle and sinew. The knight's eyes went wide with alarm and his mouth opened in surprise as his head flew off his shoulders.

Heden stood gawping. Breathing like a horse having run a league. He was amazed that his blow, intended only to scratch, had decapitated his opponent.

But he was more amazed that the knight was not dead. His body did not fall to the ground. Instead it dropped its sword, and raised its hands to where its head once was. Felt the air where once was flesh and bone.

The knight's head lay in the brush, eyes wide, mouth forming silent words. The head seemed to be talking to the body.

The body wandered over clumsily, bent down and picked up the head. The knight's hands placed the head upon his shoulders. He fitted it on like one might set a stone atop a wall, balancing it to prevent it from falling off. When he took his hands away, he was whole again.

"Alright, you made your point," the knight said, scratching his neck. His speech returned to normal. Or to its mode when they first met. Heden didn't know what normal was anymore. He was lost at sea. His mind whirred, immobilizing him, as he tried to find some context, some meaning, behind the headless knight made whole again.

The knight walked forward, approaching Heden, but only reached down to pick up his sword. He looked at Heden anew. Raised his eyebrows, pursed his lips. “Maybe I was wrong. Maybe pig-headed bloody-mindedness counts for something.”

He sheathed his sword. “Might be just what you need with that lot,” he said mostly, it seemed, to himself. He looked past Heden and clucked his tongue twice. Heden’s horse walked forward.

Heden, unbelieving, watched as the knight took the horse’s reins, took Heden’s unyielding left hand and wrapped the reins around it.

“Good luck,” he said, then walked away, around a tree and out of sight. Heden’s eyes followed him but he otherwise didn’t move from the spot from which he’d cut off the knight’s head, his mouth still hanging slack.

Then he took a great gulp of air and burst after the man, knowing what he would find.

The knight had disappeared. There was only Heden’s horse. And the empty wode.

Chapter Twenty-two

He stood behind a tree at the edge of the clearing for a full turn, staring at the priory. The building the headless knight with flowers inscribed on his armor had called a chapel. Heden wasn't sure what he'd meant by that. It was an obscure term.

He watched the priory. No one went in, no one came out, no movement within. It looked deserted. His horse stepped up and put its massive head over Heden's shoulder, as though it were looking at the priory too. Wondering if they were going to approach or just stand there. Then it made a horse noise, and Heden reached into his pack and gave the beast another apple. As the horse chewed, Heden reached up and absently scratched its ear.

It stood, a narrow stone building with a single large tower, on the far side of a large clearing, maybe four acres across. The trees marking the edge of the clearing were all very close to one another, in contrast to the rest of the wode. It was a dark building, and the dirt around it looked black.

Heden was watching the priory, and not watching it. He was thinking about the knight, or whoever or whatever it was, whose head he'd chopped off. He'd seen many strange things in his years as a professional, certainly much stranger than a man putting his own head back on, but something about this knight was personal. Directed at Heden. It unnerved him in a way dragons and celestials and floating cities had not.

The knight had been testing him. Had intended to test him from the beginning, and Heden had passed. Why the test? No one else had gained the priory since the death, the probable murder, of the knight-commander. Renaldo said anyone who came in just came out again. Turned around without realizing. That was a kind of magic Heden understood. The knight mystified him.

There was a dreamlike quality about the man he fought. But nothing could be more real than the man who found him on his ass and helped him up. The man he talked to. Heden had replayed that conversation a dozen times as he followed the path that led here. It revealed nothing.

He related to the man. Understood him. Was he meant to? Was the knight he fought the real thing, and the man he conversed with the invention? A fabrication designed to find out more about Heden? He went through a dozen possibilities and then shook his head. No point. If there was anything to be gleaned, he wasn't smart enough to do it. He missed Elzpeth.

He reached up to his neck. He'd healed the wound on his arm and his shoulder, but left this one. He wanted to remember that the encounter was real. He pulled his hand away. The blood was dried, the thin cut already healing, but some dried blood came off on his hand. Real alright.

The horse sniffed the air, and Heden noticed there were two troughs of water in front of the priory. Looked like there was water in them. He saw no well. Could be rainwater. Didn't matter. The horse needed water.

Heden and the horse walked into the clearing.

The sky was bright blue, the day brilliant. Large white clouds drifted by. It was beauty Heden was not immune to. He missed scenes like this in the inn. He checked the ground. It looked as though it had been churned and then matted down. If by horses, there was no obvious sign. But he knew he was terrible at reading the ground.

As he approached the priory, Heden saw a large stained glass window set on the north wall. He led the horse to one of the troughs. It slurped up the clear water while Heden looked around again, taking in the whole clearing. He didn't know what he had expected, but at least some horses. Knights rode horses, didn't they? Maybe a pavilion.

He approached the archway entrance, no door, no way to defend the place, and looked in. A foyer led to a long, narrow nave and several small rooms branching off. At the end of the nave, past several prayer benches, was a small altar on a raised dais. Where were the knights?

Feeling like an interloper, he walked into the priory.

The stained glass window dominating the north wall was large. It seemed odd to Heden, then he realized. He'd never seen a church oriented in this way. The entrance west, the nave leading east to the dais. Usually the entrance was north or south, so the stained glass window would be above either those entering or the priest at the altar. Why the difference here? Was it significant? No way for him to know.

He stood in the middle of the priory. Even empty it felt intimate compared to the cavernous enclosure of Llewellyn's cathedral. He looked at the window. The glass artwork depicted a scene he recognized: Godwin the Vigilant, Saint of Cavall, fighting Saint Pallad the Black, Saint of Nikros. He knew the story. Godwin lost. The glass depicted their final battle. It was, Heden thought, a strange moment to commemorate, but then he often felt that way about the stories of saints.

He turned and continued up the nave, his boots loud on the flagstones. The altar was typical. Raised. A stone rectangle with pictures of knights in Cavall's service carved into it. Behind it, nested into a cubby hole at the back wall, Heden saw a font about four feet high.

Something about the font triggered Heden's instincts. He walked around the altar and examined it.

He resisted the urge to try to move it or inspect it to see if it hid anything significant. Sometimes even writing hidden away from view was useful, but this was a priory and he reminded himself it held nothing secret. No dwarf would arrive and use a metal pole to make the altar slide away revealing a complex underground chamber.

He leaned against the altar and looked at the font. There was a little water in it. This meant someone had tended it recently. It looked exactly like a bathing pedestal for birds, such as noblemen had in their castle grounds.

Then he saw it. The font was of a different stone from the altar, the flagstones, the wall. Everything else was granite. Hard to work, requiring master masons to ensure the building didn't collapse under its own weight. But the font was limestone. It was, Heden realized, much older than the rest of the building. It was weathered, heavily so. Heden suspected the priory was built around it. He imagined the small stone pedestal, its bowl filled with water, alone in the forest with no building around it. Sunlight reflecting off its water. Something that could not happen now. This priory had started off as a simple shrine, a font hidden away miles inside the forest. How old was this place?

He touched the font. Ran his hand around its edge and put his fingers in the water. He said a prayer to Lynwen. Not much of one. Thankfully no response. He continued his survey of the priory.

Along both walls, five on one, four on the other, were several crests painted on wood about seven feet up each wall. Each was very simple, and all followed the same theme. Each had a white field with a solid green circle in the middle. Each was adorned very discreetly with one additional element, no two alike. This crest had crossed swords. This one stylized shields. Each had a different number of elements, no two the same. Two shields, seven crossed swords. A sprig of holly with six branches. Three horses rampant.

Heden noticed two things. Beneath each crest was a hook to hang a shield and below that a wooden brace, as though to hold a spear or a lance. They were all but one empty.

The one held a large metal shield. A knight's shield. With the green circle on a white field, the sign of the Green Order, Heden surmised, and in the middle of that green circle, one yellow star. The sun.

Kavalen.

Without thinking, he reached up and lifted the heavy shield off its hook. The shield had been heavily damaged and some minor attempt at repair had been made.

Heden turned it around. The shield had been pierced twice. Its owner, he knew, was dead. And the shield hung in memoriam.

"Replace that shield upon its hook," a soft voice spoke from behind Heden, causing him to jump almost out of his skin. He turned, alarmed, and saw a figure framed in silhouette in the entryway. "Or my lance will find your heart."

Chapter Twenty-three

The shadowed form in the archway resolved, and Heden saw a woman pointing a long spear at him. It showed a telltale dullness and weather-beaten quality that Heden associated with constant use and a sharpness that didn't need enchantment to kill.

She was slim and lithe, but clad in chainmail with hard leather underneath. She had a shield strapped across her back, a dagger on her belt, and a sword in a scabbard. She seemed in her late twenties. She wasn't crouching, but was coiled and ready to strike. She had long red hair streaked with blonde. Bleached from hours and days in the sun.

In addition to her arms and armor, which gave every impression of being well used and expertly repaired, she was covered in what looked like moss and vines. The moss grew from every crevice, and the vines twined around her arms and legs, some had sprouted small leaves. All in all, she looked like part of the forest had come alive. She was a strange clash of civilization and feral wildness.

"I, ah…" Heden began. "I'm not here to, ah…"

The girl frowned at him and cat-footed forward into striking range. Heden didn't move.

"Replace that shield ere another word passes thy lips, or by the wode I shall strike thee down," she said, her voice low.

He took a deep breath, aware that this woman could make a bad decision forcing Heden to hurt her even in her own defense, and carefully turned and replaced the shield on its hook.

When he turned back to face her, he found her spear tip at his throat. He stood rigid, wondering if he was fast enough to grab it and kick her away, but the length of the spear made this unlikely. And he wasn't a young man anymore.

"I'm here to help," he offered.

"Silence, lout," she said, and used the spear tip to push down on the collar of his breastplate. "Or you will bleed your life out here on the priory floor."

Delicately, she used the tip of the spear to fish a metal necklace out from under the collar of his breastplate. How had she seen it there?

She slid the spear point under the necklace and pulled, and the whole necklace came out from under his breastplate and leather. His talisman hung from it.

She stepped forward, grabbed the spear under her right arm, halfway up its shaft, and leaned in to get a closer look.

"You bear a saint's talisman," she said. The spear was no longer at his throat, but uncomfortably close nonetheless.

He didn't say anything. She threw him a dark look and pressed the spear hard into his neck.

"I said…" she began.

"Alright, alright," Heden said, raising his hands and backing away a little. "Yes, that's my talisman. You're right."

She pulled the spear away and let the talisman fall to his chest.

"A priest then?" she asked, straightening up. He was glad she didn't ask him which saint. "A priest sent hither from Ollghum Keep?"

"Sort of," Heden said, frowning. He rubbed his neck. They now stood at a respectful distance and though she was still tense, it no longer seemed that she was going to attack him.

"You're a knight," Heden guessed.

"That I am *not,*" the woman said angrily.

Heden's eyes darted around.

"You're not?" he asked as though perhaps he'd somehow come to the wrong place.

"Is it not *obvious?*" she asked, then shook her head, letting her hair fall behind her face in a manner she seemed to think was meaningful.

Heden shut up. He could not remember ever regretting silence.

"My mistress shall be here anon," she said, uncoiling. "We shall wait for her, and she shall find me guarding thee."

"You're a squire," Heden realized.

"I am that," she said. "Why how now, do you look so amazed?"

"How old are you?" Heden asked.

She leaned on her spear and cocked her head at him, challenging him.

"Eight and twenty years, I have."

Heden blinked.

"You're twenty-eight? You're a squire and you're twenty-eight? Isn't that a little late to get started?"

"My mistress accepted me when I was thirteen," she said proudly.

Heden was silent for a moment.

"You've been…hang on, you've been a squire for fifteen years?"

"Upon this solstice I wouldst have been a knight," she said, relaxing a little. Her face betrayed melancholia. "Earning my spurs, I would have been the youngest to take the Green since the lady Isobel."

"Why are you talking like that?" Heden asked, frowning.

"What sayest thou?"

"Yeah, like that."

She grimaced at him and relaxed a little.

"The Green is an ancient order," she said carefully. "The knight's cant is traditional."

Having decided Heden was no threat, she walked around him to one of the long walls of the nave, to one of the crests. She placed her spear on a small wooden stand. There was one before each crest. Each knight was permitted one squire, and this was where the squires put their spears while at the priory. She placed hers under the crest of the second knight.

"Why are you covered in moss and vines?" Heden asked. She ignored him.

"Thou art no man from Ollghum Keep, though ye may have come by there. I can tell from your speech and manner. What is thy name?"

It seemed as though she had not completely mastered the knight's cant. Her words sounded forced, not elegant.

"Do you have to talk like that? I mean, is it required?"

She turned from admiring the knight's crest and gave him a very cynical appraisal.

"What is your name?" she spoke deliberately.

Heden tried to smile winsomely in gratitude. He hoped it didn't look like a grimace.

"I'm sorry." Heden tried smiling again. "My name's Heden. I came here from Celkirk. Where were you born?" he asked.

She laughed derisively. "This is of no matter to you."

"Well, that's probably true," Heden admitted. "But I'd still like to know."

She seemed a little disarmed by his honesty, and there was something else. Something he didn't quite understand. He took advantage of this.

"You haven't told me your name," he reminded her.

She seemed to realize she'd been rude. "I am named Squire Aderyn."

"There," Heden said, smiling genuinely. "That wasn't so bad."

He remembered his assignment. Kavalen, the dead knight. But this woman was a more immediate puzzle and Heden instinctively believed solving her now would be fruitful later. He decided not to mention the knight he met earlier. Explaining how he chopped a knight's head off and then watched him put it back on didn't seem like the best way to make a first impression.

"What are you doing here alone?" Heden asked.

"I have come to prepare the..." she began without thinking. Then she spun around and became defiant. "I need not answer you!" she said. "I am a squire of the Green, this is our priory, *you* are the interloper!" She put her hand on the hilt of her sword. "Who art thou and why cometh thou here?" The cant was back.

"I'm here because something's happened," he said lamely. Not sure how to phrase it. She reacted by looking at the floor.

"The baron sent you here?" she asked, lowering her voice. "To ask for our aid?"

"No. No, not exactly. I mean, yes in one sense, sure. She knows I'm here. She wants me to succeed. But the Hierarch of the Church of Cavall the Righteous sent me." He used the formal term for the bishop out of instinct.

"We have had no messenger from Ollghum Keep," she observed and leaned against one of the prayer benches. "'Tis passing strange."

Heden was careful not to respond right away. His instincts told him that just coming out and telling her the forest wouldn't allow anyone up here would be a mistake.

"Do you know anything," he said slowly, not sure if this was a good question to ask, "about an army of urmen marshalling to the north?"

Her face lost its expression. She became still and didn't answer. Heden took that as a yes.

"The hierarch sent me," he said, walking forward slowly like a man approaching a wild animal, "because a knight has died."

She looked down and said, "Thou must speak to Sir Taethan, he will be here anon."

"Taethan," he said. "Is he the commander of the order now?"

She shook her head in disbelief at the foolishness of his question, more to herself than anything else, and did not answer.

Instead, still leaning against the end of one of the prayer benches, she gave him a knowing look. "You are a handsome man, though passing old." Heden raised his eyebrows. "Have you been with many women?" Her eyes flitted to the archway, the entrance to the priory.

"What?" he asked flatly.

"Women," she reiterated. She pulled her chain shirt down over her leather armor, and inflated herself slightly. She then indicated with a flourish of her hands the inward and outward curves relevant to her point. "You are familiar with the phenomenon? Spear and distaff? Jousting on the fields of love?"

"I'm sorry?" Heden asked, and found himself absurdly blushing and speechless. It suddenly felt warm in the priory.

She laughed. It sounded like birdsong. Her eyes danced. She walked up to him and stood too close, looking up at him with blue eyes and sculpted red lips.

"You are, I can tell. You have won many a tournament, I judge. And though aged, you are still young enough to know to be flattered and flustered when the time comes for it, well played." She flounced away.

She had caught Heden off guard and now he knew what was strange about her. She was proud, strong and confident but that wasn't it. She behaved like someone who'd spent very little time among people. She said whatever came to mind. Fifteen years as a squire in the wode, and she had almost no experience with anyone who was not a knight.

"When was the last time you went home? Or saw Ollghum Keep?" Heden said.

She ignored him again. He thought he knew the answer. Part of him was annoyed by the fact that she ignored so much of what he asked, but he respected it. She didn't answer when she thought the question wasn't important. And she was avoiding telling Heden a lot.

She went into a small room to the left of the altar, and came out a few moments later with a huge chest on her right shoulder and a huge wooden maul in her left hand. The chest was so big, it looked like it would crush her. She didn't even seem to notice the weight.

"My mistress will be here anon," she said as she walked past him, towards the archway leading outside. "You will wait for her here and she shall take your full measure."

She left the priory and Heden alone. He waited a few moments, looked at the stained glass depicting the last battle of St. Godwin, and put Lynwen's talisman back under his plate and leather. He wished he could remember more about Godwin.

He shrugged, and walked outside to see what Aderyn was doing.

Chapter Twenty-four

"What are you doing?" Heden asked, leaning against the archway of the priory.

Aderyn ignored him. She drove another stake into the ground with the maul. Spread out around her were huge, brightly colored sheets, pinions, ropes and flags with many crests, all taken from the chest. There was a riot of color in the scattered sheets, but the dominant color was green.

"What is all this?" Heden asked, looking at the colored fabrics on the grass.

"Canst thou not see?" Aderyn asked mildly.

"We're back to that?" Heden said with a sigh.

"Hast thou not eyes?" She grunted loudly as she swung again. Though she was half Heden's weight, she was strong. She needed only two attempts to drive a stake into the ground.

Heden sighed and walked around the woman as she worked. It would take her all day at this rate, but she seemed resigned to the task. Heden smiled. He recognized the attitude.

"No, I can see it's a pavilion, I'm asking why you're bothering to set it up."

"The stakes mark the center of the jousting field. Then," she said, nodding to a large circle where no grass grew, "I stake off the melee. Then the tent where there will be food and drink. Whenever the knights gather together," she said, grunting as she drove another stake into the turf, "there is a tournament."

"Every time?" he asked.

"Every time," she said, and stopped to wipe sweat from her brow. She drew her flaxen hair back in an impromptu ponytail to keep it out of her face.

"You're going to erect a whole tournament pavilion in your armor?" Heden asked.

"Never remove your armor in the forest, except to bathe," she said. Heden got the sense she was quoting someone. "We are never safe, even here."

Heden took in the idyllic scenery and tried to imagine an army of urq swarming out of the forest. Even with his experience, it was hard to imagine.

"How often do you all get together?" he asked.

"Once a year," she said, with a shrug. "Sometimes more."

Heden watched and thought.

"You're saying the order only gathers together once a year?"

She ignored him. She'd already answered him and he was just trying to catch up.

"But they must…they must see each other between tournaments."

She hammered another stake into the ground. It was going to be a large pavilion with several tents.

"Each knight," she said, "has a demesne covering perhaps a dozen leagues."

"A what?" Heden asked.

"A dozen leagues," she replied dryly.

"No, you said something else before that."

She stopped hammering and thought.

"Demesne?" It sounded to Heden like "deh-main."

"That's it."

"It is the knight's territory."

Heden tilted his head. "I've never heard that word before," he admitted.

"It is a life of solitude and quiet contemplation," Aderyn said, going back to work. "A knight may go months without meeting another soul to speak to."

"Quiet contemplation," Heden said, watching her work. Watching the strength of her body. She could have used that hammer to crush a man's skull in one blow.

"It is a noble calling," she said.

"Quiet contemplation until a thyrs attacks."

She smiled without looking at him. "Then it is a test of mettle."

"Or an army of urq," he said, ignoring her for once.

She stopped smiling and stopped hammering.

"That rarely happens," she intoned. Then went back to work.

"Let me help you," Heden said.

"Leave," Aderyn said immediately, hammering another stake into the ground.

"What?"

She turned to look at him and leaned on her maul. "If you wish to be a help, then leave us. Leave now, leave the forest, return to your world and leave us be."

"I can't do that."

"You could," Aderyn said. "I have taken your full measure and I surmise you have quit the field before."

"You're wrong," Heden said. "Besides, I was sent here to fix whatever's wrong."

Aderyn just shook her head. "There is no way to fix what is wrong," she said. "You can only make it worse." She had dropped the cant. And for some reason, Heden believed her.

"Do you know what happened to Kavalen?" Heden asked.

"All the forest knows," she said, taunting him a little.

"But you won't tell me," he said.

"You must speak with Sir—" She stopped abruptly, and her whole body tensed, though she didn't take her eyes off Heden. Heden straightened up. It looked like she was about to attack him.

He turned and looked behind him, but saw nothing. He heard her maul hit the ground.

He turned back and saw her sprinting in two layers of armor to her horse. Her running footsteps the only sound in the suddenly silent forest.

Heden realized he'd left his backpack in the priory. His heart was racing and he wasn't yet sure what…

The ground shook, like a distant tower toppling. Heden's legs went a little weak. He became disoriented, and imagined the threat could be behind any of the trees surrounding him. *Not now!* he thought, and fought to master himself.

Aderyn reached her horse, searched through its saddlebags and quickly donned her helm, a shield, and pulled a sword from a scabbard.

The ground shook again. And again. And then several times in rapid succession, the dull roar of impact getting impossibly loud in Heden's ear. The ground shook violently, the water in the troughs spilled out, but the granite priory didn't budge.

Bursting from the trees into the clearing was something shaped like a man. A huge man with skin tanned dark brown, wearing animal skins and improvised armor stolen, it seemed, from all manner of man and urq. It wielded a small tree trunk and its teeth were rotting. It had a thicket of chestnut brown hair on top of its head, and its huge eyes burned with hatred. This was a thyrs. Men for whom the thyrs were mythical called them giants, and why not? But any folk of the north, the folk of Ollghum Keep, called them thyrs, or thyrswights, their own name for themselves.

"I'VE COME TO KILL A MAN!" the thyrs bellowed. It seemed massive, but Heden's instincts took over and he compared the giant to the trees. The trees were much taller. This was a minor giant of the hills. Not one of the really big ones you got in the mountains. It had been years since Heden had dealt with anything like this, and even then he had a whole company with him. But he wasn't a prelate then. His heart stilled. He was unarmed, but thirteen years of this sort of thing came back to him.

Aderyn stood in the center of the clearing, the stakes of the future pavilion surrounding her. Her horse stood proud next to her, neighed a challenge and stamped its front hooves.

"I will have to do!" Aderyn called out a challenge. "I will settle your feud with Sir Nudd and end your life ere you take another step if you do not leave this place and return to your home!"

Black gods, Heden thought. *Would I have done that at twenty-eight? I'd have probably shit my pants.*

The thyrs looked around, seeming to ignore Heden. It peered down at Aderyn.

"LITTLE KNIGHT," it pronounced, drawing the words out. Heden thought Aderyn grew in stature. "I'LL CRUSH YOUR BONES AND SUCK OUT YOUR BRAINS!"

Aderyn didn't even wait for the thyrs to finish its sentence. As soon as it was obvious the thyrswight wasn't going to turn around and leave, she ran forward, closing the distance between them. With several paces left to go, she hurled herself high into the air, her speed and strength supernatural, her sword poised to stab downward into the naked right thigh of the huge man-like creature.

Heden weighed several options carefully, and all in an instant. Calling upon powers beyond the need could have dire consequences for him. Summoning a dominion or assuming the mantle of Cavall could result in Heden being a slave to his god for years and questing through who knows what foreign lands or underground worlds.

He said a quick prayer, pointing at Aderyn. Warding her.

The thyrswight took advantage of Aderyn's advancing leap, and swung its club like one might swat at a fly. Aderyn's attack seemed fast, but not compared to the giant's reaction.

Its tree-trunk club hit Aderyn square in the chest, at the apex of her leap. There was a crunching sound, and a loud grunt. The blow hurled Aderyn up and over the clearing, into the forest beyond. Heden's head craned up and over and back, watching her sail through the air until the forest behind him swallowed her. The sound of breaking tree limbs continued for several moments, getting quieter and settling down over time.

Aderyn's horse turned and rode off into the forest after her.

The giant grunted to itself and smiled. It took two steps forward, crushing some of the pavilion's stakes under his thick-soled feet. It looked around the clearing as though he'd just conquered it and was now seeking other challengers. Then it looked down at Heden, apparently noticing him for the first time.

"WHO ARE YOU?" the huge figure asked, sniffing. The words came out like "Oooeruuu?" It was aware of Heden, but didn't seem to care about him one way or the other.

Heden realized something was expected of him.

"Uh," he said, and cleared his throat. "Hello," he said loudly. He kept looking over his shoulder, wondering if he should go help Aderyn. But he felt as though standing his ground was safer.

The thyrs sneered at him. "LITTLE MAN," it said. "NOT EVEN A KNIGHT!"

It seemed as though the giant figure was considering crushing him outright. Heden sighed and pulled the talisman of Lynwen from under his breastplate and leather.

Heden didn't know the situation with the thyrs, and this meant he had no idea what kind of prayer would be effective. He didn't think the creature was evil. It might be safe to blind the thing, or turn its legs to stone, but these were minor orisons and might not work on so strong a creature as a hill thyrs.

Before he could finish praying, and therefore technically before his request was complete, something behind Heden caught the giant's attention.

"WHUT?!" the giant grunted, confused. "ALIVE?!"

He knew what the giant saw, but turned to look anyway. He had to see it.

Aderyn was winded, bruised, bleeding, and she'd lost her helmet, but she was grinning like a madwoman, bracing herself against a tree at the edge of the clearing, her horse behind her. Heden's wards had protected her, but more, she had a vitality, a courage beyond anything Heden had seen in many years. He was in awe.

She stepped into the clearing, pushed her hair away from her face and nodded. "Aye, Burran," she said. "Your father couldn't kill me. What makes you think you can?!"

She's taunting him, Heden thought. *If he gets mad enough he might really hurt her.*

Burran roared, tendons standing out on his neck, and Heden's ears rang. In response, Aderyn barked a sound like "hai!" and her horse started to gallop forward. She grabbed the pommel of the saddle as the horse rode past, and swung herself up.

The horse lowered its head and seemed determined to bear down on the thyrswight.

Aderyn pulled a javelin from a quiver on the horse's saddlebags. Heden realized that, having stopped his prayer, he'd missed an opportunity to fell the thyrs and thereby end this conflict. There was something about watching this squire fight the giant that mesmerized him.

Burran braced himself, a gap-toothed smile on his face. Aderyn, commanding the horse with her knees, spun her mount around halfway across the clearing and hurled the javelin. Before the javelin found its mark, the horse spun around and Aderyn readied another.

Heden watched as the thin piece of wood with a sharp metal tip sunk into the giant's right shin, burying itself in the bone, causing Burran to cry out and grab its leg.

Seeing the result of her first throw, she hurled another. Putting her whole body into it, bracing against the horse. She grunted with effort and this time the javelin pierced the giant's hand and stuck in his thigh. The horse never stopped moving, always ready to leap away should the thyrs lunge forward.

"NO FAIR!" Burran keened, and fell to one knee. Aderyn stopped the attack and, eyes wide, breast heaving with effort, she readied another javelin and watched to see what the giant would do.

What it did next was die.

Without warning, Burran arched his chest up as the tip of a lance burst forth, pushing his hide armor out and poking through it a few inches. He howled and fell forward, bracing himself on the floor of the clearing.

"OOOAAA, NOOOOO," he cried piteously. "NOOO," he said, "NOT DIE."

As he slowly lost the strength to hold himself up, Heden saw the butt of the lance poking out from his back. The entire lance had buried itself in the giant's chest. As Burran fell, he revealed the creature that killed him.

At first, Heden was certain he was seeing an elgenwight in plate armor. One of the elk-men of the wode. They were huge, the bucks as tall as fifteen feet. They had the head, arms and torso of a man, and the body of a horse, with huge antlers sprouting from their forehead. Like most of the wise creatures of the wode, they were created by the celestials, and they were among the deadliest foes in the wood. More so than the brocc, the urq, most of the thyrs.

Heden blinked and looked again. It was a man. A man on a horse, both in heavy armor. But two massive antlers sprouted from the man's helmet, projecting forward like a dozen spears. They were deadly, half-covered in what Heden assumed was dried blood. The warhorse was one of the biggest Heden had ever seen. The man had to be eight feet tall. He had several weapons on his person and strapped to the horse, one a massive two-handed sword. With his eyes shrouded in his helm, the huge blood-covered antlers projecting forward, and his heavy plate covered in moss and vines, he looked like a demon of the wode. Menace boiled off him like steam.

The horse bore a white caparison over its armor with a green circle at its center.

The green knight had killed the giant.

Chapter Twenty-five

The giant was taking a long time to die. Heden stood and watched, a look of horror on his face as the massive creature made terrible noises and wept to itself. Even with its breast pierced, its inhuman health kept it alive.

Aderyn on her horse, the vanquishing knight on his, took no notice of the huge hulk dying before them. They rode up to each other. Aderyn looked like a child compared to the huge knight.

The knight removed his ornate helm. Heden got a closer look. There was no doubt as to the blood on them, no question about their function. They were not ceremonial.

The knight had long, dark green hair, at first Heden thought it was black. The top of his head was bald, the bald spot forming a perfect circle, his straight hair falling down to his shoulders. He had a boyish face, but was obviously older than Aderyn.

He nodded at her once.

"Sir Nudd," she said, bowing in her saddle. "Your aid was not required. It was only a hills wight."

Sir Nudd got off his horse and walked around the dying giant. Anywhere south of the duchy of Gaeden, this man would be called a giant. He said nothing to Aderyn, who quickly dismounted and stood by her horse with Heden behind her. Once the knight had completed his circle, noting the two javelins sticking out of the giant's right leg, he stood before Aderyn and nodded to Heden.

"This is Brother Heden," Aderyn said, her voice unsteady. She was still recovering from the fight, her body coursing with unspent energy. "The Bishop of Cavall sent him."

Sir Nudd glanced at Heden and frowned, then looked back at Aderyn.

"About Commander Kavalen," she said, and looked down.

Heden was only half paying attention. He was seriously considering healing the giant's wounds, and also hating himself for not acting, and hating more than he knew that he would not act. *Black gods,* he thought. *What's wrong with me?*

Sir Nudd looked at Heden and appeared to sense his thoughts. He went back to his horse, removed the two-hander, and walked up to the weeping giant lying facedown in the dirt. The ground was soft with its blood and drool and tears.

Nudd brought his sword down onto the giant's head. The blow was not enough to kill the giant, though it cracked his skull. The creature made one last desperate effort to pick itself up and get away, but all it managed to do was turn its head and look at its assailant with huge dark eyes, red with tears. It moaned briefly, no words, just pleading.

Sir Nudd continued. It took several blows, but in the end the thing was dead. Heden watched its eyes dilate, become huge black pools. It made the dead giant look like it had died in terror. Which it had.

Heden found it took deliberate effort to draw air into his lungs. He was on the verge of tears himself. He looked at Sir Nudd as though for the first time, and saw the huge knight looking back at him, puzzled.

What's wrong with me, Heden wondered, trying to pull himself together.

Sir Nudd approached with heavy footsteps and looked down at Heden with some sympathy, maybe some pity. His armor was old and been repaired several times. Heden guessed it weighed as much as a man. The man smelled of moss and brackish water. Of earth and mold. In places, Heden couldn't see the armor, and he wondered whether the knight wore armor covered in vegetation, or vegetation covered in armor.

His shield was polished, but the polish couldn't cover the dents and damage done to it. The device engraved on his shield was seven small birds. They looked to Heden like stylized hummingbirds. Sir Nudd turned to Aderyn and held up three fingers.

Aderyn nodded. "I told him to speak with Sir Taethan," she said.

The knight nodded. He turned and snapped his fingers, and his horse walked up to the trough next to Heden's and Aderyn's horses and began drinking. The knight walked in long, slow strides to the priory, entering without having said a word to Heden or Aderyn.

The clearing was quiet. Aderyn and Heden both stood still and looked at the priory. At some point, the birds started chirping again.

Aderyn broke the spell, looking around the clearing at the scene of the battle with a combination of confusion and loss. Eventually she climbed atop the giant's back and began the laborious process of pulling Sir Nudd's lance out of the dead giant's back.

"Sir Nudd," Heden said.

Aderyn yanked the lance out of the corpse and, exhausted, threw it onto the ground in front of Heden.

"He is the strongest of us," Aderyn said from atop the dead giant, wiping sweat from her brow.

Heden nodded, recovering himself. "I bet."

Aderyn hopped down to the ground in front of Heden like a bird and stared at him. He avoided her gaze.

"Thou hast never seen a giant felled before?"

He ignored her. He was getting sick of the knight's cant.

"What happens to it now?" he asked, looking at the blood pooling around his feet. He didn't bother moving out of the way.

Aderyn looked at the massive corpse and shrugged. "It is not seemly for the Green to have the corpse of a hills wight here at the priory," she said. "Some might consider it boasting. Imagine perhaps that we are issuing a challenge. And the thyrs are, if not our allies, at least not our enemies."

"This wasn't an enemy?" Heden said.

"This was an exceptionally stupid giant, rejected by his mate." Aderyn wiped some of the sweat from her forehead and tried to manage her hair. Her bruises were yellowing, healing quickly, and she was no longer bleeding. "Seeking to blame his failings on the Green. His people will understand," she said, turning to look at the corpse. "Though not if we leave it here without ceremony."

"There's a ceremony?" Heden asked. He couldn't look at the giant's face anymore. Its wide, staring black eyes and gaping mouth were too much for him. He turned and looked at the forest.

Aderyn nodded and began pulling the pavilion materials away from the blood.

"Soon Sir Brys will arrive and see the corpse and order the three dastards—" Her hand flew to her mouth and she turned, hoping Heden hadn't heard her. She tried again. "Sir Idris and his two…" She stopped and Heden was reminded that she'd spent almost her entire life among the knights and the forest. Talking to anyone who was not a knight was very unusual for her. She wasn't used to people listening to her.

"Three other knights will clear the body away, take it into the forest. They will perform the ceremony and the body will be accepted by the wode."

Heden kept quiet, let her talk. Then changed the subject.

"You going to finish that," he said, referring to her continued preparations with the pavilion, "with this thing sitting here?"

Aderyn didn't look at him, she just went back to work. "My duties remain," she said. "I shall erect the main tent over the body of Burran and keep the sun off him until Sirs Brys and Idris arrive."

Heden watched her go through the motions. Fighting the hills wight, she seemed more alive than anyone Heden had met in years. Now she looked like a walking corpse.

"Would you have killed the giant," Heden asked, "if Sir Nudd had not arrived?"

She stopped working and just stood there, her back to him. She didn't speak for a moment.

"But Sir Nudd did arrive," she said, not turning to face him. "So 'if' is no matter at all."

"It bothered you, that he took matters into his own hands."

Heden expected Aderyn to rebuff him, but through blind fumbling he'd hit upon the right question.

"He would not have done so, ere Kavalen's death," she said, her voice hollow.

Heden knew he'd gotten lucky, and let it drop for now.

"Nudd doesn't talk," Heden said.

Aderyn, hefting the maul to return to work, stopped and shot a violent look at him. "Sir Nudd," she said.

"Isn't that what I said?" Heden asked.

Aderyn shook her head. "The proper form of address is Sir Nudd. I am Squire Aderyn. His father could call him…by his given name alone. You," she said, turning back to the stake and hefting her maul, "may not."

"Sir Nudd," he said. "Sir Nudd—I apologize. He doesn't talk a lot."

She started hammering another stake into the ground. "He swore an oath of silence upon taking the Green. Few are strong enough for that oath. We are lucky to be among him."

"The hummingbirds," Heden said, nodding. He knew it would be something like this.

"What?" Aderyn said, not taking her eyes off her task.

"His device is seven hummingbirds."

"He is the seventh," Aderyn said.

"Yeah," Heden said, "but hummingbirds are…in folklore they're noted for their silence." Aderyn stopped hammering and turned her brilliant, blue-eyed gaze to Heden.

"They were the messengers of the ancient Gol gods," he said, staring at the dead giant's horror rictus. "Because they hover and fly silently. One of them brought a message to Áengus when he went into the World Below to rescue Eithne. It was the only creature that could get past the guardians, because it flew so quietly."

Aderyn stared, amazed by Heden's knowledge. He glanced at her and shrugged.

"I always thought it should have been an owl," he said. "Hummingbirds make a terrible buzzing sound. Can't count the number of times I had the piss scared out of me by an owl flying past me like a ghost."

Aderyn went back to hammering stakes. The sun was no longer overhead. It was midafternoon.

"Sir Nudd seems sad," Heden said. Back to work.

"He was always of a melancholic disposition," Aderyn replied. Heden wondered if she was trying to ignore the dead giant as much as he was. He turned his back on her and looked at the sun dipping below the level of the trees. He guessed it was three o' clock.

"Not helped much by Kavalen dying," he said.

Aderyn grabbed the maul just beneath its head, and strode over to Heden.

"You!" She said, spinning him around to face her. "You will not speak to Sir Nudd of Commander Kavalen." She punctuated her words by tapping the hammer against his breastplate. Heden saw the tendons on her forearms straining, the muscles in her arms rippling. She seemed impossibly strong.

She stared into his eyes. He was listening, trying to understand, and obviously concerned. He wondered if she was angry at him for being here, or at Nudd for killing the giant. Her eyes softened, she looked down and let the head of the maul fall to the ground, the shaft loose in her hand.

"It would destroy him," she said, looking at nothing.

Neither of them said anything. Heden wanted to reach out to help her, but she seemed as distant now as she was strong a moment ago.

Heden gently reached down and took the maul from her loose grip. When she didn't resist, he walked away with it.

After a moment, she turned and saw he was hammering a stake into the ground.

"You were right about not taking your armor off," Heden said. "That's good advice."

She watched him work, not knowing what to make of this man.

Chapter Twenty-six

The main tent of the pavilion was just begun, the sun almost at six of the clock, when the knights Aderyn called "the three dastards" arrived. Heden heard them laughing to each other in the woods before they emerged into the clearing. Aderyn stiffened when she heard them. Neither she nor Heden had spoken since he began helping her. The thyrswight's corpse lay where it fell. Heden had prayed over it so that its flesh would not decay, nor collect flies. He'd also closed the giant's eyes. It didn't help. The memory was enough.

Aderyn kept her back to the knights. Heden took a step backward, so he could look her in the eye. She gave him a sheepish look, as though apologizing in advance for them. He tossed the maul to her. She snatched it out of the air as though it didn't weigh thirty pounds.

Heden walked forward and leaned on one of the pavilion stakes. He crossed his arms, waiting for the knights to notice him.

They walked into the clearing like three men carousing through the streets of Celkirk. They were laughing and talking about something Heden couldn't make out. Their horses followed behind.

They all wore plate armor. Like Nudd and Aderyn, they each sprouted moss and lichen, wrapped with vines. Their plate was green-tinged, as though made from an emerald metal.

Like Nudd, and unlike Aderyn, they all had green hair. Heden saw their helmets packed away on their horses. Each helm sported a full set of deadly antlers.

The largest of the three was the best outfitted. Obviously got the best choice of armor. The other two were missing pieces. The gorget for the neck; the elbow coverings. The well-outfitted knight walked in the center and the other two looked to him for approval as they laughed and japed.

The lead knight locked eyes with Heden right off, but otherwise did not change his attitude, laughing with the others. When he stopped in front of Heden, the other two turned with surprise. They hadn't noticed him.

The leader, still smiling, slapped the flank of his horse, and soon there were six horses at the water troughs.

The two sycophants were different in appearance but similar in bearing. The one on Heden's left was a little taller than Heden, but fit like all the other knights—no fat on any of them. He looked like a brawler. Like a thug in armor. His face was red and pockmarked with scars, giving him a look of permanent anger. The other one was a little weasel of a man, Heden's size. He looked from the lead knight to Heden and sneered.

Heden said nothing. He watched the knights and relaxed on the stake. The lead knight looked him up and down, while his flunkies walked around Heden, pointing to his outfit and laughing. Looking to their master for approval.

After the once-over, the lead dastard saw Aderyn and walked over to her, ignoring Heden. The other two seemed disappointed. No words had passed between them.

Heden turned to watch them. Unusually, he felt the urge to go to Aderyn. Protect her. Something he knew she would resent. He shrugged and followed his instincts.

The knights and the squire were already talking.

"I required no aid," he heard Aderyn say as he approached. She seemed much diminished since the fight against the giant. This did not seem like the same girl who hurled two javelins from horseback, unerringly striking the hills wight. Hitting his leg in a manner that would have let him escape without a fatal wound. "Sir Nudd need not have acted."

"It is not yours to decide," the tall one said. "Burran's quarrel was with Sir Nudd in any case, it was his right to end it as he saw fit."

"Would that I had put Burran down myself," the weasel one said, with a sniff.

"But did not and so have no reason to speak," the big one said. The thug looked at his counterpart and sneered.

There was something about the way Aderyn was talking to the knights. Apart from the way she deferred to them and seemed a little afraid of them. Then Heden saw it.

She would not look at the thug, the meaty one to the left of the big knight.

"Who told you to erect the pavilion?" the big knight asked.

Aderyn looked for a moment at Heden and then met the lead knight's gaze. "No one," she said. "I need no instruction on the tradition."

"Do you not?" the knight asked.

"What does that mean?" Heden asked. The two flunkies spun around. "You saying she did something wrong?"

Aderyn gritted her teeth. *Sorry, kid,* Heden thought.

The big knight ignored him. Heden couldn't see his face. The other knights wanted to act, but were looking at the leader for approval.

Aderyn saw whatever look was on the leader's face and responded.

"His name is Heden," she said. "He is a priest."

The big knight turned slowly and looked down at Heden. Aderyn was now behind the three knights, who could not see her. She gave Heden a dangerous look and shook her head deliberately.

"And what import doth he surmise that carries here?" the big knight said, looking at Heden. Talking to Aderyn.

Before Heden could reply, Aderyn prompted, "He's come about Kavalen." This seemed to change the knight's demeanor somewhat. "The bishop sent him."

"The bishop?" the weasel-faced knight challenged. "Who is the bishop to us?"

"Silence, lout," the big knight said absently. "Squire Aderyn," he said, and Aderyn stepped around to his front. "Tie off a rope and secure Burran's feet. Use your courser to pull the body into the forest."

"But sir," she said, pointing to the corpse. "He must weigh twelve tons!"

The knight said nothing, but when Aderyn went to comply, he stopped her, grabbing her shoulder and pointing to Heden.

"Introduce us," he barked, as though reminding her of a duty forgotten.

Aderyn looked ruefully at Heden and said, "These are Sirs Idris," indicating the main knight, "Cadwyr," indicating the thug without looking at him, "and Dywel," nodding to the weasel.

Aderyn stalked off to get some rope.

"Well how now, little priest," Idris said, watching Aderyn walk away. "Why comest thou here?"

"You know her horse will kill itself trying to pull that giant," Heden said.

"You came to guard our squire's horse?" Idris said, smiling at Heden. The other knights laughed. Idris let them. "How now, acolyte," Idris said, deliberately insulting Heden. "We have no food needs blessing, the priory is tidy, you may remove yourself and quit this place, lest some harm comes to thee."

"Yeah," Heden said, and the three of them clearly did not like his mode of speech. "I took the prelate's cloth five years ago."

Sir Idris kept his eyes on him, no reaction, unwavering. The other two's heads whipped around and they looked at Heden as though he might explode at any moment. Heden got the distinct impression that Idris had guessed Heden's rank before he insulted him.

"Kavalen's dead," Heden said. "You're down one knight."

"Commander Kavalen," Idris corrected, but without much enthusiasm.

"Sure," Heden said. "You're still down one knight."

"Thou hast not answered my question, little priest. Why comest thou here? What concern is the Green to you?"

Heden knew he and Idris were going to come to blows sooner or later, and Idris knew it too. They were just probing each other, testing to see which issue could reasonably be used to push the other to violence. Heden liked it this way. Everyone knew what was what.

"There's a ritual," Heden said.

"Do you know it?" Cadwyr asked.

Heden didn't look at the thug. He just cocked his head in appraisal of Idris. "Yes," he said.

"Well, then speak it, man, and leave this place," Cadwyr said, dismissing Heden with a wave.

"Did you know there's an army of urmen marching on Ollghum Keep?" Heden asked. This seemed to affect Idris, shutting him down somewhat. The other two knights looked at Idris with some alarm.

"Thou must speak to Taethan," Idris said, watching Aderyn trying to get a rope around the dead giant's ankles. Heden noticed Idris didn't use the knight's title.

"Yeah," Heden said. "But he's not here and you are."

"Then thou must abide here until he arrives!" Sir Idris exploded. He mastered himself quickly, grimacing as he did so, angry at Heden, and then angry at himself for showing his anger.

"Why don't you tell me what happened?" Heden said.

"Speak to Taethan," Idris said, gritting his teeth.

"I will," Heden said. "Why don't you tell me what happened?"

"What happened is past and of no matter now. Only Taethan matters," Idris said, and he seemed to be sulking a little.

Heden frowned at this change of course. The other knights were pointedly ignoring Heden and watching Aderyn.

"Okay," Heden said, realizing that perhaps he'd been asking the wrong questions. "Tell me about Sir Taethan." He was careful to use the knight's proper title.

There was something in Idris that Heden had seen before. The last time was with the dwarf at the Sun & Anvil in Celkirk the day before. It was hatred and respect.

"He is the perfect knight," Idris said, biting the words off sarcastically. Heden thought he was quoting someone.

"The perfect fool, more like," Dywel said, laughing.

"The perfect ass," Cadwyr added, amused. They both seemed unaware of Idris' attitude towards Taethan.

"Aye," Idris said, annoyed. "And as thou art each an expert on fools and asses, thou wouldst know well."

"Will he take command of the order?" Heden asked.

Idris was done.

"Dost thou surmise that thy station as a priest and prelate of Cavall wouldst earn thou e'en the tiniest measure of protection here?" he asked. Heden noticed that, like Aderyn, the knight's cant came and went.

Heden made a show of looking around. "What is there to be protected from?"

Idris laughed. "You knowest well."

Heden nodded slowly, deliberately. He did know. He wondered if Idris was dumb enough to try something here, knowing it would either result in the death of a knight or of Heden, and that this would be disaster for the order in either case.

"You want to take out your frustrations on me," Heden said. "You go right ahead."

As if on cue, Dywel smiled and took a step forward. Idris slammed a mailed fist into his chest and held him back.

"Sir Idris here is smarter than you," Heden said, not taking his eyes off the lead knight. "He knows the order needs me for the ritual."

Dywel looked up at Idris, uncomprehending. These knights were not used to complex issues. Idris was better at it.

"Do what thou must," Idris said. He wasn't angry anymore. He was in control again. "Remind Taethan of his duty. Then speak the ritual, and leave."

"Or stay," Cadwyr said. "And take our measure."

Heden threw the thug a glance, and went back to Idris.

"When did Kavalen die?" Heden asked.

"Six days ago," Idris replied, sighing wearily. This met Heden's understanding of the timetable.

"And you're, what? Returning from his burial?"

"Where we are from and what we have done is of no concern to you!" Dywel, the weasel, said, pointing defiantly at Heden but staying one pace behind Idris.

"You don't seem very upset about burying your commander."

Cadwyr put his hand on his sword, and Idris looked down at him, keeping him in check. Dywel noticed this and leaned forward to sneer at his compatriot.

"He was a fool," Sir Idris said, and as he spoke, he seemed to become nobler. It was unusual for anyone to care what he thought, Heden guessed, and part of him liked the attention.

"And deserved to die?" Heden asked.

The other two knights scoffed and shook their heads. Idris looked at him blankly.

"Perhaps," he said. "Ask Taethan."

Never 'Sir Taethan,' Heden noted again.

Cadwyr and Dywel were frowning at something going on behind Heden. Idris was ignoring whatever it was in favor of watching Heden's response. Heden turned and saw Aderyn talking to another knight. His horse had already taken up with the others, and his helm was held under his left arm. The new knight pointed at Idris, and Aderyn turned to jog over to them, the knight watching from afar.

"Sir Brys would have words with you," Aderyn said to the three knights.

Idris frowned and looked across the clearing, through the pavilion, at the other knight. He stalked off, and the other two followed. Heden waited a few moments, staring at Idris' back, before he followed with Aderyn at his side.

"They knew about the ritual," Heden said.

"What?" Aderyn said, not understanding.

“There’s something going on,” Heden said, his eyes boring a hole into Idris’ back.

“What is this ritual?”

“I hate knights,” Heden said, scowling.

“Remember that you are a trespasser here!” Aderyn hissed at him. “An interloper!”

“Whatever,” Heden said.

Chapter Twenty-seven

"I do not recommend further contact with Sirs Idris, Cadwyr, and Dywel," Sir Brys said to Heden once introductions had passed between them.

They stood away from the three knights as they used their horses and their own strength to slowly pull the corpse of the giant out from under the tent and into the forest. Aderyn had withdrawn into the priory so Heden and Sir Brys could talk. Brys had relieved Aderyn of the burden of moving the giant, and given it to Idris and his two cronies. Brys had some authority.

"You know Squire Aderyn calls them the three dastards."

Sir Brys pursed his lips and looked out at Heden from under a dark brow. "A dastard is a coward," Brys said. "No man can be a knight of the Green and a coward."

Heden nodded. He took Brys' meaning and did not dispute it. But refined it.

"Not in battle at least," Heden said. Brys looked away. Did he nod? It was hard to tell. Brys was Heden's size and his age. He had short, unkempt green hair and a sharp beard that traced the length of his jaw and ran up to a moustache, also green.

"Commander Kavalen did not think them cowards," Sir Brys opined, giving Heden an opening.

"What did they think of him?"

Brys sighed. "That is of no matter now," he said.

Heden scowled, frustrated.

"How do you know what he thought of them? Did he tell you?"

"I was his lieutenant."

Heden absorbed this.

"Where are you from?" Brys asked.

"Celkirk."

Brys nodded.

"You know it?" Heden asked.

"Does that surprise you?" Brys asked.

"Ah...yeah," Heden admitted. "Aderyn didn't even know what Corwell was."

Brys gave him a sharp look. "Squire Aderyn," he corrected.

Heden adjusted the pack on his shoulder and threw Brys a skeptical look. "You people throw that stuff around pretty casually."

Brys raised an eyebrow.

"The titles, the cant. I can't tell if you take it all seriously or not."

Brys looked for a moment at the grass, then up at Heden. "We used to," he said. Heden felt suddenly sympathetic. Then, whatever weakness Brys was admitting, it vanished.

"Would it pleaseth thou should I affect our traditional mode of speech?"

"Do you want to get punched?" Heden asked without any real threat.

Brys smiled. Heden liked this knight.

Sir Nudd emerged from the priory and began helping the three dastards. The process started going much quicker and the spirits of the knights rose. Heden and Brys watched them.

"Looks like Sir Nudd," Heden said, making sure to use his title, "decided those guys had enough punishment."

"The Knight Silent is the strongest of us," Brys said, watching the mammoth knight pulling on the ropes, dragging the giant's corpse. "He is also the gentlest and most forgiving."

"You knew he'd come out to help them," Heden said.

"If I did," Brys said, turning back to face Heden's questions, "it is because Commander Kavalen taught me."

"You spent a lot of time with him?" Heden asked. Brys nodded.

"Ader…ah, *Squire* Aderyn said you might go a year between meeting another knight."

Brys weighed this thought. "She exaggerates. She is Lady Isobel's squire. They range for leagues alone. I would spend months at a time with Commander Kavalen. But then, months alone, 'tis true."

Heden nodded his understanding.

"Squire Aderyn said you were a priest of Cavall the Righteous," Brys said.

"I was made a prelate five years ago," Heden said, carefully giving a nonanswer to a nonquestion.

Brys shook his head. "She would not know what that means." Heden accepted this.

"But you do," Heden said.

"Cavall teaches that man cannot live where injustice thrives," Brys said without answering. "He called the unjust society 'the wasted land.' Where men live false lives."

Heden was impressed. "Yeah," he said.

"That should one man die unjustly, it is the death of all." Brys was meditating on something. Heden thought something was expected of him, but didn't know what. Sir Brys reminded him of Duke Baed. It was a powerful memory and bought Sir Brys much with Heden.

"Do you believe that?" Sir Brys prompted.

"Yes," Heden said.

Brys watched Heden, watched how he responded. Heden's simple answer seemed to satisfy him.

"And how did you conclude that we needed your aid? Did the baron enlist you?"

"No, the bishop sent me."

This seemed to provoke some reaction, but Heden couldn't read it.

"Ah," Brys said, taking a long breath. "You bring the ritual."

"Yeah," Heden said. And like the three dastards, Brys frowned at the way he spoke.

"Have you read it?"

Heden nodded. "Someone has to ask Cavall for forgiveness. Someone outside the order," he said. "Me."

Brys betrayed no reaction.

"That means I have to know what happened. And I have to decide it's worth asking Cavall to forgive you."

"And how were you instructed to determine that?"

How did I end up being the one interrogated? Heden wondered.

"They didn't really tell me anything. I was told to use my judgment," Heden countered.

"Then there is no matter here," Brys said dismissively. "You knew nothing of us before Kavalen died. You have no authority here. You are not of the wode, so your instructions do not matter. Your title does not matter. Cavall, the bishop. Your judgment. None of it."

"Kavalen mattered," Heden said. He wasn't going to let Brys just run him over. Baed could talk to him like that, when Heden was a younger man and not a prelate. This knight was not Baed, and Heden was older now.

Sir Brys looked like Heden had stabbed him. Heden felt like he was playing shere against him.

"To some of us more than others."

"He didn't matter enough to you to save him," Heden guessed.

Brys did not deny this, nor deny that he knew how Kavalen died.

"Sir Idris called your commander a fool."

Brys said nothing. He looked pained.

"What happened between them?" Heden asked. "I can tell Idris didn't kill him. But something happened."

Brys didn't look at him. "Talk to Sir Taethan," he said reflexively.

"You son of a bitch," Heden said. Brys had given him nothing, his reaction betrayed nothing. Heden had no idea what was going on.

Brys grabbed Heden's tunic and clenched the wool between his mailed gloves, but held Heden at arm's length. "Do not speak to me thus," Brys said. "Thou base and churlish knave." He was really angry, Heden thought, noticing that some of the knights reverted to the cant when they were angry, some to plain speech. Heden again thought that if he knew more about knights, he'd know what that meant. For the first time in years, Heden missed having a team he could talk to, work problems out with. He never thought that would be true.

He knew better than to react. Brys' grabbing him was the knight's way of controlling himself, not lashing out. The man had a bloody great axe on his hip; he wouldn't use his fists in violence.

He released Heden.

"Why do you pretend that the order is important to you?" Brys asked. "You didn't even know we existed two days ago."

How does he know that? Heden wondered. Lucky guess, maybe. He didn't deny it.

"I didn't care about any of this until I met Lady Isobel's sister and watched her bet the lives of all her subjects on you people."

"Ollghum Keep can still be saved," Brys said, and Heden wondered if he was telling Heden, or convincing himself.

"Okay," Heden said. "Sure. So what the fuck are you doing standing around here?"

Brys gave him an angry look again. "Talk to Sir Taethan," he reiterated.

"Why?" Heden demanded. "What does he know? Why does everyone keep saying that?!"

Brys didn't respond. Heden had no idea what was going on, he didn't know how Kavalen died or why, and no one would tell him anything.

That's not true, he thought. *They're telling me something.* He looked at Sir Brys brooding and then watched Idris and his thugs working together with Nudd. Then he looked at the priory, where Aderyn waited.

"Talk to Taethan," Heden quoted. Brys looked at him out the corner of his eye.

Heden started walking around Brys, stalking him. "Because Taethan killed Kavalen?" Heden asked, watching Brys for any reaction. Sir Brys stood his ground and ignored Heden. "No," Heden said. His question had been rhetorical. "If he had, I'd know. I'd see it. From you maybe, but Aderyn definitely. If she thought Taethan killed Kavalen, I'd know."

"You like Squire Aderyn," Brys said.

Heden nodded. "I do. She can tell when I'm being stupid, and ignores me." Heden thought for a moment. "Plus, she's not a knight yet. So she's not an insufferable self-obsessed maniac yet."

Brys took the assault without comment.

"Taethan knows what happened," Heden said.

Heden took Brys' silence for affirmation. He thought some more.

"He's your brother in the order." Heden was working through it, watching Brys for some reaction. "If you just tell me what happened, you're betraying him. You all are. So you point me in the right direction, and hope I figure it out."

Brys, eyes cast down, frowned and took a deep breath. He was questioning his own motivation, something Heden recognized. He was on the right track.

"He did something awful, did something terrible so you wouldn't have to. I can understand that. *Believe me*," Heden said with import. "Whatever it was, you hate him for it, and respect him for it. That's why I can't read any of you.

"Kavalen was going to do something, or had done something, and Sir Taethan took it on himself to stop him. Or punish him. Said he was doing it for the good of the order. And maybe you believed it. So you let him do it. You let him do some awful thing, and hoped that would be the end of it. But Halcyon doesn't accept it. You think I didn't notice Aderyn's hair?"

Brys was shocked, had been shocked as soon as Heden had forwarded the idea that Sir Taethan had done something awful. He took a step away from Heden as though in horror. As though Heden had betrayed him. The knight couldn't know how much his face betrayed him.

"She's not a knight yet," Heden said. Brys turned away. "Because Halcyon won't allow it. Not until I perform the ritual. You thought 'Let Taethan deal with Kavalen and everything will be back to normal,' but it didn't work out that way. Halcyon rejected it. So here I come, ritual in hand, prepared to deal with everything. So everyone gives me this 'talk to Taethan' horseshit hoping you can all close ranks and let me get on with the dirty work you wouldn't do. That's fine. Listen to me," he said, grabbing Brys, turning him around. Brys wouldn't look at him.

"I'm telling you: that's fine. It's why I'm here. It's what I do. Just give me one thing: look at me and tell me I'm wrong," Heden said.

Brys looked at him, eyes red, on the verge of tears, and Heden didn't know what to believe. When Sir Brys finally spoke, it was like the words were being torn from him.

"Sir Taethan was the best of us," was all he said, his voice rough. "He is beyond your judgment."

Heden released him. Heden could tell when someone was lying to him, which was why Brys was making him so angry. He wouldn't say yes or no, he evaded, evaded, evaded. It was a strange talent for a knight who spent his life alone to have.

"What are you saying?" Was Taethan dead? No, that didn't make sense.

Brys refused to respond.

Heden gave up. Brys had obviously given up, and he felt bad pressing the man.

"You're not like them," Heden admitted, by way of apology. "That's the only reason I..." Heden gave up. "It's just that...you're the first one of these people I can talk to." Brys shot him a look. Heden regretted the "these people."

"I'm sorry," Heden said finally. "I'll talk to Sir Taethan."

Brys bent down and hefted his horn-studded helmet. He seemed to have recovered himself from Heden's onslaught.

"Make no mistake, Brother Heden," he said, helmet under his arm. "You and I, we can talk to each other, yes. I think we understand each other. But as sure as green leaves in spring, we are enemies."

He said it so casually, Heden had to replay it in his mind.

"You're just going to say that?" Heden asked.

"You are wrong about a great many things. Not least of which: I am like them," he said. "Do not judge our outward bearing and appearance," Brys said, fitting his helmet on. He looked far more imposing with the massive helm, its bloodied antlers projecting forward menacingly. His eyes barely glinting out from under the visor.

"We are all more alike than we are different. And we will all oppose you," he said without malice.

"All of you?" Heden asked, frowning.

"Speak with Sir Taethan," Brys said.

"Right," Heden said, giving up.

Chapter Twenty-eight

The two men stood there looking at each other for a moment, and then Aderyn ran out of the priory and looked with happy anticipation at the forest.

"Lady Isobel has arrived," Sir Brys said without feeling. Heden couldn't tell how Aderyn sensed this, or how Brys could tell without looking that Aderyn had come out of the priory.

A few moments later, a tall, willowy woman rode out of the forest on a heavy warhorse. Her face was noble and lean. Her helm was strapped to her horse. She had green hair, streaked with silver. He would have known this was the baron's sister, even if no one had told him.

She looked at Brys and Heden with no expression, then smiled as Aderyn ran across the clearing, under the tent, and to her mistress.

"Come," Sir Brys said. "We should retire to the priory."

"Okay," Heden said, watching behind them as Lady Isobel handed over her shield and lance to Aderyn.

Heden followed Brys into the stone building. Brys went to the altar, knelt and prayed. Heden sat down at a prayer bench, rested his arm on the armrest nearest the aisle and watched.

The prayer was simple. Heden was surprised at how simple, but in the middle of his muttering, Brys extracted something from his person and placed it in his mouth. It looked like a leaf. He chewed it and swallowed it. *A sacrament,* Heden thought. Made sense. They were servants of the forest. Or the other way 'round; Heden was beginning to lose track.

When Brys was done, he rose, pushing himself off his knees with some difficulty. Heden knew the feeling. Age.

The knight walked back to Heden.

"So who's missing?" Heden asked. He was suddenly tired. Exhausted. No rest since before Vanora woke up yesterday. Was it only yesterday?

Brys did not sit down; he leaned against one of the prayer benches. "Sir Perren," Brys said. "He will not be joining us."

"Why?"

"Why is no matter."

"Sounds better when you say it," Heden said, yawning. "I usually just tell people to go fuck a pig."

Brys looked at him with disgust. The knights did not like Heden's mode of speech and liked it even less when he swore.

Heden shrugged, not apologizing, but sympathizing. *We each have to put up with the other,* he was saying, *for a little while at least.*

Brys' manner softened.

"How long has it been since you slept?" he asked.

"Two days," Heden said.

"Not so long," Brys said with a little smile.

"Long days," Heden said.

Brys nodded.

"What's with the, ah..." He gestured to Brys' armor, festooned with moss, lichen, and vines. "The greenery?"

Brys looked at Heden for a moment, and it seemed to Heden that Brys was judging the question, working out whether it was alright to answer, or else tell Heden to talk to Sir Taethan.

"Squire Aderyn told you we might go months without meeting another knight?"

Heden nodded.

"But we still communicate," Brys said. "We pick a spot, a tree usually, that seems particularly blessed by Halcyon—" Heden didn't bother to ask how one might tell such a thing. "—and meditate. We cast our minds out into the wode and find the mind of another knight. And this way our demesnes do not overlap and we know where to look for trouble."

Heden absorbed this. It was not unheard of. "She said something about quiet contemplation," he said.

"You thought she was being poetic," Brys said.

Heden nodded. "Doesn't answer my question though," he said.

Brys sighed. "Sometimes a knight may be like that for weeks. In that time, the forest grows over the knight, protects him."

Heden thought. "What happens if..."

"The wode protects us. It alerts us to any nearby danger to our bodies."

Heden couldn't put words to it, but this seemed unnatural to him. It was like a parasitic relationship.

"So who's going to be the next knight-commander?" he asked.

Brys looked at the stained glass window. Saint Godwin, the Vigilant.

"Halcyon decides," he said.

"Is that..." Heden began. "Is that your way of saying 'Who knows?' Or does..."

Brys turned from the image of St. Godwin and gave Heden a look.

"Halcyon decides," he said.

Heden nodded. He didn't like badgering Sir Brys, but liked doing nothing and feeling useless even less.

The three dastards and Sir Nudd came in, all smiling. Whatever else was true, Nudd seemed to like the other three. When they saw Heden, they stopped laughing, and Nudd resumed his earlier sadness.

The huge knight walked up the nave, between Brys and Heden, and knelt to pray.

The three dastards swaggered up to Heden.

"This is normally a time for celebration," Sir Idris said accusingly, looking down at Heden. "All of us gathering."

"Oh did me being here spoil it?" Heden asked, without moving. His eyes flitted to Sir Nudd, trying to watch the man pray and keep an eye on these three at the same time. "The death of your commander didn't put a damper on things?"

Dywel, the weasel, moved forward again and this time it was Sir Brys who stepped forward to stop him. Heden noticed the little knight had waited an instant, to allow someone to hold him back. Heden had his full measure, and knew he could take the knight if it came to that.

"You did not know Commander Kavalen," Sir Idris said, his jaw clenching.

"No," Heden said. "And if he hadn't been *murdered,* I'd have never heard of him. Or you. Or had to come up here in the first place."

No one said anything. Idris' lapdogs looked to him for a reaction. Brys was watching Dywel. But no one bothered to deny that Kavalen was murdered.

Black gods, I know something, Heden thought.

Then: *Yeah, exactly what I guessed back in Celkirk.*

Lady Isobel walked in with Aderyn following behind. Aderyn looked nonplussed. Heden wondered what had passed between her and the lady.

Isobel was beautiful and regal. If anything, more regal than her sister the baron. She was obviously the older sister. Heden realized this meant the lady Isobel had rejected her hereditary barony to join the Green Order. Probably sixty years ago, if Heden was any judge of age.

The antlers on her helm were not small like Aderyn's; they were among the largest of the knights' but thin and spindly, not the heavy, roughhewn blades of Sir Idris' helm. Pointed and deadly nonetheless, and covered in dark brown stains.

Her armor was highly polished and reflected the light with a green tint, but the effect was muted—or perhaps enhanced—by the effusion of moss and branches and even a few small mushrooms growing on her. She smelled like rich soil. If Heden had seen her when he was a lad, he'd have thought he was seeing one of the deathless, risen from her grave. She was thin and her face narrow. Her eyes a pale blue.

The lady looked at the assembled knights arrayed around Heden, each either confronting him or ignoring him. She walked up the center aisle of the nave. They all retreated from her. No one said anything.

She approached the altar and knelt before it elegantly. She prayed for several minutes in silence, removing a leaf from a pouch on her belt and eating it as she looked up at St. Godwin fighting St. Pallad.

Heden looked at Aderyn. She glanced at him, and looked away.

After a long silence, Lady Isobel rose, turned and walked back down the nave. She was looking at her boots.

She stopped before Heden, and locked eyes with him.

"Mine squire hath spake to me of thee and thy seeming interest in us," Lady Isobel said, her voice light.

Heden didn't say anything.

"Thou must know by now, thou shalt not gain e'en the smallest bit of purchase 'gainst us."

Heden had to remind himself that while Lady Isobel was the oldest of the knights, she wasn't actually a thousand years old. She wasn't any older than Heden's mother. She spoke the knight's cant so naturally, so fluently, she seemed part of the past come alive.

Heden realized Lady Isobel was done talking, and everyone was looking at him. He shifted in the bench to get more comfortable.

"I am named Heden," he opened, looking at the other knights, then back at Isobel. "Named for my grandfather's father. My father is Efan and his father was Gowan."

Sir Brys, standing behind Lady Isobel, smiled discreetly and turned away.

Isobel stiffened almost imperceptibly.

"Thou thinks to shame me, reminding me of the proper forms of introduction," Isobel observed. She looked at the other knights, each expecting her to do something. Heden didn't think they were all expecting the same thing.

"Verily," she said, straightening. "I am shamed. I am the lady Isobel," she began, looking more regal in shame than any of the others in pride.

Heden cut her off. He looked relaxed, but he knew he was fighting for the lives of the people of Ollghum Keep and he wanted to keep Lady Isobel off-guard.

"I know," he said. "Knew as soon as I saw you. I met your sister. She gave me a message for you."

Lady Isobel was about to say something, her mouth open, but she stopped. Closed her mouth. Saw Heden anew.

Two tricks to me, Heden thought. *Your deal.*

"The message..." Lady Isobel began, and Heden saw her steel herself against emotion. "The message is no matter. Absolve this Order Green, then thou mayst present it to me."

"I thought you'd say that," Heden said. "With all of you standing around here like one o'clock half struck, no less."

"I," Lady Isobel said slowly. "I do not get your meaning."

"Horseshit," Heden said. Aderyn drew her sword.

"Knave!" Aderyn said. "Thou forgets thyself!" Heden ignored her and continued.

"Your sister is waiting for you and your band of moss-ridden blackguards to ride out of the forest and save her people." There was not a knight in the room who was not angry now, and showing it. Even Sir Nudd loomed over the rest, frowning angrily at Heden. Brys was looking between Isobel and Heden. Isobel was aware she was under assault, and the only one not angry. Not at Heden, at least.

"But that's not going to happen, is it? Those people are all going to die, aren't they?"

"What happens to the folk of Ollghum Keep is their fate, just as..." Sir Idris began, sneering. Heden snapped his fingers at Sir Idris without looking at him, bringing him up short. Idris was furious and surged forward.

Now it was time for Cadwyr and Dywel to stop him. "Not here!" Dywel hissed.

"Not in the priory!" Cadwyr said. "And not a priest!"

Heden, ignoring them, held up a hand and then pointed at Lady Isobel.

"I'm asking you straight," he said. "Those people at Ollghum Keep. Your sister and her family and all her subjects. They're all going to be torn apart by urq, aren't they?"

"There is still time to act," Lady Isobel said, her face clouded.

"Did you know the forest won't let anyone up here?" Heden asked.

All the knights looked at Lady Isobel. Not all of them had heard this.

She took a moment to confess her answer. The priory became cold.

"Yes," she said flatly, not looking at Heden.

Heden hadn't expected this. The other knights were frowning. Brys seemed upset.

"You did?" Heden asked. "You knew that and you…"

"How could it be otherwise?" Isobel said. "In any event, it is no matter."

"That's a popular attitude around here," Heden said, looking at Sir Brys.

"You are a cleric," Lady Isobel said. "I couldst see that e'en had my squire not said the words to me. Of what saint do you avail yourself?"

Heden looked around, unsure of what was going to happen next.

"Saint Lynwen," he said, and looked away.

"Who?" Sir Brys said.

Lady Isobel raised her eyebrows in appreciation. "Indeed?" she asked, a small smile on her face.

Now it was Heden's turn to be uncomfortable. Isobel obviously knew who Lynwen was.

"Who was Saint Lynwen?" Aderyn asked, not minding admitting ignorance.

"She was a whore," Lady Isobel said delicately. "And then a murderess. And then a saint. Never very popular. And only ever has one follower at a time."

Idris and his men laughed at the idea.

"And always a man," Isobel said, locking eyes with Heden as the dastards laughed. He was embarrassed, and looked it.

"A saint and a whore," Cadwyr laughed. "I think I know which our little priest here 'worships,'" he said, leering. Dywel and Idris joined in. They could not fight him here, but they could laugh at him.

"What..." Aderyn asked, confused. Not knowing how to react to the news. "What does that mean?"

"It means Cavall forgave her," Heden snapped. He ignored Cadwyr and looked meaningfully at Squire Aderyn. "It means a man is better than the worst thing he's ever done."

Heden looked back at the other knights and saw Brys' eyes unfocus, thinking about Heden's words. Heden looked back at Lady Isobel. He was shaken.

Trick to you, milady, Heden thought. And went back on the offensive.

"Okay," Heden said. "Squire Aderyn told you about me. Sure. You know what I'm here for. Well I know what you're going to say to me, too. 'Talk to Taethan.' Save it. He's not here, and you know how Kavalen died."

Lady Isobel suddenly stooped as though possessed of the old age he knew she had, and which she heretofore had given no quarter to.

"I'm here to absolve the order of the unrighteous death of Knight-Commander Kavalen," Heden said formally. "But that's not going to happen, is it? And you know it."

"The ritual may yet be spoken," Lady Isobel said. "The blame upon Sir Taethan's head, cleric, if it is not." Everyone was quiet now, watching the two of them intently. Sir Idris had his hand on his sword. Sir Nudd towered over them all.

"No no," Heden said, leaning forward. The air sparked with restrained violence. He knew he was risking his life here. One knight, maybe. But if two tried to take him. "You don't get out of it that easy. You know. And you could act, and you could save those people. You're just as responsible as anyone, and you know it."

"I cannot do what must be done," Lady Isobel said; it was some kind of admission, and it seemed to be destroying her. Aderyn wasn't angry at Heden anymore, but was openly worried about Lady Isobel. "I cannot speak the words that must be spoken. The wisest bear the heaviest burden, and so Sir Taethan must act, if he be not crushed under the weight of the knight's perfection." It sounded to Heden like a speech she'd practiced.

"And like that," Heden said, "your sister dies. And all those people."

"And more besides," she said quietly. Heden frowned, trying to guess at her meaning. Where would the army of urq go, after Ollghum Keep? Did she know?

"The lady Isobel has come the farthest," Sir Brys said, coming forward and putting a hand on her shoulder. "And overcome great adversity to be here. If we are to proceed with this inquisition, let it be anon, when we are rested."

"Though your words are crude," Lady Isobel said to Heden, ignoring Sir Brys. He took his hand away as though stung. "Your bearing is true. You man yourself well," Lady Isobel said, raising an eyebrow. "Many lesser men would be routed by the might assembled here against you. But you hold to your purpose. Squire Aderyn said you cared not for the order, nor even your duty. I know not. But thou carest about the folk of Ollghum Keep. Care about mine sister besides. And for this, we shall honor ye, even whilst thou defame us."

Sir Brys frowned at this. "I have no sister," he said. "Ollghum Keep or no. If this man hath come here to speak the ritual, then have him speak it." Sir Idris nodded. "If he hath come to pass judgment upon us, then he must quit the field. He knows not the traditions or our service. He is not worthy to pass judgment. Priest though he be."

Brys was setting himself up opposite Lady Isobel. Sir Nudd looked between them. Idris and his knights obviously supported Brys, but this was only because he was saying what they wanted to hear. Even Aderyn seemed confused, not knowing who to listen to.

Lady Isobel was the eldest. But Brys was the second-in-command. Heden was watching a struggle for control over the Green Order.

"You want me to leave?" Heden said to Brys, but then looked at every knight to make the point. "Tell me what happened to your commander."

No one spoke. It seemed Brys and Idris were both about to but Heden cut them off.

"And if anyone says 'Talk to Taethan," again..." Heden threatened.

"No one will say that to you," someone said from behind him. The voice rang out like a bell.

Heden knew what to expect when he heard the voice. He turned in his seat. The knight was standing in the archway. Heden couldn't make him out; he was silhouetted in sunlight.

"For I am here," he said, his voice young. "Little good though it will do you."

Chapter Twenty-nine

His plate gleamed and shone. It looked like an antique. He held his helm tucked under one arm. Its horns were not as large as Isobel's but at least as large as Brys'. They were deadly, and covered in blood like the rest.

He carried many weapons. A dagger on his belt as well as a longsword in a scabbard. On his back was the same kind of longspear Aderyn had waved at Heden when they met. There was also a quiver of javelins on his back. Heden had seen men walking around with more weaponry on them, but only for show.

He was absurdly handsome. He looked like a figure stepped out of a stained glass window. His fair complexion and fine-boned features would have made Gwiddon envious. It was hard to tell how old he was. Heden guessed, based on what he knew of Aderyn and how long one had to be a squire, he was in his late thirties.

Seeing this knight, tall, young, his green hair hanging straight down to his shoulders, his face honest and open, standing there in his perfectly made and maintained armor made all the other knights look shabby by comparison. Even the lady Isobel.

Taethan walked up the length of the nave, ignoring everyone in the priory. Heden watched the other knights' reactions.

Isobel looked distant. As though trying to remove herself from the world around her. Brys showed open frustration with the knight, as though he wanted to reach out and shake him. Nudd faced away from them all. Idris and his cohort looked disgusted with the knight. For once, it seemed Cadwyr and Dywel didn't need to look to Idris for a cue.

In every way Heden could tell, Taethan's ritual at the altar was identical to Isobel's. Heden was searching for any sign of "the perfect knight" as the others called him. He certainly looked the part.

When Taethan was done, he did something none of the other knights did. He walked to his crest, three horses rampant, removed his longspear from across his back and moved to place it on the brace under his device.

Just before he placed it in the curve of the wooden brace, he turned to look at the other knights, and let the spear drop. None of them reacted.

Taethan walked back down the nave and approached Heden. The other knights refused to look at him.

The knight looked down at Heden. No sense of judgment on his face. Heden turned and put one arm over the back of the bench, looking up at the knight whose face seemed carved from marble.

"You know what I think?" Heden opened without preamble. No introduction. Taethan didn't react.

"I think every single knight in this place knows exactly what happened to your commander."

Taethan watched him, no expression. Just listening. Heden expected some attitude, but was receiving none.

"You should have heard them. They acted like they'd never heard of Kavalen," Heden said, dropping the title to see how Taethan would react. Nothing. "Everyone said talk to you. I bet," he said, "that you think that's as much a pile of horseshit as I do."

Taethan pursed his lips, but Heden couldn't tell if it was in reaction to what Heden said, or to how he said it.

"You want me out of here as much as they do," Heden said, his voice dropping a little. "Okay. You tell me how your commander died, and I'll get out of here and leave you to…whatever you do."

Taethan looked to the other knights as though checking to see if they would interject. He turned back to Heden.

"Did you know," Sir Taethan began, "that your father prays for you, every morning?"

Heden peered at him and grimaced.

"You don't know my father," he said, pointing a warning finger.

"Only you," Sir Taethan said, and he pulled at his mail gauntlets, tugging them off. "You have two brothers and two sisters, but he doesn't pray for them."

"Why don't you use the cant?" Heden asked.

Taethan dismissed the question. "It's not compulsory," he said, echoing Idris. "Why does your father pray for you alone?"

"I know why," Heden said. "I know better than you. Probably better than he does. Why do you think the bishop sent me? You think he drew names by lot?"

Taethan adjusted his armor and moved his helm to the crook of his other arm. Heden noticed the moss growing on him. It wasn't as obvious as on Isobel. Heden wondered if he strategically picked parts off and left others. How much of this covering was for show?

The knight was expecting some kind of elaboration from Heden. Heden wasn't going to give it.

"A test? Is that what this is?" he asked. "You want to see if I'm…what? What quality do you think I need, to speak the ritual? How about this: I didn't kill my commander."

This upset the other knights. Taethan said nothing.

"Who says we need this lout?" Dywel rasped. "We serve Halcyon, not the bishop. She will choose the next commander. Run him out of here." Dywel spat the last words out.

"You think I came here for my amusement?" Heden challenged, looking from knight to knight. "Curiosity? You think I'm going to head out just because I've had my feelings hurt?" Heden shook his head and leaned back against the bench. "We've got a lot to learn about each other," he said.

"As servants of Cavall, we owe respect to the hierarch," Sir Brys said, meaning the bishop. "But not servitude. We serve the Wode." He looked at Sir Dywel without approval or affection. "I agree with Sir Dywel. Brother Heden," Brys said, looking at him from halfway across the priory, "we neither seek your judgment nor respect it. This is Halcyon's priory, not your whore saint's. If you will not speak the ritual now, you must leave."

Heden looked to Isobel to see how she'd react to Brys making that kind of statement. She seemed lost in thought.

"What do you think?" Heden asked Taethan. "You think Halcyon's just *busy*? You think that's why no one's been chosen to replace Kavalen? Or do you think she's waiting for me?"

Taethan shook his head slowly. "I hope one, fear the other, and know not." He seemed sad, looking at Heden.

"Tell me what happened to Kavalen," Heden said to Taethan. "If there is justice to be meted out, you can do it. Or I can do it, I don't care. But I can speak the ritual and one of you can take over and the people at Ollghum Keep will have a chance."

None of them liked hearing about the keep. They collectively fidgeted and avoided Heden's gaze. Except Taethan.

"What about you?" Heden said, looking at Sir Nudd. "Are you going to stand there and hope your oath protects you from doing the right thing? You *can* speak, you know," he said. "You know what happened to Kavalen, you could tell me if you thought it was important enough."

Sir Nudd frowned sadly and held up three fingers. The third knight. Taethan.

"Balls," Heden said, giving up.

"You are a priest of Cavall," Isobel said, straining to understand Heden. "Sir Nudd's oath of silence is a burdensome thing; it weighs upon him like all the rock of this priory. Thou knowest that more than any likewise. Why wouldst a priest, any priest, attempt to provoke Sir Nudd into breaking it?"

Taethan looked sharply at Isobel. Then at Heden.

"Who said he was a priest?" Taethan asked, surprised. He looked to the other knights, to see if any of them had an answer.

He looked at Heden and was obviously disappointed. Without taking his eyes off him, Taethan said: "Did he ever tell you he was a priest?"

No one responded. Brys stood up and looked angrily at Heden. Aderyn was confused, looking frantically from Brys to Taethan to Isobel.

"Did he say anything other than letting you all assume he was a priest?"

Brys walked up the nave and stood behind Taethan. The other knights, but for Isobel, were in various states of suspicion and outrage. Heden squirmed on the bench. Taethan knew too much about him, and then too much more.

Brys was about to say something damning, when Isobel spoke.

"He said nothing of the kind," she said. She wasn't looking at anyone, she was off on her own.

Her voice was clear and calm, but her pronouncement had an authority none could ignore. Heden didn't believe that some people were born to rule. But he believed some people were better at it. Hard to know Baed and Richard and not think that. Isobel ranked among them. Her sister was a pale imitation.

"It was pure surmise on our part. A fanciful illusion he invited us to share."

"He's not a priest?" Aderyn asked, confused.

"I knew it," Cadwyr sneered.

Idris shot him a look. "No you didn't."

Nudd just frowned sadly and turned his back.

Aderyn looked at Heden plaintively. "Why didst thou lie to us?" she asked. And in that moment the cant sounded perfectly natural.

"I apologize," Heden said. "It's a…it's a bad habit I've picked up."

"You should be proud of yourself," Dywel said, looking to Idris for approval. "You're very good at it. A practiced liar."

Heden ignored him and looked at Aderyn. "Most people assume I'm still a priest and I…I let them," he said.

Aderyn looked back and forth between Taethan, Isobel and Heden. "But he," she began. "He warded me when I fought the giant," she said.

"Tell them what you are," Taethan said. His voice was light and free of care.

Heden looked down at the flagstones. He didn't like being the center of attention.

"I'm an arrogate," he said.

Isobel stood up sharply, shocked, and turned to face Heden. Taethan smiled widely, cynically. The others were confused. Aderyn watched them all, trying to judge how she should react.

"What is that?" she asked, and now there was anger at her own ignorance.

"Tell her," Taethan said.

"How did you know my name?" Heden asked. "When you came in here? None of the other knights had a chance to tell you about me."

Taethan looked as though Heden had just complimented him. He said nothing. Heden found it difficult to talk.

"You tell her," Heden said, refusing to take Taethan's bait.

"It's an ancient tradition," Lady Isobel interjected, not taking her eyes off Heden. Her attitude towards him had changed. There was respect now and, Heden thought, awe.

"Prithee," she said, "almost as old as ours."

Taethan seemed a little put out that Lady Isobel was letting Heden off the hook. He interrupted.

"They are agents of the church," Taethan said.

Heden nodded.

"Then priests after all," Brys said, seeming confused but obviously wanting to learn that Heden was trustworthy. Wanting to find a way to shape events to fit his worldview.

"Nay," Lady Isobel said, shaking her head in disbelief. Like she'd found some plaster statue had turned out to be a priceless artifact. "They must first be annulled. The arrogates serve the church by leaving it, and taking on those duties abhorrent to Cavall."

"Abhorrent?" Cadwyr said, interested in spite of himself.

"Awful things," Isobel said. "I thought the tradition dead because it destroyed those who attempted it."

"Hasn't destroyed him," Dywel said, looking to Cadwyr, who nodded approval. "Maybe he's lying about this, too."

Lady Isobel cast a glance at Dywel and Idris hit him on the shoulder lightly with his mailed glove, then pointed at Dywel and Cadwyr, scolding them.

"Thou knowest the truth now," Isobel accused, turning back to Heden. "Should have known it from the start."

The knights accepted this. Lady Isobel had spoken and none seemed willing to gainsay her. Heden wondered at what it meant that he'd been able to deceive the knights in the first place. Isobel's response seemed to indicate that it should not have worked. Like Heden, like most priests who served Cavall or his brother Adun, the knights should have been able to sense truth, but could not.

"How long hast thou been an arrogate?" Lady Isobel asked.

"Three years," Heden said.

Lady Isobel nodded, as though confirming a suspicion. "And has it aged thou?"

Heden shrugged. "Not as much as not being an arrogate did," he said. *Choke on that,* he thought. *"Ask Taethan," my ass.*

"What would prompt one to do such a thing?" Brys asked. "Why does the church need someone like you?"

Heden didn't respond to either question.

Taethan walked forward. Heden felt like a criminal, with the knight standing there before him. He averted his gaze. Something he hadn't felt the need to do with the other knights. It seemed like, until Taethan, Heden had never seen a knight.

"They don't understand," Taethan said. "Tell them."

Heden shifted under his gaze. "It's not just the church," Heden said. "I…an arrogate is sworn to find good men who've done or might have to do awful things, and absolve them. Take on their transgressions. Usually things Cavall forbids. Sometimes that means doing it yourself. Which means violating the speech of Cavall."

"Give them an example," Taethan said, pushing him.

Heden gave them the canonical example. "A giant is pillaging your herd," he said. "It's a big, stupid thing, can't be reasoned with, but it's not doing it out of malice, it needs the food. You need the food. So you decide to kill the giant. But that would make you a murderer," he said, and Aderyn interrupted him.

"Not in defense," she objected. "Not to defend your land! The law permits!"

Heden looked at Taethan and tried to hold his gaze. "You tell that to the farmers who've come back from killing the thing. Covered in blood. Can't speak to their wives, can't sleep with them, ignore their children. You ask them if the law matters. They're the ones who had to go out and *do* it." He bit the words off. "They still feel like murderers."

Taethan, some secret knowledge firing him, held Heden's gaze. Heden couldn't meet his gaze. He looked at the floor, and then at the back of Sir Nudd.

"They know the giant had as much right to live as anyone."

Sir Nudd half-turned, aware the comment was directed at him.

"So you do it for them. You murder the wretched thing, so they don't have to. So they can go on being…normal people."

Brys stared at him.

"That isn't justice," he said darkly.

"No," Heden agreed. "But it's…human."

Taethan nodded approval at Heden's explanation and turned to the other knights.

"That is an arrogate," he said.

"What an awful way to live," Sir Idris said. Heden noted the rare moment of compassion or introspection from him.

Heden shrugged. "It's not so bad."

As Taethan retreated and tucked his mail gloves into his belt, Brys walked forward and confronted Heden.

"You lied to us," Brys said frankly, pointing an accusing finger at Heden. "Not an auspicious way to begin."

"He goes," Idris said. "He is not fit to judge the death of Kavalen, he has no authority to judge, and he has worn out whatever welcome we were foolish enough to grant."

"Aye," Cadwyr said.

"That's what I said," Dywel said, looking between them.

"He must stay," Isobel said. "For he is the only way."

This seemed to satisfy Aderyn.

Brys and Nudd both looked at Taethan. Taethan turned his back on Heden.

"It doesn't matter," Taethan said. "The result is the same."

Nudd held up two fingers. The second knight, Isobel. He was siding with her.

Heden stood up and looked at each knight.

"Someone needs to explain something to me, because I don't get it." They all turned away from him, could see where he was going and wanted to ignore him. This angered him more. "All I want to do is grant absolution or justice to whoever killed Kavalen. So you can go do your duty. So you can save the people at Ollghum Keep. Every time I bring the keep up you all look like you're going to vomit. You hate that you're all sitting here while the urmen march. I can see it. But you won't ride out against them because of what happened to Kavalen. Fine. I don't know why that matters, but I can see it does."

He looked at Brys.

"So tell me what happened. Let me do my job, so you can do yours."

Brys said nothing. Heden got very angry.

"Why are you all *fighting* me on this? What possible reason could you have for sitting on your asses and doing nothing while people die?" Why did Taethan matter so much?

Brys was pained, and looked at Taethan, who seemed in some kind of meditation. Lost in thought.

"He goes," Brys said finally, ignoring Heden's plea. That made it four against, two in favor, and one abstention.

Heden stepped forward.

"Don't do this," he said, his voice low.

Brys turned and looked at the stained glass window.

"You are an interloper here. You may return to the hierarch and explain to him that you failed, and more that he was wrong to send you."

"If I leave here," Heden said, clenching his fist, "then that's it. No one replaces Kavalen. No one else will come up here. And a thousand innocent people die."

Nudd turned back to them, and walked over. He was almost twice Heden's height. He was one of the biggest men Heden had ever seen.

Sad, in some kind of pain, Nudd pointed to the archway. Heden liked Nudd and didn't want to fight him. More, he didn't want to cause him any more pain.

Idris put his hand on his sword's pommel. Aderyn looked confused.

Heden grabbed his pack from the floor, turned and walked down the nave to the archway. His boots rang out on the stone floor. No one said anything.

He walked outside into the center of the clearing. Saw the setting sun stabbing wan fingers of light through the trees. The warm light of the priory bled out into the clearing.

Heden dropped his pack on the ground.

"Shit," he said.

Chapter Thirty

The sun had set, its light thin. Heden could see a few stars in the sky and the rust-colored Dusk Moon hanging over the trees. Small, turning slowly. Three times an hour, just like the Dawn Moon. No one in the city paid the two moons any attention, but they still used the word "turn" to mean a third of an hour. Most didn't think about where the word came from.

Out of habit, he marked the facing of the moon, so he could count the turns and know how much time had passed. Though only appearing, and at its brightest, during dusk, it would still be visible for several hours, only disappearing at midnight.

It had not yet been a full turn since he left the priory. He hadn't moved. He didn't know what he was going to do, but he knew he wasn't going home yet. He was thinking about heading to the keep, against his own judgment, to see if he could help.

The knights in the priory argued loudly. It meant nothing to Heden. He didn't know what they were arguing about, and didn't care.

He heard the absence of sound behind him that indicated someone was inexpertly trying to be quiet, and turned around.

Aderyn was standing behind him, watching him watching the moon.

Heden turned back to the Dusk Moon twirling slowly in the sky.

"You didn't finish the pavilion," he observed.

She sniffed, but otherwise did not move. He could feel her eyes on him.

"The jousting field is complete," she said. "The melee is staked off. But the tent…Lady Isobel declared there would be no tournament."

Heden thought about what this meant. What it meant for Isobel to make such a decision, whether Brys objected. He heard the knights inside, arguing.

"I guess they've got enough to fight over," he said.

Aderyn watched him. Her attention was difficult to bear, he wasn't sure why. It was like a shaft of sunlight bearing down on only him, and he didn't feel worthy of it. He sensed that her attitude towards him had shifted and there was something akin to sympathy and interest in her gaze. He decided to test that.

"I asked you a question earlier," Heden said, turning to look at her in the moonlight. "About the giant. If it bothered you that Sir Nudd took matters into his own hands." Aderyn looked away. "You told me he wouldn't have done that before Kavalen's death."

She nodded, eyes cast down.

"But you didn't tell me everything. You were ashamed by Nudd's behavior…."

Her head whipped up and he thought she was going to chastise him again for not using the knight's full title. But he'd underestimated her.

"It was a cowardly attack!" she admitted, as much to herself as to Heden. Her face looked possessed in the starlight.

Heden nodded, he understood. The attack affected her because of what it meant about the order. She wasn't just angry at Sir Nudd, wasn't just ashamed, she was afraid.

"Stabbed from behind," Heden said.

"And with no warning. No declaration, no mercy, no chance to surrender or quit the field."

"I've known a lot of knights," Heden said, "I'm not sure any of them..."

"We are not 'any' knights," Aderyn hissed. "We are the Green Order. Not even Dywel would have done such a thing before the commander's death."

Just saying that pained her. Heden wondered what kind of knights these men and women were, before Kavalen's death, to inspire such loyalty. He had no idea. They must have been close to magnificent. Part of him would have liked to see that, see these knights who kept to the traditions for a thousand years. Part of him didn't believe it.

"Well," Heden said, embarrassed somewhat by the silence and the strength of Aderyn's reaction. "If I leave, then no one replaces Kavalen. And then no one to lead you, and the order dies."

He tried to say it smoothly, dramatically. Like Gwiddon would have. Aderyn didn't respond. Heden took a breath and looked south, thinking of home.

"Why do you not ride to the keep?" Aderyn asked, curious. "You were a prelate. Does your service as an arrogate forbid..."

At the sound of his title, Heden interrupted her.

"It's not that easy," he said.

She frowned at him. He turned and saw her confusion.

"You think I ride down there and bless their soldiers, heal the wounded. Maybe do some fighting myself."

She looked in the direction of the keep, and then back to him. It was obvious he thought her idea was worthless, and equally obvious she didn't know why.

"Right now, fear is the only hope those people have."

"I do not understand," Aderyn said.

"Every day more people flee the keep. Flee their neighbors, maybe even their families. They've been thinking about running for weeks, but they're afraid of being called cowards. Even traitors, for abandoning their friends.

"But those people," Heden said, nodding southwest, "the ones who shit themselves at the idea of having their heads cut off and spit upon pikes by rampaging urmen, the ones who run. They're the ones who'll survive. The people who stay at the keep are the ones who'll be eviscerated.

"And what happens if I show up?" Heden said. He turned to Aderyn to make sure she understood this was not a rhetorical question.

"What happens if a prelate of Cavall shows up and announces he's going to help?"

Aderyn ruefully held his gaze. "The people stop fleeing."

"And?" Heden asked.

"More people die when the urq come."

"I can't stop a whole army by myself," Heden said. "It takes men to hold a keep, more than me, and more than they've got. All I'd do is give those poor bastards enough hope to convince them to stay behind. Fight and die. And for what?"

"I had not considered that," Aderyn admitted darkly. She found Heden's reasoning sound, but very distasteful. "I had never considered the virtue of cowardice."

Heden didn't say anything. He wasn't sure if she was mocking him. He thought maybe she had a right. There was a time when he'd have gone to the keep and damn the consequences. But those principles died a long time ago.

"Anyway," he said, kicking the dirt under his boot for no reason. "What are you doing out here?"

"I am to scout the urq," she said, drawing herself up.

Heden glanced at her, then went back to star-watching. He was counting the constellations. For some reason, he couldn't return her gaze. He felt like he was staring at her when he did so.

"What does that mean?" Heden asked.

He heard her footsteps as she approached him.

"We are a day from the keep," she explained. "They are two days from here, but they are an army and move slowly. I can move quickly. I will find them, observe them. They will not see me. And I will report back on their position and movement."

Heden nodded and looked at her again. She was staring at him. He wondered if she volunteered for this because she knew he was out here.

"Sounds like make-work," he said.

She screwed up her face, trying to understand what he meant.

"If you mean 'something to do while the knights do nothing,' you are likely correct. But it is my duty, and I will discharge it well."

She walked in front of him, so he couldn't ignore her as easily.

She set her shoulders.

"I have decided you will accompany me," she said.

Heden raised his eyebrows.

"You have?"

"I have," she said in plain agreement as though there was nothing strange about this.

"What do they think about that?" Heden asked, throwing his thumb over his shoulder towards the priory.

"Well, they are arguing," she said, as though it wasn't obvious. Heden thought he got a little sense of what she thought about her idols' indecision.

Heden slung his pack over one shoulder.

"Beats heading to the keep," he said.

She smiled.

"Come, arrogate," she said, raising an eyebrow. "And see how a squire of the Green comports herself."

She turned and ran off into the forest. Heden almost missed it, but she spoke a prayer under her breath, and her speed was that of a deer.

Heden sighed and shook his head, put his other arm through the second strap on his pack, tightened the buckles, spoke his own prayer and ran off after her.

Chapter Thirty-one

Keeping low to the ground, her strides long, leaping up over rocks and bushes that would slow them down otherwise, Aderyn led him through the darkening wode.

Heden marveled at her, but remembered when he and his company spent days doing this. Were they ever that young? *Young,* he thought. *She's already twenty-eight.* Heden was already musing on age and mortality at that age.

They made little noise. Mostly the soft and regular clink of her mail against hard leather armor. It was quiet enough and they moved quickly enough that should they come upon any urq, the enemy would not have enough time between hearing the sound and Aderyn and Heden being upon them.

The first time she stopped, after about a half-turn, she turned and looked for Heden and found him standing right behind her. Both of them were breathing hard. She nodded once in approval and seemed to wait for him to catch his breath. He shook his head and waved her on, and she dashed off again.

They would stop about every turn and Aderyn would orient herself. This was a combination of smelling the air, checking the trees and trying to find stars through the thick canopy of leaves. When she did this, she reminded him of someone he knew long ago, someone he considered a brother, now dead.

It was midnight before they stopped to rest. Four or five hours running. Heden watched the Dusk Moon finally wink out, only a small black circle where once had been a reddish disk. You had to know where it was to find it.

Aderyn pulled her pack off, and plopped down on the dead leaves and moss and vines that made up the forest floor, her back against a tree. She opened her pack and took out what smelled like salted pork and dried fruit.

Heden worked to lower himself to the ground, his joints popping. He wasn't hungry, even after the run. There was no tree he could sit against and still see Aderyn, so he just lay down amongst the fallen leaves, putting his pack under his head.

Aderyn ate, and Heden watched the sky through leaves now seeming black.

"How far to the urq?" he asked.

Aderyn bit off a bit of jerked pork. "Three hours," she said, munching. "But it will be after dawn before we come upon them.

Heden turned his head to look at her. She swallowed.

"There is a stream only a few hours away," Aderyn said. "Always take the chance to fill your waterskins and always take the chance to bathe." She was quoting again. Then she sniffed the air pointedly. "Good advice for everyone," she said. Heden took her meaning and sneered. At himself more than her.

"And in any event," she said, picking some of the moss off herself and throwing it away. "I no longer wish to be a..." She looked at Heden quizzically.

He didn't realize what she meant at first, but then remembered his words in the priory.

"A moss-ridden blackguard," he said.

"That was it," she nodded, not without humor.

"Well, you're not any kind of blackguard, moss-ridden or otherwise," Heden said. He meant to compliment her, but he spoke so matter-of-factly that she couldn't tell. The fact that everything he said sounded so final, impartial, made her happy. Made it sound like truth.

He looked at her and smiled a little. "I doubt you ever will be."

She smiled back at him. Then she stopped and cocked her head.

"But the other knights," she said. "You hate them somewhat." It wasn't a question.

"I rarely meet one who isn't a lout and a braggart," he said, trying not to swear.

She understood. She didn't agree or disagree, but she knew what he meant. It was a point of view.

"I think it's the oath," he continued. "It's meant to be a burden but I think most of them look at it like a badge of station. An excuse to act like a horse's ass."

Aderyn nodded very slightly, it was hard to tell under the bright starlight. Heden wondered at her silence. Did she agree? Was she afraid to agree?

He turned to her, a mischievous look on his face. "Remember that," he said. "When it comes time for you to swear your oath."

She pursed her lips. "I have already sworn," she said. He couldn't tell if she was chastising him for not knowing that, or regretting something.

"When you became a squire?"

She nodded. "It is the first thing the squire does, for if one cannot hold the oath as a squire, how then as a knight?"

"Good point," Heden said. He hadn't known that. Of course, back in the civilized world, a year was the standard term of service for a squire, before becoming a knight-errant. Here in the forest, a lifetime as a squire, then a second lifetime as a knight.

"Sir Nudd took the oath of silence," Heden said.

Even in the dark, he could tell she was anticipating his next question, and waiting ruefully.

"What oath did you swear?" he asked.

She deflated a little.

"Chastity," she said.

Heden didn't say anything. She seemed to think chastity was…unfashionable? He couldn't tell. She didn't like admitting it, in any case.

"The same oath Lady Isobel swore," Heden said.

Aderyn gaped. "How did you know?"

"Just a guess. Guessing it's a pretty popular oath among the womenfolk."

She seemed like she was going to protest.

She looked at the ground. "Sir Taethan swore it," she said. "The only man among them."

Heden looked at her. This was interesting. He was glad she recruited him for this. He was learning more here about the knights than he had at the priory. Maybe that was her goal.

He closed his eyes and exhaustion overtook him. It was now the second night without sleep. Only last night, he'd been hunting through kethat warrens searching for a carter's missing family.

"All men need sleep," she said, and it sounded like she was quoting something again.

Heden nodded.

"Not now, though," he said. "I can keep going for a few hours." His body was ready to collapse, but his mind was racing and would not let him rest.

Aderyn, looking at Heden with wide eyes, like he was a wild animal, got up and approached him timidly, her small hand outstretched. Heden allowed it. Didn't move. Didn't look at her. She placed her hand on his breastplate. Her face was lit by stars.

She spoke a prayer. Heden recognized it. The air seemed clearer, his vision sharper. Tension and exhaustion began flooding out of him. He was refreshed, no longer needing sleep.

"You will have to sleep anon," she said. Heden nodded his understanding.

"Thank you," he said, seeing her as a person and not as a puzzle to solve. She gazed at him, her hand still on his chest, her eyes wide. They stared at each other like that for a moment, then Heden looked at her hair, and she looked away.

"You could not have done that?" Aderyn asked, and went back to sitting against the tree, finishing her rations. Her voice was rough. She cleared her throat. "Is it because you're an arrogate?"

Heden shook his head and took a few deep breaths.

"It's because I forgot," he said, smiling. "I must have learned," he took a breath, tension and exhaustion flooding out of him, "seventy prayers? A hundred?" He wondered. "Some of them twenty-five years ago. Haven't used any in a while. You forget a lot."

Aderyn was impressed. "All the prayers of all the knights, even Isobel and Kavalen, do not number more than a few dozen."

"You have other talents," Heden said, nodding to her sword.

Aderyn accepted this, but said, "You use a sword as well."

Heden shrugged. "Lynwen allows it," he said. "A lot of Cavall's saints do. But I'm not very good with it."

"You became a priest when you were very young," she said, changing the subject.

"Same age as you became a squire," he said, trying to smile a little.

"Is that why you are not wed?" she asked. She was looking at his neck. There was no torque around it.

He was reminded that she'd gone her whole life with nothing approaching intimacy besides the fellowship of the order. None of the knights had.

"No," he said. "Priests of Cavall and Adun can marry. So can arrogates," he said, preempting her next question.

"Then why?"

"Because the woman I love," he said, trying to make it sound like it was easy to say, "does not love me."

This surprised her.

"But there are other women," she said.

"Not for me," he said, and that was it.

Her face softened and she looked at him with a new expression he didn't understand.

"I knew you had not sworn an oath of chastity," she said, smiling. He found it disconcerting.

"It's not the same thing for priests. We don't swear oaths when we take the cloth. It's more like a test. Had to take an oath to become an arrogate, though."

This interested her.

"What oath?" she asked, sitting forward, wrapping her arms around her legs.

He gave her a sideways glance. "It's a secret," he said.

"This is not fair!" she declaimed.

Heden shrugged, but did not budge. "The whole ceremony is filled with ritual and secrecy. The bishop had to go look it up. I'm the first arrogate this age. Probably the last."

This mystery seemed to gain him more respect with her.

"Was it the bishop who asked you—"

He cut her off. "A friend suggested it," he said, not wanting to name St. Lynwen for a couple of reasons. "It was the right thing to do." He failed to add he no longer felt like he was up to it. "Part of my job as a priest of Cavall was judging people, bringing justice to people. Looking at everyone as though they're guilty of something. I was having a hard time with that.

"My friend saw I was having…difficulty but knew I didn't want to just give up on Cavall. She knew about the arrogate tradition." Had been one, he remembered. "And suggested it. Taking people's burdens rather than their measure."

"A man is better than the worst thing he's done?" she quoted. Heden was impressed she made the leap.

"Yeah," he said. "It's harder than it sounds. But once you start, once you start…seeing into people's hearts. It's hard to stop. Doesn't matter what you think of someone, how much you disapprove…once you see the kind of pain they're in." He left it at that. He didn't like talking about it.

Her stare bore into him. The brilliant stars above them were not distracting enough. Heden found it impossible to ignore the strength of her attention, so he changed the subject.

"Where is Kavalen's body?" he asked.

He didn't look, but heard her shift as she leaned back, disengaging somewhat. His question had worked.

"You think if you saw his body, you would know what happened to him?" she wondered.

Heden shrugged. Not easy lying on his back, but he'd had a lot of practice. "I'd know something," he said. "If I knew any less than I do now, I'd forget my own name."

"There is a ceremony," Aderyn said. "And the knight's body is accepted back into the heart of the forest. It is not a simple burial. You could not gain his corpse even if you knew where it was."

Heden thought about this. She was telling the truth. He considered pressing her, but decided against it. He didn't want her to close up on him.

The sounds of the forest enveloped them. Heden enjoyed it. The forest could be a pleasant place. Then he remembered the urmen.

"Why are we on foot?" Heden asked. "Why not take the horses?"

She shook her head. "Not for this. Not for scouting. And not your horse. Mine can be quiet where yours cannot. And find its way through the wode at night with nary a misstep. But even my horse cannot mask its smell, and the urq like horseflesh."

Heden knew this was true.

"Horses when we want them to know we're here," she said. "On foot when we don't."

Heden nodded his understanding. Aderyn gave him a look, making certain he was ready. She watched him a little too long, seeming to make a decision about something, then nodded and stood up, smiling. Heden got up as well. It took him a little more work to manage it.

"We go," she said, then turned to lope off into the forest, like a cat chasing pray.

Heden watched her go, admiring her youth, before he started in after her.

Chapter Thirty-two

It was maybe an hour later and a large ravine navigated before they stopped again. They were covering miles at a time. A relentless pace. Their way lit by starlight.

They stopped because something brought Aderyn up short. At first, Heden not seeing her clearly in the darkness, he thought they'd come upon the urq. Then he remembered they were first going to a stream. The urmen should still be hours away. And there was no stream nearby.

He looked at her, expecting to see her sniffing the air again. He couldn't tell what she was looking at, something on the ground.

"The urq?" he asked.

She shook her head. "We are in the territory of the brocc," she said. The quasi-mythical badger-men who called the southern wode home. Where Heden grew up, far to the south, they were a story told to children at bedtime. Heden had met them though; they were anything but myths. They didn't mind men, but only the men who lived close to the forest had any kind of relationship with them.

"Not even an army of urq would test the mettle of the brocc," she explained. Heden knew this to be true. Where there was one, there were thousands, and they were incredibly fierce fighters, but difficult to interest in anything except the defense of their territory.

Heden approached slowly and looked around, not seeing what she was looking at. She appeared to be staring at the base of a tree covered in lichen and mushrooms, a large bush growing around it.

Heden stared at it again, and like it were a cloud that suddenly coalesces into the shape of a bird or a horse, he saw it.

There was a knight lying against the base of the tree, illuminated by starlight.

"Sir Perren," Aderyn said.

He'd been there some time; the undergrowth had almost completely enveloped him. Heden could see his armor and his sword. A lump that was probably a shield. Heden remembered Brys explaining that the forest would grow quickly to protect the knight, but Heden had a hard time imagining that Sir Perren had been here less than a year. And Brys had known he was in this state. He'd said Sir Perren would not come to the priory.

"Is he alive?" Heden asked.

Aderyn nodded.

"But all the knights are at the priory," he said. Aderyn frowned, pained. Looked like she was struggling with a difficult decision. Or a difficult realization.

"He attempts a casting. He casts his thoughts out, far beyond this demesne," Aderyn explained. She was only half paying attention to Heden.

Heden looked at the nightmare picture of a man physically and mentally merging with the wode. "Who is he trying to commune *with*?"

Aderyn turned away, her mouth open, breathing heavily, looking at the stars.

"Commander Kavalen," she said.

Heden was horrified.

"Can he…is that possible?"

"Sir Perren was closest to the wode. He would sometimes say "we" instead of "I" and flew into a rage if he found an urq or kethat harming a tree."

Heden stared at the lichen-covered face of the knight.

"The death of Commander Kavalen has driven him mad," Aderyn said. Perren was trying to will the power of the forest to resurrect Commander Kavalen. It didn't look to Heden as though the forest was trying to protect him; it looked like the forest was trying to consume him.

"Well, we can wake him up at least," Heden said, stepping forward.

"No!" Aderyn hissed, grabbing him. He stopped, trusting her. He took a step back.

She looked down at Sir Perren, thinking how to explain it, then turned back to Heden and pointed at Perren's body.

"It is a thing Sir Cadwyr would do," she explained. Heden took her meaning, an oafish thing. Disrespectful.

They both stood and looked down at the knight, his features thrown into sharp relief by the bright starlight.

"We leave him," she said. "He is in no danger here."

It looked like he was being eaten by danger.

"What..." Heden stopped and thought, and turned to Aderyn. "Squire," he said formally, and she took notice. "You know about the sack of Ollghum Keep."

She nodded.

"You know what I'm trying to do."

"You would save those people," she said with maybe a touch of admiration. Heden was getting some sense of why she was here with him instead of back with the knights who refused to act.

He pointed to Sir Perren.

"Would Sir Perren help?"

This was a difficult question for Aderyn. She looked at Perren, unsure how to answer. Then she took a step forward and crouched down to look into the knight's sleeping face.

"If you're asking," she whispered, looking at the gaunt knight, "whether Perren would make a difference." She thought for a few moments more. The forest continued to make various noises, crickets and other nocturnal animals trying to find mates.

She stood up and squared her shoulders, took a breath. Made a decision.

"Sir Perren is lost to us," she said.

"What does that mean?" Heden asked.

"He may never wake." Her voice was hushed.

Heden thought about this. Thought about the timeline. Kavalen had only died a few days ago. How could Aderyn know this?

"Isobel tried to contact him," Heden said.

Aderyn raised her eyebrows, impressed at Heden's insight.

"Is this unusual for him?" he asked.

She nodded again, her jaw set.

"This is his reaction to Kavalen's death," Heden realized.

"Lady Isobel said Sir Perren was an oracle." Aderyn didn't like thinking about what this meant. "His fate was the fate of the order."

"That's why no one will tell me anything," Heden said. "They've already given up. On the keep, on the order. On everything." Their behavior made more sense to him.

Heden looked sharply at Aderyn. "How do you feel about that?'

She shrugged.

"I thought nothing of it. Milady has been in a melancholic mood since the death of Commander Kavalen. She will regain herself."

"And Perren?"

"I am not Sir Perren's squire," she said.

"Okay," Heden said, ignoring that, since it didn't make any sense to him. "What if I just woke him up, whether you liked it or not."

"It could kill him," she said.

"Figures," Heden said ruefully.

"The wode keeps him alive thus," she explained. Heden looked at the knight against the tree; it was hard to see in the starlight. He thought he saw the vines that grew over Perren pulsing with nutrients, but it was probably just his imagination. He decided it was his imagination.

"To wake him now would be like ripping a baby from its mother's womb."

"Great," Heden said.

"Come," Aderyn said. "It will be dawn in an hour, and we near the stream." She took his hand gingerly, and he let himself be led away as they abandoned Sir Perren.

Sir Perren made no objection.

Chapter Thirty-three

Heden didn't trust water and women. For reasons passing understanding, every time Heden had been near water with any woman, she'd always taken the opportunity to get naked and lured Heden into doing the same. Ostensibly for the purposes of cleanliness, but that never turned out to be the real reason.

When Heden was younger, and very uptight about these things, it bothered him. Now he was far less uptight, but had another reason to avoid such situations. As he thought about it, it didn't seem fair.

Maybe Aderyn would be different. He looked at her in the new morning sun, watched her take out a comb missing several teeth and untangle her hair, the closest to vanity she could come to out here, and decided that in this respect, she was exactly like any other girl.

She looked at him with a discreet smile and cocked an eyebrow, as though she knew what he was thinking. He tried to ignore her. He was not sure he could resist her, if she tried anything. And never completely sure that resisting was for the best.

She hopped down lightly from the large rock they'd both been standing on, down to the stream below. It was wide and so deep in places as to be black. It burbled past, gathering in great large pools, and the broken terrain here created small waterfalls and rivulets. It was beautiful. He understood why she wanted to stop here.

Taking more care, he followed her down. She had already dropped her pack by the edge of the river, and was disentangling her hair from the links that held her cloak around her neck.

There was a small waterfall, no more than six feet high, but it broke the river neatly and no one bathing above could see anyone bathing below, and vice versa. It was an easy climb to make.

"I'll wash up there," Heden said. "And meet you on the other side." He looked up at the light blue Dawn Moon and marked its face. "One turn," he said. Trying to act like he was in charge of this expedition. "Remember our mission."

"I have never forgotten it," she said with no inflection. No reproach. He nodded to himself—still suspicious of her—and turned, heading upstream.

Looking around to make sure Aderyn was nowhere in sight, feeling only a little self-conscious, he stripped his armor off. Breastplate first, into the pack. Then his leather armor.

Pulling the hard leather off, revealing his woolen underclothes, released a potent aroma. He held his breath and stuffed them all into the pack.

Naked, he held the pack in one hand, and stepped into the water, ankle deep.

It was cold. He strode into the water, enjoying the feel of it on his naked skin. This was something he missed about the life, something he never got to do in Celkirk.

Keeping his pack over his head, he waded out until he had to swim. He was a strong swimmer, having done a great deal of it as a boy, and soon he was across the river. He dropped his pack on the ground and removed a cake of soap. A product of the city; he'd never had any with him as a campaigner. He smiled to himself at his foresight.

He looked up, considering getting out the oil and cleaning his armor, but saw the Dawn Moon had already made half a revolution, and so, cake in hand, he dove back into the river.

Its water was clear and clean. Potent enough to wash more than just dirt from him. The pool that formed before the waterfall was deep, and he dove down, scrubbing the soap into his hair.

He enjoyed the momentary luxury of losing track of time, emerging and floating in the water, his eyes closed. He knew that when he opened them the Dawn Moon would be waiting, but he also knew that in the proper meditative state, he could expand that time.

Eventually, his meditation was broken by the memory of the urq they were scouting and the people of Ollghum Keep. He opened his eyes just as the Dawn Moon finally turned to the same facing he'd noted before leaving Aderyn. He sighed and willed his limbs to move again, and swam towards shore.

Heden walked out of the water. Naked. Clean. He felt like a new man. Felt ready to go back to the priory right now and confront Sir Taethan and extract from him the truth about Kavalen. He could be home tomorrow. But first, the urmen.

He dried himself with a cloth from his pack, and then pulled out a fresh pair of woolens. Happy with himself that he thought to bring more than one pair. He dressed and armored himself. Whatever apprehension he had about Aderyn doing something foolish was forgotten.

He finished dressing and stretched himself, his joints popping, his muscles relaxing. He breathed the forest air. Strange how you got used to smells. The stink of the city eventually vanished, then the sweetness of clean air eventually became something you took for granted.

He turned to go down and find Aderyn, and startled. She'd been standing only a few feet behind him, watching him. Standing on the yellow grass in bare feet.

She was naked. He shouldn't have been worried about the water. He should have been worried about after the water, when she was clean again.

He expected her skin to be pale from constantly wearing the armor, but she obviously spent a lot of time under the sun naked. Her skin was brown and smooth. Though she had many scars, to Heden's eye they in no way marred her beauty.

She wasn't standing before him like a knight, she was shy. Presenting herself for his approval. Heden could not draw a breath. He felt like a spell had been cast upon him. She took a deep breath and suddenly parts of Heden's clothing no longer fit properly. For many years as an adult, he believed that an artfully dressed woman could be far more alluring and irresistible than mere nudity. He no longer believed that.

She was youth and health and sun and innocence and lust. She was like a goddess of summer.

"I will never be a knight," she said to him.

Heden forced himself to look away. He turned around, forgot how to breathe.

"You can't know that," he said. Turning away hadn't helped, her image was burned into his mind.

"Go, ah…" he said, pointing downstream. His throat was dry. "Go put your clothes on." He got the words out quickly.

He heard her walk up behind him as she slipped her hands about his waist. She pressed herself against him, held him tight. She laid her head against his cloak.

"It is my oath to break," she said, apropos of nothing.

She must bind her breasts, Heden reasoned, *when she's in her armor.* He shook his head, these thoughts weren't helping.

She took a deep breath. "I watched you in the water. You have the body of a knight."

Heden understood this was a compliment. He took her hands around his waist and pulled them away, but did not let go of them.

"Wasn't there something about your armor? Uh, always…always staying in it except to bathe?" He tried to push her away.

She pulled her hands back and slowly turned him around to face her. He looked down at the top of her head, her thick red hair curlier from the water. She was looking at his breastplate. She slid her hands up his sides, to the buckles that held it on, and began to undo them.

"I think," she said delicately, "that there is yet more bathing in our future."

Heden was overwhelmed by what she was doing, what she was asking. His knees went weak and his legs went out from underneath him. He fell to his knees before her, his hands on her waist. She seemed to writhe with anticipation, mistaking Heden's gesture.

"Please," he said. "Don't do this to me."

She ran her fingers through his hair. "And what am I doing to you?" she asked, delighted in the effect she was having on him. The more he resisted, the more she was enjoying herself.

"I can't," he said. "I swore."

"An oath?" she asked, idly. "Let us break them together."

"Worse," he said. "A promise. There's a woman…" A woman who, in all likelihood, would not care what happened here. Would think him mad for rejecting Aderyn.

"But she is not here." He could hear her smiling.

"I really wish you hadn't said that," Heden said.

She laughed, stepping impossibly closer to him. His hands slipped around her. He took a deep breath and almost gave in. Came closer than he ever had in his life to breaking a promise that no one in the world cared about anymore except for him.

He pushed her away.

"You swore an oath," he said.

"It is no matter." There was a little something in her voice.

"Stop saying that," he gasped. "You're about to do something you'll regret."

He felt her stiffen. "Then it will be my regret to have," she said. "It will be something of mine." She softened, seeing him on his knees. "Besides," she said. "I know you will not let me regret it."

Black gods, he thought.

She knelt with him. He didn't think things could get more difficult, but he found it easier to worship the goddess who stood before him than confront the woman who knelt with him.

She had never been with a man in her life. Heden realized with a dull ache that there was no way she could understand what he was dealing with. Would take his fidelity as rejection. She had no experience to compare this to and would think there was something wrong with her. She was old enough to know better, but had spent her whole life alone in the forest. The thought of her confusion and self-loathing if rejected broke him.

"I want to do this," she said, putting her hands on either side of his head. She looked at him, struggling to avert his gaze.

"And so do you," she said, pulling him forward and kissing him, delicately.

They kissed like that for only a moment before she advanced her cause, pressing her body against him, wrapping her arms around his neck.

Fuck it, he thought, unbuckling his breastplate. She laughed and helped him with his leather armor.

They looked at each other, his armor on the ground clad in his woolens, her armor and clothing nowhere in sight. He marveled at her, not disguising the effect she had on him. She seemed deliriously happy, and that made him smile.

They embraced and kissed again, this time longer.

Then, in his mind's eye, he saw a pair of smiling eyes, and a woman's cynical, knowing laugh rang out like she was standing there watching them. Calling Heden a manly fool.

He opened his eyes and looked at Aderyn again, realizing what they were both about to do. Destroy what amounted to decades of fidelity between them.

He pushed her away abruptly.

She looked at him, worried that something had gone wrong. That he was unwell.

"We can't," he said.

"It is too late for 'can't,'" she said, shaking her head and pulling herself back to him.

He kept her at arm's length.

"Listen, please. This isn't your fault." He knew saying it was meaningless, but he had to try. "You deserve…" She deserved more than he could give her.

"Do we not deserve to be happy?" she asked, yearning. As concerned for his happiness as her own.

"We won't be happy if we betray our oaths."

This pained her. She could see it on his face, could see he was telling the truth about himself.

"I do not see how we can be happy any other way."

Heden had underestimated her. She had thought a lot about this. Probably had been thinking about it since the priory. Heden hadn't noticed. She had probably run through this scenario several times on the way here and thought through what he might say.

"You're going to think," he said, "that there's something wrong. With you. But you haven't done anything wrong."

"How not? How have I…how have I failed you, explain to me, say the words and I will—"

"Aderyn!" he said, putting his hands on her shoulders. "Squire!" he reminded her. She didn't like being reminded of that. He looked her in the eye, stopped pleading with her and just looked at her until, when she looked back in anticipation, he said the words she needed to hear.

"We only fail if we break our oaths."

This angered her.

"They broke their oaths! There will be no more order! Why cannot you and I…"

"What do you mean they broke their oaths?" Heden asked. He couldn't help himself.

"Ah!" she cried. "Stop it! They are gone, I am here. We are here, now!"

He shook his head. He had passed the test, and all that remained was trying to get her not to hate herself for it.

He stood up and started putting his armor back on. She made a sound like a defeated gasp.

Even facing away from her, he couldn't get the memory of how she looked, and how she wanted him, out of his mind. *I'm going to have trouble sleeping for,* he thought a moment, *a year.*

"You're going to be a knight," he said. "The urq can't stop it. Even the other knights can't stop it. Forget them." *Forget me.* "Hang on to that. You worked for it your entire life, and you are going to be a knight."

He could hear her stand up. She was staring at him. He didn't want to turn around and see her expression.

"Go put your armor on before I change my mind."

She didn't move.

There was a sound like a saw biting wood.

"Ragh! Ragh! Ragh!" It was urq laughter.

Heden turned and saw a dozen, more, hairless blue-black figures emerging from the woods, each wearing light armor, carrying various weapons. Each covered in blood-like red powder. He recognized them. Bloodrunners. Elite scouts.

The urmen had found them.

Chapter Thirty-four

Of course, Heden thought. *Urmen use scouts too. We tarried here too long.*

Even squatting on their tiny legs, each urq stood larger than a man. At night their dark blue skin looked black as pitch, but here in the sunlight it glowed a deep indigo. Their long, massively muscled forearms stretched from their shoulders all the way to the ground. They used them to lope faster than a man could run. Their build gave them the use of heavy weapons and bows no man could lift or fire.

Each sported a thick layer of hard fat protecting almost as well as armor, and so some wore no armor at all. Most left their potbellies unarmored; it was a sign of masculinity among them. They had small, piggish yellow eyes and huge mouths full of wide, flat teeth. Two white tusks, each needle-thin and perfectly straight, jutted up out of the lower jaw and rose up to their temples, acting as natural protection from injury to the face or eyes.

Dull red powder coated them, sometimes on their shoulders or their forearms, or all over their bodies. It looked like blood but Heden knew it was rust. The Bloodrunners destroyed iron as part of a ritual.

Heden could not count how many stood on the other side of the river. They leered from behind every rock and tree. Dozens. The fierce, intelligent Bloodrunners knew how to effectively use cover and squad tactics, but Heden could call upon the incarnate power of a god, should it prove necessary. And it would not. He had many other tricks up his sleeve. The only problem was Aderyn.

The urmen watched Heden put his armor back on but interrupted once it seemed Aderyn might go do the same. Typical for the urq, they theatrically announced their presence. They liked inspiring fear. But it cost them the initiative.

Heden watched Aderyn search for her armor while trying not to panic. Heden sensed this and spoke her name. "Squire Aderyn."

She turned to look at him. Her eyes wide. She started to speak, but Heden interrupted her. He put his left hand on his breastplate, held up his right hand and prayed to his saint.

Aderyn, naked, gasped as a flash of light blinded them both. When Heden's eyes recovered from the glare, the squire stood before him in a full set of golden ornamental plate armor. She had no weapon and there was no helm, but the articulated plate armor covered the rest of her body like no real armor could. She was a warrior-goddess. The plate's winged filigree made her look like she'd stepped out of a stained glass window.

It was a gift. From Heden's saint to Aderyn. A reward. For what, Aderyn could not know. But Heden knew. Aderyn could not have worn that armor if she and Heden had succumbed to temptation.

"How long will it last?" she asked him, marveling at her hands and arms covered in flexible, impenetrable golden metal. The only sound was the urq marshaling. He could hear them. They had only moments before the bloodshed began.

Heden seeing her outfitted thus, she was no longer an object of desire. More than anything, he wanted her to succeed. To become a knight. To become the kind of knight she believed in. He had no idea if this was even possible now.

"Nothing lasts forever," he said cryptically. Her eyes shot up to meet his, reacting to his answer. An answer to no question she asked.

The sun sparkled on the river behind them, and the moment was over. He turned, hand reaching to the pommel of his sword to draw it from its sheath, and saw the full might arrayed against them.

He reeled. There were hundreds of urmen, all Bloodrunners. They'd poured out of the forest while he'd prayed. Heden hadn't though there were this many Bloodrunners in all the tribes in all the thousands of miles of the Iron Forest.

One of them held aloft a great torch, a great red guttering flame. It was their battle standard. A sorcerous thing, it fed on the blood of their enemies. Heden had seen one before, and he suddenly couldn't see anything else. His eyes fixed on it, and he stopped breathing.

It was like unmooring a boat. His eyes no longer saw the urq in front of him. His mind translated to another episode like this.

The urq, dozens of them, boiled out of the forest, leaping, loping, hurling themselves towards the river, towards Heden and Aderyn.

Aderyn smiled a wolfish, feral grin and crouched, ready for battle. Glad for the challenge. Ready to prove herself, test the mettle of the Green against the might of the Bloodrunners.

Like an arrow fired from a bow, she surged forward to meet the Bloodrunners. But she sensed she was alone. Turning as she ran, she saw Heden still standing there, unmoving, unseeing.

"Heden!" she shouted. She instinctively ran faster, trying to cover more ground, engage the urq as far from Heden as possible, give him more time to ready himself. What was wrong with him? She didn't understand it. She could not reconcile what she knew of him with someone who would be gripped by terror at a few dozen urmen.

Trusting Heden to defend himself, the squire of the Green slammed into the descending line of scouts. Their armor was makeshift. Traded for and stolen. Their weapons all axes taken from men and huge two-handed swords that no man could wield.

She identified one urq using a shield, small for him, perfect for her, and launched herself into the air, speaking a prayer to Halcyon as she did so.

Her right heel connected with the urq's head, slamming into it like a battering ram. She aimed her attack precisely to avoid the urman's tusks, as they would deflect and absorb any such attempt. For an instant the prayer made her limbs like stone mauls, and the blow threw the urq back, flinging its shield up in the air. She grabbed it before he hit the ground, and whirled on another urq closing in on her.

At some point in the metal shield's history someone, probably the urq she'd stolen it from, had given it a serrated edge. She dodged one massive axe swing, then sliced the sharpened edge of the shield through the thick layer of muscle and fat that had until this point protected the urq's pink intestines. He went down instantly.

Now she had an axe.

And still Heden did not move. She was effectively keeping the urmen off him, but there were too many. Eventually they would swarm her and have him.

"*Heden*!"

This was a bad one. He was with the Sunbringers going out into the forest to preempt the sack of Hoddenhill. In the real battle his company was victorious but he was badly wounded, his ribs crushed. Heden grasped his chest with the memory of it.

He seized up, arms and legs locking in a whole-body clench. He wasn't even aware of it, only of the vision of explosions as huge trees snapped like twigs and men screamed while an army of urq, their blood-red flame empowering them, lay waste to the town. Heden could do nothing. He heard the screams and saw the blood-soaked smiles of urq stamping in the blood of the townsfolk.

"*Heden*!" a voice cried. It was Stewart Antilles, the Hospitaller. A troll had swung his terrible mace and crushed Heden's breastplate. Stewart ran in full plate mail across the field to save him. He wouldn't arrive in time. Heden was dying.

"Heden, it's me! It's Aderyn!"

It was the nightmare logic of the dream, events happening out of order, repeating. He felt the slam of the troll's great maul hit his chest and bear him through the air.

But this time, instead of hitting the ground, he splashed into water. He gasped, swallowing water. He was drowning, his clothes heavy and soaked, his steel breastplate bearing him down while several thick arms grappled him under the surface.

He looked down through the murk, grabbed the arms and felt them. They were urmen. Urmen trying to drown him. He suddenly panicked and thrashed about. He wasn't sure what was happening or how he could stop it, but he was drowning.

Aderyn watched as Heden, borne into the water by five urq, finally burst into action. He might have been able to save himself but she wasn't taking any chances. She hacked at the neck of an urq that stood in her way, and in spite of its great strength and the thickness of its skin and density of its bones, more than a match for any normal man, it was unequal to the power of the Green. The urman's skin split from its collarbone down to its beating heart, and it fell while Aderyn leapt into the water.

She dove into the air dropping her axe and shield—they would only hinder her—and breathed deeply before hitting the water.

Even in the deep water, the strong current, her divine armor hindered her not at all. But the urq could hold their breath much longer than a man. All they had to do was outwait Heden, and their opposition would be halved.

Though the arrogate struggled, he had no air and could not speak a prayer or reach any weapon. Add to this his disorientation, the heavy pack on his back adding to his weight, and he was almost dead.

Aderyn expelled some air in a prayer, and the five urq holding Heden down stopped worrying about him and grabbed at their throats. Each started to kick its tiny legs and swim up to the surface, but Aderyn knew that air would do them no good. She ignored them and swam down to Heden, whose struggle lessened. He was drowning.

The river water started to cloud. Great billowing gouts of black ink erupted from the mouths of the urq. They were bleeding out gallons of their ichorous blood into the river. Twisting and writhing in the clouds were the thorny vines summoned by Aderyn's prayer. The vines erupted from the urmen's throats, ripped out of their mouths, tore out their tongues and snapped their jaws with the strength of growing trees.

In moments the urq were dead, their bodies floating up to the surface. Aderyn swam under the cloud of blood and found the limp form of Heden. Grabbing him by the edge of his breastplate, she pulled him up and began to swim to the other side of the lake.

She heard a distinct sound in the water around her, unmistakable. Like dragonflies zipping past her ears. Heavy black urq arrows shot into the water, trying to slow her escape. The arrows lost all momentum once they hit the water—she knew she was in no danger. The urq probably did as well, but wanted to make sure she knew they were there and she wasn't getting away.

She stayed underwater as long as she could. Swam as far as she could. Eventually she had to come up for air. She wasn't sure if Heden was alive or not—he'd been underwater some time without moving—but she couldn't leave him behind. She had to make the attempt.

As she kicked with her legs and strove through the water with one free hand, she felt the sudden flood of water against her bare skin and realized Heden's divine armor had faded abruptly. She was naked again. But maybe far enough away now.

Needing air, she surfaced. The urq loosed more arrows. She looked to the far shore. Roughly four dozen urq archers, four units, fired black arrows at the water. Their massive bows could easily clear the river, wide though it was. But at the moment only Aderyn's head was visible above the surface. A small enough target to keep the odds in her favor.

As she swam she pulled Heden's head above water. She didn't know if it would help, but she knew keeping him underwater was no good.

Finally reaching the far shore, she dragged Heden's waterlogged body out of the river and onto the wet ground, laying him down on a bed of moss and decomposing leaves.

Arrows thudded into the ground near her. She didn't have long. She could deal with one or two arrows, but each one would slow her and make her vulnerable to more arrows until eventually the urmen decided to ford the river.

She stopped, looking at Heden's breastplate, and suddenly didn't know what to do. An arrow struck less than a foot from his head, its black, raven-feathered shaft buried six inches into the ground.

She couldn't tell if his heart was still beating without listening for it, and she wouldn't be able to hear it through the breastplate. But she was completely naked. His breastplate was the only armor between them. And he needed armor more than she did.

She put her hand on his neck and felt for a pulse, trying to concentrate as arrows rained down around her. Were they getting closer? More accurate?

She felt a faint throb. His heart was dying, but not yet dead. He wasn't breathing. His face turned blue.

She rolled him onto his stomach and pushed on his back. Water gushed out of his mouth. She did it again and this time there was water and a sound, like vomiting.

An arrow slammed into her back, just under her ribs. She looked down and saw the sharp obsidian arrowhead protruding several inches from her stomach. No pain yet, just shock. There wasn't much time. She'd been hit by arrows before, but never while so defenseless.

The urq's triumphant war bark carried sharp and clear across the water.

Aderyn tried a prayer over Heden, rolled him over. He coughed, more water came out of his mouth, but he wouldn't breathe normally.

Another arrow pierced her right calf, pinning her leg to the ground.

"Ugh!" she grunted, and worked to pull herself free. She snapped the arrow so she wouldn't be pulling the muck-covered arrowhead through her leg.

The urq barked again, a different shout: the command to advance. The arrows stopped as the urq leapt into the river.

Aderyn looked down at Heden, his lungs working to draw in air, and nausea gripped her.

She looked down at the arrow protruding from her stomach and felt the blood-covered tip. There was no need. She knew by the blood in her veins.

Poison.

She slumped forward, losing control of her muscles. She looked down at Heden, tried to stay upright, stay conscious. He seemed to be breathing, but he was not yet conscious. Her prayer might have worked…if she'd done it sooner.

She collapsed on his unconscious form while the river, clogged with madly swimming urq, roared behind them.

Chapter Thirty-five

Heden opened his eyes and felt paralyzed. His arms and legs would not obey him. It took him a moment to realize this was because they were pinned under a weight.

Aderyn.

She lay on top of him, breathing but unconscious. He blinked a few times. His mind was clear now. He felt like a tree had fallen on him, but the panic that took his mind from him was over.

He sat up and held Aderyn in his arms. He surveyed her body and saw the problem, knew she'd been poisoned. This was no matter, as Brys would say. He unceremoniously ripped the arrow from her torso and cast it aside. Pulled the broken arrow out of her leg.

He heard a sound, like the sound of the running river, but louder, rougher. The urmen were getting closer.

He stood up. There were something like two hundred urq swimming across the river, shouting and goading each other on, the closest only a moment from shore. This was only one scouting party; there would be at least two.

"Black gods," Heden said with dread marvel.

The urmen climbed ravenously out of the water and laughed at the frightened man and the naked woman.

Heden's problem was his experience. It had been so long since he'd fought urq, since he fought anyone, he suddenly couldn't remember any prayers. Or rather, could remember too many, and most useless.

Then he remembered his pack. It had many easy solutions within. The leather was wet, but waterproof.

He prayed over Aderyn, a more potent prayer than the one she'd said over him, and her wounds closed, the poison purged from her veins. Her eyes flashed open, instantly awake and aware.

"Heden," she said.

"Hello," he said, smiling.

They could both hear the urq coming towards them. The urq could be quiet as flying owls when they wanted to, but this time they wanted the humans to know they were coming. It was a terror tactic.

She tried to cover her nakedness. She wouldn't look him in the eye. "There's so many of them," she said.

Heden reached into his pack and pulled out the long, thin blade of *Starkiller.*

He turned his back on her, wanting to give her some privacy, and faced the urq company with the dwarven artifact blade in his right hand.

"Not for long," he said.

The urq loped towards them, bristling with weapons.

He raised *Starkiller* to the sky and spoke a single word.

"*Starfall,*" he said in Elemental. His sword flared violet, and the blue sky above turned instantly black, revealing a night sky studded with stars.

The urq stopped, some still crossing the river, and looked up in awe at the darkness. It was the last thing any of them would ever see. The stars above began to rain down like small white comets, making a hissing, slashing sound in the sky. Each unerringly struck a single urq. Each urq evaporated from the impact, leaving only a scorched and smoldering crater and the smell of burnt flesh.

The *starfall* lasted a while. There were a lot of urmen to kill. Eventually Aderyn stood up to get a better view, and still the stars came down. She looked up in awe at the black sky and the falling stars, and then looked at Heden, his sword upraised to the heavens, summoning their power to earth.

Once the spell was done, Heden looked around, the sky still dark. It would slowly lighten, was already lightening. He had no real understanding of how it worked, and of whether the knights at the priory or even the people at Ollghum Keep saw the night sky.

The river was choked with urq corpses, the ground before them sizzled, hot with cooking meat and fat. Satisfied that the urq were all dead, and feeling a little self-congratulatory that he had remembered what the sword could do and so did not need to call on his god or saint, he smiled to himself and then turned to Aderyn.

She didn't smile back. She was still naked and looked at Heden with open fear. He turned away. He fished in his pack and pulled out some of his clothes. He held them over his back. He heard her walk up to him and take the clothes.

"If you can do that," she said as she dressed, "you could save everyone at the keep."

He shook his head. Everyone looked to him to do the impossible.

"Good against a few hundred urq. They have *five thousand*." He quoted Baed: "It takes men to hold the field."

There was silence as she considered her next question.

"What happened to you at the river?" she asked. "Was it the wode?" The wode, they both knew, could pervert perception.

The question gave him goosebumps. He didn't like to remember, but knew he had to talk about it. Not talking about it gave it power over him.

"Just me," he said, coughing. "Just me."

He sensed she was dressed, and turned. She had tied his too-large shirt tight around her, and had rolled up the legs of his leather pants.

"Are you…" she started. She was confused. "What possesses you?"

"Just fear," he said. "And memory. I can't control it."

"What memories?" she asked, fear and awe mixing.

"This place," he said. "The wode. Any forest. It's hard," he said. "I spent a lot of time, years, in places like this. A lot of terrible things happened."

"Nothing will happen while I am here," Aderyn urged.

Heden coughed and laughed at the same time. What kind of woman would say that? Then he reminded himself. The kind who'd been a squire for thirteen years.

He was overwhelmed with emotion. This often happened after an episode. Though there was not usually anyone there to see it. Thankfully.

"I..." she said, then turned away. "I must go find my armor," she said, as though recovering from a dream. "It is not seemly for a knight to be seen thus." It would be a while before she could talk about what just happened. Probably she would feel better with her armor.

As he heard her walking away behind him, Heden tested something.

"You will be a knight," he said, his back to her. It was not a question.

He could hear she'd stopped. Had no idea what she was doing.

"Aye," she said quietly. And went back to find her things. Heden put *Starkiller,* for which he had no scabbard, back into his pack. He left the river behind, not wanting to see the ruin of the urmen any longer, and walked back into the forest at a leisurely pace.

By the time Aderyn found him, it was broad daylight again, thick pillars of sunlight streaming down from the tops of the trees, as though the sunlight itself were holding up the canopy of leaves.

He heard her striding towards him through the wode. He turned and saw her, and whatever had passed between them before the urq seemed to be gone. He relaxed. She, on the other hand, did not.

"We've got to get back," she demanded.

"What's wrong?" Heden asked. They had found what they were looking for, had known the army was there and where it was going before they'd even left the priory.

"They're too far south," she said, "too fast. Someone must be told."

Heden did some quick mental calculation. The scouts usually kept a day ahead of the regular army. Sometimes ranging farther afield, but usually a day. Farther meant any situation they came upon would be changed by the time they reported back.

They had just obliterated several units of urq scouts. This would blind the army for a little while at least. But where were they?

"How far from Ollghum Keep are we here?"

Aderyn looked to the south. "A day for us," she said.

That meant the urq army was at best two days away from the keep. Heden had no idea they were that close. He'd lost all sense of direction as they ran through the evening. And because of the way he'd found the priory, he had no real understanding of where the priory was in relation to the keep.

"I've got to go back," Heden said.

Aderyn nodded. "The knights must be told. We leave immediately."

"No," Heden said. This brought her up short. "You tell the knights. I'm done wasting my time with them. I'm going to tell the people of Ollghum Keep that the Green Order has abandoned them. I don't care what the baron says," he said mostly to himself. Aderyn had no knowledge of Heden's argument with the baron. "I'll start a riot if I have to, but someone's got to do something."

Heden turned to walk away. Aderyn grabbed him.

"If you speak the ritual," she said, looking up at him, pleading. He found it hard to return her gaze. "The knights will be free to act. To stop the urq."

"I can't," Heden explained. "It doesn't work that way. The ritual doesn't absolve them, *I* do. I have to *know* what happened. I have to *believe* Kavalen didn't die in violation of his oath. Then the ritual can be effected."

"Then there will be no order," she said, pulling back and looking at his breastplate blankly. "And I will be no knight." He didn't know what she meant. They were talking about one knight, their leader, but still only one dead knight. He grabbed her shoulders. She could have stopped him, pulled away, but she let him.

"Then tell me what happened to Kavalen."

"I was not there," she said, looking at the ground. "And what I know, I cannot say."

"Even if it means those people die?" he asked. He realized she probably never met the people of Ollghum Keep. They were an abstraction to her. And now it was too late.

"If you were right about our oaths," she said, looking up at him. "Then I cannot tell you."

Heden pushed her away. He rubbed his temples. This place and these people were going to drive him mad, everything was intertwined with everything else. It was a huge knot. There was no thread he could pull at that could unravel it. Everything he said and did seemed to make it tighter.

She stepped closer to him.

"Take me with you," she said.

He swung about, trying to disguise his horror. She had not given up the war, only the battle.

I underestimated her again.

"I can't," he said.

"If we spent more time together, away from this place," she began.

"That's what I'm afraid of."

She didn't disguise her anger this time.

"I saved you," she reminded him. "And you saved me." He saw it in her eyes and realized what was going on. She had lost faith in the order, but found it anew in Heden.

Heden could not bear the burden of being responsible for destroying Aderyn's knighthood. He knew if he stayed here any longer, she would say the right thing, or he would talk himself into something.

She would hate him for it, but maybe she needed to hate him to get on with her life. "Tell the knights," he said. "Don't tell the knights, I don't care. I'm going to Ollghum Keep, and then home."

He wasn't that good a liar. She could tell he cared and it pained her to see him lie to protect her.

He turned away and darkly said: "You're on your own."

He forced himself to walk away. Leaving her alone in the forest. Whatever her answer was, he knew he wasn't it. And she would have to find it here.

He found he was furious at the baron, at Sir Taethan—for reasons he didn't exactly understand—at Gwiddon and the bishop. But most of all, angry at himself.

He tromped through the forest, trying to put some distance between himself and Aderyn before wrestling the carpet out of the pack. He wanted a good clearing to take flight from.

As he looked for a likely spot, not watching where he was going, his foot snagged on a root and he pitched face-first into the dirt. He pushed himself up and brushed himself off, turning to look at what had tripped him, and saw it.

He'd come back the same way they'd left, and here was Sir Perren, still sitting against the tree. Heden could see him clearly now in the daylight.

But now he was dead. Had been dead for what appeared to be weeks. Heden was certain he'd still been flesh and blood last night. But now his face was a withered, desiccated husk of skin pulled tight over a protruding skull, the only part of him now visible. His body, his arms and legs, were all covered in thick ivy at the base of the tree.

Vines grew out of his gaping mouth and eye sockets. They were already flowering, drinking in the sun. They were beautiful.

He feared what it meant. It was an omen, and more, a terrible reality. A knight had been killed here and as far as Heden could tell, the murderer surrounded him.

The forest itself.

Chapter Thirty-six

Heden spoke a prayer, and five men, each red-faced, shouting, holding various improvised weapons, in various stages of drunkenness, fell to the ground. The inn went silent as all eyes turned to Heden, everyone thinking he'd just killed five men.

In concert, the men on the floor all started to snore loudly. The inn relaxed.

Renaldo had frozen in place as his attackers slumped before him, his rapier still pointed at where the lead ruffian had been standing. He had one leg on the back of a chair, another on a table with food and drink now scattered over it, and his off-hand reaching up for the candleholder that hung from the ceiling.

"There were only five of them!" he objected.

Heden walked up to him, gingerly stepping over the sleeping idiots, as Renaldo uncurled himself from his fighting pose.

"Playtime's over," he said to the Riojan troubadour.

Renaldo looked away, disgusted, and then turned a scowl on Heden. "Good entrance," he admitted reluctantly. "Terrible sense of timing, though." He sheathed his rapier and smoothed the ruffles out of his expensive silken tunic, the red vest matching his red hose.

"It's time for you to get out of here," Heden said.

Renaldo's look changed. He stared at Heden.

"If it were anyone but you saying it, friend. Give me time to collect my earnings. There are many in town who owe me for a week's gambling profits."

Heden grabbed Renaldo's tunic and pulled the little man forward. Initially, Renaldo tried to object but once Heden started to whisper in his ear, he stopped struggling and listened.

"There are five thousand urq less than two days' march from here."

He released Renaldo. Taking time for one perfect, comedic beat, Renaldo replied: "They can keep their money. When do we leave?"

"We?" Heden said. "No."

"We!" Renaldo said, turning and grabbed his lute. "Yes!"

"No, I'm serious," Heden said. "You can't go where I have to go." For one thing, Heden hated flying two on the carpet. He looked around the packed room at the people still seeming to enjoy themselves. "You don't seem to have had much effect on these people."

"No?" Renaldo asked. "I doubt there is a man here who was present last time we met. These are farmers and tradesmen from outlying villages, newly arrived. I have spent my time inspiring the citizenry to take matters into their own hands and travel south to safer lands." He stopped suddenly, looking past Heden, mouthing the words he had just spoken. His hands assumed positions on the fretboard and strings of his lute and he mimed playing a few fictitious notes as he mouthed the words again, his head moving back and forth.

"Not bad," he said and looked back at Heden. "In any event—" He slung his lute over his shoulder and draped his cape over one hand. He pointed accusingly. "—you owe me a tale, and as I surmise you are not yet dead, it is not too late."

"Listen, Renaldo," Heden said. "That army…I just stopped here to tell the baron the order isn't coming. And give you the word so you could get out."

"How did the baron react to that?" Renaldo asked.

"Don't ask," Heden said darkly. "Let's just say it's me here telling you to leave and not the baron telling everyone to leave. I'm caught up in this now so unless you *really* hate urmen and want to kill a few before you die, you've got to get out of here."

"You're staying?" Renaldo asked, suspicious.

"I'm…it's complex." Heden didn't know what he was going to do.

"You and I against five thousand urq?" Renaldo pondered the issue. Heden was getting impatient. "I know many withering insults in urqish." He appeared to make up his mind. "You don't happen to know three more dependable men? I would feel more comfortable with five against five thousand. It is more…dramatically it has…" The Riojan waggled his hand. "You understand."

Heden stared at him.

"I'm leaving," Heden said, turning to leave. "You're on your own."

"Ahp!" Renaldo held up one hand, stopping Heden. Heden gave him one last chance.

"Now before you turn and stride away purposefully like a man exiting stage left, which you are very good at, I might add. You're a natural entrance-and-exit man, audiences love that. Before you go I want to point out that I am a far more subtle and clever man than you. More handsome as well, but that is no matter."

"What?" Heden asked, confused.

"I would never grab you in front of all these people to whisper some point critical to the plot in your ear. Far too obvious."

Heden stared at him for a moment, parsing what he just said.

Renaldo's eyes flickered almost imperceptibly to a spot behind Heden and to his left. There was no way anyone else in the room could have seen it even if they were looking for it.

Heden didn't acknowledge Renaldo's meaning, but Renaldo smiled widely as he realized Heden had it.

Heden grabbed a passing patron—easy to do in an inn packed with townspeople and refugees—pulled out his hand and plunked a crown in it. "Get to the stables," he told the bearded farmer, "and get me the fastest horse in town. There's another crown in it for you if you're back in half a turn."

Heden didn't even pay attention to the man's response but, having turned to stop the man, used the opportunity to look as discreetly as possible in the direction Renaldo indicated.

There was, among the press of people, a small table in the corner at which sat a polder. A small man-like creature about three feet high. He had a mass of curly blonde hair atop his wide face and appeared to be sleeping, his head lying back against the wall, his mouth open, a half-empty bottle of strong liquor in front of him.

Heden would have thought nothing of it, but for the fact it was the only table at the inn with only one patron at it.

Heden turned back to Renaldo.

"Okay," he said. "Now it's time for you to go."

"Very well, if you insist. I heard tell you were a prelate," Renaldo said. "Where are you from?"

"Celkirk," Heden said. He didn't bother telling Renaldo about the Hammer & Tongs. He'd enjoy it more finding out on his own anyway.

"I have not been there. A week's ride on a fast horse, I hear. Too far, I think. Perhaps I shall continue east."

Heden extended his hand.

"I hope we meet again," he said awkwardly.

"Oh we will," Renaldo said, doffing his elaborate cap and taking the proffered hand. "The gods are terrible at second drafts. And once they cast a man in a role, they never change their minds."

With a smile and a discreet flourish, the Riojan troubadour was gone.

Chapter Thirty-seven

Heden sat down at the table and for a moment the polder pretended to wake up, then saw who was sitting across from him and clucked his tongue. All pretense gone.

The little man gestured for a barmaid's attention and indicated he and Heden would both have a drink. Heden noticed he was ordering another drink without having finished his own.

The polder was short, typical of his race. He had dark green eyes and a small button nose in the middle of a round face framed by blonde locks. He looked young, but his skin was weathered. Most polder couldn't grow beards, but this one had light blonde stubble on his chin and jaw.

"Figure you know who I am," Heden opened. He didn't ask the polder's name and they both knew why.

The polder looked around the room, taking a reading of it. He registered everything and everyone. Heden had seen it before.

"The minstrel," the polder said. His voice was an odd mix of age and youth. Weary in expression, light in tone.

Heden nodded, confirming the polder's suspicions.

"Figures," the little man said.

The barmaid brought their drinks. Heden studied his opponent. There were many reasons why someone might send an assassin to kill him. But this was more like a spy making contact.

"Why don't..." The polder stopped to reconsider what he was saying. He finished his first drink while he talked. Downed it in one smooth gulp. It didn't appear to have an effect on him. Heden noticed a degree of unease. Unfamiliarity. Probably not faked. "Why don't you tell me what you know about the Green Order?" he asked.

The Green Order.

How many people knew Heden was up here working on the order? And of those people, who could possibly care? No one had heard of them in...Heden cut the thought off. Obviously someone *had* heard of them. Kavalen's death was more complex than Heden guessed. It was a situation he already had only a tenuous grip on, and now for the first time in many years he felt like he might be in over his head.

Heden stared at the little man. "Man" was, he knew, technically incorrect, but people treated polder as smaller humans, even though they were no more humans than the urq.

Heden picked up his glass and took a drink. It was powerful stuff. He coughed once, discreetly, and put the glass down.

"You're from Celkirk," Heden said, an educated guess.

The polder didn't say anything. He just sat there, eyes wide and bright, waiting.

"Someone in Celkirk hired an assassin to come look into the order," Heden said. The reality of what he was saying, the sheer enormity of what was happening around him, was too large to take all at once. He had to break it up into little bits.

The polder screwed up his face.

"I'm not an assassin, man."

Heden raised an eyebrow.

"You kill people for money?" he asked.

"Well, yes," the polder said, annoyed. "I mean, sometimes. What's that got to do with it?"

"If there's any other definition of assassin, I've never heard it."

The polder shook his head, his ringlets dancing in a manner that belied his serious bearing.

"My people were wrong about you," he said. "Ah well."

Heden raised his eyebrows. "A spy?" he asked.

The polder twisted his mouth and shook his head. "We're terrible spies." He meant members of his species. His people were stereotyped as jovial cooks and often…

"You're a thief," Heden said.

The polder sniffed. "Proud to say it."

Heden nodded. Thieves and assassins hated each other, and this little man obviously felt very strongly about the subject. This meant he was guilded. Unguilded thieves worried about guilded thieves, guilded thieves worried about assassins. There were only three thieves' guilds in Celkirk—that narrowed it down.

"But you're not here," Heden said, "to steal anything."

"No," the polder said, starting on his second drink, "my vest buttons down over many duties."

"Like killing people," Heden said.

"Sure," his opponent said, as though it weren't an important point.

"But not me," Heden said.

The polder shrugged. "If I needed to."

"No."

"Pretty sure I could," the polder said, smiling.

"Nope." Heden explained. "The minstrel saw you. I don't know what kind of thief you are, but I know you're the kind who was sniffed out by a man who plucks a lute and begs for a living."

The polder's smile fell away. The room, though packed with drinking men and women, suddenly got colder.

Heden tried some more of the uske, but couldn't down more than a sip. He wiped his mouth. "Drinking," he said. "Sloppy. No professional would risk losing his edge."

Heden realized he was putting his life in danger. The knights left him in a foul mood and he wanted to see how far the thief could be pushed.

The polder sat up and leaned forward, angry, scowling.

"You shouldn't feel constrained by these people, all these innocent people," the polder said, pointing around him but never taking his eyes off Heden. "Thinking they might get hurt if we went at it. Because I'm here to tell you that if you push me far enough you'll be dead and I'll be out of here and the only thing these people will know is that someone got stiffed on the bill."

Heden was impressed. But he'd noticed something about the polder, and so pushed. He leaned back in his chair and put his right arm over the top of the high back, relaxing. Insulting the polder with his attitude. "You like talking," he said, smiling. "If you were any good, you'd keep your mouth shut and then maybe I'd be afraid."

The polder frowned at the insult with quiet confusion and outrage. He situated himself in his chair.

"Do you…" He stopped, looked at Heden anew and started again. "Listen, I know what happens if one of us kills a priest, especially a Cavallite, but don't think that's going to…" He was flustered. Heden was right about him. "I know you're not a priest, so whatever these ignorant pigfuckers usually give you because they're too stupid to see that you're…it's not working on me. Forget it. You get nothing."

Heden nodded. He had guessed the polder knew he wasn't a priest.

"I'm not a priest," Heden said.

"No," the polder said. "You *were* a priest."

"I was a priest," Heden said.

"That's what I just said," the polder replied, looking around as though to see if perhaps no one could hear him.

"What am I now?" Heden asked, as though taking the trick in Tanip.

"What…" the polder started, and then sat back in his chair and gave Heden a respectful appraisal. "I don't know what you are anymore," he admitted. "I know they kicked you out, but you still work for them."

"I could tell you didn't know," Heden said.

The polder's face lost none of its outrage and hostility. He sat forward again and stabbed a finger on the table.

"Don't push me. My curiosity is the only reason you're still alive right now."

Heden relaxed and smiled a little. "I know."

"You know," the polder said.

"Yes. You wouldn't try anything until you knew."

"I wouldn't," the polder repeated.

"No," Heden said. "Because you don't know how to get into the forest." Heden played his trump card. "That's why you're here waiting for me. You knew the forest wouldn't let anyone in, but you heard about a prelate who maybe did it. You knew they meant me, even though I'm not a prelate anymore. So you wait for me, find out what I am and what I know. Maybe you don't have to go in and find the order, maybe I'll tell you something that makes your whole trip moot.

"You never for an instant considered making a move on me because if I don't tell you what I know, then you go home empty-handed, which upsets your guildmaster. Let's say you kill me. You'd still have nothing. Your guildmaster is upset and you've got the church and all my friends coming after you too." Heden opted not to emphasize that his friends would be by far the most dangerous group to upset. "Better just to go home empty-handed and report to your betters."

The polder opened his mouth to object, let it hang open for a moment, then shut it and pursed his lips, nodding in approval at Heden's reasoning. He looked around the inn. Then looked back at Heden and nodded.

"You're good," he said.

Heden shrugged. "Threatening people probably works most of the time," he said, trying to make the polder feel better.

"It really does," the little man said smoothly.

"I'm pretty hard to threaten," Heden said. "Probably about as hard as you." He smiled. "Plus, I had an advantage."

"What advantage?" the polder asked suspiciously.

"You've got half a bottle of uske beet in you," Heden said, nodding to the empty glasses.

The polder didn't say anything.

"You think that means I can't take you?" he asked, his voice quiet.

Heden held out his right hand, steady as a rock.

The polder just looked at it. Heden saw him clench his fist reflexively, trying to stop the small tremors he thought no one noticed.

After a moment of staring at Heden's hand, the polder said: "That doesn't mean anything."

Heden was done embarrassing him. He'd made his point. He pulled his hand back. "I'm an arrogate," he said.

The polder took a few deep breaths, not liking how Heden just confronted him.

"Okay," the polder said and nodded, filing the term away. He composed himself. Happy to move on. "I don't know what that is."

"You could find out." It wasn't information to trade for, no reason to be secret. He explained the basic principle.

The thief accepted his description without question, just a nod.

"How'd you get into the forest?"

"Flying carpet," Heden said. He chose not to reveal the real method, in case the polder could duplicate it.

The polder whistled, impressed.

"You said you were a prelate."

"I was before I was annulled."

The polder was impressed. "That's high up," he said.

"Pretty high," Heden said, nodding slowly.

"So how would you, ah…how would you deal with someone like me? Here?" The little man tested him.

"Well," Heden said, playing along. "That depends on what I thought about you. Let's say I hadn't seen you down that drink like water."

The little man gave him a look, which he ignored.

"You'd be fast," Heden said. "Faster than me. And you'd be close to their best, if they sent you out here alone. So you have some talent," he said, referring to the normal man's ability to tap into magic with proper training. "Probably a mistake for me to get this close to you," Heden admitted. This seemed to surprise the polder.

"So I'd call on a dominion."

"You can do that?" the polder said, impressed and a little alarmed.

"Yep," Heden said.

"Quick enough?"

"I speak its name, that's it. It's not like speaking a prayer. The dominion *is* the spoken prayer of Cavall."

"How can you do that if you're not a priest?" the polder asked.

"The church dismissed me," Heden said. "Cavall did not."

The polder nodded. This was something he had not considered.

"I saw a dominion once," the polder said. "In Celkirk."

"Two years ago?" Heden asked.

The polder nodded.

"That was Radallach," Heden said.

"You're on first-name terms with a dominion of Cavall?" The polder was a little overwhelmed.

"No, Sir Radallach is the Medial Templar of the White Hart."

"The Hart?" the polder said. "The Hart can summon dominions?"

Heden nodded. "They're sponsored by the king and the church."

"And you know this Radallach?"

Heden nodded. "And his master."

"You have some powerful friends," he observed.

"Radallach is a piece of shit and someone should have put him down years ago."

"Okay," the polder said. "You have some powerful enemies."

"I just don't like knights."

"Well, me neither," the polder said. "So there's that."

Heden smiled. The polder smiled back. He looked idly at Heden's drink.

"What about you?" Heden asked.

"What about me?"

"Let's imagine you knew I'd been a prelate and what I could do. How would it go?"

"Oh," the polder said, now relaxed. He seemed to enjoy talking to Heden now, and Heden imagined he didn't get to do it often. He rubbed his hands together briefly.

"You see, you think you have to be fast because I'm so close to you here." Heden nodded agreement. "But really, distance is nothing. If I concentrate—" He snapped his small fingers. "—I'm across the table, across the room, no problem. There's not even a flash, just *blink* and I'm there."

"That had to be hard to learn," Heden said.

"You have no idea," the little man said slowly. "For years I thought it was a myth. Even when I saw my instructor do it, I thought it was a trick of the eye." Heden nodded and indicated for the polder to continue.

"Well, at the same time," he said, leaning back. He picked up the empty glass from his first drink and just held it. "I'd have my dagger out, same principle, and then through your breastbone and into your heart and that's it."

"Nice," Heden said.

"So the question is: can you call on the dominion before I get my dirk in your heart?"

"It's a short name," Heden said.

The polder just snapped his fingers again, meaningfully.

Heden nodded.

"So we call it a draw," the polder finished.

Heden opened his hands, displaying his palms. Yielding. He liked this little man and thought he sensed something behind the drink and violence.

"Okay, let's trade," Heden said.

"Trade," the polder said flatly.

"Sure," Heden said. "You can't get into the forest, I can. You know why you're here, I don't."

The polder shook his head slowly as he thought it through.

"Not sure how my masters would feel about that."

"How do you feel about it?" Heden asked.

"I feel like they don't care how I feel about it," the polder said ruefully.

"How about this? I'll tell you what I know; you decide whether to give me anything."

"Just like that," the polder said.

Heden shrugged. "Just like that."

"Why would you do that?"

"Goodwill to trade on later."

Silence for a moment.

"You sure you're not a spy?" the polder asked, mocking suspicion.

"I was going to ask you the same thing," Heden said. He smiled widely, genuinely. It seemed to disconcert his opponent.

The polder shook his head, his curls vibrating, as though he were trying to shake a thought loose.

"You understand how unlikely it is I'll ever be..." the polder began. He tapped the table with his middle finger, and looked up at Heden from under bushy eyebrows. "Listen, 'goodwill' is not my business. I told you, I'm not a spy. If I were, okay. But I'm not. Goodwill doesn't get you anything with me."

Heden shrugged. "I think it will."

"You do," the polder said flatly.

"Yes," Heden said.

"Why?"

"I'm a good judge of character."

The polder stared at Heden for a moment with his mouth open, looked away, stared out the window, realized his mouth was open, clapped it shut and looked back. He blinked.

"Ah..." the polder said, completely off balance as a result of Heden's trust in him.

"One of the knights of the Green Order was murdered," Heden opened.

"We know that," the polder said, taking a deep breath. Happy to be on familiar territory.

"How do you know that?" Heden asked. Who could know that? Who could even know there was anything *to* know?

The polder shrugged. "Just a simple servant, me." Heden accepted this; there'd be little reason to give a thief that kind of background.

"So you're not here to kill Kavalen?" Heden asked.

"Was that his name?" the polder asked, raising his eyebrows innocently.

"I'm guessing you know it was," Heden said.

"Good guess," the polder admitted. "No, I'm not here to kill their commander."

"Or me," Heden said.

The polder looked at him for a moment, judging some thought. Then made a decision. "No one knows you're out here but me," the little man admitted. "I found that out myself."

Heden nodded. "Thanks," he said, gracious for information the polder didn't need to give.

"I'm trying the 'goodwill' thing. It doesn't come naturally, just so you know."

"It gets easier as you go," Heden said, amused. Then his amusement vanished. "You checked into me in Celkirk."

The polder nodded. "Yep. You know there's a trull staying in your inn?"

Heden looked at him, his skin tightening. "She still there?"

The polder shrugged. "Was when I left." He looked at Heden and then frowned, trying to figure out why Heden was apparently angry. Then he saw it.

"Man I didn't…look I don't care if you've got fifty trulls back there working in shifts, why do I give a shit?"

Heden nodded.

"But you left some pissed-off people back there," the polder said, smiling. He seemed to enjoy the idea.

"Pissed off about the girl?"

"Oh yeah. Everyone's staying away for the moment, seems like a lot of people are afraid of you. Got a lot of interesting reactions bringing your name up."

"I bet," Heden said, relaxing a little.

The little man made a gesture, prompting Heden. "So, who killed the commander?"

"I don't know," Heden said.

"You don't know."

"Nope," Heden said.

"Well then what the fuck good are you?" The polder was a little upset.

Heden shrugged. "I've been wondering that for about three years now."

The polder shook his head. "Shit."

Heden watched him.

"You don't have a guess?" the polder asked hopefully, aware it was unlikely.

"All the other knights act like another knight, Sir Taethan, did it."

The polder pursed his lips, filing the information away, and nodded. "I can tell you don't buy that."

"I don't know what to think," Heden said. "They shut me out and then told me to go fuck a pig."

"Did they really say that?!" The polder was delighted at the idea.

"No."

"Oh."

"It's just an expression."

"That's disappointing."

"They're all committed to some kind of conspiracy of silence. They didn't want me anywhere near the place. Wouldn't talk to me, wouldn't help me. Won't let me help them."

"Help them do what?" the polder asked.

"I perform the ritual that absolves the order of Kavalen's death."

"Why you?"

"I'm…" Heden thought about it. The same question the mysterious knight he met and decapitated asked him. "I'm not sure."

"And the knights turned you away."

"Yep."

"That doesn't make sense. What did you find out?"

If the polder was trying to get Heden to reveal something useful about the order, Heden knew he was going to be disappointed.

"Well," he said, "he's certainly dead."

The polder waited, and when it became apparent there was no more he raised his eyebrows and said, "That's it?"

Heden shrugged.

"You don't know who killed the guy."

"Nope."

"You don't know how he died."

"Nope."

"You don't know where his body is."

"Ah, no."

"You have any idea why anyone would want him dead?"

"None."

"No idea why you were sent up here."

"Not really."

"And no idea why no one will tell you anything."

"I know what your assignment is now," Heden said.

"You do?" the polder replied, surprised.

"You were sent here to cheer me up."

The polder barked a laugh. Heden smiled. They liked each other. Heden liked having someone to talk to about this, and the polder seemed very at ease in the role. No argument.

"So why are you here?" the polder asked, indicating the inn.

"Going home. Giving up. Maybe convince some of these people to run while they can. Seems like the Green's going to do what the Green's going to do whether I'm there or not. No reason to be there and watch them all feel sorry for themselves until it kills them. Plus I hate knights. Not entirely sure why I was sent there."

"Maybe you weren't sent up here to do anything," the polder forwarded.

"What do you mean?" Heden asked as he rolled the idea around in his mind. He liked the taste of it, but wasn't sure if it made sense.

"In my experience," the thief said, looking at Heden's drink again, "smart guy like you ends up wandering around looking like an idiot, it's because he's been sent to catch fog."

Heden thought about this. It seemed obvious now, but at the same time made no sense.

"Plus," the thief said, "you hate knights."

Heden nodded, thinking about it. He was no longer looking at the polder. He wasn't looking at anything. "Yeah. So I'd be the guy to send…"

"If you wanted someone to get disgusted with it all and leave."

"Which is what I was doing."

"'Was?'"

Heden nodded again and came back to reality.

"Either I was sent to do a job," Heden said, "and so maybe I should stop feeling sorry for myself and go back and do it, or I was sent *not* to do a job in which case fuck that."

The polder smiled and toasted him.

Heden smiled back.

"What about you?" Heden said.

"Well," the thief said. "Not going to tell you what I'm here for, but I'll say I'm satisfied that things are going the way my masters would like."

Heden accepted this, but there was a little doubt, which the polder saw.

The thief shrugged. "Can't get into the forest anyway," he said. "Didn't know that when I left. You got a fucking flying carpet, nothing I can do about that." He sighed. "So I stay here awhile, keep an eye out to see if you come back out of the forest and then maybe discreetly follow you and see what you found out."

"Don't want to just wait here in the inn? I could just come find you."

"Heden," the thief said, "you're never going to see me unless I want you to."

This confirmed Heden's earlier suspicion.

"You let the minstrel see you."

"I'm three foot eight and this place is packed with people," the polder said, gesturing. "You think I couldn't avoid being seen if I didn't want to?"

"You deliberately made contact with me," Heden said, working it out as he spoke, "because you were sent here to kill someone, not me, but you don't know who and don't know how to find out. They just told you 'the Green Order.' So you blow your own cover, see if you can find out what I know. Maybe I find out what you need to know so you can kill the man you were sent to kill." Heden thought of Sir Taethan for some reason.

The polder frowned at Heden's sudden insight.

"Nobody likes smart people, you know that, right?" he said.

Heden frowned. "I'm liked."

"No you're not," the polder said, hopping off his chair. Heden watched the top of the polder's head bob around the table until he was standing next to Heden, keeping a professional distance.

"Let's imagine," the polder said, putting a fist on his hip, "you found out who killed Kavalen and then performed this, uh, ritual. What happens to the murderer?"

"I'd take him back to Celkirk," Heden said, making a half-turn in his chair to stay oriented on his rival.

"Good," the polder said, fishing some coin out from a purse at his belt.

"Giving you plenty of opportunity to kill him," Heden said, getting coin from his own purse.

"Yes," the polder said bluntly. He watched as Heden put down three crowns to cover the drink he hadn't touched.

"Why do the people you work for," Heden said, hoping the little man noticed he never asked who those people were, "want to kill a knight who murdered a knight?"

The polder reached out and picked up Heden's nearly full glass as though it were his own drink, and drank half of it.

"I have no idea," he said, stifling a belch.

"That bothers you," Heden said, saying nothing about his drink.

"I'm used to not knowing," the polder said without contradicting Heden.

"No you're not," Heden said, looking at his drink in the polder's hand. "You're used to being sent to kill someone without knowing why, but this is different. This time they couldn't even tell you who. They expected you to figure it out yourself, which is not your strength."

Heden was being confrontational, pushing the polder to see how he'd respond. It was a risk, but it paid off.

The little man didn't bat an eye, showed no signs of feathers ruffled. Heden's respect for him grew.

The polder drained the rest of Heden's drink, put the glass back, wiped his mouth with the hairy back of his hand.

"I'm not doing bad so far. I know who you are, and I know what you know, and you don't know who I am and don't know what I know." The polder pointed to the glass as he turned to walk away. "Plus, I got your drink off you, free. So…I win." He started to leave.

About ten paces to the door, he half-turned and, without looking at anyone, obviously uncertain and confused at his own uncertainty, the polder said: "My name is Aimsley."

He stood there, having said that, stared widely out the window for a moment, shrugged to no one and left.

Heden stood up, poured himself a drink from the bottle the polder had left, half-empty, and drank it in one gulp. His throat burned and tightened up, but he clenched his jaw, grimaced and forced it down.

He watched the people around him, the townsfolk, the villagers and farmers, and it was clear the inn was emptier than the last time he was here. Some people would never leave their homes, even should the World Below erupt and vomit forth its legions. The drink slowly spread out, warming him and relaxing him. He imagined it loosening a knot in his mind.

The urq, the sack of Ollghum Keep, the Green Order were not just an obscure problem at the edge of civilization. Someone wanted to destroy the order, and sent Aimsley the polder assassin to make sure they didn't leave the priory. Didn't do their duty.

Heden felt manipulated, but he couldn't tell by who or what. But he knew that if the Green Order fell, then the people who hired Aimsley won. Had beat him.

Shaking his head at the absurdity of what he was about to do, he vowed to try to save the Green Order one last time.

Chapter Thirty-eight

From the air Heden could see the knights standing outside the priory. Their pinions flying, their mounts readied, preparing for something. He circled overhead. The knights all looked up at him, but none of them seemed to give him more than a moment's thought. As though men on flying tapestries were something they saw all the time.

They gathered around the line of posts that marked the jousting field. Heden landed the carpet on the large, grassless circle of the melee. Sir Brys saw him and approached. The other knights ignored him. Isobel, Taethan and Nudd were on one side of the joust, the three dastards on the other. Taethan and Nudd helped Isobel with her armor. Cadwyr and Dywel helped Idris with his. Aderyn was nowhere to be seen.

Heden rolled up the tapestry, began feeding it into his bottomless pack.

Brys stood by and watched the laborious process. The pack slowly consumed the tapestry.

"That is a useful pack," Brys said.

"Yeah," Heden said.

"Why a tapestry?"

Heden worked to stow the thing away. Once he was done, he slung the pack over his shoulder, straightened his breastplate and stretched his arms. Then he looked at Brys and shrugged. "Why not?"

Brys frowned at him. Heden realized he was being an ass.

"It was a gift from a friend. From Qartoum."

Brys shook his head. The name meant nothing to him.

"It's a desert land," Heden said. "Not sure why carpets or tapestries are significant. Never thought to ask." Heden looked up at the blue sky and the thin wispy clouds. "Seems strange now that you bring it up. Seemed perfectly natural while I was there."

Brys accepted this.

Carpet stowed, Heden looked at the field. Saw Idris, now fully outfitted in plate from head to toe, being helped onto his horse by Cadwyr and Dywel. Isobel waited patiently on her horse, lance ready. It was a long, lethal thing, with a sharp, gleaming point.

"I thought she canceled the tournament," Heden said.

Brys stood next to him, also watching.

"This is not part of the tournament," he said.

Heden didn't understand.

"This is a quarrel between knights," Brys explained, folding his arms over his chest.

Heden looked at the knight. He was a hard, pragmatic man. Not driven by hubris or idealism. Of all the knights, Brys seemed the most sensible. Heden had to remind himself that this perspective and intelligence opposed Heden. And Brys wanted to command the knights. This put him at odds with Isobel at least, and possibly Taethan and Idris as well.

Heden wondered what kind of man Kavalen must have been, to have kept this motley band together. He doubted any of the knights could take his place. Maybe they each knew it.

Brys ignored him. He didn't seem particularly happy with what was going on, and Heden decided not to ask.

Heden strode across the field to Lady Isobel. Taethan challenged him with a look but said nothing. Nudd stood silent behind the lady knight.

"What's going on?" Heden demanded.

Lady Isobel's helmet covered her face. Her armor still covered in twigs and moss and small mushrooms, the metal looking green and opalescent in the sun, she looked down at Heden from her horse imperiously.

"What hast thou done with mine squire?" she asked.

"I left her in the forest," Heden said.

"And why wouldst thou do such a thing?"

Heden grabbed the reins of her horse, pulling it towards him. "She wanted to come back here and warn you about the urq. I went and told your sister that you weren't coming."

This obviously wasn't what Isobel wanted or expected to hear.

"How did..." Isobel began, and then stopped. "What was my sister's response?"

"Does it matter?" Heden said. "She'll be dead soon anyway."

It was a calculated gambit. Heden didn't have much in the way of leverage over these knights and he wanted to see what Isobel would do if denied something she wanted.

She stared at Heden for a few moments. Heden had no idea what she was thinking. Then she looked across the field at her opponent preparing.

"Thou art surely right," she said, composed. No reaction. There was nothing she could do from here. There was no point in being sentimental about it. And she had an enemy to face. And that was that.

The wrong sister became baron, Heden thought. If this woman was back at the keep, the urmen wouldn't stand a chance.

Lady Isobel looked down through her helm at Heden's hand on the reins of her horse, and Heden let go. She spurred her horse on, and the large animal trotted away.

Idris and Isobel took their positions on either side of the jousting run. They looked like two knights in a dream, each in full plate. Their lances long and deadly. Their horses towers of muscle and speed.

Taethan had joined Brys by the melee but now Brys was walking to Sir Nudd, leaving Taethan standing there alone. Heden eyed Sir Taethan, gritted his teeth and walked over to the knight.

Taethan said nothing to him, just watched from a distance as the two knights sat atop their horses, lances pointing skyward. Neither moving.

Heden turned and watched as well, he and the knight now standing next to each other.

"You're wasting your time here," Taethan said. Heden glanced up at him. He looked like a saint. Noble and powerful. Heden turned back to Idris and Isobel.

"My time to waste," Heden said. Neither of the knights moved. The sun beat down. "Where's Kavalen's grave?" Heden saw no reason to waste time. He didn't think Taethan would tell him anyway.

Taethan raised his eyebrows in reaction but did not look at the arrogate.

"There is a ceremony, and the dead knight is accepted into the heart of the forest. There is no grave, as you think of it." This was essentially what Aderyn had said.

Heden imagined the dead knight's body being consumed by moss and vines like Sir Perren's body. Or being absorbed by the soil and turned to peat. It was a nightmarish thought. But Taethan did not appear to be lying.

"What's Sir Nudd doing?" Heden asked, covering his eyes in the bright summer sun and looking at the Knight Silent gesticulating at the Knight Lieutenant.

"He pleads with Sir Brys to stop the joust," Taethan said.

"Doesn't look like Brys is going for it," Heden said. He forgot the knight's title, but Taethan didn't seem to mind.

"Brys says he cannot stop the joust," Taethan said. As though he could hear them. "He has not the power, and if he had the power he has not the right. And if he had both the power and the right he still would not."

"Lot of bloody-minded people around here," Heden observed.

Taethan looked down at him. "Your time to waste." He threw Heden's words back at him, but without malice.

"Alright," Heden admitted. Nudd looked like he was giving up on Brys. He tramped over to Cadwyr and Dywel, the bald spot at the top of Nudd's head red in the heat.

Lady Isobel and Sir Idris still sat on their horses, motionless.

"I knew I'd regret coming back," Heden said, shaking his head at the two knights.

Taethan said, "You have no interest in the joust?"

Heden glanced at him, and then turned to look at the two knights facing each other across the jousting field.

"It's a sport for rich idiots," Heden said.

"You speak of the tournaments they have in the south," Taethan said.

"Yeah," Heden said. "In the south."

"It is different here."

"I can see that," Heden said. He'd been watching the two knights for what seemed an entire turn. "How long are they going to sit there?" he asked. "Isn't there a trumpet or a scarf or something?" Heden looked around to see if anyone was acting as anything other than a spectator.

"The true joust is a test of mind as well as body," Taethan intoned. "There is no signal to react to. Only knowing the other knight. Neither wants to run first, neither wants to run last."

"Why not?" Heden asked, interested in spite of himself.

"Running early gives your opponent more time to watch you on approach, more time to react. Forces you to commit to a strategy before he does. Running late means your horse will not reach full gallop and therefore your blow will not be sufficient, should it land."

Heden thought about this.

"So what do they do?"

Taethan smiled. "They watch each other," he said. "And think."

"Exciting," Heden said.

"They study each other," Taethan continued, ignoring him, "and when the moment is right, they will both run."

"At the same time?" Heden asked, narrowing his eyes.

"Because each will know in the instant that it is the right instant."

Heden was intrigued.

"It is hard to explain," Taethan said. "Squires run early or late. Knights never do."

Heden watched the two knights, each sitting stock-still on their horse, lance up, each gazing at the other. The sun beat down, baking them in their armor.

"You have seen the joust before?"

Heden nodded. He didn't bother saying that the last time he'd been the guest of the king. It was the kind of thing Taethan wouldn't have cared about in any case.

"The popular joust is a sport," Taethan said. "It's ceremony and show. For the crowd," he said, looking down at Heden.

"The Green joust only for each other. It is how we resolve some disputes. And to train in the use of the lance against a real opponent, and so keep to the old ways."

At the end of his sentence, both knights spurred their horses on and began thundering down the field. It was impossible for Heden to tell who ran first, it seemed exactly as Taethan described. Simultaneous.

The hooves of their great chargers kicked up dirt. There was no sound in the clearing but the explosive barrage of hoofbeats and the clash of armor as their shields rang against their plate. The horses closed the distance so fast it seemed as though they were being pulled along by some outside force.

They both leveled their lances as they charged. At very nearly the last moment, Lady Isobel appeared to turn her lance sideways, perpendicular to the direction of her charge. Heden stared, forgetting everything but the joust as Sir Idris' lance reached the point where it would either hit or miss. The point of the lance was so small, Heden couldn't immediately tell that Idris missed.

He then charged at full speed into Lady Isobel's lance, which had been held crosswise like a barrier. The blow rocked Sir Idris, Lady Isobel's lance shattered and the force nearly threw Idris from his horse. The whole thing happened in less than four seconds.

"Black gods!" Heden tried to unpack what he'd just seen.

Taethan looked at him, surprised.

"Sir Idris leveled his lance at the head of Lady Isobel," he said.

"Okay," Heden said, following. He watched the two knights circle around. Each was given a fresh lance.

"The chest makes a bigger target of course, but the plate is designed to deflect any such blow. Even a blow to the shield, if dead center, can throw a man. It is difficult, the head. The most difficult. Lady Isobel saw this, and wagered that Sir Idris would miss."

"That's a wager with Cyrvis," Heden said.

Taethan tilted his head, indicating that perhaps it wasn't as bad a wager as Heden believed. "It is easier to see when yours is the head the lance is aimed at," Taethan said. "Idris having taken the hardest of all possible strategies, typical for him, Lady Isobel countered with the easiest."

"I get it," Heden said. Taethan finished anyway.

"By turning her lance crosswise, she ensured that Sir Idris would encounter it. She gains the surety of the cross-lance, losing any chance of missing, but at the possible cost of stopping Sir Idris' lance with her head. The cross-lance is not as heavy a blow as the point but it can unseat a man."

"What if Idris hadn't missed?"

"Then Lady Isobel would be dead."

Heden wheeled around, as though seeing the field for the first time. "Are you saying they're jousting to the death?"

Taethan nodded solemnly. "I told you, this is no tournament."

"Cavall's teeth," Heden swore. "What were they fighting about?"

Taethan looked at Heden and said nothing.

"Who leads the order," Heden concluded.

Taethan nodded. "And what to do about you, but they're much the same thing."

In the absence of Heden performing the ritual, without Halcyon to name a new leader, they were trying to solve the problem themselves.

"You have to stop this," Heden demanded.

This piqued Taethan's interest. He looked down at Heden as though seeing him for the first time.

"And why is that?" Taethan asked.

"It's not worth it," Heden said.

"That is for them to decide," he said.

"No it's not," Heden said, thinking madly. "Halcyon decides. Isn't that what Brys said?"

"Sir Brys," Taethan corrected automatically.

"*That's* what matters to you?" Heden raised his voice in outrage. "You should be out there talking some sense into them!"

"If I thought I could," he said, "I would. If I could, I would take the blow myself, though it meant my life. No knight should have to kill another."

Heden replayed what Taethan had just said, listening for any sign of falsehood. He detected none.

"And they fight for many reasons," he continued, sounding like a man defeated. "I think perhaps neither truly wants to win. Though each must strive for victory."

Sir Idris was trading up for a longer lance.

"Sorcery?" Heden asked.

Taethan shook his head. "There is no need for a sorcerous weapon here. And it would be cowardly."

"Then how's he going to hang on to that thing and ride a horse? It must be ten feet long."

"Twelve," Taethan said. "The weight is no matter."

"Magic," Heden said, as though this proved his point. Taethan shook his head.

"At the gallop," Taethan explained, "the horse is smooth, all its weight is moving forward." He mimicked the motion with his hands. "Not up and down. It cannot be sustained long, but it does not need to be."

"But..." Heden began.

"And the lance," Taethan said, demonstrating, "is not grasped using the whole hand thus. The butt is precisely weighted to offset the shaft and tip. A well-made lance can be held perfectly still at the full gallop using only the thumb and middle finger."

Heden watched.

"At the last, at the moment of impact, you wrap your whole arm around the lance, and put all your weight behind it. It must be precisely timed," Taethan said, enjoying talking about it. Admiring the skill.

"I bet," Heden said.

"The longer lance is harder to manage," he admitted, "but it grants an obvious advantage."

"Another wager," Heden said.

Taethan nodded.

Taethan and Heden were silent. Waiting for the knights to spur their horses on. Heden's mouth was going dry. He held his breath in anticipation.

So quickly, so violently that it startled him, Heden saw the two knights spur their horses on. Once again, at exactly the same moment. The next few seconds drew out to a seeming eternity.

Idris' longer lance hit Isobel's left shoulder, but caught on a rondel and tore it off. Isobel shifted with the blow but this didn't affect her right side, and she maintained her form. Her shorter lance smashed into Idris' shield, piercing it and ripping it from his grasp.

"That shield was useless," Heden observed. The blow rocked Idris. As the horses of the two knights trotted around, back to their starting positions, Idris looked clearly hurt.

"Rare for the lance to hit the shield thus," Taethan said. "Normally it is deflected. Lady Isobel has had much practice."

Heden remembered Nudd, who used his horse and lance to run a giant clean through.

"Watch," Taethan said, putting a hand on Heden's shoulder. He pointed to Isobel. "Lady Isobel will grant Sir Idris the chance to yield."

"Why would she do that? Honor?" Heden asked.

"Or mercy. The blow to the shield was a warning, I think."

"You're saying she stripped him of his shield on purpose."

Taethan shrugged. The gesture was not natural for him. "One never knows. Only the man on the horse can tell what his opponent was thinking."

Lady Isobel was already in position. Idris was getting another lance from Cadwyr.

Isobel let her lance drop slowly to the ground until the tip was touching the dirt. Cadwyr and Dywel pointed and Idris saw it. He appeared to ignore it.

"The offer," Taethan said.

Idris finished mounting and, with no shield, accepted a new lance from Dywel.

He guided his horse into position and lifted his lance until the point was directed at the sky.

"Refused," Taethan said. It seemed to Heden as though Isobel's head dropped slightly.

The two knights faced off against each other again. Moments passed. Time slowed.

"Who's going to win?"

"Lady Isobel," Taethan said.

"You know that?" Heden frowned.

Taethan nodded.

"Why?"

"Because hers is the purer heart," Sir Taethan stated matter-of-factly.

Heden stared at him.

"Is that a joke?" Heden asked.

Taethan ignored him. Heden tried a different tack, trying to home in on this knight.

"What would…what would Sir Brys say, if I asked him the same question?"

Taethan smiled a little, not looking at Heden.

"He would say the same."

"For the same reason?"

Taethan shook his head slowly once. "He would say: because she has the greatest insight into the mind of her opponent."

Heden understood. Now he was testing Taethan.

"And what would Aderyn say?"

This seemed to surprise the knight. He looked down at Heden.

"She would say Idris," Taethan admitted. "Because he is the stronger."

Heden and Taethan watched the knights. Then Taethan looked slyly at Heden and said, "Who do you think will win?"

"Isobel," Heden admitted.

"And why?"

Heden realized he believed it for the same reason Taethan did. He believed Isobel *had* to win because of her dedication to the order and the purity of her service. How could it be otherwise?

He didn't answer. He wasn't sure how to explain that he agreed with Taethan.

Suddenly Idris reached his now-shieldless left arm up, and wrestled his helmet off his head, throwing it into the dirt. He faced the lady, without a helm.

Isobel's horse balked at this, but she brought it back in line.

Taethan took a measured breath, as though recovering from a blow.

"What does he think he's doing?" Heden asked.

Sir Taethan's eyes seemed to dance around the field, seeing everything and nothing. It was like a ghost had passed through him.

"He seeks to shame her into withdrawing."

"What?" Heden said.

"You would not understand," Taethan said. "He is a noble fool." He shook his head and was overcome with sadness.

"Ah Isobel!" Taethan whispered. "Ah Idris!" He seemed in physical pain watching the two knights.

Idris' face looked flushed red.

"I don't understand," Heden said. "What difference does it make, he's just as dead if she hits him with that lance, helmet or not."

Taethan pulled on his breastplate as though it constricted his breathing.

"Please, arrogate. Be silent," Taethan said. "Be silent and bear witness."

Taethan's cheeks were wet. Heden realized they were tears.

Heden looked at the other knights. They all seemed distraught. Brys lunged forward as though to grab Lady Isobel, but Nudd reached out one massive hand and restrained him.

"Wait," Heden said, getting a flash of what was about to happen. "Wait!" he shouted and started to run forward. He wasn't sure what he was going to do, but he was compelled. He couldn't stand by and watch anymore. He broke into a full run. "Don't!" he bellowed.

The two knights at the same instant spurred their horses into the full gallop.

Isobel's helm afforded no expression of emotion, if there was any. Idris gritted his teeth and held to his lance, appearing to once again aim at the lady's head. Heden watched as the green bled out of Idris' hair, leaving his natural black behind. He would not die a knight.

The last thing Heden saw as he ran forward was Idris' face covered in sweat and tears. He too was weeping. Heden would add Idris' grimace of pain and fear and anger to the catalog of desecration he'd accumulated. The giant's dead face melded with Idris' as Heden's legs fell out from under him.

Idris couldn't see properly, so his lance came nowhere near the lady Isobel.

Her lance hit his breastplate square and pierced it clean through.

The blow separated him from his horse, his arms and legs thrown forward; the forward force of Isobel's horse and lance lifted Sir Idris up, into the air and back several feet before Lady Isobel released her lance and the knight fell to the ground before her. Dead.

All of the knights ran forward as Lady Isobel wheeled her horse around.

Heden stumbled to his feet and ran to the fallen knight.

Cadwyr and Dywel looked around, confused, at the other knights.

Nudd stared down into the unseeing eyes of Sir Idris, his hair wet with sweat, tears and blood. It was jet black. His mouth was open in a look of surprise.

Brys stepped forward and pulled the lance from Idris' breast. There was a wrenching sound and a squeal as the wood scraped against the twisted steel. He threw the lance away.

"What are you all standing around for?" Heden asked, looking at the knights.

He dropped to his knees before Sir Idris and began to pray. In spite of Heden's words, no power manifested.

"Heden," Brys said. Heden ignored him and continued praying. "Heden!" he said loudly and pulled Heden off Idris.

The arrogate scrambled around to face Brys. He looked as though he was going to throttle the knight.

"You forget yourself!" Sir Brys hissed. "He is dead!"

"Damn you," Heden said, "I can bring him back!"

"He was a servant of Cavall!" Brys shouted at him. "Cavall does not permit! He died at the hands of his sister!"

Heden realized Brys was right. Cavall would not grant Heden the power to return Idris to life. He'd been killed by another servant of Cavall. A betrayal of everything Cavall granted power for in the first place.

Brys' words made all the knights turn and look at Lady Isobel. She had dismounted and walked over to join them.

Brys saw the looks on the faces of Nudd, Cadwyr and Dywel. He turned quickly and looked at the helmed form of Isobel.

Isobel looked from one knight to the other. She reached a mailed glove up to her helm and felt it once, as though trying to sense something underneath. Then she pulled the helmet off, slowly. Deliberately. Heden knew what he was going to see.

Her hair was grey. No longer green streaked with grey, just dull grey. The grey of an old woman.

The other knights looked at her in shock.

"Halcyon!" Dywel hissed in fear.

"Milady," Brys said. "Isobel!" The word was torn from him. Isobel looked at him, disoriented, confused, and pulled some of her grey hair forward as though showing it to Brys.

Heden watched at Brys and Isobel and saw something between them. Brys loved her. He loved her for who knew how long, and she had sworn the vow of chastity.

Taethan walked up behind them. They didn't notice him at first. All eyes were on Lady Isobel. She turned and saw Taethan, held her hands out in front of her, pleading.

"What have I done?" Lady Isobel asked him.

Taethan looked at her with naked fury. His fists clenched. His teeth bared.

Everyone looked between Lady Isobel, shattered and confused, and Sir Taethan, the perfect knight, a tower of rage. Something was happening. Something Heden didn't understand. All the knights were watching Taethan, and Taethan's anger was directed indiscriminately.

He looked from one knight to the other, and then down at the forms of Idris and Sir Dywel, the weasel, cradling the dead knight's head in his lap and rocking back and forth.

Speaking to the knights, he hissed, "Nikros and Cyrvis have your bones," and he turned and strode into the priory.

"What will he do?" Cadwyr asked. Dywel was sobbing, Idris' dead face looking up at him, unseeing.

Brys and Isobel stared at each other. His need was evident, but she could see no way to bridge the gap. She seemed helpless.

Taethan came out of the priory and, ignoring the knights and Heden, turned to walk north into the forest. He carried his shield, his sword and his spear.

Heden looked at the knights, watched Taethan disappear into the forest, and ran to the melee where he'd left his pack.

He scooped the pack up as he ran past, slung it over one shoulder, and ran into the forest after Taethan.

Chapter Thirty-nine

Heden jogged into the forest after Taethan. He couldn't see the knight and soon had run so far into the wode that he was beginning to get disoriented. The trees were massive, primordial things. The ground was thick with dead leaves and ferns and vines and bushes. The sun was up there, somewhere above the canopy of leaves, but Heden couldn't orient to it.

He heard a noise behind him and turned. Taethan had stepped out from behind a tree. A tree Heden had just run past. Where had he been standing?

"You should stay at the priory," the knight said. He appeared melancholic. Haunted.

Heden looked around, as though maybe Taethan was talking to someone else.

Before Heden could respond, Taethan turned, walked straight into the tree, and disappeared.

Heden cursed and then spoke a prayer granting him endurance. Turning to face what he believed was west, and therefore in the direction of the urq army, Heden ran as fast as he could.

The knight wanted to lose him, but Heden was no acolyte. He made a lot of noise but covered a lot of ground.

He stopped, catching his breath, leaning against a tree. He looked around. Taethan could be behind him, in front of him. Could have gone in another direction entirely. Heden could, in fact, be getting himself lost. There was no way to know.

He considered whether to pray for guidance or continue running when Taethan stepped out of a tree ahead of him. He heard Heden's heavy breathing and turned to see the arrogate leaning against a tree.

He paid Heden the compliment of looking surprised.

Heden gasped air but pointed at the knight.

"You kicked me out of the priory," Heden answered.

The knight recovered from his surprise and looked on Heden with something like pity. This annoyed him.

"The keep then," Taethan said. "You may do some good there."

The knight turned and walked back into the tree.

This time would be harder. Heden knew he was going west, trying to intercept the army of urmen. Heden began running again. There was no sound in the forest but his breathing and his boots crunching leaf and branch beneath them.

This time, calculating the range of Taethan's ability, Heden stopped and looked around, trying to guess which, if any, tree Taethan would emerge from.

He didn't hear a noise behind him, but rather the sudden and suspicious absence of noise. Taethan had probably never met a professional thief, and so did not know the difference.

Heden turned. He'd overshot by forty feet or so. Sir Taethan was standing before the tree he'd just emerged from. He managed to look annoyed at Heden and regal at the same time. Heden hated knights.

"The people at the keep," Heden said, breathing heavily. "Are going to die whether I'm there or not. The smart ones have already left."

"Home then," Taethan said, closing the distance across the forest floor, stepping easily among the roots and ferns. "You hate the forest. You hate us. Sirs Perren and Idris are dead and Commander Kavalen's death cannot be absolved."

Heden found it easy to agree with the knight. That was frustrating.

Taethan turned and walked into the tree.

"Black gods," Heden said wearily and ran off west again.

He had to bet that Taethan didn't really want to lose him, just wanted to test him. If he really wanted to lose him, he could double back or step out of a tree a thousand paces north or south and Heden would never find him again.

This time, Heden stopped at a tree much larger than its brothers. He put his hands on his knees and bent over. His lungs burned.

Taethan walked directly out of the tree and came up short when he almost ran into Heden. He pursed his lips and rested his forearm on the hilt of his sword.

"Why just the two of us?" Heden said, recovering from his sprint. He stood up. "Tell me what happened to Kavalen. Help me speak the ritual. You can lead the order...."

Taethan grimaced at this, like he tasted something sour.

"Or Brys, or even Isobel," he said. "I don't care! Tell me what happened." Heden was almost pleading. "And I can absolve the order, speak the ritual, and you can stop the urmen. The five of you could do it."

Taethan shook his head. "I no longer know the difference between guilt and innocence," he said. "I cannot tell if we are all guilty, or none of us."

"Tell me and I'll figure it out. I'm good at it."

Taethan shook his head.

"I go to stop the urq," Taethan said. "I will find my answer there."

"Balls," Heden said. This visibly offended Taethan. Heden understood what he meant. He would test himself against their army. Typical knightly behavior. If he was innocent, he would triumph.

"You'll just die like anyone else and you'll get me killed with you."

Taethan peered down at him with something approaching suspicion.

"Would you die to save the people of Ollghum Keep?" Taethan wondered. It seemed the knight was asking the question rhetorically. Weighing the idea to himself.

Heden shook his head. "Stupid question. If we die, they die anyway. That kind of solution is no solution. I reject it." It was hard for Heden to keep the venom out of his voice. "But I'd fight with you to save them."

Taethan looked at him with naked respect.

"Don't look so honored," Heden said. "I'm not here to die valiantly; I'd fight with anyone if I thought we had a chance."

"Because you wish to kill many urq," Taethan suggested. "This is not unusual, many men feel the same way. It comes naturally to them."

Heden shook his head again. "No," he said. It wasn't a response. It was an order. He pointed to the knight. "I hate killing. It sickens me. Especially urmen."

"You would prefer to kill men?" Taethan asked, raising a perfectly sculpted eyebrow.

Heden shook his head. "I prefer to save people from doing something awful. The urq are driven. It's in their blood, they were made that way. Men have a choice. If they choose evil, well then it's up to people like you. You're welcome to it. I walked that road for thirteen years, I'm sick of it. But sometimes they have no choice. That's where I come in."

Taethan nodded. "Lady Isobel thought more highly of you when she learned you were an arrogate than when she thought you were a prelate."

"She's a romantic. It's awful. She was right when she said it destroyed people."

"It has not destroyed you."

"I'm bloody-minded," Heden said, sneering.

Taethan frowned and looked at Heden's beaten iron breastplate, a dull contrast to Taethan's emerald-tinged gleaming plate. He seemed to make a decision and started walking, not disappearing into a tree.

Heden moved to keep up with him.

They walked through the forest, keeping a brisk pace but not running. Taethan looked ahead, never making a misstep. Heden had to keep his head down to avoid turning his ankle on an exposed root or catching his boots on a grasping vine.

After several minutes of this, Heden broke the silence.

"What happened to make you drop the cant?" Heden asked.

"Why do you hate knights, Heden?" Taethan asked, as though not having heard anything Heden had said.

Okay, Heden thought. He couldn't force Taethan to answer his questions.

"I've never met one who wasn't a power-mad self-obsessed braggart."

Taethan raised his eyebrows at this and looked at the man. "Indeed? Not a one?"

Heden glanced up at him and then back down to the forest floor. "I was going to say I hadn't made up my mind about you, but then I remembered where we were going." It was just like a knight to attempt an army of urq just to prove a point.

"Mmm," Taethan said.

Heden looked around. He hadn't noticed it at first, but Taethan's cryptic response made him think.

"Where *are* we going?" he asked.

Taethan, maddeningly, kept his mouth shut.

"This is north. We're headed north, the urq aren't this way."

No answer.

They walked briskly, occasionally breaking into a trot or speeding up to hop over some thick undergrowth. Heden knew there was meaning in Taethan's decision to switch direction.

“Something’s going on here,” he said, thinking furiously. Wishing someone smarter was here. Wishing for Elzpeth’s intellect or the abbot’s insight. “Something’s driving you people to some horrible extreme. You’re all living in some kind of nightmare.” Heden remembered Perren’s twisted, lifeless face, the vines growing out of it. “But it’s not the real world. It’s something you’ve created for yourself out of pain and fear and you don’t know how to get out.”

He said it quickly, before the idea could get away. He was out of breath when he finished and breathed deeply afterwards. *That sounded good,* he thought. *All that time with the abbot, not wasted.*

“That’s what I’m here for,” he said, not thinking, but realizing it as he said it. “I’m here to get you out of this.”

They walked in silence for a while.

“That’s not good news for you, by the way,” Heden explained. “That’s called the blind leading the blind.” Heden wondered again where they were going. They were miles north now.

Taethan glanced at him and kept walking, saying nothing.

“Yours is a fell insight, Heden.”

“How do you know my name?” he shot back. He’d asked the question back at the priory and gotten no answer but a metaphorical boot up his backside.

“I prayed to Halcyon,” Taethan said. As far as Heden could tell, it was the first straight answer the knight had given.

"That's how you knew about my father," Heden said. Taethan had spoken personally about Heden's father back at the priory in a way that made it seem like Taethan had met him.

"I'd forgotten about her," Heden said. "She told you I was coming."

"She told me a great many things."

"Oh," Heden said drolly. "Good."

"She told me you were more lost than I," he said.

"Well that's a matter of opinion," Heden bit back.

"She told me you were possessed by fear and pain. She said you couldn't survive in the forest anymore. Your memories take hold of you and unman you. I asked what could do that to a man and she told me about Elemein and Parlance. And a man named Stewart Antilles."

"You didn't know them," Heden growled. He had to restrain his instinct for violence. He felt that the memory of people he loved had just been desecrated. But Taethan continued smoothly.

"I could tell she was keeping something from me, something darker than death. But she would say no more on that matter."

Heden kept pace with the knight.

"What else did Halcyon tell you?"

"She told me you and I are the same," Taethan confessed, and it was clear the idea worried him.

"Well that's horseshit," Heden said.

"That's what I thought at first," Taethan said. "Though, of course, not in those words."

"But now that you've met me…" Heden said, trying to smile like Gwiddon.

Taethan stopped suddenly. Heden smelled moisture in the air, and the sound of birdsong was suddenly very loud.

Taethan was a head taller than Heden and looked at him with open judgment.

"Now I'm certain it's horseshit," the knight said.

Heden barked a laugh.

Chapter Forty

"Where are we?" Heden asked.

They stood at the edge of a huge lake that stretched before them like the mirror of a vain god. It was so big, the far shore disappeared into the line of trees beyond. To the east, he saw a fawn drinking from the water, picking its head up regularly to look for predators. It took no note of the two humans.

"This is the center of our demesne," Taethan said, walking until he was standing ankle-deep in the water. "We are still hundreds of miles south of the center of the wode. But for us, this is the heart of the forest. It is sacred to us. All the wode knows this is our holiest of places, more so than the priory, and none would disturb us here."

"Alright," Heden said, accepting this. "So what?"

"I wanted to see it once more before I died," Taethan said, looking out over the water as though in prayer. His face sparkled with reflected silver light.

"Black gods," Heden said. "You're not making this easy for me." Taethan looked to him quizzically.

"Everyone said, 'Talk to Taethan.' By the time you finally showed up, I was so sick of them I was willing to believe you were the only innocent person in the whole forest."

Taethan turned back to the lake as though ignoring Heden.

"I don't know what you're guilty of," Heden said. "But you're guilty of something. It's killing you. I know the signs."

"I am sorry that you are a part of this, Heden."

"What?" Heden asked. Taethan was deflecting so much, Heden was off balance.

"I believe you when you say you would stand alone against the urq for the sake of the people of Ollghum Keep, if you thought there was a chance."

"Well," Heden said, uncomfortable. "I'm still a…a servant of Cavall, I…"

"But moreover I do *not* believe you when you say you hate knights. Hate the order."

"You don't," Heden said.

"I watched you run after Idris, a man you had every reason to despise. Trying to will the joust to stop. In that moment, I believe you would have given anything to save his life, including your own."

Heden found the memory of it difficult. And it reminded him of something worse, something Taethan could not know about. Elzpeth.

Taethan looked at him with compassion. "Do you know how I know that?"

Heden was having trouble breathing. He nodded. He remembered Taethan crying out the names of Idris and Isobel.

"Because you felt the same way," Heden said thickly.

Taethan nodded, smiling ruefully at Heden.

Something opened up between the two men, some shared pain or grief. It was powerful and Heden didn't like it.

"Don't—" Heden cleared his throat. "Don't read too much into that." He found the sudden intimacy with the knight difficult. Found any such intimacy difficult. It seemed this knight suddenly knew him too well. "I would have behaved like that with anyone. I'm an arrogate. It's my *job*. I just enjoy it more when knights are involved."

"Did you ever wonder why Culhwch never became a saint?" Taethan asked.

"Can we stay on one subject?" Heden asked.

"Who's the greatest knight who ever lived?" Taethan asked.

Heden knew Taethan was trying to make a point. He gave in.

"Culhwch I guess," Heden answered.

Taethan stood before the lake like it was an altar and he was waiting for his god's judgment. A sparrow landed on the ground before him and hopped around, searching the edge of the water for worms.

"Culhwch wanted to be the greatest knight on life," Taethan said. "It was all he thought about. He hungered for it, the thought nourished him."

Heden wasn't stupid. He knew Taethan was also describing himself.

"But he was weak," Taethan said with a shrug. "He was perfect, physically. No man could defeat him in battle. But he was vain and, in his vanity, he broke his oath. He lay with a woman who was married to another. They say she seduced him. As if that mattered."

"I never heard this story," Heden said.

"There was a tournament," Taethan continued. He had entered into some kind of reverie, and Heden found himself borne along. The lake, the air, the timelessness of the place mesmerized him. "At a place called Tabernan.

"Culhwch jousted for his illicit lover's favor, knowing she could not award it to him. He defeated seven knights in a row. He challenged them all, and they were honor-bound to accept, even though they knew they could not beat him. And he knew it too. He would beat every knight at the tournament in his passion and frustration. You would call him 'bloody-minded.'" Taethan smiled but did not look at Heden. It was as if he couldn't see the arrogate. Couldn't see the lake. Only the tournament in his mind.

"The eighth knight, before he rode out, removed his helm and gave it to his wife, bent down to kiss her and his son. He left his helm with his wife and rode out with his face bare, his wife screaming. He knew the gods had chosen him for a purpose. He knew it meant his death. He found himself unable to resist."

Heden remembered Idris doing the same. The knight had been reenacting this story, and everyone at the joust knew it except Heden.

"To ride out without one's helm is to admit that you are the weaker knight. It shames your opponent in the hope of making him yield. For who would joust against a man who was so vulnerable? But Culhwch was blind; his passion for love consumed him."

Heden knew what happened next. He felt like he was there.

"Culhwch rode out, heedless of his opponent's state. His lance pierced the knight's breastplate. Ran him through. Lifted him up, off his horse. He was dead by the time he hit the ground."

Heden saw Idris' lifeless face staring at him.

"Seeing the dead knight on the ground, his wife and son weeping over him, his face bare, Culhwch saw what he had done. He had broken his oath. He broke it when he lay with the woman, broke it when he challenged the knights. Killed a knight who'd deliberately rode out displaying his weakness," Taethan said. His face held a mixture of puzzlement and awe.

"He dismounted and went to the man. Culhwch was already a legendary knight. Everyone believed it was only a matter of time before Adun granted him a miracle and made him a saint.

"The perfect knight would be able to perform a single miracle. He had waited for this all his life. The spectators had been waiting for it. The sign that the gods recognized his virtue. But in order to be the perfect knight, one must be devoid of all vanity. All pride. Want. Desire.

"Culhwch's vanity had led him to murder. And the guilt of it, the knowledge of it and everything he'd done, everything he'd failed to be, consumed him. He knelt beside the fallen knight. The widow and her child stepped forward. All the tournament gathered around, pressed in." Taethan used his hands to emulate their motion. Heden watched as Taethan, transported, reenacted the scene. "They were waiting to see him perform his miracle."

"He lay his hands upon the dead knight, and prayed." Taethan held out his hands as though laying them on the breast of Idris. "'Adun,' he said to himself. 'I thought I served you all my days, but now I see I served only myself. I was vain, and I was prideful. I should be punished. But this man is innocent. He did no wrong. Do not punish him for my failure. Oh lord, I beg thee, spare this man's life. Spare this man's life.'

"The crowd, of course, heard none of this. It was for the ears of Adun alone.

"Moments of silence passed, and the dead knight gasped a heaving breath. And then another. And then another. He breathed normally and his eyes opened. He saw the crowd assembled, saw his wife and son, and knew not why they looked on him with wonder.

"The crowd proclaimed 'a miracle!'" Taethan threw up his hands and turned, as though praising the forest. He smiled widely, caught up in the reaction the crowd must have felt. Exulting at the knight who performed a miracle and would be sainted. "They cheered and stamped and, with the wife and son, bore the once-dead knight away." He stretched a hand out to the forest as though he could see them.

After a moment, he dropped his hand and dropped his smile and turned back to face the lake as though awaiting judgment.

"Culhwch remained on the field. He remained, kneeling, weeping, sobbing, where he'd laid hands on the knight.

"He cried," Taethan said. "While the others cheered. Because *he alone* knew the truth. He alone knew there *had* been a miracle. The miracle was that Adun had permitted Culhwch, who was not worthy, to perform a miracle. He alone knew that Adun had judged him, and found him wanting. His life wasted. All his oaths broken.

"Culhwch could be a knight no more. Adun had meted out his punishment."

Heden didn't know what to say. Wasn't sure Taethan could hear him anyway. The sounds of the lake intruded, breaking the reverie.

"Do not judge my fellows too harshly," Taethan said, looking down at the water lapping at his feet. "It is I alone who bears the burden. I liked what you told Squire Aderyn."

"What?" Heden asked, rattled by the change of subject.

"'A man is better than the worst thing he's done,'" Taethan said wistfully.

Heden just stared at him, trying to understand the meaning of Taethan's story. He knew it wasn't about Sir Idris. It had something to do with Kavalen and Taethan. Something to do with the overwhelming guilt Taethan bore and which he was awakening in Heden. There was something Taethan wanted to do, but couldn't, and so looked to Heden to solve.

"I know why you brought me out here," Heden said suddenly.

This piqued Taethan's interest. He looked to Heden with something like hope.

"You *want* me to figure out what happened."

Taethan said nothing.

"You set out to stop the urq on your own. You had no idea I would follow you, and when I did you tried to lose me. But then you changed your mind and brought me here."

Heden took Taethan's silence as affirmation.

"You brought me here and told me that story because if I can figure all this out without you breaking your oath, then we can go back to the priory. I can speak the ritual, and then the Green can ride out and save Ollghum Keep."

Taethan picked up a rock and skipped it across the lake. He ignored Heden.

"Well you're going to have to give me a little more help." Heden bit the words off. "I know this has something to do with your guilt. You're blaming yourself for something and you're obsessed with..."

His obsession with death.

"I know how Kavalen died," Heden said abruptly.

This intrigued Sir Taethan. "Indeed?" he said. "Prithee."

"He killed himself," Heden said.

Taethan just stared at him. Once again, Heden found himself unable to read the knight's reaction.

"He killed himself and you could have stopped it but you didn't."

"Why," Taethan began. "Why would I stop him, should he wish to end his own life? Is there no reason—"

"No," Heden said. "No, I don't buy it. Death is never the answer."

"Never? A man can see such things," Taethan said, shaking his head. "Commit treachery by action or inaction. And sometimes, methinks, understanding alone can consume a man with misery."

"Cavall's teeth!" Heden said. "How are you still a knight?" He gestured to Taethan's curly green hair. "You're so obsessed with death and guilt and judgment. The one time I think one of you bastards is going to actually do something, take some action, even if it's suicide against the urq, and you come up here instead. You asked me why I hated knights. This is why! You're so self-absorbed. Like your pain and your guilt is the only thing that matters. You're paralyzed."

"That is no matter," Taethan said. "The matter is why you, who know as much as I, are not."

"Because unlike you I know my pain doesn't matter!" Heden threw the words at him like an assault. He was coming to understand the knight. He thought the statement would affect him. He was right. Taethan didn't take it well.

"You are a man of fell insight, arrogate," Taethan said for the second time. "If your judgment weighs so heavily on me, how much more heavily it must weigh on you."

"This isn't about me."

"It is as much about thou as I," Taethan said, shaking his head. "I hope you pass your test."

"What are you talking about? I didn't have anything to do with Kavalen."

"Is it not plain? We are being tested, you and I. We have each offended our god, betrayed our friends and our oaths. There must be a reckoning before absolution. The order was my test. I have already failed, I fear. For the sake of us all I hope that you pass your test."

"Which is?" Heden asked, afraid of the answer.

Taethan looked at him with a mixture of sadness and affection.

"Me."

Heden was speechless.

They stood there by the lake for some time. Taethan meditating on the perfect beauty of the waters and the forest and the sun and the sky. Heden just staring at him.

"I..." Heden opened his mouth to speak and heard a terrible noise.

It was the sound of thunder far off, but there were no clouds in the sky. It came again. Heden remembered the giant. Were they under attack?

Again, the thunder. And this time the whole surface of the lake, miles across, rippled with it. The water flooded up to them, soaking them up to their knees before rushing back out. They backed away from the lake.

Taethan's eyes were wild, searching the tree line.

The pattern of the explosive sounds was irregular. Inhuman. Six heavy explosions in rapid but uneven succession, then a pause. Then the pattern repeated.

The trees deep in the forest to the west swayed—something was looming over them. Something larger than the massive trees, two hundred feet high. Heden's heart beat rapidly. The sound was becoming deafening. He was starting to panic, he felt it creep over his skin and clutch at his hammering heart.

"I thought you said no one would attack us here!" Heden shouted over the din. The sound suddenly stopped.

Taethan turned and gave Heden a look. He drew his sword. "We may be in trouble," he admitted.

Chapter Forty-one

The thing loomed over the trees. It had to be close to three hundred feet high. Inarguably the largest creature Heden had ever seen. There was a kind of thrill in seeing something new. Feeling frightened for the first time in years.

"What is it?!" Heden asked.

"It would not come here but to find us!" Taethan said. "I fear I have led us both to our deaths, arrogate!" He had his shield and sword at the ready. Heden wondered what possible use they could be.

The trees bent and then snapped in explosions of wood and sap. Whatever it was, it stepped out from the forest.

It was made of vines and thorns and trees. Mostly thorns. It was like the forest come alive. It had six legs and a massive body with a short neck and an eyeless dog-like head. Its head alone was as large as the whole priory.

Taethan stared up at the thing in a kind of awe.

The creature's head turned this way and that, orienting to what, Heden didn't know. Until it faced Heden and Taethan and its mouth opened and the thing convulsed like it was shouting. There was no sound. It was still at least a mile away.

Heden watched as the sheer force of the creature's report caused the surface of the lake to ripple outward. When the bow of the disturbance reached Heden and Taethan, they heard a clarion call wash over them. Like the sound of a thousand trumpets blowing. It blew Heden and Taethan's hair back and smelled of bark and flowers.

Heden recognized the sound.

"That's a celestial horn," Heden said. The elves sounded it before battle, but this was a hundred times louder. He turned to Taethan, grabbed the man, tried to shake him and make him forget his awe.

"Why is that thing sounding the battle call of the sky elves?"

"It is an Yllindir!" Taethan said.

"An..." Heden translated in his head. It meant "lifedeath" but life in the sense of the place you lived. And death in the sense of "an assault." Heden had never heard the proper term before, nor seen one, but he knew the celestials made such things. He knew they were large, but had no idea how large.

"It's an elven siege engine?" Heden said.

"Aye," Taethan said, bracing himself for battle.

Heden stared at the thing and for a moment could not maintain his terror. He sighed and his face betrayed his exhaustion.

"Typical," he said.

"What?" Taethan called out.

"Why aren't we running?" Heden asked, the fear returning.

The creature began to walk forward on its six legs. The ground shook terribly. It stepped into the lake.

"We could not outrun it. And after it devours us, it would head to the keep. The urmen must be driving it south."

"Okay," Heden said, looking around. "So what do we do?"

"Do you have a shield?" Taethan asked. He was looking warily at the siege engine as though he might have to leap aside at any moment, even though the thing was still half a mile away and so big that there was no reasonable way to evade it.

"No!" Heden said.

"It will be no matter soon," Taethan called out. "Ready yourself!"

Heden looked up at the thing. Though still hundreds of yards away, it towered over them. It stopped moving and reared up on its four hind legs.

It spread its two front legs outward and then convulsed in one massive shudder. It seemed to Heden as though dust fell off it in great gouts, but he quickly realized it was too far away for dust to be visible, and whatever it was, the spray of material arced menacingly towards them.

Thorns. Each as big as a horse. This was how the siege engine assaulted its targets.

Heden turned and ran for cover. The nearest tree was thirty feet from him. He didn't think he was going to make it. The ground under his feet darkened as the sky above was clouded with falling thorns.

Heden didn't reach the cover of the trees before the thorns started to fall. They hit the ground all around him, driving deep into the earth. Wherever one hit, it erupted in twisting, blossoming vines that prised the ground apart like a ploughshare.

A thorn stabbed into the ground only a few feet behind Heden, and the impact flung him through the air. He smashed into a tree upside down, and then flopped onto the ground. Thorns slammed into the tree, each doing serious damage and then further weakening the tree with twisting vines. This was the weapon that felled the indestructible walls of the elementals. A tree stood no chance against it, even one of the massive trees in the Iron Forest.

Heden pushed himself up, his ears ringing, just in time to hear the tree behind him crack and splinter under its own pressure. He got up and ran as fast as he could.

Taethan ran up to him, his shield dented. They both stood and watched as the tree started to fall. It was huge and most of it would fall into the water.

"Watch out!" Taethan called, pointing to the left.

Most of the tree line behind them was in a similar state. Hammered by massive thorns and then pulled apart by vines, twenty trees fell forward.

"Black gods," he said. The Yllindir would destroy the forest in its attempt to kill Heden and Taethan. The trees were hundreds of years old and toppling like the towers of a ruined castle. They hit the surface of the lake, each with a loud crack that forced Heden and Taethan to cover their ears.

Heden thought madly. He could summon a dominion…but what could it do? A dominion was only roughly as powerful as a celestial in any case, and this thing was built by the celestials. Had survived in the forest for thousands of years. Heden had spent so many years thinking if worst came to worst, he could always call upon a herald of Cavall and end all dispute, that he found himself unable to recall the dozens of prayers he knew that might have been a help.

He looked at Taethan.

"Come on," Heden said, throwing his backpack to the ground. He opened it and began pulling his carpet out. "Help me with this. I'll fly us out of here."

Taethan watched Heden laboriously extract the carpet from the pack. He pointed.

"I am not getting on that thing!" he said as the Yllindir got closer.

"Yes you are," Heden said. "Don't worry, it's impossible to fall off it. We'll get out of here and get the other knights."

"It would only follow us to the priory!" Taethan called out. The engine walked towards them again. Each footstep an earthquake. Heden yanked the carpet the rest of the way out of the bag. It flopped down on the ground, unrolling slightly.

"Good!" Heden said. "Then it'll be the order against that thing and maybe we'll have a chance!"

"A thousand elementals could not stand against it!" Taethan yelled.

This situation was all too familiar. Except usually Heden was arguing with five or six other people about the looming certain death. In a way, it was refreshing to be here with only one person to argue with.

"Well, I don't have any better ideas!" Heden called out. He started unrolling the carpet. Taethan was probably right, this thing could take down a whole army of elementals and they had nothing to…

Heden's head shot up.

"I have a better idea!" he said, thrusting his arm back into the pack.

The engine was almost upon them. Heden pulled his hand out of his pack, removed and thrust *Starkiller* into the air.

The sword burst into blinding almost-light. It hurt Heden's eyes; the space behind his eye sockets exploded with pain. He kept his arm up and blinked furiously, trying to see the engine react.

It stopped, rearing up in what seemed like alarm. In this position, the same from which it launched its catapult-like volley of thorns, it seemed like a god of the forest. So large that Heden couldn't even see its massive head from the ground.

But it had stopped, that's what was important. The dwarf sword was made to kill elves and by extension anything they made, though it had a special taste for the star elves. The Yllindir feared it. Seemed to fear what it could do. Heden didn't know how long that could last.

He tried to remember what else the sword could do. It had been years since they found it, and he'd never been the one to wield it.

Starfall was a powerful spell; Heden didn't know the full range of spells the dwarves put in the thing, but he knew one that was more powerful than *starfall*.

In the language of the dwarves, in Elemental, he spoke the word.

"*Cometstrike*," he said, and a hideous screaming sound came from above.

The summoned comet was massive. It burned white, a long tail trailing behind it. It screamed out of the sky like a hot ingot of metal.

It smashed into the rearing elven engine of destruction, tearing through it and smashing into the lake with a huge explosion, sending a gout of water a hundred feet into the air. The Yllindir's legs buckled. It had no bones, no skin, just a web of branches and vines, and the comet destroyed much of it.

Heden put *Starkiller* back in his pack and looked at Taethan, who gaped at what he'd just seen.

"Was that a dominion?" Taethan said.

"What, that? No, dominions are like humans with huge wings and metal skin. That was a bloody great rock called down from the sky."

"Can you do it again?" Taethan was awed.

"Not at the moment," Heden said, getting on the carpet. He reached out for Taethan, tried to grab the awe-struck knight and move him.

"You were wise to bring such an artifact," Taethan said, allowing himself to be guided by Heden.

"Well, I get lucky every once in a while," Heden said.

"No," Taethan said, pointing up. "You don't."

Heden turned around.

The Yllindir hadn't stopped, hadn't fallen to the ground or collapsed into the lake. It had just stumbled and lost its orientation. Though the comet destroyed a significant part of its mass, and left a smoking empty column of burning vegetation from its back just behind its head down through its gullet, the Yllindir seemed otherwise unfazed. It had no brain, no spine, no organs to attack. Heden wondered how much of it had to be destroyed before it stopped functioning. The celestials designed it well.

It righted itself and turned to bellow at the two tiny humans before it.

"Shit," Heden said.

"It was a valiant effort," Taethan said, impressed.

"Yeah, and it's about to be a valiant retreat, get on." He pulled the knight onto the carpet and spoke the command words.

The carpet rose, and when Taethan's legs buckled on the unexpected and uneven surface, Heden pressed him down into a sitting position, then sat behind him.

They were only a few yards off the ground, but climbing.

"Hold on to the sides," Heden said. "Flying two is tricky, your weight throws me off."

"I am sorry!" Taethan shouted, his brilliant green curls caught by the wind.

Heden willed the carpet up and away. They climbed quickly and at a steep angle.

"Don't look over the sides!" Heden said.

Taethan looked over the sides.

"Aaahhh!" he shouted and pulled back, clinging tighter to the edges of the tapestry.

Heden took the carpet up as fast as he could, but he'd begun his ascent right under the Yllindir. He looked behind him.

Having reared up again, the engine used one massive foreleg to swipe at or grasp the carpet. Heden couldn't tell which: it had no proper foot, just a tangle of twisting vines and thorns that swung towards them.

"Hang on!" Heden said, then rolled the carpet in a tight but elaborate circle, flying over then under the rapidly moving thorny limb. The carpet would always right itself so its riders could not fall off, but Heden knew that could be pushed.

At the height of the twisting circle the carpet inscribed, he looked up, which was down, and saw the Yllindir's massive leg below him.

It was at that moment that Taethan threw up.

Heden ignored it and finished the carpet's roll, then sped up and away, leaving the Yllindir behind him.

"It's okay," Heden said. "We're away. We made it." The wind made it difficult to talk. The forest stretched out below them, an infinite field of green leaves.

"I do not know," Taethan said, wiping vomit from his mouth with one hand, while grasping the edge of the carpet tightly with the other.

"I do!" Heden shouted. "Trust me!"

"Look!" Taethan said, pointing behind him and down.

Heden turned the carpet to get a better look.

Far below them, but not far enough, the Yllindir was still in its rearing position. It shuddered again, and another volley of thorns erupted from all over its body. Thousands of them, all speeding towards the carpet.

"It's just one damned thing after another," Heden muttered.

"What?"

"Hang on to something!" Heden said, laying as flat on the carpet as he could with another man on it.

"On to what?!" Taethan asked.

Like a thousand massive thrushes speeding past, the wave of thorns clouded the sky around them, thrumming the air. As soon as Heden saw how thick the volley was, he knew there was no way the carpet could avoid getting hit.

A thorn erupted through the carpet between Heden and Taethan, and they began to drop.

Then another tore the edge off behind Heden. They were now almost in free fall.

Heden's stomach rose, his whole body seized up in one massive convulsion of terror, and as though in a nightmare he dropped out of the sky. Wind whistling past, he thought of a prayer that would save him. Taethan too.

Eyes blinded with tears from the biting air, he tried to find Taethan, but could not. He couldn't see. He was still holding on to what was left of the carpet. He couldn't tell if it was one piece with a hole in it or two pieces, and he couldn't see Taethan.

He started to speak the prayer as he saw what he thought was the ground rushing up to meet him. There was no time. He was going to smash into the ground below and be killed.

There was no danger of hitting the ground, however. The Yllindir swung one massive foreleg and batted them both out of the sky like gnats.

The light of consciousness went out of both of them as their bodies sailed out, inscribing a beautiful geometric arc over the forest.

Chapter Forty-two

Consciousness returned. Heden's eyes opened to a blurred landscape, he couldn't focus. His head hurt, his chest hurt. His whole body tingled in that unique way that spoke of broken or shattered bones cured by a priest.

His head swam, he couldn't control it. He tried to move. He was slumped against a large tree. It dwarfed him, its size disoriented him.

He managed to sit up under his own power and noticed his breastplate lying a few feet away. Someone had taken it off him. Looking up, he saw the path he'd taken as he'd fallen through the branches. A hole in the forest stretching up and away at a sharp angle. For some reason this made him laugh.

"You're delirious," a voice said, reacting to his laughter. He looked around, vision still blurry. Then he smelled something wonderful. Broth and bread and meat. Someone was cooking something? Out here in the forest?

Head lolling, he finally narrowed in on the speaker.

She was about forty feet away from him, crouched on her haunches, cooking something over an open flame. She wore a heavy brown-and-green dress and had long brown hair. As he watched, a squirrel scampered up to her and held out a tiny nut. She plucked it from the small animal's hands and said, "Thank you," with a small bow. The squirrel dashed off.

"Hello," Heden said. *I must be dreaming.*

"Give it a few minutes," she said. "You're not as young as you used to be. Once you've had one concussion—" She seemed to be talking to herself now. "—it gets easier and easier to rattle your braincase."

Heden lay back. "Dreaming," he said. He closed his eyes and fell asleep.

Sleep didn't last long, and he woke to deep hunger and the delicious smell from before. He started to see her crouched in front of him now, offering a bowl of soup.

She looked about his age, and was beautiful. It was her eyes. They were golden brown and danced with wit and intelligence. She had dark copper hair, almost brown.

"Normally I'd say sleep is best, but we need to talk." She waved the bowl of soup under his nose. "This is better than sleep, anyway."

He tried to take the bowl of soup. It took him a moment to coordinate his hands, but he managed it. He held the stone bowl and smelled the soup, taking a deep breath.

"I smelled bread," Heden said.

"Yup," she said, reaching behind her. She dropped a fresh loaf in his lap. It was still warm.

"I made it," she said.

"How?" Heden asked, frowning. His head throbbed.

"Wasn't hard," she said. She got up and walked back to her little camp. "You learned the prayer when you were fifteen. The soup I made the hard way. Comes out better."

Heden sipped the soup. He put the bowl in his lap and broke off some bread.

"How long have I been out?" he asked, dipping the bread in the soup.

"Few hours," the woman said, crouching to tend the fire and stir the soup. "You were a mess," she said. "You would have gotten through it on your own." She sampled the soup, concluded it was good and kept stirring. "But you wouldn't have enjoyed it."

Heden breathed deeply. As his body recovered, his mind cleared. The woods around him seemed real now. He blinked a few times and his eyes seemed to be back to normal.

Where was Taethan?

What happened to the Yllindir?

Who was this woman?

He took a sip of the soup and forwarded a hypothesis.

"You're a witch," he said.

She smiled widely to herself. "Good guess," she said, her voice like a bell. "But no. I'm, ah, the cause of witchcraft in others." She looked at him slyly from the corner of her eye.

He thought for a moment.

"Fallara," he guessed.

The woman frowned and shook her head. "That crone? She couldn't cook to save her life."

He put his head back against the tree. It hurt to think. Once he stopped trying, it came to him.

"Halcyon," he said.

She didn't react in any way Heden could see.

"Before you ask," she said, "Sir Taethan is fine. You'll meet up with him once I'm through with you."

That sounded ominous.

Before Heden could stop himself, he asked, "What did I do?"

He regretted asking it. It made him sound like a child, but it seemed to impress the woman. She nodded to herself.

"Well for one thing, three of my knights have died while you stood by gawping."

"Three?" he asked.

"I'm counting Kavalen," she said, and there was low menace in her voice. But it was casual. It didn't appear directed at Heden. "With Idris and Perren that's three."

Heden didn't say anything. He was reeling from the concussion and the fact that he was talking to a saint again. This one seemed bafflingly normal.

She stood up and kicked dirt on the small fire, quenching it.

Looking down at the dying fire, she put her hands on her hips and, obviously talking to herself, said: "And I don't hold out much hope for the other six."

"What happened to Aderyn?" Heden asked.

Saint Halcyon turned and looked at him askance. "You won't see her again," she said, crossing her arms. Heden couldn't tell if this was good or bad. "None of the knights will. That's a wager I've made with myself." Heden didn't know what she meant.

"Perren and Kavalen weren't my fault," he said.

She sighed and walked over to him. She made a gesture as she walked and a small toadstool near him grew enormous, allowing her to sit comfortably.

"We didn't pick you for this because we wanted you to stand by and gasp while the knights..." She stopped, and then said something else. "...died."

"How did you pick me?" he asked, frowning. The act made his head hurt again.

"Suggestions," she said. "Nudges. Coincidences. I mean I could just appear before the hierarch and tell him what to do but that's not a good idea. No rules against it, but it sets a bad precedent. And that's pretty much all we have."

"Why don't you speak like them?" he asked. When it seemed like she didn't understand, he went on. "Like Isobel."

"The cant?" she asked. She lay back against the toadstool and crossed her legs. *Nice legs,* he thought. Heden wondered if there was any situation so bad that he wouldn't notice a woman's legs. Probably not.

"The cant is their tradition, not mine. They created it."

"Created?"

She nodded. "One of the knight-commanders came up with the idea a few hundred years ago. When the order was even smaller than it is now. She thought that's how the original knights talked. Back when life was...I don't know...simpler? Course these knights don't know that. They think the cant is a thousand years old. Have no idea that no one spoke like that even then."

"It's fake," Heden said, reeling at the idea that the knights were acting out a kind of theater and didn't even know it.

She shrugged again, pleasingly. "Not if they're serious about it. Which they are. Or were." Her face clouded. Heden felt ashamed, though he didn't know why. "Doesn't matter either way. As long as they keep the pact, I don't care what else they get up to."

"You mean chastity and purity and all that," Heden said.

"No, the *pact*. Not the oaths, they made those up too. I can't imagine any better way to take the fun out of life. Chastity? They can keep it." She smiled at him and he smiled back.

After regarding him for a speculative moment, she smoothed her robe over her legs.

"All those things, the vows, the cant. Chivalry," she said. "They're just there to remind them of things they feel people take for granted. They think people speak too quickly, too often and with too little thought. The cant makes them think before they open their mouths. But they don't need the cant to be knights. They only have to honor the pact."

"What's the pact?" Heden asked.

She looked around at the forest. "This," she said. "The forest and everything in it. And men. It's all that really matters. I know it's hard to imagine now, but for thousands of years before my knights the border of the forest would shift, north, south. Wiping out whole cities over centuries or being cut back to almost nothing. It was a war. As much as the one you fought in. But it happened so slowly, men couldn't see it. The tide of centuries is meaningless to us. So I invented the order to keep the peace, and since then—" She spread her hands. "—things have been nice. The forest and the men all get along."

Heden nodded. He understood.

"I'm sorry about Idris," he said. She nodded, accepting his apology.

"At the river," she said, "you kept your promise to Reginam. That counts for something."

"Not on my own I didn't," he said. "I had a vision of Lynwen."

Halcyon smiled. "You did enough," she said. "The two of you needed and wanted each other as much as two people can. Lynwen didn't force you to do anything; it was still your will. Your choice. We just gave you a nudge, you did the rest."

Heden remembered his time with Aderyn. He had a vision of her standing before him at the river. "I'm not sure she chose the right vow," he said, grimacing. He wanted to keep talking about Aderyn because he felt like he was in trouble and this helped avoid it.

"The chastity vow is perfect for her. For the same reason it's meaningless to Isobel and Taethan."

"I don't understand."

"Aderyn is a passionate woman. In every sense, and in every sense that is good and right. Denying that, bottling it up…gives her power."

"You're saying Taethan and Isobel don't get power from their oaths?"

She shook her head. "Isobel gets her power from dedication. She was never a creature of lust. Nor Taethan."

"What does he get his power from?"

She looked at him. "Heden, I can inspire you. But I can't tell you anything you wouldn't be able to figure out on your own. There *is* a rule against that."

He thought for a minute. "He's pure," he said.

"No," she said.

"They all think he is."

"What do you think?"

He shook his head. "I do not know," he said. It frustrated him.

"Well, you better figure it out," she said. "It's the only thing that's important in all of this and if you of all people can't see it—" She sighed and stood up. "—then that's it and we're back to the beginning."

He played back what she said. It took a few moments to pick out the important phrase.

"What do you mean: me of all people?" he asked.

She looked at him with naked pity. "Heden, I'm sorry." She seemed moved by some great sadness. "I'm sorry for everything that led you here. And I'm sorry for everything that's going to happen. If it's any consolation, everyone agrees." He had no idea what she meant by "everyone." "If you can't do it," she said, "no one alive can."

"It's because I'm an arrogate," he said.

She nodded as though it should have been obvious to him earlier. "Yes."

"You want me—" He felt like he was wading through molasses, trying to push through solid fog. "—to take Taethan's burden on...."

"No, Heden, not that," she said sadly. "But you're right next to it. And by Cavall I hope you crack it." She smoothed out her dress, and the toadstool went back to its original size.

"That's it?" he asked. She seemed to be saying their meeting was over.

"I will tell you one more thing," she said.

"Something I couldn't figure out on my own?" he asked, raising an eyebrow.

"Let's call it a piece of advice. Nothing wrong with that." Heden wasn't sure who she was defending herself to. Possibly Cavall or the other saints.

She looked at him as though sending a favored son off to his apprenticeship.

"The perfect knight may have no place in an imperfect world. But you do."

"What?" Heden asked. She was talking about Taethan. Saint Halcyon looked at Heden and shook her head.

"Lynwen likes you too much, she'd never say this. You're not the hero, Heden. Stop trying to solve the problem. Do your job."

Heden drew himself up at that.

"My job," he said, perhaps confrontationally, perhaps unwisely, "is to absolve the order of Kavalen's death."

Halcyon shrugged, mimicking Heden's favorite gesture. He noticed a honeybee land on her shoulder and then realized there were several there. He saw many buzzing around.

She nodded, though to what or whom Heden couldn't know. "Well, that's it," she said. "Time for me to go." She turned and began to walk away.

"Wait," Heden said. She stopped and turned. "Tell me Aderyn's going to be okay."

She looked at him with something like affection and nostalgia. "I can't tell you that Heden, it's not up to me. I will tell you that we were all very impressed back there at the river. Don't waste it. She kept her oath too. Find a way to honor that, if you won't honor your own."

"What does that mean?" Heden asked. He was beginning to feel like he'd forget all this—had she given him any answers? Was this all going to slip away, as his meetings with other saints had, leaving only a memory of light?

"It means," she said, brushing the bees off her shoulders. They took flight but seemed to orbit around her. "Chastity is one-sided. Fidelity is not."

Heden looked at her blankly.

"You're faithful to a person, remember. Not an idea."

"I don't understand."

"Well," she said, sighing again. "I don't talk to mortals that much anymore, it's probably my fault. Sorry." She smiled winsomely and turned and walked away.

As she turned and disappeared behind the nearby tree, Taethan came walking out from behind it. He'd lost most of his armor but seemed otherwise no worse for wear. Someone had tended to him, just as Halcyon had tended to Heden.

"That was a bloody great swarm of bees," the knight said, using what was left of the carpet, in one hand, to ward off the cloud while he brushed them off his linen shirt with the other hand.

The knight stood over Heden, offered him his hand. Heden took it and rose unsteadily to his feet. Bees crawled all over both of them.

"What did you do, land in a beehive?" Taethan asked.

Chapter Forty-three

Lacking horses, or flying tapestries, they walked. Both men limped like aged war veterans. Heden compulsively replayed the conversation with Halcyon in his mind, looking for meaning. Sir Taethan intruded on his thoughts.

"You seem withdrawn," he put forward with some hesitation. Heden didn't respond immediately. He looked down at his feet eating up the miles. This was how you did it, miles without a mount: head down, one step at a time.

"I don't like talking," Heden said without looking up. "I like quiet."

"It's just that," Taethan said after a moment, "you talked a great deal before we arrived at the lake."

Heden didn't reply.

"I had grown used to it," Taethan admitted.

Heden glanced at him and read his expression.

"That had to be hard to say," Heden said without sympathy.

Taethan shrugged, trying the expression out.

"You're not going to tell me what happened to Kavalen," Heden said. "Not sure what there is to talk about. At this point, we get back to the priory, I can go home. Dunno why I bothered coming back up here, except to almost get killed."

Taethan, he knew, was trying to bridge the gap between them. Heden was reminding him that Taethan put that gap there and it wasn't going away as long as Kavalen's death remained a mystery.

The two men continued to crunch through yellow and red leaves. For a while, neither spoke. Eventually, Heden let him off the hook.

"What did you think of Lynwen?" he asked, taking a guess at what Halcyon had meant when she said Heden's saint was "busy."

"I found her..." Taethan began. "Difficult."

Heden nodded. "Yeah."

"She does not seem to think very highly of you," Taethan said, his frown deepening with confusion.

"Well," Heden said with some resignation. "That's only because she knows me."

"Were you speaking with Halcyon?"

"It was more her talking and me listening. She said a lot of things that didn't make sense to me."

"Saint Lynwen did the same."

"Did she come on to you?" Heden asked.

"Did she...?"

Heden glanced at him.

"Did she try to seduce you?" he asked.

Taethan blushed.

"Don't worry," Heden said. "She knew you'd refuse her."

"She knew?" Taethan asked, not sure what that signified.

"Yeah," Heden said. "If she thought you'd, ah…succumb," he said, "she'd never have bothered with you."

"That does not make sense," Taethan said.

"You haven't known many women, have you?"

Taethan said nothing.

"Well, Lynwen is like most of them, only more so."

"And you are her only follower," Taethan observed.

Heden suspected this told Taethan more about him than he found comfortable.

"How did that come to be?" Taethan asked. It was the most personal question he'd asked thus far.

"How far to the priory?" Heden asked.

"Half a day," he said. "If you don't want to talk about it…"

"Half a day," Heden repeated. "That's not long enough for me to tell the story."

Heden watched the ground being eaten by his boots step by step, but he thought out of the corner of his eye he saw Taethan smile.

"We have no mounts," Taethan said. "I'm afraid we are ill prepared."

"I was prepared," Heden said, "before that thing ripped my carpet in half."

"Can it be repaired?"

"I dunno," Heden said. "What's left is still usable, but no more riding two," he said. "Pity."

"There was no danger I'd get on that thing again in any case," Taethan said.

"Feel like walking anyway," Heden said.

"Myself as well," Taethan said.

They continued their slow journey to the priory. Neither had the strength to muster a prayer to grant them speed.

"If that thing," Heden began.

"The Yllindir," Taethan offered.

"Yeah," Heden said. "If it showed up at Ollghum Keep, could the Green stop it?"

"You mean a fight?" Taethan asked.

Heden shrugged. "You tell me."

Taethan marched with Heden through the forest. They looked a pair.

"Lady Isobel could stop it," the knight said eventually.

Heden glanced at him, read his expression, then went back to watching where he was going.

"Okay," Heden said. This was good news. He'd been thinking how futile everything was now. The celestial siege engine would make short work of the keep, Green Order or no. "How?"

Taethan seemed reluctant to answer. Heden let him work it out. Silence seemed to bother him now.

"Do you know the fae?"

"Yeah," Heden said, nodding. "Yeah I do."

"They can influence the Yllindir."

Heden nodded. "That makes sense." Both were created by and servants of the elves.

"And Lady Isobel is counted as an ally of their queen."

"Okay," Heden said. Taethan didn't seem to mind questions that furthered the rescue of Ollghum Keep. Heden was worried the presence of the Yllindir rendered any attempt at rescue moot.

"If the urq are controlling the Yllindir..." Heden began.

"They could not control it. The urmen hate the elves and everything they make. And even a million urq would be like gnats to the Yllindir."

"Yeah but I don't like coincidences," Heden said. "The urq marching south, the Yllindir. There's a relationship. What did the Yllindir want at the lake? Why go there? Who did it expect to find there?" He looked at Taethan.

"The lake belongs to us all," the knight said.

Heden took this in as they walked.

"That lake is holy to you, right?" Heden asked.

"It is our most sacred place."

"And everyone knows that?"

"All the wode."

"Even the urq?" Heden asked.

Taethan did not reply. Heden took this as a yes.

Heden looked at Taethan's bloody clothing under what was left of his armor. They had almost died at the lake. At the lake Taethan led them to.

"You took us to the lake," Heden said, his eyes flitting to Taethan and then away, afraid of what he was discovering, dread coming over him.

"You took *me* to the lake."

Taethan looked at Heden, his face somewhere between fear and hope. Heden knew he was right.

"I'm the only one trying to do anything about what happened," Heden said. "And you took me to the lake."

Taethan tilted his head expectantly.

"You knew the Yllindir was going to be there," Heden said flatly. "You planned to go get killed fighting the urq alone at Ollghum Keep. But you hadn't reckoned on me. The two of us might be able to stop the urq army," he said. "So we *couldn't* go to the keep. So we go to the lake, where you knew the Yllindir would be. It would make short work of both of us. Then your problem is solved. The urq get Ollghum Keep, the gods only know why, I can't interfere if I'm dead, and you get to satisfy your self-obsession and guilt by getting killed in the process."

Taethan looked confused. "What a horrible way to think," he said. "Lynwen was right about you."

"You killed Kavalen," Heden concluded, ignoring him.

Taethan turned in disgust and continued walking back to the priory as quickly as he could.

Heden ran to keep up with him.

"You killed Kavalen so the urq could sack Ollghum Keep," he said.

"I was wrong about you," Taethan said. "You are a fool."

"What's so damned important about the keep that it was worth murdering your commander? Why is your silence more important than those people? Why isn't anyone trying to save them?!"

Taethan wheeled on him.

"Why do you pretend to care for the people of the keep?" Taethan asked.

"Have you met any of them?" Heden shot back. "When was the last time you met anyone who wasn't another knight?"

"*You* have met the people of Ollghum Keep, yet you are here."

"Yes!" Heden said. "I'm here, trying to get you lot to do your duty."

"But you do not need us!" Taethan said. He pointed to Heden's backpack. "I saw what you did to the Yllindir. And I saw the sky go black when you fought the urq, though I was leagues away. Do not pretend impotence; you have power enough to stop an army!"

This brought Heden up short. He put his hand on the pommel of his sword, though *Starkiller* was in his pack.

He remembered his speech to Aderyn. "*It takes men to hold the field,*" so said Duke Baed. But Heden had *Starkiller.* The ancient dwarven blade could turn the tide. Why had he brought it?

He'd brought it to defend himself. That's what Taethan forced him to see. He'd brought *Starkiller* because he needed something to rely on, so he wouldn't have to rely on Cavall. Because he didn't trust his relationship with Cavall. Because he was afraid that asking his god for help would mean…having to do the right thing.

This was not a truth he was prepared to face. He evaded.

"The people of Ollghum Keep," he said slowly, "are your duty. You are mine."

"You are a bumbling knave," Taethan said, containing his anger. "You deserve that harlot as a saint, and she deserves you."

Whatever else was true, Taethan was not acting like a man who was guilty of the crime Heden just accused him of. Heden could read his face and see truth, and what he saw was frustration, which frustrated Heden.

Heden nodded. "Sure," he said. "I could have told you that. Maybe you didn't kill Kavalen, okay, but you know who did and right now knowing and not telling me makes you a coward." It was the strongest insult Heden could think of, designed to provoke the knight.

"Draw your sword," Taethan said mildly.

Heden raised his eyebrows.

"I'm not going to fight you, you idiot. I came up here to save you."

"Draw it," Taethan said tensely, but quietly. "They don't understand Tevas well enough and will think we're really fighting. I'll draw mine as well."

Heden spent no time absorbing what Taethan was telling him. He stepped back as though he were about to fight Taethan and wrenched open his pack, drawing *Starkiller*. Taethan drew his blade.

Once they both had their weapons in hand, Taethan called out a name.

"Pakadrask!" he shouted.

"Green Man."

The voice was a growl, deep and resonant, like thunder coming from a cave.

Heden spun around. There was a fallen and rotting tree a dozen yards away. It might as well have been a stone battlement, so thick and high was it. Atop it squatted a large urman wearing heavy armor. Several dozen urq also stood on the tree. The thing was fifteen feet high so there was no way to tell, but Heden guessed there were many more urmen hiding behind it.

They were so quiet. And Heden had been distracted interrogating Taethan. Maybe he'd been close to the truth, but now it didn't matter.

For the second time in as many days, the urq had found them.

Chapter Forty-four

How many were there? Heden couldn't tell. It could be a hundred, hidden behind the massive fallen tree. Taethan goaded them.

"I alone would be sufficient," the knight called out. "But you see we are two and therefore you are outnumbered," he said, his voice iron. "Your master sent you on a fool's errand; you must know you cannot defeat a knight of the Green."

The urq laughed. It sounded like someone striking stones together.

Their leader, Pakadrask, stood on his small but powerful legs and raised his massive arms. The urmen went silent.

"Where is the rest of your armor, Green Man?" Pakadrask asked, pointing down at Taethan with his brutal axe.

"Do you remember the White Falls?" Taethan said. "I had less armor then! And the falls ran black with your blood!"

The assembled urmen riled at this, sniffing the air, many banging sword and axe against shield.

Pakadrask turned his attention to Heden.

"What about you, little one?" Pakadrask said. "Are you strong and brave, like the Green Man?"

Heden just sniffed and looked around the forest, ignoring the urq before answering.

"Try me and see," he said.

The urq shouted at that. They liked it. They looked forward to fighting Heden.

"They are bold," Taethan said. "They have some ally behind the fallen tree they want to show off. Put fear into us."

"Let's get this over with," Heden said. "Where are your friends?" he called out to the urq leader.

"Enh?" Pakadrask sneered, questioning.

The other urmen looked worried and glanced behind the massive fallen tree.

"Behind the tree," Taethan yelled. "Don't be shy, let us see your smiling face."

Pakadrask sneered at the men's attempt to thwart his dramatic reveal. He snapped his fingers, and his urq began to stomp and shout with battle fever.

Its footsteps made little sound, because the thing knew to move without announcing its presence. It stepped up onto the tree and towered above them. Larger than the hills thyrs. It was a tall, hairless humanoid, perfectly formed. Its skin looked dull grey, but Heden recognized it and knew that close up it was white with flecks of black, like granite. Exactly like granite.

Heden turned to Taethan, who was doing his best not to look surprised.

"I just want you to know," Heden said, "I'm actually a little worried right now."

"Wait," Taethan said.

Heden turned back in time to see two more mountain thyrs step up onto the fallen tree.

"If I die out here," Heden said to Taethan, "I'm going to be really angry with you."

"The giants hate the urq!" Taethan objected.

"Well why don't you explain that to them?" Heden said, and then spoke a prayer.

The urmen didn't seem to notice or mind. So Heden warded himself and Taethan.

"This is my friend," Pakadrask said, gesturing to the tallest of the three thyrs. "Hrannat," he said. The stone giant's massive, implacable face grinned.

"What will you tell your master," Taethan called out, pointing to the stone giants, each almost twenty feet tall, "when we have sent your men to Grole? When you have wasted these powerful allies 'gainst us?" The urq obviously didn't like hearing the name of their god spoken without fear by a terran. "When you come back alone, when you have failed, what will Kadakav say?"

"Lord Kadakav!" Pakadrask barked. "King Kadakav!" he shouted.

"King of nothing," Taethan said. "Lord of fools! You cannot hope to stand against the order," Taethan said.

"Order? I see no other Green Men," Pakadrask said. The urq cheered at this. "Just you and your squire," he sneered.

"Alright," Heden said, wearily.

He spoke a prayer and a gust of wind exploded into Pakadrask, throwing him backward off the log. It was meant to make him look the fool and anger the urq, provoke them. It worked.

The urq shot off the log like a volley of arrows, some leaping and tumbling when they hit the ground, streaming towards the two men.

Heden turned to Taethan and shrugged. He was tired of talking and knew they were going to fight as soon as he heard the urq speak. They didn't come here to negotiate.

Heden wasn't worried about the urmen. He realized he maybe should be; he and Taethan were exhausted, recently wounded, lightly armored, but the real problem was the thyrs. The two men together could probably handle one. But three? And three aided by a company of urmen?

Taethan began a prayer. The two smaller mountain thyrs watched the larger, their boss. He seemed content to watch how the urq fared.

As five score urq thundered forward, Taethan finished his prayer and a thin line of emerald-green vines twisted and snaked their way out of the ground under the blanket of leaves. At first they seemed meaningless; the urq would stomp them underfoot. But they were waist-high by the time the line of urq slammed them. They snagged the urmen and continued to grow. They caught ankles and legs and arms and lifted dozens of urmen into the air.

The urmen behind came up short and watched, bright yellow eyes wide as their compatriots fought and struggled to hack at the ropey vines. But soon they no longer had mastery of their arms, bound in green. Then they started screaming.

The vines ripped the urq apart. Vitriolic blood rained down. Heden and Taethan waited.

For the urmen, fear was at worst a brief inconvenience. Soon their drive to hunt and kill overcame it, and they attacked the line of snaking vines, hacking at them. It wasn't clear if any tool, any strength, could overcome the power of the Green, the power of the wode made manifest, but then the tall stone giant gestured, and one of his lieutenants stepped lightly off the fallen tree.

The mountain thyrs strode forward, urq fighting to get out of his way, and waded into the vines. Even at twenty feet tall, they only came up to his eyes. He collected fistfuls of them, and though they wound around his wrists, they could gain no purchase. He pulled and uprooted them, grabbed more, yanked, and the vines died in his fists. Urmen ran forward, barking, shouting.

Sir Taethan sighed and spoke another prayer. The light around them brightened. The sunlight piercing through the veil of leaves strengthened until each shaft of light was solid white, too bright to look at directly.

There were only a dozen such shafts. Heden wondered what the point was. Then the beams of light started moving.

They searched and strove, like living things. Like there was a giant eye behind each beam, up above the canopy of leaves, peering down looking for urq. They moved smoothly until one oriented to a single urq and then suddenly flared even brighter, cooking the screaming urq where he stood.

Dozens fell thus. Heden was impressed.

The searching shafts of light faded, another three score urq cooked into smoking, blackened husks. The acrid, oily smell of burning fat and flesh now stuck to Heden's nostrils.

But still more urmen came. When they were close enough, Taethan burst into action. Even hurt, even without his full plate, he was devastating. His weapon sliced and stabbed about him, felling urq faster than they could come. It took no apparent effort on his part.

Taethan's prayers and battle skill were among the best Heden had ever seen. Urmen lost their heads, their arms. Their pink guts rippled from their fat bellies. He tripped them, he knocked them down. One urq charged him and received Taethan's boot in his chest, knocking him back and flipping his axe up in the air. Taethan caught it and smashed it into another urq's head while slicing across the eyes of yet another with his sword.

The urmen knew of no way to fight but to rush the knight. Their normal tactics were useless. Their shamans melted the ground into soup; Taethan leapt over the morass. Their godcallers cursed him, but his purity protected him.

Halcyon granted him power and there seemed no limit to it. Heden realized that this lone knight might be the last stand of the Green Order. Halcyon would give him whatever he asked for.

Heden watched as for a brief period Taethan's sword transformed into a long and snaking whip vine that could snap through a dozen urq, slicing them open in an instant. He liked that.

A dozen urq stood atop the tree and pulled on massive bone bows. Heden nodded, he'd anticipated this.

Their black arrows sped towards Heden and Taethan and hammered into them, but apart from the heavy thuds, each enough to knock an unprepared man over, the tips of the arrows could not penetrate even their exposed flesh. Heden had warded them well.

Seeing this, the lead thyrs gestured to creatures Heden couldn't see behind the tree. They pushed up a great rock, which the giant grabbed easily.

"Watch out!" Heden said, trying to get some distance.

The thyrswight threw the huge boulder at Taethan, who ducked out of the way and then leapt into the air. When the rock hit the ground behind him, the impact threw dirt high and knocked several urq off their feet, but Taethan was already in the air and so remained unaffected.

Heden was impressed. Taethan was minding the giant just as Heden was, and needed no warning.

For his part, Heden was dealing with fewer urq. They seemed much more interested in Taethan, the known quantity. Heden slashed and stabbed about him with *Starkiller*, the dwarven blade drinking the blood of the urmen greedily. Its eerie light sparked and flashed with each blow.

The three thyrs remained otherwise disengaged. They were watching the knight and the arrogate, looking for weakness, judging strength.

Heden heard an urq barking orders. He knew it was Pakadrask. The urq commander climbed back atop the tree and, seeing the giants doing nothing, shouted at them and pointed at the knight and the priest.

The lead thyrs shouted to the companion who'd uprooted the vines, and tossed him a heavy stone maul. The shorter thyrs waded into battle with it. It was crudely shaped, but so large it needed no special craftsmanship to wreak its havoc.

The giant swung about, trying to hit Taethan. Many urmen were killed in the process. Those remaining didn't seem to notice. Taethan avoided one blow, two, but the giant surprised him by smashing the ground when Taethan expected another blow, knocking the knight into the air. The giant was ready for this—it was a tactic he'd tried before—and as the knight rose into the air, the thyrs swung his maul around again and smashed Taethan in his unarmored chest, sending him flying.

Had he landed, wounded, amongst the urmen, it would have been trouble, but through sheer luck the thyrs sent the knight flying to Heden.

Heden ran to Taethan and saw he'd been knocked out. Heden touched the knight with *Starkiller* and said a potent prayer. Taethan opened his eyes, no disorientation, and extended his hand to the arrogate.

Heden helped Taethan up and for a moment the two men grasped forearms like soldiers and looked into each other's eyes. There was gratitude from Taethan, but not for the help: for the kinship. Heden was moved, and as the urmen ran to them and the giant strode towards them, Heden felt a bond with this knight, unlike any knight he'd known before.

The feeling lasted only a moment, and then the urq were upon them.

The knight and the former priest fought, back to back, each man's sword arm acting as shield for the other. While Heden was nothing like the fighter Taethan was, *Starkiller* made up the difference.

Soon they were surrounded by urq with rust-covered skin, and Heden knew Pakadrask had unleashed his elite upon them. Bloodrunners. But he had no patience for this. He spoke a word in Elemental and the whole squad of them, twelve at least, fell as *Starkiller* unleashed blue-black lightning arcing between them, each arc detonating an urq and leaving behind a pink mist before leaping to the next.

In an instant, the elite urmen were down, leaving a confused and frightened army. Their Bloodrunners had died in the blink of an eye without scratching the humans. The urq had never seen anything like this power. Many ran.

But the giant did not. He strode forward, banging his stone maul against the ground.

"If you were saving anything for later!" Heden shouted over his shoulder as the two men fought together. "There are two more where this one came from!" The other two mountain thyrs stood on the fallen tree, their leader with his arms crossed, watching to see how one thyrs would fare.

Heden felt Taethan's left shoulder pressing back against him, and they wheeled until Taethan was fighting and facing Pakadrask, who was commanding his urmen and the thyrs.

"You wish to see the power of the Green?!" Taethan called out. "You would pit your might against mine?" He killed another three urq, and he and Heden strategically withdrew. Neither wanted the pile of urq bodies to rise so high that they couldn't maneuver.

"The Green is broken!" Pakadrask howled, his long white tusks slicing through the air with every word. "This is your last stand!"

"Prepare to meet your god and be shamed before him!" Taethan hurled back.

He spoke a prayer and Heden was surprised when he heard it. It was just a name. Like one might summon a dominion. What was the knight doing? What power did he call?

The earth trembled. The urq stopped attacking. Heden stopped attacking. The thyrs ceased its march towards them. They had to concentrate to keep their footing. They looked around wildly.

The fallen tree the urmen used as cover began to rise. Taethan's prayer animated it, infused the dead tree with some dark forest spirit.

Branches grew like rising smoke. As though time had sped up. Vines grew and lashed themselves to the other trees, pulling the tree upright as more branches pushed from below.

Urq fell from the thing like beetles. The two thyrs lost their balance and fell backward. Behind the tree Heden could see what seemed like an entire army of urmen waiting for battle. But this couldn't be the whole thing; the urmen had a keep to assault. Heden had underestimated the size of the real army, if this was only a fraction they sent to kill Taethan.

The tree rose with frightening speed until it was upright again, its leafless branches scraping the canopy of green leaves above. It was a raging thing and it hated the urq. Without mouth, without eyes, it radiated hunger for these twisted mirror mockeries of men.

Vines reached out and wrapped themselves around the urq, thrust themselves into urq mouths, erupted from urq eyeballs and ears. Some urmen were merely picked up, flailing about trying to cut the vines, and some succeeded. But those were merely grabbed by other vines, sometimes before they hit the ground.

As the tree spirit maneuvered forward, Heden unable to see how it propelled itself, black branches would suddenly thrust out, like lances twenty feet long, skewering several urmen at once.

"Wow," Heden said, mouth slack, eyebrows raised.

Pakadrask ordered and many urq attacked the tree god, ran at it and chopped at its crumbling, decaying bark. But each blow let off a cloud of black spores from the tree. The urq couldn't help but breathe them in, cough once, twice, and then fall to the ground. They died squirming, their small yellow eyeballs popping out of their heads.

The thyrs before them knew this was Taethan's work. It ran at the knight, needing only three strides to close the distance, and pounded its stone maul into the ground as it did so. Arcing from the point where the club struck the forest floor came a brilliant white lightning bolt that stabbed at Taethan. But Taethan was ready.

Taethan dodged as soon as he saw the thyrs bring its maul down; he knew what the mountain thyrs could do. But leaping out of the way gave the giant the opportunity to grab Taethan in its massive hand after its club had smashed into the ground.

The giant pinned Taethan's arms to his side, clasped the knight to its chest and began to crush him. Taethan couldn't breathe, couldn't attack. The other two thyrs watched, grinning. Enjoying watching their friend kill a Green Knight.

Heden ran forward, prepared to attack the giant, but Pakadrask interposed himself, an axe in each hand, and assaulted the priest.

The urq commander was a skilled fighter. Much more skilled than his men. Heden recognized the fighting style. Pakadrask had been a Bloodrunner. Experienced beyond a normal urman and now a commander besides.

In spite of this, Heden was not afraid.

He lashed out with *Starkiller* and one of Pakadrask's axes exploded, sending shards of metal into the urman's forearm.

Heden tried it again with the other axe, but this time there were just black sparks. There was some form of sorcery on the remaining axe. He frowned and stepped back. The urmen could not create a sorcerous blade. Where had Pakadrask gotten this axe?

Pakadrask, his left arm bleeding, grinned at Heden, his flat white teeth smeared with blood.

Heden was not a swordsman—he had to rely on *Starkiller* to fight for him. But his prayers made up for it. He blinded Pakadrask, but the urq kept pressing the attack and fought by sound until he managed to shake off the blindness.

Heden encountered worry, and looked to see if Taethan was still alive.

The knight was unconscious, limp in the thyrswight's arms. Heden saw this and began to summon Ailil, a dominion, to settle the matter. But fate intervened.

Whatever prayer Taethan had used to manifest the demon tree spirit wore off. The urq army was decimated, but enough were left to be a problem as long as the three giants still lived.

The tree ceased moving, slowly began to topple over. Heden watched as it fell towards the giant holding Taethan. Pakadrask stopped and watched as well.

The mountain thyrs turned at the last moment and saw the huge tree about to fall on it. Mouth open, it tried to step out of the way, so the tree would only glance him.

But at the last moment, a pointed branch thrust out from the tree and, with the entire weight of the two-hundred-foot-tall tree behind it, drove itself into the giant, through its skull and down through its chest, impaling it, ripping it apart, and finally crushing it.

Taethan's unmoving body fell to the ground next to the dead thyrs and the now-lifeless tree.

Heden tried to close the gap again and get beyond Pakadrask, but the urman commander had slipped behind him.

Pakadrask wrapped his remaining massive arm around Heden's head, twisting and exposing the man's neck. Heden began a prayer, and then his shoulder and collarbone exploded in pain. He saw coming into view from below two needle-thin, blood-red tusks.

Pakadrask had pierced Heden's breastplate with his tusks, which went clean through Heden's chest and neck. He was biting down at the same time, into Heden's shoulder.

Heden swung around, pulling Pakadrask with him, and tried to stab the urq with *Starkiller*, but the urq was unreachable.

Heden found he couldn't breathe, and the weight of the urq commander drove Heden to his knees. The other urq stood by, watching their master take the priest down. Many glanced at the tree, afraid it still had the power to kill.

Pakadrask twisted and Heden felt his neck would snap. He looked at Taethan's unconscious form and thought that if he wasn't dead now, he would be once the urmen finished with Heden.

As his vision narrowed, Heden found himself feeling guilty over the knight's death, over his own inability to learn the truth. He had failed here, and it was costing him his life, but more he felt he had failed Taethan, and he wasn't sure how or why. He would die confused and ignorant here in the forest.

Figures, he thought.

Something hit him. Something big smashed into him and ripped the urq commander off him, sending Heden spinning and falling on his face.

Face down in the dirt and leaves, he heard hooves beating past him. A horse. A big one. He pushed himself up and looked forward and saw a caparisoned steed with a knight atop it. A Green Knight. Though helmed, given his size there was only one knight it could be.

Sir Nudd.

His lance had unerringly pierced Pakadrask's ribs, jutted through his chest, but the urq was still alive. His strength inhuman. Nudd tilted his lance up, and Pakadrask slid down it, impaling himself further, the lance protruding from his back, covered in black oily blood.

The lance held in one hand, Nudd drew a great two-handed sword with the other. Pakadrask's eye went wide; he gritted his teeth, scrambling to grab the lance, prevent himself from sliding closer to Nudd. He knew what was coming.

As though it were light as a rapier, Nudd's two-handed sword swung around and Pakadrask's head flew off into the forest, landing where Heden couldn't see.

Seeing their commander killed, the urmen went into a blood rage. They forgot Taethan and Heden, forgot the deadly tree spirit, stopped running away, turned and swarmed across the forest floor towards the knight. He and his horse were so large, they made the urq seem small.

Sir Nudd swung about him with his broadsword. His horse stamped and bit, turning slowly, crushing urq skulls and ribs with its mighty hooves. Apart from Nudd and his pack and weapons, there was a body wrapped in white cloth strapped to the horse's back.

The body of Sir Idris.

Heden watched, dumbstruck for a moment. He saw Taethan lying, unconscious, a few yards away. He made a quick calculation.

He crawled to the knight and examined him. He was unconscious, ribs shattered, but Heden could fix that. First, he asked Lynwen for aid, and strength and health flooded back into him. His wounded shoulder and neck healed and became stiff, almost too stiff to move.

He watched Nudd swinging his sword about him like a whip, and urq fell in pieces. Each swing took out two or three of them.

One urq used his heavily muscled arms to lope forward and launch himself over the fray at Nudd, but the knight simply reached out with one hand, the other stabbing his impossibly heavy sword through the fat of another urq, and grabbed the tusk of the screaming urq as it arced through the air.

Tusk in hand, Nudd twisted and snapped the urman's jaw in one fluid motion, pulling it down behind him as he twisted out of the way. The entire episode took no more than three seconds. Nudd was impossibly strong. He could have carved up this entire band with his bare hands.

The urmen finally tore Sir Nudd's horse out from under him. The beast screamed in pain as they ripped it apart. Heden's heart raced at the terrible sounds.

For a moment, Heden couldn't see anything but a beating, thrashing pile of urmen tearing into the still-living horse, but then Nudd regained himself. He stood. Though his horse was now mortally wounded—would be alive for only a moment more and in pain all the while—Sir Nudd began hewing about him again, defending the dying mount. His face was grim, but his eyes streamed tears. The only sign of mourning for his steed.

Bodies piled around Sir Nudd, but nothing could stop him. No urq, certainly. Heden watched, dragging Taethan's body as fast as he could, and wondered, as urq after urq fell, *How many would it take?* How many urq was enough? Nudd's labor seemed effortless.

None, Heden realized with admiration. No amount was enough. The only hope the urq had was to ignore the knight—he was only one man and now had no horse. But they were driven with hatred for the knight who killed their commander.

Heden stripped off Taethan's armor, preparing to pray over him and bring him back again. There were still two thyrs. Did Nudd know that?

Urq archers climbed back atop the fallen tree, their fear of what it had done mastered. From their vantage point above the battle, they loosed a dozen black arrows. And a dozen arrows thudded into Nudd. It seemed only to enrage him further, but Heden knew this couldn't last. The arrows were almost certainly poisoned and Nudd had not warded himself.

Heden started to pray, but stopped when he heard a sound like a thunderclap from behind. It took him a second, looking at the still-raging battle, to reconstruct what had happened.

Nudd was still standing, but his armor had peeled off him and was now smoking in a husk at his feet, some small, sharp scraps still clinging to him.

The lead thyrs, his second behind him, had stabbed the ground with his own lightning maul, loosing a bolt that slammed into Nudd, burned and blistered him and peeled his armor off.

Sir Nudd was not down yet, but was now largely unarmored and poisoned, and two thyrs faced him. He was the biggest of the knights but next to the mountain thyrs he seemed a child.

His flesh smoked. He seemed disoriented. He didn't seem aware of what had just happened. Though many urq died when the lightning hit him, there were many more. An endless supply, who ran at the knight in an attempt to avenge their leader.

As the urq blades cut into his seared flesh, he continued to fight. The two thyrs surrounded him and swung at him with their mauls. He deflected one, dodged another, but then the lead thyrs caught him and smashed his collarbone. Heden heard a snapping sound.

He watched in silent horror as something appeared ready to burst out of Nudd. His chest swelled, his face turned red as though he were about to vomit, and then as if torn from Nudd violently, Heden heard something he would never forget.

"KAVALEN!" Nudd cried at the last. His tears mingled with blood. Though one arm was now useless, he hewed about him mightily, his two-handed blade a blur.

"KAVALEN!" he shouted again, the first words he'd spoken since swearing his oath. Heden saw the knight's hair slowly bleed its green out, revealing dull brown. Nudd was a knight no longer. He seemed to physically diminish, but Heden couldn't be sure if it was just a trick of his perception. The thyrs hit him again. And again.

Summoning the last of his strength, he continued to fight. His oath broken, his unnatural power deserted him. His massive strength waned, but it seemed it would take hours to bring him down. Moments ago, he could not be stopped by any number of urq. Now, there was no way he could survive.

Heden looked around. The urq were ignoring him. They wanted a piece of the Green Knight's flesh. To eat the body of the man who killed their master.

Using the kind of logic one acquired over a decade of campaigns, Heden picked up the unconscious form of Sir Taethan and slung the knight over his shoulder.

Around Nudd, the bodies of a hundred urq, two hundred, lay dead or dying. The urmen swarmed over him and Sir Nudd disappeared under a pile of stabbing, slashing, beating blue-black arms. Heden could see the knight no longer.

He turned and, with Taethan on his back, ran for the priory.

Chapter Forty-five

The sound of battle faded until eventually Heden could hear it no more. He alternated walking a few paces, then jogging a few, Taethan on his back, until he felt safe. He found a large boulder without any trees growing around it and laboriously climbed atop it, eventually resting Taethan's body on top of the rock. From this vantage point, it would be very difficult for anyone to sneak up on him while he tended to the knight.

Normally he would be concerned over how much aid he had asked Cavall for thus far, but all such concerns fled at the sight of the man almost dead before him. Being roughly carried by Heden for over an hour hadn't helped.

Heden prayed, and Taethan's wounds mended quickly. He could sense the presence of Cavall's power, and someone else's. Halcyon's.

Taethan opened his eyes.

"We're alive," he realized.

Heden nodded.

"You saved me," Taethan said. He held out his arm. Heden grasped it at the elbow. A fraternal handshake. "I owe you my life."

"It was Nudd," Heden said, releasing the knight.

"Sir Nudd?" Taethan asked, confused.

"You were out," Heden said. He explained what happened.

"We must aid him," Taethan said. Heden nodded knowingly.

"We can't," he said.

"Cannot?" Taethan said. "You would leave him to…"

"Nudd is no longer a knight," Heden said.

Taethan gaped at him.

"Nudd?" he asked, almost like a child, his face fallen.

"He saved me," Heden said, sitting back on the rock. "He killed that urq commander. He…he called out."

"Oh, Nudd!" Taethan cried.

"He called out Kavalen's name as his battle cry. His last words."

"This world!" Taethan said, looking to the sky. "Halcyon aid me!"

It seemed the knight wanted to weep but his own pain overwhelmed him.

"I don't know how much of Pakadrask's unit will survive," Heden said, trying to ignore Taethan's pain. "Some of them were running as soon as you brought up that tree thing. We've got to get back to the priory if we have any chance of…" Heden thought about how much had been lost already. "Anything," he said finally.

Taethan didn't seem to be listening. Heden didn't blame him. He extended his arm again. Taethan took it reflexively, and Heden lifted him up.

"You ready to go?" Heden said, examining him for any permanent damage.

Taethan just looked down at him.

"How do you bear it?"

Heden didn't want to look the knight in the eye, wanted to pretend he didn't hear what the knight had said. But he felt he owed him something. What, he wasn't sure.

He looked into the eyes of the Green Knight.

"It's not easy," he said. He knew it sounded glib, but it was the truest thing he could think of.

Taethan wouldn't drop it.

"Tell me," he said.

Heden didn't know how to answer questions like this. He remembered the lake, its beauty, and then the Yllindir arriving. He remembered Elzpeth and everything they had, and then Aendrim. He remembered asking his father a similar but much less meaningful question and, not for the first time, found himself quoting a farmer in his seventies who'd never been more than five miles from home.

"You have to take the good with the bad," Heden said simply.

Taethan looked like he'd been poisoned, like he might throw up at any moment. Heden knew what he wanted to say.

"Some people get a bigger helping of bad," Heden said, agreeing with the knight's unspoken objection. "Not much you can do about that."

He knew the answer didn't satisfy. But then, what answer could?

"Complaining about it doesn't seem to help," he said. "Come on." He turned and climbed down the rock.

When he was on the ground again, he looked up and saw Taethan looking down at him. The knight hadn't moved.

"I no longer think it matters," Taethan said.

Heden looked around the forest impatiently, and looked back up at Taethan, waiting for him to explain.

"Whether you speak the ritual," he said.

"Maybe it never mattered," Heden allowed himself to say, remembering what the polder and Halcyon had said.

"You may be right. It is a kind of tragedy. I would undo it, if I could."

"You should have thought of that before Kavalen was murdered."

Taethan surprised Heden.

"You are right," he said. He paused in thought and then began to climb down the rock. Heden wondered if that was as close as he'd get to a confession.

Once both were on the forest floor, they began heading south again. Neither spoke.

Heden didn't know how much time passed, maybe an hour, before Taethan spoke again.

"There are only five of us now," he said.

Heden kept his mouth shut.

"Four dead."

"Going to be a lot more than four dead," Heden said, "if we don't get Isobel to stop the Yllindir."

"The keep," Taethan said, nodding.

"Yeah. What, did you forget?"

"Not exactly," Taethan said. "I…I admire your ability to focus on the next problem."

"Thanks," Heden said with no gratitude. "Wouldn't mind five thousand urmen fighting for survival and territory instead of killing humans they don't give a shit about, either."

Taethan absorbed this, saying nothing.

"Don't get me wrong," Heden said. "I don't mind a dead urq, I don't mind that at all, but I like to think they're off somewhere in the wode fighting the trolls and the brocc."

At this, a war scream sounded just behind them, and an urq launched itself at Taethan. It had followed them alone from the battle.

Both men, exhausted, were surprised. But it was just one urq. The blink of an eye and the thing lay against a tree twenty feet away, unmoving.

Heden and Taethan walked up to it, sheathing their weapons. It was still alive, breathing. Its eyes open, but unseeing.

Taethan took off his linen shirt and began to tear it into bandages.

"What are you doing?" Heden asked.

Taethan didn't answer.

The urq wheezed; black blood, thicker than human blood, oozed from its wounds. Its yellow eyes were wide and unfocused. It was in shock.

This is what the dragons thought of us, Heden thought.

"This thing would kill you if it had the chance; you know that better than anyone."

"It's helpless."

"What does that have to do with it?" Heden said thickly, looking around the forest.

Taethan continued to minister to the creature. He tensed and his movements became jerky, angry at Heden.

"You realize," Heden said, "that what you're doing right now probably means the death of more men."

Taethan surged to his feet. He stopped himself from assaulting Heden.

"Stop *testing* me," Taethan said, staring at Heden, their faces inches from each other.

"Is that what I'm doing?" Heden asked.

"Why are you so blind?" Taethan demanded. "Why can't you see what's happening right in front of you? You know why I'm doing this, by the gods, stop acting like you don't."

"You're aiding the enemy."

"Don't act like you don't understand! Don't *blame* me because you don't know what's happening at the priory!"

This threw Heden. He tried using his ignorance like a weapon.

"There are a lot of things I don't know," he said. "I came up here to find out and I get 'talk to Taethan.' Well that didn't do a lot of good, did it? You don't want to talk to me, you don't want to tell me what happened. You sure as shit don't care if it destroys the order, but by Cyrvis' thorny prick you care about a fucking urq."

"I'm helping this creature because I have to!" Taethan shuddered with barely controlled violence. *Finally,* Heden thought. *We're down to it.*

"Why do you call it a creature; why don't you call it an urq?" Heden was not intimidated. The opposite. He felt he and Taethan were both walking the same awful path, but only one of them could see it.

"Do you think that I am doing this for the *urq*?" Taethan said.

Heden didn't reply.

"I'm doing this because of who I am. Because I'm not going to give that up. Not because of the urq. Not because he deserves it, not because of what he's done or what he might do. Not because of what *they think*," he shouted. Heden knew he meant the rest of the order.

"And later?" Heden asked. "When it's killing the innocent people at the keep?"

"Damn it, man! Why are you doing this?! Why are you pretending like you wouldn't do the same thing? Why are you acting like *them?*" he demanded, pointing in the direction of the distant priory.

Heden shook his head, trying to preserve his sense of self in Taethan's onslaught.

He looked at the dying urq. It heard none of this, its body desperately trying to maintain life for another few moments. Heden saw the giant, Nudd's spear sticking out of its back, make one last vain, horrible attempt to save itself, push itself up, and only end up turning its head to look at Heden. Pleading. Terrified. It didn't know why it was dying. Heden didn't know why Nudd had killed it.

"It's a creature born and bred to hate and kill," Heden said slowly, trying to keep perspective. "You took an oath—"

"My *oath*? Do not dare to speak of my oath, thou base and churlish knave," he said. "You defame it by your presence. I swore to preserve life."

"Human life."

"All life!"

"Is that what you told Kavalen before you killed him?" Heden dared.

Taethan lunged at him, his speed remarkable. Heden braced himself and the knight grabbed him by his breastplate at the shoulders, lifted him off the ground and bore him backward, slamming him into the trunk of a tree. Heden's head hit the bark and he almost lost consciousness again. When he'd shaken the impact off, he heard Taethan shouting at him.

"What kind of man are you?!" Taethan roared. "Why did you come here, why are you doing this?"

"I came to absolve the order of…" Heden began.

"No!" Taethan said, pulling Heden's body away from the tree and then slamming him back into it. "You! What do you want?! Is there nothing left of the priest? Is there no man in there?" he howled, and slammed Heden into the tree again.

Heden looked into Taethan's face, twisted with rage, his eyes red.

"I don't know," Heden confessed, and the confession took something out of him, took away some defense he had stored. He was afraid of what it meant, and his fear showed. "I don't know what else to do."

In a flash, the hate was gone. As quickly as it had arrived. Taethan shrunk. Like a puppet whose strings were cut, he sagged but did not collapse. He let Heden go. He looked beaten.

Heden felt the same. He'd deliberately provoked the knight and felt like shit because of it, and he'd still not gotten what he wanted.

Heden watched Taethan's reaction, and something clicked. Heden peered at the Green Knight.

"Compassion," he said.

"What?" Taethan asked, uncomprehending.

"That's what Halcyon meant. What she hoped I'd figure out." What gave Taethan his power.

Taethan ripped some cloth in two and handed a strip to Heden.

"Are you going to help me or not?" he asked.

"The other knights must *hate* you," Heden said. The sheer weight of Heden's understanding of the knight struck him like a blow. Taethan bowed his head.

"Every time they do their duty, they see you judging them," Heden pronounced. Taethan seemed to diminish with each sentence.

"You were a priest," Taethan said miserably.

"They love it. Defending the forest, killing the urq and thyrs who push things too far."

"Have you no mercy?" Taethan pleaded.

"But you've got so much compassion you can't stand it. You do it, and it kills you a little each time."

"You were a good man once," Taethan said. "What happened to you?"

"They hate that. They hate being reminded of how awful it is. Hate being reminded of what it's like being human. And you hate reminding them. But you don't know how to stop it. You'd give anything to stop it. You're so full of compassion, you're sick with it." He pointed to the dying urq. "You can't help but feel what it feels. And it's destroying you."

Taethan didn't look at Heden; he just held out the strip of white cloth, and waited. Waited to see how much Heden understood.

Heden knew what the offer meant. It meant all of Heden's judgment of the knight was judgment of himself as well. Meant admitting that whatever Taethan had done, whatever had brought Heden up here, whatever happened to Kavalen, it was exactly the same thing Heden would have done, and for the same reason.

Heden reached out and took the torn piece of blood-stained white linen.

He held the cloth limply in his hand and watched the perfect knight turn and tend to the enemy. He didn't know what to think. His mind was empty but for understanding of Taethan. The knight who had lived such a different life from Heden and yet the two of them had ended up living the same false existence. Fearing what it meant, Heden felt closer to this knight than he ever had anyone in his life.

He looked at the urq. The once strong and deadly creature now seemed feeble and childlike.

Heden bent, his joints popping, kneeled awkwardly on the ground, tore off a strip of white cloth and began to bind the urman's wounds.

Chapter Forty-six

Neither of them spoke the entire way back to the priory.

It was after noon by the time they stepped out of the forest and entered the clearing dominated by the steeple of the stone building. It had been only three days since Heden left Celkirk. Three days without sleep. The skies were darkening. The temperature was dropping rapidly. There would be a storm.

The wind picked up, causing the tent Aderyn had left half-built to whip and flap. Sir Brys was standing outside, brushing his horse. He saw Taethan and Heden emerge from the wode and called to the priory. Isobel came out and joined him.

The knight and the former knight crossed the clearing to Heden and Taethan. Heden had a hard time looking at Isobel—she seemed small. Lost. She looked to Brys for direction. She stood next to the younger knight like they were a couple, but the two did not touch.

"Where are the others?" Sir Taethan asked.

Brys shook his head. "Dywel and Cadwyr rode off. I did not ask them where."

"Isobel," Heden said, ignoring Brys. She looked at Heden as though afraid and confused.

"Isobel, the urq are driving an Yllindir to Ollghum Keep."

Isobel grasped Brys' elbow as though for support, looked up at him. She didn't understand what Heden was saying. Brys looked from Heden to Taethan.

"Heden," Taethan counseled, putting his hand on Heden's shoulder. "It was just this morning she..."

Heden jerked his shoulder from Taethan's grasp, and snapped his fingers rudely before Isobel to get her attention. Her eyes swam around to focus on him.

"Taethan says you know the queen of the local fae." Isobel nodded, her face gaunt. It seemed she'd aged twenty years since Heden saw her.

"Can you summon her?" he asked.

She looked at him.

"Isobel, there's a thousand people at Ollghum Keep about four hours away from certain death, are you listening to me? Your sister, Isobel. Remember your sister?"

"The queen," Isobel said quietly. She started to weep, though apart from the tears she gave no indication of anything other than disorientation. She had retreated as far as she could from the world around her.

Brys wrapped his whole hand around his jaw and mouth to cover his reaction.

"She would not answer my call," she said. "I killed…I am no longer a knight. I am not worthy of her attention." All Heden could see was someone despairing at her own fall from grace while her sister fought and died.

"I don't fucking believe it," Heden said, giving up. He tried to rub the headache out from his temples. "You all deserve each other, I swear by Cavall."

"I attempted to summon mine squire," Isobel said. "But I," she began and stopped. "There was no…" She couldn't bring herself to say it. It seemed to Heden as though she didn't understand what had happened.

Heden remembered what Halcyon had told him.

"I don't think you'll see her again," he said bluntly. Isobel bowed her head. It was something he thought she knew but refused to face. Heden was not in the mood for avoiding the truth.

Brys looked at the two of them.

"What happened to you?" he asked.

Taethan began to answer, but Heden cut him off.

"We went to the lake," Heden said.

"The lake?!" Brys said, alarmed, and looked at Taethan.

"And were ambushed. By the Yllindir. And then we were ambushed on the way back by the urq. And then…" Heden was losing track of everything that happened. "Then we were ambushed one more time. But that…that probably doesn't count." He looked around the clearing. The bodies of Idris and the giant were gone.

"Sir Nudd is dead," Taethan announced.

Isobel gasped.

"Oh yeah," Heden said, feeling very tired and letting it show. "I forgot that part."

"He rode out and saved Heden from Pakadrask. Heden saved me. Nudd gave his life so we could escape."

Brys and Isobel looked at each other and nodded. Isobel smiled a little. They deemed this a fitting death for a Green Knight. Heden looked from them to Taethan and then back again.

"No-no," Heden said. "Hang on, you don't get off that easy."

"Heden!" Taethan said, trying to stop the arrogate.

"No!" he said. "They're going to hear the whole…" He turned on Brys and Isobel.

"He died howling Kavalen's name." Isobel gasped and covered her mouth. "He was so full of grief and pain it was just ripped out of him. I watched it. He couldn't control himself. I watched his hair turn dirt brown as he screamed your master's name. He broke his oath. He died in fear and pain and disgrace!"

Isobel shook her head, trying to wipe tears from her eyes. Brys tried to console her, but she pushed herself away and ran back to the priory.

"Lady Isobel!" Taethan said, and went to stop her.

"No," Brys said, stopping Taethan. "Let her go." He turned on Heden.

"You would destroy her," he hissed. "She is mortal just like you and I."

"I watched her kill Idris for no fucking reason, don't give me that shit! And you stood by!"

Heden was in the mood for a fight, but Brys backed down. His hair was still green, but the fight had gone out of him.

"I had hoped…" Brys said.

"Yeah? What?"

Brys wouldn't look at him.

"You thought she'd kill Idris and then magically Halcyon would appear and crown her commander of you lot? By Cavall, I thought the White Hart was bad."

"If we ride now," Taethan said to Brys, ignoring Heden, "we can gain Ollghum Keep an hour before the Yllindir. The siege may last days. We can still discharge our duty."

"It is no matter," Brys said, deploying his favorite phrase. "We cannot stop the siege. We cannot stop the urmen. We can't stop anything."

"Do you think Halcyon will allow you to remain a knight," Taethan said flatly, "if those people die?"

"How could she not?" Brys demanded. "What have we done but obey…." He stopped and looked at Heden.

Heden was staring at the priory. Taethan saw it too.

Brys turned around.

"What is happening?" he asked, his eyes darting all over the priory.

Smoke was billowing out the archway. A fire roared inside; they could see its light flickering through the stained glass windows.

The priory was on fire.

"By Cavall," Heden said. At the name of his god, thunder rippled across the sky and it started to rain. It would not be enough. Nowhere near enough.

"Where is Isobel?" Brys asked, running forward. "Where did she go?!" He was frantic.

"Taethan!" Heden cried, pointing to Brys. Heden started to run after the knight. "Taethan, stop him! Stop him!"

Taethan just watched in horror, paralyzed.

Brys ran into the burning church. Heden went after him.

Inside, the wooden prayer benches had been pulled around haphazardly, and several were stacked around the altar.

On the altar stood Isobel, her armor stripped from her. Her clothes stripped from her. She stood there naked, and opened her arms to Brys.

He ran past the burning benches and leapt up onto the altar, embracing Isobel in his arms.

The benches around the altar burst into flame.

The fire roared, blasting heat out through the archway where Heden stood. He could see no path through the fire. It mirrored Isobel's despair, raging just as Brys enfolded her in his arms. He saw only their silhouettes through the fire.

They kissed passionately, like lovers, and the fire consumed them both.

Heden couldn't watch. He turned away just as Isobel screamed. Howled with incalculable pain and fear and more. Heden closed his eyes, put his hands over his ears, trying to block it out. He heard realization and regret in her mad screaming.

She was trying to get away. She was gibbering, desperate to get away from what she'd started. She'd changed her mind, but Brys clung to her. She realized what she'd done, and as the fire burned the flesh from her bones, she regretted it, and found there was no way back.

There was no sound from Sir Brys.

He opened his eyes. Taethan stood before him, looking into the blazing church, his face a rictus of hellfire. Orange light and shadow played across his fine features.

Heden grabbed him by the straps across his chest. The knight recoiled.

"How many?!" Heden shouted. "Is this enough?!" He shook the knight. Taethan did not resist, but did not answer him.

"Tell me what happened!" Heden howled out his pain on the implacable knight as the air filled with the charred flesh of Isobel and Brys. He didn't even know why he was asking anymore. Nothing made sense to him.

Taethan would not answer. Could not. Heden gave up. Pushed him away. He looked at the burning priory in dull horror. Then turned to Taethan, holding his clenched fist before him, the tendons on his arms and neck standing out.

"I swear by Cavall and Llewellyn, if I had the power I would curse you, I would lay such a curse upon you it would strike you blind and dumb. Your skin would boil off your bones, your eyes would cook, you'd shit your own entrails out and you would know that *judgment* had been passed upon you!" he hissed, furious.

"Heden, please..."

Heden pushed himself away and looked at Taethan as though for the first time. What had he come here for? What had he achieved? He raised his hands as he might to protect himself from attack. He remembered the giant, the grimace of Perren consumed by the wode. Idris, Isobel, Brys.

He looked at Taethan, unable to understand his unwavering denial of everything that had happened, and he hated the knight.

"Cyrvis take your bones," Heden abjured with a wave as he turned. It was not a thing a man of Cavall could say.

"Heden!" Taethan called.

As Heden strode away, he turned and, walking backward, pointed at the knight.

"You knew!" he called out and waved to the blazing priory. "You knew and did nothing!" Eyes red with tears and anger, he pointed at Taethan. "This be upon your head, *knight*!" He spat the word out. He was shaking with rage. He could not master it. He could only leave it behind. Cut it off and jettison it to survive.

He turned his back on the knight and the priory, its fire casting a long shadow. He opened his pack and yanked out the square of carpet that was left.

He stared into the bottomless pack, rain matting his hair to his face. Remembering something Taethan had said. He had the power, though he tried to avoid admitting it. He could save the people at Ollghum Keep.

Heden laid the carpet on the wet ground, stepped on it and draw *Starkiller* from his pack.

Armed with the ancient dwarven elf-slayer, Heden willed the carpet to rise, up, out, over the forest, and speed through the rain towards the doomed keep.

Chapter Forty-seven

The keep was almost completely razed to the ground. Heden wondered if the Yllindir had been here. If it was under the control of the urq. That seemed improbable, but no more improbable than the near-complete destruction of the keep.

The walls had been pulled down. The town surrounding the keep was still on fire, but the flames were dying, whether from time or the rain or both, Heden didn't know.

The motte and bailey that formed the core of the town and gave the keep its name was now a burned-out husk. It was the main source of the black smoke. Bodies, Heden knew, provided the fuel.

Heden landed, got up and walked off the carpet, leaving it behind. No one else could use it in any case, and he was certain there was no one left alive here.

There were many heads spit upon pikes. He could see dozens in every direction. Probably hundreds overall. Each urq, killing a human, would use a specially prepared ceremonial pike for the purpose. Heden didn't look at their dead faces. Didn't want to see someone he'd met here.

There were no bodies, though. Just heads. The urmen knew that the fat from the bodies was the best fuel for firing the keep.

He walked down the town's main road to the motte and bailey, the wet soil black with soot. But he could not attain the ruined keep itself; it was still too hot. The stones in a heap were glowing faintly, had once been red-hot. Heden guessed this had all happened the day before. Possibly around the same time Lady Isobel had immolated herself. The same time Sir Brys had run in to die with her.

Heden now wondered if the lady had known the timing of the urq army's march. She was the older sister, she would have been baron and the town hers to defend had she not joined the order. So she was responsible twice. She knew her sister and the town were dying, and had chosen to die with them. He felt a heavy weight pressing down on his chest, suddenly certain this was what fueled her grief. How could it be otherwise?

She was dead, though. Heden wondered if the baron died in flames just as her sister did. Heden couldn't bear to think about it. There was nothing now here to do. The urq army was nowhere to be seen. Their tracks went nowhere but the keep, which meant they'd marched back into the forest once their raiding was done.

Was there any connection between the keep and the knights? Heden wondered. There had probably been a time when he could have saved the keep, though he hadn't wanted to face that. Was there ever a time when he could have saved the knights?

How much of this was he responsible for? He didn't know. Just the thought of it made him sick. There was someone who knew. Someone who could tell him. And he no longer had any reason to stay here. His failure was complete.

Chapter Forty-eight

The Cathedral of St. Llewellyn the Valiant was the largest stone building in Vasloria. Its massive spires towered over the other buildings in Celkirk, a statement about the power and influence of the Church of Cavall the Righteous and his most popular saint. The only other building like it was the Cathedral of St. Bróccan the Stout, the primary saint of Adun, now a ruin in Aendrim's former high city of Exeter.

Heden walked down cobbled roads to the church in the early morning, reminded of a similar walk at this same time of day but to the jail to deal with Vanora. Before he knew she was Vanora. Only a few days ago. A lifetime ago.

Even at the height of his passion for the church, his worship of Cavall, he saw the Cathedral of St. Llewellyn as a massive piece of propaganda. A monument to power, the power of the church, its influence. It loomed over everything, deliberately. It was, Heden knew, a challenge to the king, and while this upset Heden, most of all it bothered him that everyone in Celkirk needed to be reminded that Cavall was Corwell's patron deity. People should be allowed to get on with their lives. What did it say about the church he served that somewhere there were people in it who felt the need to remind the citizens who they owed their spiritual allegiance to? The king's castle was large, but a purely practical building. There was nothing practical about the cathedral.

Walking through the massive doors, Heden was relieved to discover that the cathedral was nearly empty save for a few acolytes observing the dawn rituals, keeping the place clean, and some supplicants sitting in the pews waiting for first service.

The abbot waddled around replacing the ceremonial candles. Heden's boots rang out against the flagstones. Everyone in the church heard him, and all turned to look. Many of the acolytes knew him and so did not give him a second glance. The rest looked to the abbot, who was lighting the candles with a long brass candle lighter. The grey light outside failed to project the brilliant, multicolored light of the massive stained glass windows into the room. It gave the place a larger, more cavernous feel.

The abbot turned, saw Heden, watched him as he methodically tramped down the main aisle past dozens of prayer benches, then went back to lighting the candles.

Seeing him again, Heden realized the abbot was now an old man. He wasn't old in Heden's memory, just…older. Older than Heden. Now, of course, that meant the man was in his sixties. Twenty years used to seem like an eternity, but now Heden felt they were almost the same age. He felt like he was catching up.

The abbot had a short crop of white hair on top of his head, like a cloud had nested on his pate. His pale, square face was well-jowled though it had not always been. He had thin blue eyes and a wide smile from thin red lips. Taller than Heden, he had once been fit, but service to the church in the same building for fifty years and many heavy meals had thickened the man. He also had a stiffness in his legs that gave him a comical waddle, which he exaggerated for the sake of students who needed to learn early that wisdom could play the buffoon.

When Heden stopped a few feet away, the abbot was stretching and making elaborate noises to let everyone know how much his body complained about this duty.

"I thought of you, yesterday," the abbot said, his voice that of a comic character in a play. Unbidden came the thought of a Riojan troubadour and how much he and the abbot would like each other. "A student was asking about Joran the Rector. My first thought was of digging up…enh…your old papers."

Heden said nothing.

"'Human beings are not mathematical formulae, we cannot expect mathematical solutions.' I thought you wrote that, how's that for a compliment? I'd forgotten it was Joran. I tend to do that with you. You were so good at restating his work."

More stretching and grunting from the abbot. Silence from Heden.

"Did you know," the abbot continued, ignoring Heden, "there's a whore staying at your inn? Before you ask, Gwiddon told me. Not sure why I was surprised. Seems the least surprising thing in the world to me now."

He put a hand on his back and lowered the candle lighter. He grunted theatrically and turned to smile at Heden, a twinkle in his eye.

Then he saw Heden's visage and stopped smiling.

"Ah, well. It's that then. Come on!" the abbot declared. "Let's get out of the nave. Don't want to scare the acolytes."

The abbot led the way to his quarters in one of the dozens of rooms that fit into the niches and hidden-away places in the cathedral. It was a trail well-known to Heden.

Inside his quarters—piled with books and scrolls, several busts, an astrolabe, a working model of Orden with special disks for the World Below, the Land of Faerie and the Dawn and Dusk Moons as well as a stuffed owl, all collecting dust—Heden slumped down onto a threadbare divan against the wall by the door. One he had spent hundreds of hours on, man and boy.

The abbot waddled his way around his heavy rosewood desk, making a show of how difficult it was. Possibly to hide how difficult it actually was. He carefully sat down and then let out a sigh in preparation for heavy thinking.

He raised his thick, bushy white eyebrows once, signaling Heden.

"I need..." Heden had a hard time beginning. Was afraid to start. It was taking all his willpower to keep himself together. He was forty-three years old. He didn't want to cry in front of the abbot like some bawling babe. "I need help."

The abbot knew to keep silent. Let Heden find his own way.

"I don't understand..." Heden said, looking around the room. Looked at anything except the abbot.

"I don't know...what the point of..." He found it hard to breathe. He reached up, under his collar, and fished for the talisman of Lynwen. The icon of a woman's smiling eye. He wrestled it out from under his clothes and breastplate and pulled it violently up over his head.

Once released he held the talisman, silver chain dangling, and stared at it.

The abbot watched and said nothing. Let Heden fill the space up. Heden tossed the amulet down on the divan. He looked like someone had stabbed him.

"Things went bad in the wode?" the abbot prompted.

Heden was both surprised and concerned. "You know about it?"

"Gwiddon told me."

"Oh," Heden said without feeling.

More silence.

"Things went bad," he said finally, his eyes looking out into nothing.

More silence.

"I should have stayed at the inn," Heden said.

"Tell me what happened in the wode," the abbot said, trying to keep Heden on one subject.

It took Heden a while to say anything. Time seemed to slow for the two men, neither eager to talk. Then Heden started and the whole thing came out. The abbot didn't ask any questions—he concentrated on what Heden said. Heden skipped one thing, something he didn't feel the abbot needed to know.

"At the river with the young squire," the abbot asked, twirling a quill pen in his fingers. He didn't look at Heden—he leaned back in his chair, looking at a piece of art on the wall Heden had never paid much attention to.

Heden grunted his understanding.

"Was that the only episode you had?"

"I don't..." Heden struggled. "I need to talk about the knights," he said. He desperately needed the abbot's insight. "I need to know why I was there. What was I supposed to do?" He was yearning, desperate.

The abbot held up one finger. "The river," he said, and then bit his lower lip in thought.

Heden sighed.

"No."

The abbot nodded as though he'd suspected that.

"When I first went into the forest," Heden said, "I got...disoriented. Confused."

"No clear direction, no path to follow," the abbot filled in.

Heden stretched out a little and seemed to relax.

"I panicked," Heden said. "I almost turned around." Talking about it was difficult.

The abbot hummed to himself. He thought in silence a moment, then turned and faced Heden, leaned forward in his chair and put his arms on his desk.

"The death of the giant bothered you," the abbot said.

"I didn't come here for our normal—"

"You know the rules," he said.

Heden tried to calm down.

"Talk to me about the thyrs," the abbot said.

In the state Heden was in, remembering the death of the hills thyrs was difficult. His eyes started to get red.

"It was awful."

The abbot nodded, saying nothing.

"Aderyn had the problem under control. I don't know why Nudd did what he did."

Heden was avoiding the issue, and they both knew it. The abbot didn't say anything, confident Heden would get there.

"I should have done something," he said.

"How did you feel when you saw him die?" the abbot asked, trying to help Heden focus.

Heden, eyes red, trying not to show emotion, confessed: "I felt like I was dying."

"Were you aware you felt that way at the time?"

"Yeah," Heden said.

"And how did *that* make you feel?"

"I don't know," Heden said, evading.

The abbot smiled. "You didn't feel ashamed at all? After everything you've seen? You've killed giants."

"Alright," Heden said, now ashamed that he'd bothered to avoid the issue. "I felt like there was something wrong with me. I wanted to cry, to…to weep. Why? I couldn't control myself. Like another attack. Yeah. I felt ashamed."

"Because you felt so strongly about the death of a marauding thyrswight."

"Yeah," Heden said. "When I was younger, I'd have helped Nudd. Why wasn't I on his side?"

"So," the abbot said, sitting back in his chair, trying not to look too pleased with himself, "first you felt ashamed that being in the forest could cause you to lose control of yourself, and then you felt ashamed when you found yourself caring about a dying giant."

Heden found himself drawn into his own rehabilitation by his fascination with the abbot's process.

"You think they're related?" he asked.

The abbot's head nodded in big swoops, causing his chair to rock back and forth. "I do." The abbot knew Heden had taken it as far as he could, and so gave him the rest.

"I think the attacks leave you feeling vulnerable," he said.

Heden agreed. He had felt vulnerable.

"That's good for you; it's something you're not used to."

Heden's face fell. He understood. "Not like at the inn," he said, feeling stupid for not having seen it himself. The inn was his sanctuary.

The abbot grinned. "And that vulnerability leaves you open to feel other things."

In an instant, like remembering someone's name after having forgotten it, Heden realized this was truth. He could see the death of the giant now, and his own reaction, without shame. Though the memory of the giant's eyes still brought pain, he wasn't afraid of it.

"That giant didn't need to die," Heden said with certainty.

The abbot shook his head. "Probably not," he said.

"That was Nudd, and his pain. The order collapsing."

"The squire told you as much," the abbot said. "I think your reaction to the death of the giant was perfectly healthy. You experienced grief at the death of another life. That's something Sir Nudd could not do," he said.

Heden saw the truth. "I think Aderyn was upset too."

"Well, I haven't seen her, but she'd been affected by what was happening. Maybe sheltered from it too. There's hope for her yet."

Heden looked at him, and the image of Isobel and Brys wreathed in fire came unbidden to his mind. He felt nauseous.

"Let's talk about the knights," Heden said. The abbot agreed, taking a deep breath.

"The knight you met when you entered the forest was Sir Mór." He leaned back in his chair, assuming the role of teacher once again.

"Mór?" Heden asked.

"Mór was the squire of St. Godwin."

"I know him!" Heden was amazed. "By Cavall I learned about them at school."

"Mór was called 'The Green Man.' That's probably what he meant when he told you everyone in the north knew him. He became a figure more mythological than legendary. I think there was some Golish antecedent there, some preexisting figure whose role he stepped into." The abbot enjoyed teaching again, which was fine with Heden. He enjoyed being taught. "The Green Man is the spirit that fights winter, or keeps summer safe. There's a folktale, almost certainly based on a now-lost Golish legend, about Sir Mór, the Green Knight, going into the wode to rescue the Lady of Summer. It's an allegory of the cycle of the seasons."

Heden's eyes unfocused. "Pakadrask called Sir Taethan 'Green Man.'"

"Yes, well, there's obviously a connection there, although what exactly? Who knows? Mór seems interested in the fate of the order, certainly. And he knew something about you. Knew you were, ah…a mess." The abbot smiled with affection at his pupil.

Heden managed a smile.

"What did he want with me?"

"He was testing you."

"Testing me?" Heden objected.

"Well, testing you and preparing you to be tested."

This seemed to upset Heden.

"Test me for what?! What did he think I was going to…"

"Heden," the abbot said, trying to calm him down, and then his expression turned to fondness, remembering the student from years ago. "You never liked allegory, I remember. You're very literal-minded. Probably for the best."

"What are you talking about? I cut off the man's head!"

The abbot dismissed this comment with a flick of his fingers.

"You grew up on a farm, yes?"

Heden agreed. "Okay." He played along.

"You go out and collect the harvest, you collect the grain. With what?"

"With what?" Heden asked, not understanding the question. "With a scythe or a..." He frowned. "Or a sickle. Okay, I get it."

"But that's not the end of the world," the abbot continued, ignoring Heden's disdain. "More crops will grow next year. With some work on your part of course. So you chop off the head of the Green Man with your—" The abbot pointed to Heden's scabbard. "—your scythe substitute there. His head grows back, all is well."

"You're right," Heden said. "I hate allegory. Okay, so what? He wasn't doing that just to be...just to be *poetic*."

"No," the abbot agreed, "he obviously thought you weren't up to the task of saving the order, and this was his way of seeing how far you'd go."

"Well, I went about as far as you can!"

"Yes, and he accepted that. Probably he knew what I know."

Heden got goosebumps at that.

"What do you know?" he asked, wary of the answer.

"That if you couldn't save them, no one could."

Heden sulked. He didn't like this insight.

"You don't like knights, and I think Mór somehow knew that about you. But the true knightly ideal has very little to do with the Hart and their ilk. The true knight is about purity, which is where you get that oath of chastity. That, and courage. Those were your tests. Aderyn at the river: that was chastity. Fidelity. Love unrequited, all of those in one. And then courage, a test you passed several times, but mostly I think it was going back in after you left the first time.

"We can never be sure of these things, but I think when you cut off his head, he saw that he had no right to judge you. He knew, or believed, that you had to be in the forest as much as the knights. That it was as much a test for you as it was for them. Sir Taethan knew that, I think. That's why he accepted you. He saw a man going through the test of knightly virtue and I think he judged you a truer knight than any of his brothers."

Heden's face went blank.

"There's something I didn't tell you," Heden confessed.

This didn't appear to alarm the abbot. "I'm here for *you*, Heden. By now, if you don't want to tell me something, I trust you."

That helped. "When I came to, after the Yllindir almost killed us. Taethan and I were separated."

The abbot didn't say anything.

"Halcyon brought me around."

The abbot took this in stride. "You mean…when you awoke, you felt her presence in or around…"

"No, I mean she was there," Heden said. "She was actually there, I met her. I talked to her." *I looked at her legs.* "She made me soup."

The abbot accepted this.

"Why do you think she appeared to you?"

This was not the question Heden was expecting.

"She wanted to help me," Heden said.

"But that's why we're granted prayers," the abbot reminded him. "The saints aren't allowed to intervene directly. So why appear before you?"

"She was afraid," Heden guessed, and in guessing discovered the truth.

The abbot nodded. "Afraid of what?"

"Afraid her order was being destroyed."

"So why not appear before Taethan?"

"I don't know!" Heden shouted. The abbot's eyes rose. Heden was at his wits' end.

The abbot let him have his frustration, and let the matter lie.

"Well," he began, returning to the larger issue, "my first reaction to the whole thing is: you probably didn't make anything worse."

Heden didn't say anything. He tried to accept this. It wasn't easy.

"I failed."

The abbot frowned. "Nobody's perfect," he said.

"You sure about that?"

The abbot raised his eyebrows theatrically. "Confidence is high, as the castellan says. But one never knows. I loathe certainty."

No one said anything.

"So there's this girl back at the Hammer & Tongs," the abbot said, changing subjects.

"What?" Heden asked.

"Did you know I used to drink there, before you bought it and closed it down?"

"You what?" Heden asked, disoriented.

"I was talking with Gwiddon about the Hammer and you opening it. I miss the place."

"I can't talk about…listen, I need to know what to do about the knights."

"We've talked about them," the abbot said. "I want to talk about the girl."

Heden didn't say anything.

"What happens if you let her down?"

"What?" Heden heard him but couldn't process the question. It was too hard to switch midstream. The answer scared him too much.

"She's not a thousand people at a keep no one's ever heard of," the abbot said. "She's not a knight who spent sixty years in service to a practically monastic order. She's just a girl whose parents don't remember her. No one cares about her. What happens if she just goes back to what she knows? Back to being a whore?"

"She'll be dead in ten years," Heden said.

"I'm not asking about her, Heden," the abbot pointed out. "What happens to you if she goes back to being a whore?"

Heden shook his head.

"I don't think I could take it."

"Why not?"

"Because she deserves better."

"Everyone deserves better."

"I didn't save everyone's life," Heden said.

"But why her? Why save her life?"

Heden was silent for a moment. He knew the answer.

"She needs me."

"Ah!" the abbot said, Heden having finally said something revelatory. "And what do you need?"

"I guess I need her too."

"Well that's no problem," the abbot said. "She badly needs a father, you badly want to be a father."

"I do?" Heden asked, not entirely surprised.

"You do, trust me," the abbot said. He always said this when he was telling Heden something he already knew.

"That's not all," Heden said.

"No," the abbot said.

"I don't think..." Heden was sidling up to it. "I don't think she knows what to do with...how to deal with people who aren't patrons."

"That's it," the abbot said, not affirming, just drawing the information from Heden.

"When I first saw her look at me, she was scared. She saw something. Something in me."

The abbot let him off the hook. "She saw someone she couldn't control."

Heden breathed out, unaware he'd been holding his breath as he groped for the answer. "Yeah," he said.

"Well it's early days yet. Give it time. Give *her* time, the hard part's still ahead."

"What do you mean?"

"I mean children are hard."

Heden obviously didn't know what he meant.

"Didn't seem hard to me. She seemed pretty normal to me."

"Of course she did."

Heden scratched his eyebrow and looked at the abbot.

"She was doing that on purpose?" Heden asked.

"What do you think?"

Heden sat up. "Shit."

"At some point she'll drop that and try something else. That'll be hard. Then you'll get down to the real thing and that will be hard, too. I don't know this girl, I haven't met her, but this is a project that'll take a year or two. And you won't be able to head off to the forest for a fortnight."

"It was only three days."

"You think it felt like three days to her?"

"You're saying I should forget about the knights and concentrate on the girl?"

"What does Duke Baed say?"

"Fight the battle in front of you."

The abbot nodded. "Heden, I don't think you could forget about the knights, or the people at that keep, even if you wanted to. The knights are still there, the keep is still there. For a little while at least. But I think the knights are at the end of something and Vanora is at the beginning. You need beginnings more than you need endings."

"And I need to fight the battle in front of me."

"I think you should go to the inn."

"I will," Heden said.

"No, I'm saying I think you should go home," the abbot explained. "You've been gone three days."

"What do you mean?" Heden asked, frowning.

The abbot waited a moment for the import of his words to sink in.

"I mean three days is a long time."

Chapter Forty-nine

The war-bred urman sat at a table in the middle of the common area, on Heden's left as he came in. He was the only figure in the room. Though ten inches over six feet and dwarfing the chair he sat in, he wore normal clothing, city fashionable, from the tailor. No sword, no weapons that Heden could see, and a half-empty bottle of wine sat alone at the center the table, an empty glass next to it.

Ballisantirax was lying on the table. The urq ignored her. She ignored him, giving Heden a bleary-eyed, relaxed appraisal. But the fact she was lazing in arm's reach of the war-breed spoke volumes.

When the urman heard Heden enter, he fished in his pocket for two gold crowns and put them on the table. It was among the most expensive vintages Heden stocked. At the sound of the coins hitting the table, Balli loped down.

Heden walked in and ignored the demiurq. He walked through the common room and up the stairs, then a few moments later came down and opened the door to the cellar. He called out, his voice echoing into the darkness. No reply. He closed the door.

Then he turned his attention to his guest.

The urq called himself Bann, though he made no attempt to mask the elaborate symbol burned into his forehead that read "112" in the numbering system of the First Language. The closest thing he had to a real name. Like the urq from which he was bred, he had dark blue skin, so blue as to sometimes seem black. His tusks were much smaller than a true urq's, jutting a discreet half an inch past his lips. War-bred urq tusks never grew as long as those of a true urman. Heden believed Bann kept his tusks filed down to a fashionable size. His arms and body were otherwise of normal humanoid shape, not the elongated massive arms and small legs of the true urq.

Bann wore no sword because he was not planning on fighting Heden. He would lose any such fight, sword or no, and it would not be pleasant. So, dress well, drink well and wait. Heden guessed he'd been here for hours, waiting for Heden to return from visiting the abbot, but it would take more than a few glasses of wine over several hours to have any effect on Bann.

Heden walked to the table, cupped his left hand just under the edge, and swept the coins off the tabletop into it. He pocketed the money. It would be impolite to refuse payment.

"Bann," Heden said.

The urq's bright yellow eyes did not meet his own. With no expression on his flat face, he tilted his head deferentially.

"You done with that?" Heden asked, nodding to the wine.

Bann made a gesture with his hand, black fingernails like miniature serrated spearheads. Heden picked up the bottle and glass.

As he walked to the bar, Heden said, "Want anything to eat?"

"What've you got?" Bann said, his voice casual, but like low thunder nonetheless.

Heden went into the kitchen and came out a few moments later with some beef that was on the wrong side of fresh. It wasn't that Bann or urmen in general preferred slightly rotting meat, it was just that it didn't seem to matter much to them either way, so Heden took the opportunity to offload some of his older stuff. He put the plate in front of Bann.

Bann ripped a small piece of steak off, and began tearing delicately at the meat with his teeth. No war-breed ever used cutlery, though many of them managed to look civilized eating without them.

"Where's the girl?" Heden finally asked, sitting down.

"Back at the Rose. Came on her own."

Heden thought about this. Nothing was disturbed in here; the door to the basement wasn't open. Three days was a long time.

"Okay," he said. "I believe you. Is she safe?"

Bann took his time chewing his steak, then wiped his mouth with the back of one hand and looked at Heden for the first time since he entered the inn.

"No," Bann said, his voice a rumble.

Heden looked at the war-breed.

"But nothin's going to happen to her, uh, right now."

"Why are you here?" Heden asked.

"Reasons, I have three," Bann said, amusing himself with an archaic turn of phrase.

"Morten, bit of an embarrassment. Figured I should apologize."

Heden accepted this. "Have to start somewhere," he said.

Bann seemed to agree.

"I'll find a use for him. Don't like letting people go," he said. He was, Heden knew, fiercely loyal. Though the use Bann might find for Morten could require a glorious death.

"Don't worry about it," Heden said. "It was a mistake. We all make them."

Apology accepted, Bann reached into his doublet and pulled out a thin roll of black cloth which, when unrolled on the table, revealed three star sapphires, three rubies and a diamond, the seven gems worth something on the order of seventy-five thousand crowns.

"Second reason," he said. "You saved the girl's life. By some law," Bann said, reminding Heden that in a city as diverse as Celkirk, the laws and traditions of many species and cultures held sway, "means you own her. Miss Elowen wants to buy her from you."

Heden stared at the gems. Something was happening here he didn't understand. If Elowen was offering seventy-five thousand crowns for Vanora, that meant Vanora had to be worth something like 300,000 crowns to Elowen. Under no circumstance could a whore, even one at the Rose Petal, be worth 300,000 crowns, even summed over the course of her whole life. A tenth of that was reasonable. This meant something dangerous was happening around Vanora. Heden remembered her saying it wouldn't be easy.

Heden reached out and pulled the black cloth towards him. He looked at the gems and did some reasoning.

"Someone thinks that girl is worth a lot," Heden said.

"Miss Elowen said to apologize for the crude offer of money," Bann said. "Told her seventy-five wouldn't mean nothin' to you. But she don't understand. She could have a hundred million crowns and she'd still want five more."

"Someone with a lot of money wants Vanora." Heden could make neither heads nor tails of this. Vanora was—regardless of what Heden thought of her—in the grand scheme of things not anything special.

"Told her you'd say no," Bann said, smiling in self-congratulation.

"You brought the offer anyway," Heden said.

"'s my job innit?" Bann said. "'sides, I think you should take it."

Heden snapped a look at him.

"Lots of folks afraid of me, but you ain't," Bann said. "Got no reason to be. No reason to be afraid of Miss Elowen. But there's some in the city you should be afraid of."

Heden looked down at the gems and picked up the diamond. Gems. Not cash. This offer didn't come from Miss Elowen.

"Even though I know you ain't," Bann finished.

"You said three reasons. What's the third reason?"

Bann sniffed. "I like it here," he said, making an expansive gesture with one hand, dropping a piece of meat into his mouth with the other.

"Really?" Heden said.

"Better than the Rose," Bann said, chewing.

Heden scrutinized the face of Miss Elowen's head enforcer.

"No it isn't. You love working at the Rose."

Bann swallowed. "Better here than there," he said, enjoying the moment, "when you are about to go to there and kill a lot of people to get the girl back."

All the warmth fled the room.

"I don't want to kill your men, Bann." Heden said.

Bann took his time picking his teeth clean with his black spearpoint fingernails. Then he smiled at Heden and showed all his teeth.

"It's not my men that have her, Heden."

Chapter Fifty

The Rose Petal sat on Grape Street where Wigen intersected it, so that if you stood on the stoop of the brothel looking out, you'd see Wigen stretching away before you, and Grape running left and right.

Two men stood outside the front door to the Rose. They were leaning against the doorframe, watching the traffic pass by in the afternoon, smiling and talking. One of them was Bann's. The doorman. Heden recognized him.

The other man was Teagan.

Heden walked up and stood on the three steps leading to the door. He nodded at Bann's doorman. He looked up and down the street, looking at the people and carts making their way.

Then he turned and looked deliberately at Teagan. The man's casual grin faltered for a moment when he saw Heden and remembered their last encounter.

"Teagan," Heden said.

Teagan touched his forehead with his thumb and index finger, where a forelock would be if his hair wasn't too short.

"What are you doing here?" Heden asked.

"Captain wanted to make sure everything was okay here," Teagan said. It was the second time Heden had heard him speak. He was clad in brown leather armor that looked simple and unadorned, but Heden recognized it as very expensive. It was light, reinforced, and allowed maximum flexibility. It said a lot about how Teagan fought. Heden looked at the sword at Teagan's side. It was hard to tell in the confines of the city, but Heden didn't think it was sorcerous. He'd seen Teagan work. It didn't need to be.

"I'm here for the girl," Heden said.

Teagan, still smiling, nodded.

"You going to stop me?" Heden asked.

"You think I could?" He cocked his head and peered at Heden as though thinking about who would win.

Heden looked at the man. "I didn't come here to find out," he said.

Teagan nodded. His amusement faded as the two men stared at each other, neither breaking eye contact. It wasn't a confrontation. Each man wanted to know the other.

Finally, without breaking eye contact, Teagan spoke. "You do what you have to," he said. "Don't worry about me."

Heden looked at the doorman.

The doorman looked back and forth between the priest and the watchman, and then realized something was expected of him.

He sniffed the air dramatically. "Think I smell a pie with my name on it," he said. "Shouldn't be a moment, watch the door for me, Teagan." He walked down the stairs past Heden.

Heden looked at Teagan. Teagan opened the door to the brothel.

Heden walked up and entered the foyer. It was, unusually, empty. Teagan walked in behind him and closed the door.

Heden looked sharply behind him.

Teagan smiled and spread his hands. "Captain would be upset at me if I let you get killed in here, so…"

Heden did not know what to make of this fighting man. He'd known several in his life but none that seemed as at ease with their role.

"You going to get in my way?" Heden asked.

Teagan pursed his lips, then his open face resumed its light amusement. "That wasn't my plan."

"There's no in-between here," Heden said. A door opened upstairs and rapid footsteps followed.

Teagan smiled widely and extended his hand. "In for a copper," he said.

Heden looked at the proffered hand, thick and callused. He couldn't remember the last time he'd accepted help from anyone. He took Teagan's hand and shook it once.

"In for a crown," Heden said, and the two men stared at each other for a moment.

Miss Elowen glided down the stairs, her dress an elaborate pattern of gold and red. She enjoyed changing her hair color as the mood suited her; in this case her long straight hair was pure white. She was Heden's exact contemporary, but looked twenty years younger.

She arrived at the bottom of the stairs in the otherwise empty foyer, a place where no expense was spared to give every illusion of taste and refinement. Looking at Heden and Teagan, she sighed with something like defeat. She hurried over to the two of them.

"What are you two doing here?" She looked from one to the other.

Heden looked at Teagan and looked back at Elowen.

"What do you think?" he asked.

"Didn't Bann..."

Heden took the black cloth with the gemstones wrapped in it and threw it onto the lush carpeting. The cloth unfurled in the air and the gems spun and danced as they fell onto the floor.

Miss Elowen didn't look at them. She just stared at Heden, her face a mix of frustration and disgust.

She looked to Teagan and saw the man standing casually, looking around the welcome room, hand on his sword.

Elowen took a step forward and spoke quietly and intensely.

"You don't know what you're doing."

"Yeah, but I know I don't know what I'm doing. That should count for something," Heden said.

"Leave and forget about her. What is she to you?"

Heden shrugged.

Teagan frowned and looked around the room to his left as though hearing or smelling something just at the edge of perception.

With no warning, just an explosion of violence like a finger of lightning striking down from the sky, Teagan's body danced as he brought his sword out of its scabbard in one fluid motion; it soared around him once, there was a sick wet sound and a body materialized out of the air, its head severed from its neck.

Elowen looked shocked, something Heden wasn't sure he'd ever seen before.

By the time Heden had turned around to see what had happened, Teagan had already sheathed his weapon, and the body of a man dressed in grey and black was convulsing, blood all over the floor and divans, his head having rolled under a plush chair.

Before Heden could react, he felt a sharp pain in his back. Someone had stabbed him and he knew he was poisoned.

Grunting with pain, he spoke a prayer and two brilliant white shafts of light stabbed down from the ceiling, each enveloping and exposing a man: one behind Heden, one on the far side of the room. Two men, both clad in the same grey and black linen. Teagan and Lady Elowen shielded their eyes, but the two assassins, previously invisible, were now blind.

But they were used to operating in darkness anyway, and the one immediately behind Heden stabbed again. Even without his sight, his small razor-sharp blade found its target, and Heden went down, his knees crumpling.

The assassin who felled Heden couldn't see Teagan and so couldn't see the man gingerly step over Heden's recumbent form and pull his sword from its scabbard in the same manner as he had at the jail three days ago. Using the pommel as a projectile, he smashed his sword into the assassin's jaw from below, and with a sharp crack the man fell to the ground.

That left the other assassin, blind but too far across the room for Teagan to get to quickly.

Heden, his face red, rolled over and propped himself up on his elbow. He pointed to the blind assassin, spoke a prayer, and the man suddenly stopped breathing. He grasped his throat, started pulling at his clothes, trying to get air, but could not. Suffocating was not a quick death, and he flailed around, eventually falling onto a table and breaking it. He continued to scrabble and his feet kicked as his tongue and lips turned blue.

Heden spoke another prayer and the poison was neutralized. He panted, the redness in his face slowly fading. The man across the room slowly died.

"Wasn't sure that would work," Heden said. Teagan helped him up. "If they're good enough," he said to the fighting man, "they can fight it. Especially if they've fought a priest before."

Teagan looked at him.

"You know that, though," Heden said, lamely.

"We went through three priests in the Sword," Teagan said pointedly.

"Well whose fault is that?" Heden said. Teagan smiled.

"Salorna's swollen teat," Elowen hissed, looking at the still-spurting blood, the blood spread around the room, the still-twitching assassin who broke her table.

"I'll pay for the repairs," Heden said.

Elowen shook her head once. "Just don't destroy the place, Heden. It's everything I have."

"I'll do my best," Heden said. Elowen stepped in close.

"There are six more of them, upstairs," she whispered.

"Not for long," Heden said. "I'm taking the girl with me."

Elowen looked at him. With her heels on, she and Heden were roughly the same height.

"Are you sure you're not just being pigheaded?" she asked.

"Is that a trick question?"

"They said they're not here to kill anyone, they just want to frighten you off."

"You told them that wouldn't work?"

Elowen nodded.

"You care about the girl?" Heden asked.

It was Elowen's turn to shrug.

"Not enough to fight you over her," she said with a shrug.

"Heden," Teagan said.

Teagan was pulling a long piece of cloth off the beheaded assassin. It had been tied around his arm. It appeared to be a silk scarf.

Teagan shook it and black clouds of soot billowed off, revealing a pattern of bright yellow silk beneath.

"The Black," Heden said.

"That means the count. This is a man you maybe don't want to fuck with," Teagan offered.

"What do you know about this?" Heden asked him.

Teagan had stopped smiling. "I know I don't want to dance with the Guild of Blackened Silk," he said. "You weren't kidding about that 'in for a copper, in for a crown' shit. I wish I'd stayed home today."

"He feels the same way," Heden said, nodding to the headless man. "Now what?"

"Hope they know I'm a watchman," Teagan said. "The guilds don't like killing watchmen."

Heden turned to Miss Elowen. "He wasn't here," Heden said.

She sighed. "That means you're not going to leave any of them alive." That meant a lot of killing and a lot of expense cleaning it up.

"It's only a yellow scarf," Heden explained.

"I know what it means," Elowen said.

"Oh, I thought maybe you were concerned for me," he said with mock affrontedness.

"She's not going to want to go with you," Elowen said.

"What?"

"Violet wants to stay here."

Heden frowned and thought about that.

"Well, whatever," he said. "She's not equipped to make that decision."

"I knew you'd say that," Miss Elowen said. "Okay, it was just you. I've never seen the thieftaker before," she said, nodding to Teagan.

Teagan smiled and touched his imaginary forelock.

"I'll be in the basement," Miss Elowen said, turning and walking to a far door. "I'll wait until the noises stop."

Heden turned to Teagan.

"After you," Teagan said, pointing to the stairs that led to the upper floors. Heden prayed over both of them for a few moments, warding them.

When he was done he looked up at Teagan.

"When we get out of here," he said, "I'm taking the girl back to the Hammer & Tongs." Teagan nodded, and Heden continued, "You go back and tell Domnal what happened. If he's smart, he'll post some guards on the street to watch."

"The Black could get past the guards and kill everyone in here and none of them would ever know it," Teagan said.

Heden gave him a look.

"Well," Teagan admitted with a smile, "unless I was one of the guards."

"Doesn't matter," Heden said. "If the count knows Dom cares, he'll back off a little."

"'A little?'" Teagan shook his head.

Heden took a deep breath and turned to lead the way.

As they climbed the narrow candlelit stairs, Heden stopped. He turned and asked Teagan a question.

"You ever been in the Iron Forest?"

"Yeah," Teagan said. "Went in with eight in '22, came out with three."

Heden nodded to himself. "Never mind," he said.

"Okay," Teagan said with a shrug. He seemed to have no problem letting go of anything not immediately threatening him. Heden envied him.

The arrogate and the fighting man climbed the stairs, preparing to kill six low-ranking assassins there to stop them from rescuing a whore who didn't want to be rescued.

Chapter Fifty-one

Vanora was putting up less of a fight now, but only because she was tired.

Heden dragged her into the Hammer & Tongs, and threw her into a chair. She fell back against it like a rag doll, her hair in her face. She gave him a dark and sullen look.

"You're just like everyone else," she said. But the abbot had prepared Heden for this.

"Do you believe that?"

"You left," she rasped.

"I came back."

"This time," she said.

"Okay," Heden said. She had rehearsed this. Probably knew, or hoped, that Heden would come back for her. Maybe even left to force Heden to make a choice. Prove something. Knowing this, Heden didn't need to say it.

She filled in the silence.

"What, it's alright for you to leave on your own, but not me?"

Heden nodded. "Yes."

She shook her head. "You're just like all the rest."

She thought it bothered him for her to say this, but it didn't. Watching Lady Isobel wreathe herself in fire bothered him. This was just a problem to solve.

"Did you know someone tried to buy you from me?"

"What?" she said, pushing her hair out of her face. "I don't...who? I don't *belong* to you," she objected.

"They offered me seventy-five thousand crowns."

Vanora opened her mouth to say something, and left it that way. After a minute, it looked like she'd forgotten how to breathe.

"What...?" she whispered.

"It was in gemstones," he continued. "Rubies. Diamonds."

"Seventy...seventy-five thousand..."

"That's half what I paid for this inn," Heden said.

She looked into space. "Diamonds," she said.

"I told them you didn't belong to me."

"But...seventy-five..."

"Vanora, do you know why someone would offer me that much money for you?"

She looked frightened. Good.

"N-no," she said.

"Yes you do," he said.

She looked at the floor.

"Did you know Bann was here waiting for me when I got back?"

She was still stunned. "Bann?" she repeated.

"He wanted me to know what happened to you. Came to tell me you were at the Rose. He wanted me to go get you, and bring you back here." That was probably true, Heden thought.

Now she was frightened and confused. Good.

"Bann works for Miss Elowen," she said.

"I know."

"Why would he…I don't understand."

"Yes you do," Heden said. He stepped forward, was now standing over her. This wasn't how the abbot would do it. But he wasn't the abbot.

"How long have you been at the Rose?" he asked.

She looked up at him, lost. "I don't know," she said reflexively. "Three years."

"You were twelve when you started."

"I…I think so."

"And when did you have your first patron?"

"I don't know!" she objected. But she meant "stop asking me." "A year later, maybe?"

"Right," Heden said. She'd been groomed. Groomed for a special client. "So two years on the job, and how many patrons have you had?"

Her desperation having run its course, she went on the attack. "Why do *you* care?!" she spat. "You're not my father. You're nobody. What, you only like it when you can be the first? Is that what this is about? You like to stick it in and watch us bleed?"

It was a crude attack. She only did it to provoke him. She wanted him to hit her. He knew it. He'd seen it before. It's probably what her father did, and it's what she thought of when she thought of a father figure. He wasn't going to take the bait.

"You've had one patron," Heden said.

She stared at him. Afraid and angry at the same time.

"She told you," Vanora guessed. "Bann told you."

Heden shook his head.

"It's the count," Heden said. "You're his favorite."

She dropped her head.

"I was wrong," Heden said, almost to himself. "I told the abbot ten years. You don't have ten years, you don't have two. He runs though them about one every three years, which means you're about due."

She wouldn't look up.

"The other girls must have told you. Told you what he did."

She cradled her hands in her lap.

"Figure you've got about a year left. Maybe less."

"I don't care," she said dully.

"You better not," he said. "If I was you and I cared, I'd be shitting myself every night. You know what he does to them when he's done with them?"

"No," she said quietly, head down.

He took a deep breath. Took it easy on her.

"You liked him, at first," Heden said, doing what he did. Getting into her head, seeing everything from her point of view until things made sense. "He's handsome, still looks young. And that's not a nickname, he's a real count. And he was nice to you. It wasn't what you expected. It didn't have to be, he had plenty of time. He had you all to himself.

"Still, he moved fast. But that was okay. Pretty soon he wants to tie you up, okay. He wants to do things to you, okay. Has to be okay because you can't say no. The girls try to tell you what's going to happen. Miss Elowen tries to keep you apart, but that's not really possible in there. And maybe she hopes…hopes you'll get away. I think she hates him as much as anyone does. You think the girls are jealous of you. Of course they are. And they hate you too, because you only ever see him. But they don't need to make anything up to hurt you, the truth is bad enough.

"He used to leave all sorts of marks, bruises. Used to be, his girl couldn't even leave the building, but that was years ago and he's better at it now. Doesn't leave anything anywhere that shows. I didn't see anything when I changed your clothes. I didn't think anything of it."

She looked up at him. She wasn't crying. Tough little girl.

"How do you know all this?" she asked.

"Here's what I don't understand," Heden said. "If you knew about the count, what he did to his girls, and I was here, giving you a way out—something you had to be dreaming about every night since you realized the other girls weren't lying to you…why did you go back? That's the only thing I don't get."

Her head dropped back down again. From under her long hair came her voice.

"Three days is a long time."

Heden pulled up a chair and sat down across from her.

"You're right," he said. "And you were scared of what would—"

He said the wrong thing, or something inside her broke. Either way, she lashed out at him.

"You think I went back because I was scared? Because I didn't know? You think I'm some innocent girl?! I went back because I liked it! Do you understand? The others would whisper to me all the things he would do, they tried to frighten me, but I liked it! I never dreamed about leaving, I dreamed about him taking me away! The other girls weren't like me," she said, proudly. She swelled a little. "He said so. They didn't like it, they cried, they were afraid. I was afraid he'd stop!"

Heden sat back roughly in his chair, surprised at her revelation. *Shit,* he thought, *I need to talk to the abbot about this.* Part of him didn't like that. Didn't like admitting defeat. Another part of him liked the fact that there was the abbot to go to.

She took his introspection as shock.

"Listen," Heden said, recovering. "It's my fault. I forgive you."

"You can't forgive me!" she shouted. "I haven't done anything wrong. You can't save me, because there's nothing to save me from!"

"That's not what I mean. I mean I forgive you for leaving. I left you alone, I shouldn't have done that. Things were…fragile and I should have…it's my fault."

"Stop saying that! Why aren't you angry at me?!"

This brought Heden up short. She wasn't just telling him the truth, she was being open. She trusted him, but needed something from him, and he couldn't give it to her because he didn't understand it.

He didn't know what to say, so he went with the old standby. "What?"

Vanora was angry at him, furious. "How can you just sit there after all this?" She threw it all at him. "I'm sick! There's something...there's something *wrong* with me! I'm not normal! Why can't you see what's wrong with me? I need to be...I need to be punished or something. I need someone to see what I've done!"

She was looking at him with fear and horror, her young face twisted with pain. He looked back in shock. He'd seen that look before.

They needed someone to see what they'd done.

"Black gods," he said, standing up almost involuntarily.

Why can't you see what's wrong with us?

"Brys." He remembered his first meeting with Brys, trying to worm out of the knight what Taethan had done wrong. The look on Brys' face when Heden suggested... He staggered, took a step back.

"What?" Vanora asked, confused.

Heden started breathing heavily. He ran his hand through his hair absently.

"That's why she killed herself." Isobel!

We need to be punished.

"What?!" Vanora was now on the verge of hysterics.

"Black gods," Heden said. "It wasn't him. He wasn't horrified because I realized what *Taethan* had done wrong...he was horrified because he thought I'd guessed what *he*..."

Heden shook his head and looked around the inn, as if he'd forgotten where he was. He looked at Vanora and knew what to do.

He got down on his knees and took her head in his hands. She tried to pull away, but her heart wasn't in it.

He kissed her on the forehead and then pulled back, put his hands on her shoulders and looked into her eyes. There was fear there, but hope as well. That was his job. Fuel the hope and kill the fear.

"It's not complicated," Heden said. "It's just this. Five days ago we didn't know each other. But now we do. And let me tell you something, young lady." He tried out the phrase to see how it sounded. Not bad. "That's all that matters. You think there's more, everyone thinks there's got to be some greater significance, but that's all crap. All that matters is: we didn't know each other, and now we do. So now what? I'll tell you. We stay together, we stay here and see what happens, or you go back to the Rose and we're just two people who used to know each other. It's that simple."

Her eyes were wide with fear.

"I'll protect you from the count. And there's nothing wrong with you. Whatever you like, whatever you think you are or want to be, that's up to you. And I can get you help." He hoped the abbot wasn't busy for the next few years. "But the count is an evil man and he will kill you as soon as he's bored with you, and he gets bored fast. Now, I've got somewhere to go," he said.

"Heden!" She grabbed the edges of his breastplate at the shoulders. He slowly pried her fingers away.

"Hours," he said. "Not days. Not this time. If you leave, that's your decision. But if you're still here when I get back, then that's it. Then we're in this together and we'll take it as far as it goes."

She stared at him and saw something in his eyes. Something she'd never seen before. Something no one had seen in him in years. She threw herself around him, buried her head in the crook of his neck and started crying. He hugged her back, tight. As tight as he could.

"You're not going to leave," he said, his voice choking.

She shook her head.

He said the words again. They stayed like that a few moments, and then Heden heard the sound of something soft but heavy hitting the tabletop next to them.

He pulled away and saw Ballisantirax on the table washing herself.

He stood up. Vanora pushed herself back and tried to straighten her hair. She was sniffling.

"Balli," he said, and the black cat looked up at him with large black eyes ringed with yellow. He pointed to Vanora. "Watch Vanora," he said.

The large black cat looked at Vanora and said, "Mow."

Vanora laughed through her tears and reached out, grabbing the cat. Ballisantirax was heavier than she looked, and all muscle.

She hugged the cat, burying her head in its fur. Balli squirmed and tried to get away, her feet splayed and a look of mild alarm on her face. "Mow."

Heden looked at the two of them. *Hell of a family,* he thought. But good enough, he reckoned.

He grabbed his pack and, without saying anything else, walked out the door.

Chapter Fifty-two

He slammed the door behind him. Then he noticed the two men standing on either side of the door.

Well, one man. And one war-bred urq.

He spun around and looked at Bann and Teagan. Teagan had fired a nail; he passed it to Bann, who inhaled deeply from it. Bann had brought his sword, his huge two-handed broadsword slung over his back. It was like walking around with a ballista in his pocket.

"Heden," Teagan said, nodding. The watchman's slight smile was there.

"What the fuck are you two doing here?" Heden asked.

They looked at each other and then back at Heden.

"Well, that's a bit of a pickle, innit?" Bann growled.

Heden looked, shocked, at Bann, and then, pointing to the urman, looked shocked at Teagan. "You know he's Miss Elowen's head muscle?"

Teagan shrugged. "Nobody's perfect."

Heden looked between them.

"And you know he's a watchman," Heden said to Bann, pointed at Teagan.

"Yeah, and he's a mare," Bann said and sniffed. "We know all about this one. Figure what a man does with his time is his business, innit? Long as he doesn't try to arrest me or stick his prick up me arse."

Heden stared blankly at the door between them.

"Listen," Bann said, taking another drag on the nail. "Miss Elowen, she says to me…wol, basically same thing his boss tole him," he said, nodding to Teagan. "So we said, what the fuck?" Bann handed the nail back to Teagan, who took it without looking and took a drag from it.

Teagan nodded, smiling. "That's exactly what he said."

"Now," Bann said, adjusting his back to get more comfortable leaning against the doorframe and his sword. "We figure, you pissed off the count and he's the kind of pigfucker you wouldn't want to go dig a hole with, 'cause he'd stab you in the back and fuck you in the ass—"

"So to speak," Teagan said, blowing smoke through his nostrils and looking casually down the street.

"—and leave you in the hole to rot. So we figure, you're a busy man. You've got things to do. We don't know what; we don't *want* to know what."

"We don't want to know," Teagan agreed.

"Figure, that's your business, innit? So we come down here, and uh, mind the store while you're away." He smiled triumphantly, his teeth and tusks a yellowing white.

"He means protect the girl," Teagan explained.

"That's what I said," Bann said. "He knows what I mean, don't you, Heden?"

"I know what you mean," Heden said cynically.

"Now if you got a problem with this," Bann said, his voice like a roaring river in an underground cave. "Then uh, I think we're at something of an impasse," the urq said, using the last word tentatively. He looked to Teagan for approval.

"He means, if you don't like it, you can go fuck yourself," the man said smoothly. "We're doing it anyway."

"It's for your own good, style of thing," Bann explained delicately.

"Hers too," Teagan said, nodding behind him.

Heden could see Vanora's head pressed against the glass in the door, listening.

He nodded to himself. He had little choice. "Alright," he said. "Figure each of you will keep an eye on the other and, between you, she'll be okay."

Bann reached out and hit Teagan's shoulder with the back of his hand. "Told you he'd say that? Didn't I?"

Teagan took another drag on the nail. "You did," he said, nodding.

"I'm going to see the abbot," Heden said to them.

Teagan shrugged.

"Who?" Bann asked.

"Doesn't matter," Heden said. "I'll be back by nightfall." The two men nodded. They didn't seem to care when he came back.

"Someone might come by," Heden said. "Thin, short curly blonde hair. Well dressed."

"You want us to kill him?" Bann asked.

"No," Heden explained patiently.

"Just hurt him a little, then?"

"No," Heden repeated slower. "He's a friend."

Teagan nodded.

"Well that's as may be," Bann said, looking between Heden and Teagan, "but not all your friends get along, if you get me drift."

Heden nodded. "Tell him," Heden began. "If he shows up, tell him that you've known a lot of snakes, and you appreciate the ferret."

Bann nodded. "And that'll do the trick?" he said.

Heden nodded. He pointed to the door. "No one goes in, got it?"

They nodded. Heden started to walk away and then thought better of something and turned back. "Or leaves," he said.

"Now that goes without saying," Bann said, smiling. "Off you go now, save the world."

Heden turned and walked away.

"We'll see," he said.

Chapter Fifty-three

Heden burst into the abbot's quarters and threw his pack on the divan where he normally sat.

"How do the Hart bury their dead?"

The abbot looked at him and blinked. He didn't ask Heden what he was talking about. He put the quill down, covered his inkpot and sat back in his chair. He crossed his hands over his stomach and thought.

"Heden, you know I can't tell you that," the abbot said.

Heden pointed at him accusingly. "But you've been there for the ritual."

The abbot nodded. "And that's one reason. It's sacred."

Heden stared at him.

"You know you're one of the people who talked me into becoming an arrogate."

"This has nothing to do with that."

"If I were still a member of the church, you could tell me."

"Heden, the time you spend here with me is just as sacred, just as much a ritual, as anything I do with the White Hart."

"What's that got to do with anything?" Heden frowned, frustrated.

"You're a smart boy, you'll figure it out."

"Are you saying you talk to knights of the Hart?"

The abbot just looked at him.

"Heden, do you think that when I talk to the king," which they both knew he did, "that I mention the things you and I talk about?"

"There are something like a thousand people at the keep." Heden glowered.

The abbot pursed his lips.

"Maybe you should ask Gwiddon."

"What?"

"Gwiddon knows a lot."

"Not about the Hart," Heden said.

"Well, if he *did*," the abbot said pointedly, "but you never *asked him*, then it would be just as if he *didn't*."

Heden wasn't paying attention. He was becoming furious.

"Do you want me to go talk to Radallach? Because I will. And I will *beat it out of him*."

The abbot didn't react. Wasn't sad, nor afraid. Just thinking.

"No," he concluded finally, looking down and patting his large belly absently. "I don't want that."

The abbot ran his hand across his forehead, smoothing the stress out of it. Then scratched at the back of his neck.

"They wrap the body in samite," he began.

"I know that part," Heden said.

"And they take it into Bleddan Wode." The wode was a small forest roughly a day's ride from Celkirk. It was the local haunted wood and, like all the wodes, the truth was worse than any stories that had grown up around it.

"Hah," Heden said. "Of course they do. There's something in the forest, isn't there?"

The abbot nodded. "They give the body to the *genius locus* of the wode," he said.

Heden nodded. "It's a naiad, isn't it?" He was leaping ahead, his face an open map of his thoughts.

The abbot shook his head. "No, it's a draiad."

"Same thing," Heden said, dismissively. He stood triumphantly in the middle of the abbot's small quarters, looking around at nothing. "Same thing," he repeated.

The abbot just watched him, waiting.

"Brys tried to tell me," Heden said. "I was close, and he knew it."

"What did he try to tell you, Heden?" The abbot asked. Heden started pacing around the room.

"I didn't see it," Heden said. "He practically pissed himself in front of me and I didn't see it." He looked at the abbot. "I wanted to give Taethan the benefit of the doubt. They all seemed to hate him, but not the way you would a murderer. So I asked Brys if Taethan killed Kavalen out of duty. Maybe he thought he was doing the right thing. If he…" Heden stopped, unable to finish the sentence.

"If he arrogated to himself the responsibility of doing what the other knights could not," the abbot finished. "That would explain why they hated him. Especially if they agreed but couldn't bring themselves to do it."

Heden just stood there.

"Yeah," he said dully, realizing how his own experience had misled him. How much he had projected onto Taethan. "Brys was shocked. I thought it was because I was onto something. But that wasn't why Brys reacted that way."

"Why then?" the abbot said.

Heden grabbed his pack.

"I have to see the body!" he said.

"And you now know where it is?" the abbot asked.

"He tried to tell me, he showed me but I didn't see it. I wasn't paying attention."

"Brys?"

"No, Taethan. He said the dead knights were accepted back into the heart of the forest."

The abbot nodded. "Which you took to be symbolic."

"But that was the whole point of him taking me to the lake. He *called* it the heart of the forest. He was trying to show me where Kavalen's body was, and I didn't see it."

Heden stopped moving and stared into space as all the pieces fell into place.

"That's where Nudd was going. He wasn't coming to save us; he was taking Idris' body to the lake. To bury it."

Heden threw open his pack and fished out the remains of the carpet.

"What are you going to do?" the abbot asked, calmly.

"I'm going back."

"Is there much time?"

"There's no time," Heden said, then stopped. He stuffed the carpet back into the pack. "I won't be able to take the carpet, I'll have to..."

Silence for a moment.

"I'm sure Elzpeth would be glad to see you," the abbot said quietly.

"Balls," Heden said. "It'll have to be Negra."

"She will *not* be glad to see you," the abbot said smoothly.

"You can stop helping now," Heden said and walked out the door.

Chapter Fifty-four

Negra's shop was under her home, on Apell Street, not far from the cathedral. The symbol on the sign hanging over the door was a solid black circle with lines radiating from it. The Black Sun. Neatly incorporating one of the symbols for magic with the Tevas translation of her chosen name in the First Language.

He stood in front of the door and stared at it. He couldn't remember the last time he'd been here, the last time he'd talked to her. But it had been to ask a favor then, too.

He stepped up and knocked on the door.

It opened immediately.

"Heden," Negra said smoothly, her voice dripping with distaste.

"Did you know I was standing out here?" he asked, frowning.

She stared at him and did not answer. She was tall, one of the tallest women Heden had ever met, with pale skin, long black hair and a simple black dress. Heden had seen her in other dresses, less simple, and even though she was too slim for his taste, she never failed to make an impression. Sometimes her elegance reminded Heden of a black swan. Sometimes a snake.

"You've come to ask a favor," she said.

"How's Rane?" Heden asked.

She sighed theatrically, maintaining her aura of distaste and disinterest.

"I wouldn't know; I haven't talked to him in two years."

"Oh," Heden said. "I'm sorry," he added lamely. "I liked him."

"So did I," Negra said, leaning on the doorframe and crossing her arms.

"I need something," Heden said.

"Yes," Negra nodded. "You do."

"I'm sorry," he said. "I need a scroll."

"What kind of scroll?" she asked.

"Translocation."

"Why?"

"It's complex," Heden said, betraying a little impatience.

"Why don't you ask Reginam," Negra said, nodding behind Heden at the Tower of the Quill.

"I can't ask her."

"But you can ask me?"

"I shouldn't ask you either," Heden admitted. "I'm sorry."

"Stop saying that," she muttered, frowning.

Her look softened. "Do you want…" she began. "Do you want to come in?"

Heden did want to come in. He wanted to make everything right again but he knew now that wasn't possible. Might never be possible. And he'd hate himself afterwards.

"You know I can't do that," he said.

"No, I guess not," she said, looking at him with a little pity but no forgiveness.

She reached behind herself and without otherwise moving produced a scroll.

"You knew I was coming," he said, looking at the scroll in her hand.

"Do you know why she hates you, Heden?" Negra asked, casually holding out the scroll, waiting for Heden to take it.

Heden snatched it from her hands. "Thank you, Negra," he said, unable to meet her eyes.

"She hates you…"

"Goodbye, Negra," Heden said, turning and walking away.

"…because even after everything, she's always believed you could make it all right." Now she had to shout to be heard. People watched them, seeing a fight. "All you had to do was want it bad enough!" she shouted.

Heden trudged away, leaving her alone.

"And that makes it all your fault," she said, to no one.

She watched him until he turned onto the street that would take him home.

"Pigfucker," she said, with no malice, and turned and closed the door.

Chapter Fifty-five

It was raining at the lake. Just as beautiful under heavy clouds as under bright sun. Its surface a mass of disturbances from raindrops striking, like the craterous impacts of a million tiny catapults. Two dozen trees, each as tall as the tallest spire of the cathedral, lay on the ground, most stretching out into the lake. They'd lie here for a hundred years before finally disintegrating.

Heden made no concession to the rain. He just got wet. He looked around as though expecting to see someone else here. He didn't know who that might be. Taethan, probably. Almost everyone else was dead.

He opened his hand and the scroll, the writing burned off it, fell to the ground. He didn't move. He didn't want to learn what he thought he was going to learn, and he enjoyed just looking at the forest for its own sake. The massive, implacable trees, the lake, the sky. It reminded Heden of how fragile and small the human experience was. Something he felt he needed to be reminded of.

But soon he was incapable of justifying delay, and reached into his pack. There were songs, he was aware, that could summon the lake spirit, but he knew none of them. He was not a minstrel.

Rather, he simply attempted power. *Starkiller* was made by the elementals to serve in their last war against the celestials. The spirit of the lake, if spirit there was, was a creation of the celestials. Heden didn't know what effect *Starkiller* would have, but he knew it would do something.

Drawing the thin grey blade from his pack, lacking any sheath to keep it in, Heden immediately knew he was right. The blade hummed an eerie whistling tone that matched its unlight glow. It sensed the presence of a celestial, or something made by them.

He stood there, in the rain, *Starkiller* hanging loosely at his side, staring at the lake. Nothing happened. The surface of the water continued to sizzle with raindrops.

He stepped forward and dipped the tip of the longsword into the water. The reaction wasn't violent or startling, but was obvious. The water pulled back from the sword. Unable to move entirely out of the way, it nonetheless depressed several inches as though something heavy were resting on it. The tip of the sword appeared to disappear in the lake. Heden bent down to look. Awkwardly holding the sword in one hand, he knelt and saw that the sword was completely invisible below the surface of the water, even though he could clearly see rocks and leaves a few inches under it. Either the lake was denying the sword, or the sword was ignoring the lake.

His knees and legs were soaking at the edge of the water, and so he stood up. In doing so, he saw the naiad.

She was standing a few feet away on the surface of the lake, like it was solid ground. Like a marble statue of a young girl. Shaped like a human, but not human. Appeared female, but Heden knew she was immortal and sexless. She was short, shorter than a man but taller than a dwarf. And she was beautiful. All of the creations of the celestials were beautiful. Art was the only thing that mattered to them.

She was naked and lithe and had pale blue skin and long light-blue hair. It didn't look unnatural or sickly; it looked like the health and power of the lake made solid.

Her gaze wandered over Heden curiously with eyes that were solid blue. This made it difficult to look directly at her.

She opened her mouth and spoke to Heden. The sound that came forth was like wind chimes. Or the perfect pitch of a wet finger rubbed along the rim of a wine glass. It was a language no normal man could comprehend. Heden was no normal man.

Even translated in his head, it was still nonsense to someone unused to interpreting it. The celestials spoke in a kind of open poetry. Lacking meter or rhyme, only a fluid expression of thought.

"If we see only what we wish to see," she was saying, "how can we say we are not blind?"

She was chastising him. The presence of *Starkiller* obviously upset her, and she was asking Heden why he insisted on approaching her on his terms rather than hers. Why he didn't think about the effect on her.

“I’m sorry,” Heden said in common Tevas. He knew she could understand his language and probably speak it as well but chose not to. Sometimes the nature spirits of the celestials forgot humans existed. How to behave around them. “I didn’t know how to summon you otherwise.”

“The child sees everything anew and with wonder. Smiling at creation and destruction alike.”

You should have known better. Heden nodded. He put the sword away.

“I think,” he started. He didn’t know how to begin. He had met these *genius loci* before and so wasn’t daunted, but was afraid he might say the wrong thing and not get his answer. “I think Sir Taethan wanted me to come here,” he said. He hoped the name meant something to the naiad.

She nodded.

“You sway to the pulse of a river of blood that flows through your body,” she said with a small smile. “You believe in things that you cannot see.”

I think so too.

“Is this where the order buries its dead?”

She didn’t say anything for a little while. Just the constant sound of rain on water before him and leaves behind him.

“See the leaves fall, last breath,” she said.

Yes.

“Do you know—” Heden asked, and then paused as he realized that she could not know. “—how he died?”

"What is a star, if not the guiding light? The permanent eye that sees the impermanent. You look up and find guidance on your journey, but the stars neither journey nor guide. The stars do not see today and yesterday, only forever."

Heden nodded. She didn't know. She was an immortal water creature who couldn't understand the difference between life and death.

"Then I need to see his body," he said.

"You wish to be a child again. But if you were to truly be born anew, you would have to gouge out your eyes, cut out your tongue and grieve."

"I know," Heden said. She was warning him that a thing once seen could not be unseen. "But I have to see it. I'm trying to save them!" The words were almost pulled from him.

"The fly would spin a web to catch the spider, if he could."

There was something about talking to the celestials, their poetic expression of ideas, that made it difficult to argue with them. Heden found himself disappearing down into a warren of meaning. He was able to spin the naiad's words into anything, project whatever fears and doubts he had onto them. Other celestials didn't have this problem; it was a thing unique to humans.

"I think," he said. "I think you mean that I would try to stop you, if I knew what you know and our roles were reversed."

She nodded. He felt a little thrill for having worked something out.

"That doesn't matter," he said. "I still have to know."

"Who stands above the mountains," she said in her chiming, shining voice. "And at your word they fled, they hastened away, and sent spring into the valley."

Heden knew this reference. It was part of a celestial legend, an elven hero who fought the great mountain that held back the seasons. He was only able to succeed when he had given up everything he had.

Heden looked at her, trying to sense her meaning. Or trying to avoid it.

"Need," she said. "And want nothing."

A tiny pit opened in Heden's stomach. She wanted something in return for this information.

"I'm trying to save the Green Order," he reiterated. "That has to mean something to you. You have a pact with them, that's why you accept their dead."

She shook her head. "Need, and want nothing," she repeated.

"What is it to you?" he asked. "What is your stake in this?" he challenged.

"See," she said. "Be. Believe. Free." Each word was like the entire lake taking a breath. Like the tide coming in and rolling out.

Heden gritted his teeth. She wanted to trade. More, she wanted Heden to give something up. He knew how these things worked. Knowledge at no price had no meaning. The rain continued to fall.

Heden reached back into his pack. This was going to make the dwarf even angrier at him. *Well,* he thought, *that's not true. He's already maximally angry at me.*

He took out *Starkiller* and presented it to her.

She smiled widely. "You believe in things that you cannot see," she reiterated with approval.

She didn't take the sword, she just nodded her head behind her. Heden knew what was expected. With his mailed gloves, he grabbed the dwarven blade near the tip with both hands, swung it back over his head and then with all his strength threw it overhand into the lake. Its hum oscillated and faded as it flew through the air—the weight of the hilt causing it to spin and turn in a strange, almost organic way, like it was writhing—and then sank with a splash into the center of the lake.

She closed her eyes and breathed a sigh of relief. The sword had lain undisturbed for thousands of years when Heden and his friends had found it. Now it would lay for another thousand.

"Okay," Heden said. "Now. The body."

The naiad opened her eyes and took a breath, as though a great weight had been lifted from her shoulders.

"For the service of the terrans, they brought forth fruit, to make wine, that makes glad the heart of man." She was thanking him.

The water in the middle of the lake began to boil, froth. Something was being dredged up from far below. Slowly, the tumult moved towards the edge, to the shore of the lake where Heden stood. He didn't know what to expect. The celestials gave their servants great powers in some arenas. Was Kavalen going to walk out of the lake like some kind of watery ghoul? No. No, there were no more deathless. This, Heden knew.

A bulbous watery mass oozed up onto the shore of the lake. The water splashed away, covering Heden's already soaked boots and revealing a mass of what appeared to be vines and leaves, dark green, brown and black.

Then this too disintegrated, revealing a perfectly preserved body.

Kavalen had been tall and strong in life. He looked a little like the king. He shared with Lady Isobel a noble bearing, even in death. He had a square jaw and solid brow. Heden wondered if Kavalen was a good leader. His hair was short, but still green.

"He died valiantly," Heden said. The naiad said nothing.

He bent down and examined the body. Standing in the rotting lake vegetation, he pulled Kavalen's clothing away and saw several wide wounds cut into his torso. Heden frowned. He rolled Kavalen over, splashing around in the ankle-deep water. There were precisely seven wounds, and all in the ribs, or stomach, or back. None on his hands, or arms or legs. He didn't appear to have tried to defend himself. Heden dreaded what this meant.

His left foot ached because the heel of his boot was standing on something hard and unyielding. He bent down to clear away the vegetation and caught a glimpse of something man-made.

It was a spear. Also preserved. A short wooden spear with a wide, flat tip like the one Aderyn had first confronted him with. Exactly like it. Like the one hanging below Taethan's device in the priory. Like the weapons that had cut fatally into Kavalen's body.

Heden fell to his hands and knees and, amidst the rain, splashed around in the shallow water, revealing several other similar objects all around the body, also disgorged by the lake.

They were the spears of seven knights. All the spears except Kavalen's, Aderyn's and Taethan's. He remembered Taethan at the priory placing his spear under his crest. Which the other knights couldn't do.

Heden stood up and stumbled back a step. They had come here to bury Kavalen and throw their own spears in with him. The spears they used to kill him.

"They killed him," he said. The naiad watched but the words were not for her. "They all killed him. They stabbed him like…" Heden was reeling at this. Why would they do it? What had Kavalen done? His hair was still green. He had kept his oath.

A feeling came over Heden, a swelling, like something lifting him up from the inside. It was a sickening feeling. He started to panic, fearing another attack in the middle of the forest. New images replaced the lake and the naiad, and he knew this was no memory called up from the fear and horror of his past.

Chapter Fifty-six

"Thou 'mongst all the creatures in the wode must know it!"

Kavalen glowered at the ground. He wasn't going to repeat himself. Wasn't going to defend his actions. Wasn't going to answer Sir Perren's complaint.

"How often does such a command come? Once a generation? Never before in mine own life, and sure never again. It is not ours to choose which command to heed and which to dismiss." This was Lady Isobel. She looked the queen, but was wreathed in sadness.

The priory loomed behind them. It was just after dawn. Heden walked around the assembled knights. They could not see him. This was not real. Not even a memory. It was something else.

All the knights were there except Aderyn. Heden recognized Sir Perren. Lithe and lanky, with a great green beard. The knights, covered in moss and bracken, their helmets sporting long and lethal blood-covered antlers, looked like spirits of the wode.

Heden watched them, and though he recognized each, these were not the knights he'd met before. This was the Green Order before the fall. Each radiated strength and power, and something else besides. Health. Fidelity. They were the strength and implacability of the forest made manifest. Heden experienced an unusual sensation. Fear, mingled with respect. He saw now what the baron saw, that which made her think a single member of the order could turn back the army by defeating its chieftain. He remembered Nudd fighting off three mountain thyrs before he died. He saw what inspired Aderyn.

He saw Kavalen. The knight seemed in his early fifties, and like Heden had what Renaldo called a "fell countenance." His granite expression brooked no compromise. No half measures. His scarred face and grim bearing spoke of terrible knowledge. Knowledge gained at the extremes of life and death. It was his mastery of it that made him their leader. Now Heden knew what it took to lead the order. And just as much knew why none of the others were ready for it.

"None of us wouldst countenance it," Idris said bitterly. "But needs must. How now should we refuse? What punishment might be meted out upon us? It is not for me to say…"

"Nor for any of us," Cadwyr said.

"…but I fear refusing this command makes us traitors. And then Green no more."

Kavalen said nothing. He didn't seem in a hurry to say anything. Heden walked around him like an invisible man on a stage, and stared at the knight's clouded face.

Idris looked to Brys.

Brys sensed Idris' eyes on him, but would look neither at him nor Kavalen.

"We must consider the source," Brys said. "No reason given. Mayhap in this instance it is proper to let the urmen march."

Kavalen threw a glance at him, but did not speak. The look said a lot.

Lady Isobel looked at Kavalen.

"I pray thee, stay," she said. "Should any of us break our oath, 'tis one thing. But thou art the knight-commander. Thine actions reflect on us all."

Sir Nudd only looked at his feet and shook his head.

Kavalen took a deep breath. He looked at Taethan. The rest had made their intentions clear. But Taethan would not speak. Would take no side. Kavalen nodded then, the decision final.

"It falls to thee then," he said to Sir Taethan. "I charge thee on behalf of thine unwavering commitment, should this be judged a transgression, thou must atone for all. Yea, and mete out justice, no matter the price."

Even though Heden was looking at the past, was not physically there, he felt the power of Kavalen's geas just as palpably as if a wave had threatened to pull him out to sea. It was no prayer, it was a curse. The last words of a dying man, given strength and power by the gods.

This, then, was Taethan's failure. Kavalen charged him to heal the order, but Taethan could not. The crime was too great.

Kavalen knew what was going to happen. Saw the future just as clearly as Heden was now seeing the past. He was going to disobey an order. Ordered to allow the urmen to march on Ollghum Keep, he was going to fight them. Try to stop them.

Kavalen knew his own knights would cut him down. Would have to, to preserve the order. Stop him from committing treason and thus breaking their oaths. And so he charged Taethan to judge them.

But Taethan was incapable of judgment. And so the crime of his brothers paralyzed him.

Kavalen looked at his assembled knights, each proud and full of conviction, then removed his longspear from across his back, turned and walked away. His horse, in response to no signal, trotted up to him and kept pace.

Once Kavalen was in the wode, Idris looked at Brys. Dywel and Cadwyr watched Idris. Perren looked to Brys as well, waiting. Nudd stood silent by Lady Isobel.

Brys nodded to Idris, and the two knights removed their longspears and started slowly after Kavalen, in no hurry. Cadwyr, Dywel and Perren followed.

Nudd waited. Eventually, without saying anything, Isobel followed, and Nudd went after her, acting like a man heading to a funeral.

Only Taethan stayed behind. Eventually it was just Heden and Taethan in the clearing. Taethan looked like his friends had just gone off to die.

"Well it's just you and me," Heden said to the vision of Taethan.

Taethan looked to the sky and said, "What else could I do?"

Heden started. It seemed like Taethan was responding to him, but he realized this was not possible.

Heden didn't know what would have happened if the Green Order obeyed the command to stand down and let the urmen overrun the keep. But that was not the past; this was. And whatever else, the cold-blooded murder of their commander was enough to break the order. Unless Taethan could set it right.

"I am trapped," the knight confessed in pain. "Halcyon aid me; I canst see no way out."

"No," Heden said, kicking at the illusory dirt. "That was my job."

Chapter Fifty-seven

And, so far…Heden had failed.

He collapsed in the shallow water once the vision released him. He shook his head. The naiad was gone. Back to the massive lake that was her home.

Kavalen's lifeless body, skin grey, half-rotten, lay beside him. Rain fell on them both. Spattered on Kavalen's grey skin, mottled black and purple.

"Who gave the order?" Heden muttered. It was the only thing he needed now. He knew the rest.

He splashed around and grabbed the body of Kavalen.

"Who gave the order?!" he yelled at the corpse.

It had to be Halcyon. Who else? Who else had the authority that would make the order bend to their will? But why would Halcyon do it? She gave no indication either way when she manifested before Heden. She must have made a mistake, and appearing before Heden was her attempt to set it right.

He understood now, everything that had happened at the priory. The knights were not mourning the death of Kavalen; they were mourning the death of the order. And they knew they were the murderers. Halcyon had given them a command they could not follow, but they had to follow. The contradiction had destroyed them, inflicted the order with a kind of madness.

They killed their commander. They all took turns stabbing him with their spears until he was dead. He'd received the command to stand the order down. To not move against the urmen. But Kavalen couldn't live with that. He decided to ride to the keep anyway.

The other knights feared what disobeying an order meant. Feared it would mean dissolving the order. And so, thinking they were preserving the order, all rode out to stop him. All except Taethan.

They had been waiting all this time for Taethan to absolve them. It wasn't Heden's ritual they needed, it was Taethan's forgiveness. And he wouldn't give it.

Taethan was not the murderer. Heden felt a flood of relief. Taethan had kept his oath. Was the man Heden thought he was. Heden breathed in the moist cold air. There was hope. Hope for everyone. Hope for Heden. If Taethan was not false, maybe doubt was unnecessary.

This is what Halcyon meant. Heden had been trying to solve the murder of the knight, and when the order rebuffed him, he attacked Taethan. Made the knight stand in for all his comrades. But the knight didn't need Heden's judgment, he needed Heden's compassion. And Heden was too blinded by his own hatred of knights to see it.

Heden plunged his hand into the pack and pulled out the small square remains of the flying carpet. The naiad was gone. Their meeting over. The body of Kavalen lay on the shore. Maybe it would start decomposing now; maybe it would be accepted back into the lake. Heden didn't care. There were still some knights left alive, and Heden now believed he had the key to save the order.

Chapter Fifty-eight

Having navigated there by carpet before, it wasn't long before Heden saw the clearing and the spire of the priory. It was now a black finger of rock, the stained glass windows burned out. Under the grey sky, it seemed like a bloodless corpse.

Before he landed, he could see something had happened in the clearing.

It looked like an entire war had taken place in the few hundred yards surrounding the priory. He put the carpet down, pack slung over his shoulder, and walked randomly among the carnage. His feet stamped in rainwater and blood.

There was blood everywhere. The yellow grass was stained black almost through the whole clearing. Heden walked among small pieces of flesh and saw that most of the bloodstains were deliberate. Someone had coated their hands in blood and smeared it on the grass. The faint tang of iron stung his nose. It had happened recently.

The pieces of flesh were so small. Someone had deliberately cut up the bodies and flung the pieces around. He saw a finger. And then a horse's hoof. And then the heads.

Two human heads were spit upon ceremonial pikes in the center of the clearing. He hadn't seen them from above. The pikes were only about two feet high.

It was Cadwyr and Dywel.

The urq had been here, had reveled in the destruction of the green knights. They'd been driven into some kind of blood frenzy. And Heden noticed the knights' hair was now brown and black. Green no more. They'd fallen from grace before they died. Their hair was stuck to their pale faces by the rain that now did the same to Heden's. Their faces were each a rictus of despair, swollen bulging eyes turned to the grey sky, mouth agape, frozen in a howl.

Heden reached a hand out, preparing to pray and receive a vision from Cavall of what happened here, when he saw Cadwyr's mouth had something fleshy stuffed into it, covered in blood. Heden didn't bother to find out what. He suspected it was the knight's genitals, but this wasn't something he needed to confirm. Aderyn hated Cadwyr for some reason, maybe the urq knew why. But the knight was dead now, and Heden knew that whatever it was, it didn't matter anymore.

With the dastards dead, that meant the Green Order was now…

He heard a sound coming from the empty priory. He turned and saw Taethan's horse walk out from behind the priory wall. It neighed at Heden, recognizing him. Heden just stared at it through the rain.

The horse turned and drank from the trough of water, but stopped. Heden thought he saw body parts in it. Then the horse just lifted its head and stared at the priory's archway. It neighed again.

Taethan.

Sir Taethan was still alive and was now the last Green Knight. He was in the priory. Heden knew it, knew it like he knew his own name.

He dropped his pack without thinking and ran into the burned husk of the priory.

Grey light flooded through holes that once held stained glass. The windows had melted when Isobel and Brys had immolated themselves. The light coming in was no longer multicolored. The charcoal-like prayer benches were still there, like the black bones of a burned carcass.

Heden could sense Taethan was there. Could feel the priory was not devoid of all life, but he could not see the knight.

He walked slowly down the nave, his boots ringing out on the flagstones and leaving puddles. The rain fell heavily outside. Steam boiled off Heden's wet clothes. Part of him wanted to run, look wildly for the knight; part of him was afraid that when he found Taethan, his hair would no longer be green.

"Taethan," Heden said, dropping the honorific. Aderyn said only a relative could call a knight by his given name. His voice echoed off the walls. He looked down each burned bench as he walked towards the bare altar.

"Taethan, I know you didn't kill Kavalen," he called out.

No reply.

"It was them," Heden continued. "They all did it. They hunted him down like a boar and took turns stabbing him with their spears until he was dead." Heden found it hard to talk. Hard to finally pronounce judgment.

Heden looked to the altar. By rights, Taethan should be there, but Heden could see he was not. Where was he?

"I couldn't figure out why Halcyon didn't strip the murderer of his knighthood. But now I know. Kavalen gave the matter to you. And Halcyon counted on you to absolve them. That's why they didn't kill you too. They knew you were their only chance at redemption. They craved it. They needed justice even if it meant their deaths!"

Heden stopped for a minute and listened as his voice echoed off the stone walls. Could he hear breathing? He wasn't sure and couldn't tell where it was coming from.

"But you wouldn't do it," he said. "You refused. They hated you because you didn't join them in murdering Kavalen, and then they hated you because you wouldn't judge them.

"That's why she sent me. To take that responsibility from you. But you wouldn't give it." *And I couldn't see it.*

"Taethan!" Heden called out. Was he in one of the rooms? "Taethan, I'm here to forgive you. No man could shoulder that burden, do you understand me? I know what I'm talking about. It wasn't your fault." Even the perfect knight. "It wasn't your fault!"

Heden stepped up onto the base of the altar. He was going to turn and look down the nave when he saw the font, the ancient font behind the altar.

It was filled with blood, and a man's hand rested on it.

Heden pulled himself around the altar and saw the recumbent form of Sir Taethan behind it. His wrists were slit, two garish gashes like gasping mouths. There was tacky blood all around him, sticking his armor to the floor. But his hair was still green. The Last Green Knight. Heden was not too late. He started forward but Taethan's words froze him in place.

"It doesn't matter," Taethan said, reading his mind. It looked like he was fighting to stay awake. "I am a servant of Cavall like you." Heden realized what this meant. Tragedy. One servant of Cavall could not save another who'd attempted his own life. Cavall would not permit it. He didn't mete out power to his servants to use in self-destruction. That's why the slit wrists. Taethan knew Heden was coming, and wanted to make sure the arrogate couldn't save him. He'd done it hours ago. He was taking a long time to die.

"You'd have made a good knight," Taethan said, gasping for breath. His fine-boned face and delicate features were beautiful, even in death. He slumped down further, head resting on the short pillar of the font. "Better than me…do you see why?" he asked in desperation. He needed Heden to see.

Heden found it hard to focus, his eyes filling with tears. He was rooted to the spot with impotence and rage and grief. It was like the priory itself was dying before him.

"Because," Taethan said, his voice becoming quieter with each phrase. His face was twisted in pain, but Heden couldn't tell if it was physical pain or something else. "Because you know the world, and can stay here in it. You're strong enough." The words were being pulled from him in surges. "This awful horrible world. All the pain. You hate it too," the knight said, and Heden watched the color start draining from his hair. The green was vanishing, replaced by blonde. Beautiful blonde hair framing a dying face.

"You hate it," Taethan said, breathing shallow, his eyes closing. "But you're strong enough to take it. I couldn't...." He stopped, he was weeping.

"Why?" Heden asked, and it took all he had to get the words out. "Why did Kavalen have to die? Who...who ordered it?" Heden's rage was growing and he couldn't stop it. *"Who gave the command?"*

Taethan was fading fast. It was killing Heden. Both men were dying.

"The bishop," Taethan whispered.

Heden's blood turned to ice in his veins.

"What?" he asked, his voice a graveyard.

The bishop gave the order. Who could have commanded the Green Order to stand down? The bishop. He lied when he told Heden he'd never heard of them. That's why the knights all instantly hated him. He'd been sent by the same person who commanded them to let Ollghum Keep fall. And then he sent Heden to the forest to...what? Why?

Because the bishop had to send someone. Had to be *seen* sending someone. So send the man least likely to make a difference. The man the bishop could be sure would be completely ineffective. The most damaged man the bishop knew.

Taethan reached out with a thin arm, bright red blood painted on chalk-white skin.

Heden, bishop forgotten, surged forward, fell to the ground and wrapped his hands around the man, pulling him forward. He clasped Taethan's body to his own, as though he could grant Taethan some of his own health and keep him alive. He pressed his ear to Taethan's breast, listening to the heartbeat fading, struggling.

"No!" Heden cried, holding Taethan tighter. "No!" Heden couldn't see through his tears anymore. He loved this man. As much and as strongly as he loved anyone.

"Heden," Taethan whispered, then bent and kissed Heden's rain-matted hair.

Heden heard Taethan's heart beat once, twice, and then no more.

"Gods!" he cried, hugging the dead knight. "Cavall!" he cried out in unending desperation. "Please!"

He pulled himself up and held Taethan's perfect face in his hands. His skin was already cooling, his lips blue. It was happening so fast. The knight's eyes were still open but his jaw hung slack and his pupils were completely dilated, wide and black with no life behind them. It was the giant again, and Heden could do nothing. Again. Taethan's dead visage was a nightmare Heden could not wake from.

All his pent-up anger and frustration poured out of him and he couldn't stop it. The desperate feeling that he could at least save one of them. That he could save someone. Anyone. A man he loved, a man he thought of as a better version of himself, his brother, everything Heden would never be. Every hope flooded out of him and he sobbed. All that work, all that pain and struggle for nothing. He couldn't stop himself. Everything that was important to Heden had just died in his arms. His chest was being crushed by it, and he knew he was dying.

He couldn't be inside the priory. He couldn't stand it. He lurched to his feet, unsteady, like one of the deathless, and ran outside, pushing himself into the rain. It no longer felt cold; it felt hot on his skin. His legs gave out, and the rain beat him down until he collapsed in the mud. His fists sank into it, his tears disappeared into it.

He vomited, not even realizing it. Then he choked. He was numb. There was nothing left but tears, weeping, his whole body convulsing and he couldn't stop it.

He couldn't save Taethan. Couldn't save Isobel or Nudd, or Ollghum Keep, or the giant, or Mathe, or the boy in the jail a year ago, or the people of Aendrim. And he couldn't hold it back anymore. In killing Kavalen, the knights had killed the order, and with it, Taethan. And Taethan's death was Heden's death. The man he had been for three years died in the mud outside the priory.

What was left was something older, something almost unrecognizable.

A weapon, aimed at the bishop.

Epilogue

Sir Mór stood at the edge of the clearing, watching Heden. The arrogate looked like a beaten animal, collapsed on the jousting field, half-buried in mud, weeping in the rain. Mór had come to test the man again, finally. But no test was now necessary. No test was possible.

Mór, less a man and more an agent of a power, felt some impenetrable field around the priest. No god projected it. It was the man's reality. His sense of self pouring out so strong that Mór could not approach him, could not judge him. The man was judging himself with an authority greater than any the forest could muster. Making Sir Mór irrelevant.

The man before him was now a crucible, burning away everything he had been until that moment. Mór watched with sympathy, wondering what could survive the process. Glad it was no longer his worry.

The Green Man turned, forgetting Heden, and looked with purpose north into the forest. In an instant, his horse was there. He mounted and rode off, in search of what, only the forest knew.

Heden saw none of this.

Ratcatchers continues in Volume 2:

Thief

Acknowledgments

Alpha Readers

Natalie Elspeth – "It feels like you put your whole life into these first chapters."

Austin Baker – "Pretty cool."

Aaron Contreras – "Polish, polish, polish!"

Beta Readers

In every instance these volunteers provided critical feedback that led to significant edits. The book within would be very different without them.

Chad Nicholas, Doug Burke, Hyrum Savage, Ian Harac, Ian Welke, Jason Bell, Jason Durall, Josh Baker, Manny Vega, Paul LaPorte, Robert Djordjevich

Sine Qua Non

Heden is the result of many influences, but first he came from a conversation with John Wick way back in 2003 about Sin Eaters.

The next major influence was a piece on *This American Life* about a veteran returning home from Iraq finding himself unable to function at home.

Most of the heavy lifting on this book was done while listening to *Where You Go I Go Too*, by Lindstrøm, for which I thank Brian Chan and his passion for introducing people to new music.

Made in the USA
San Bernardino, CA
14 November 2019